HELEN
BIANCHIN
The Marriage Bed

D1381954

HELEN
BIANCHIN

COLLECTION

February 2016

March 2016

April 2016

May 2016

June 2016

July 2016

HELEN BIANCHIN
The Marriage Bed

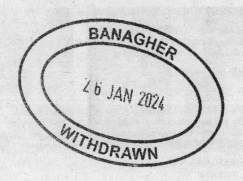

BANAGHER

2 6 JAN 2024

WITHDRAWN

MILLS & BOON

® and ™ are trademarks owned and used by the trademark owner and/or its licensee. Trademarks marked with ® are registered with the United Kingdom Patent Office and/or the Office for Harmonisation in the Internal Market and in other countries.

First Published in Great Britain 2016
By Mills & Boon, an imprint of HarperCollins*Publishers*
1 London Bridge Street, London, SE1 9GF

THE MARRIAGE BED © 2016 Harlequin Books S.A.

An Ideal Marriage? © 1997 Helen Bianchin
The Marriage Campaign © 1998 Helen Bianchin
The Bridal Bed © 1998 Helen Bianchin

ISBN: 978-0-263-92150-2

09-0616

Harlequin (UK) Limited's policy is to use papers that are natural, renewable and recyclable products and made from wood grown in sustainable forests. The logging and manufacturing processes conform to the legal environmental regulations of the country of origin.

Printed and bound in Spain
by CPI, Barcelona

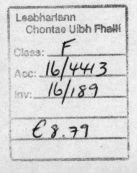

AN IDEAL MARRIAGE?

HELEN BIANCHIN

Helen Bianchin was born in New Zealand and travelled to Australia before marrying her Italian-born husband. After three years they moved, returned to New Zealand with their daughter, had two sons and then resettled in Australia.

Encouraged by friends to recount anecdotes of her years as a tobacco sharefarmer's wife living in an Italian community, Helen began setting words on paper and her first novel was published in 1975.

Currently Helen resides in Queensland, the three children now married with children of their own. An animal lover, Helen says her two beautiful Birman cats regard her study as much theirs as hers, choosing to leap onto her desk every afternoon to sit upright between the computer monitor and keyboard as a reminder they need to be fed...like right now!

CHAPTER ONE

IT DIDN'T MATTER how far or how frequent the journey, returning home had a significant effect on her emotions, Francesca mused as the jet banked over the harbour and prepared its descent.

Sydney's cityscape provided a panoramic vista of sparkling blue ocean, numerous coves and inlets, tall city buildings, the distinctive bridge, the Opera House.

Brilliant sunshine held the promise of warm summer temperatures, a direct contrast to those she'd left behind in Rome the day before.

The Boeing lined up the runway and within seconds wheels thudded against the Tarmac, accompanied by the scream of engines thrown into reverse, followed by the slow cruise into an allotted bay.

Collecting baggage and clearing Customs was achieved in minimum time, and Francesca was aware of a few circumspect glances as she made her way through the arrivals lounge.

The deep aqua-coloured trouser suit adorning her tall, slender frame was elegantly cut, her make-up minimal, and she'd caught her dark auburn hair into a loose knot atop her head. The result was an attractive image, but downplayed her status as an international model.

There were no photographers or television cameras in sight as she emerged onto the pavement, nor was there the customary chauffeured limousine waiting at the kerb.

Francesca reached for her sunglasses and slid the dark-lensed frames into place.

She wanted, *needed*, a few days' grace with family and friends before stepping onto the carousel of scheduled modelling assignments, contracted photographic shoots and public appearances.

Cabs formed a swiftly moving queue at the kerb and she quickly hired one, providing the driver with a Double Bay address as he slid out into traffic exiting the international terminal.

Cars, buses, trucks—all bent on individual destinations. Warehouses, tree-lined parks, graffiti decorating— or desecrating, depending on one's opinion—numerous concrete walls. It could be any city in the world, Francesca mused.

Yet it was her city, the place where she'd been born and raised of an Italian immigrant father and an Australian mother who had never quite come to terms with the constraints of marriage.

Francesca retained a vivid recollection of voices raised in bitter recrimination, followed soon after by boarding school, with vacation time spent equally between each parent.

Happy families, she mused with a rueful grimace as she reflected on the years that had followed. Three stepfathers: two who'd bestowed genuine affection and one whose predilection for pubescent girls had become apparent during a school vacation soon after the honeymoon. Acquired step-siblings who had passed briefly in and out of her life. And then, there was Madeline, her father's beautiful blonde wife.

The modelling career which had begun on a whim had succeeded beyond her wildest dreams. Paris, Rome, New York. She had an apartment in each city and was sought after by every major fashion house in Europe.

'Twenty-five dollars.'

The cab-driver's voice intruded, and Francesca delved into her shoulder bag, extracted two notes, and handed them to the driver. 'Keep the change.'

The tip earned her a toothy grin, a business card and the invitation to call him any time she needed a cab.

Francesca slid a coded card into a slot adjacent to double glass doors, and stepped into the lobby as they slid open.

The girl on Reception offered a bright smile. 'Nice to have you back.' She reached beneath the desk for a set of keys and a slim packet of mail. 'The hire car is parked in your usual space. Paperwork's in the glovebox.'

'Thanks.'

Francesca rode the lift to the top floor, deactivated her security system, then entered her apartment.

Beeswax mingled with the scent of fresh flowers. Delicate peach-coloured roses stood in a vase on the sofa table, with a card from her mother. *'Welcome home, darling.'*

A bold display with strelitzia and Australian natives

reposed in the middle of the dining room table, with a card from her father, who had inscribed an identical greeting.

The answering machine recorded no less than five messages, and she played them through. A call from her agent; the rest were social. Seven faxes, none of which were urgent, she determined as she flicked through the pages. All, she decided, could wait until she'd had time to shower and unpack. Then she'd go through her mail.

It was good to be home. Satisfying to see familiar things and to know that she would enjoy them for several weeks.

Oriental rugs graced the marble-tiled floor, and there were soft leather sofas in the large lounge area. A formal dining room, modern kitchen, two bedrooms with *en suite* facilities, and floor-to-ceiling glass. Ivory drapes flowed on from ivory silk-covered walls, and the marble tiles were ivory too. Framed prints in muted blue, pink, aqua and lilac graced the walls, the colours accented by several plump cushions placed with strategic precision on sofas and single chairs.

Understated elegance combined with the rich tapestry of individual taste. Lived in, and not just a showcase, she assured herself silently as she took her bags through to the main bedroom.

Unpacking could wait until later, she decided as she stripped off her clothes and entered the *en suite* bathroom.

A leisurely shower did much to ease the strain of too many hours' flight time, and she riffled through her wardrobe, selecting casual cotton trousers and a matching sleeveless blouse, then thrust bare feet into low-heeled sandals.

Collecting shoulder bag and keys, she rode the lift down to the underground car park.

Sydney traffic was swift, but civilised, and far different from the hazardous volume of cacophonous vehicles that hurtled the city streets of Rome.

Italy. The birthplace of her paternal ancestors and the place where she'd met and married world-renowned racing-driver Mario Angeletti three years ago during a photo shoot in Milan, only to weep at his funeral a few months after their wedding when a spectacular crash claimed his life. Last week she'd stood beside an adjacent grave site as her widowed mother-in-law had been laid to rest.

Nothing could be achieved by focusing on the sadness, she rationalised as she drove to the nearest shopping complex.

Her immediate priorities were to access Australian currency and do some food shopping.

Minutes later she parked the car, then crossed to the bank.

There were several people queuing at the automatic teller machine, and she opted for the bank's air-conditioned interior rather than wait in the blazing heat, only to give a resigned sigh at the lengthy column of customers waiting for vacant teller locations.

For a moment she considered saving time by utilising her bank card at the foodhall, then dismissed the idea.

The man in front of her moved two paces forward, and her attention was captured by his cologne. A light, musky exclusive brand that aroused a degree of idle speculation over the man who wore it.

Impressive height, dark, well-groomed hair. Broad shoulders, the muscle structure outlined beneath a fitted polo shirt. Tapered waist, well-cut trousers. Tight butt.

Accountant? Lawyer? Probably neither, she mused. Either would have worn the requisite two-piece suit during office hours.

The queue was dissipating more quickly than she'd anticipated, and she watched as he moved to a vacant teller.

Mid-to-late thirties, Francesca judged as she caught his features in profile. The strong jaw, wide-spaced cheekbones and chiselled mouth indicated a European heritage. Italian, maybe? Or Greek?

The adjoining teller became vacant, and she moved to the window, handed over her access card and keyed in her PIN code, requested an amount in cash, then folded the notes into her wallet.

Francesca turned to leave, and collided with a hard male frame. 'I'm so sorry.' The startled apology tumbled automatically from her lips, and her eyes widened at the steadying clasp of his hand on her elbow.

Dominic's scrutiny was unhurried as it slid negligently down her slim form, then travelled back to linger on the soft curve of her mouth before his eyes lifted to capture hers.

There was something about her that teased his memory. Classical fine-boned features, clear creamy skin that was too pale, gold-flecked brown eyes. But it was the hair that fascinated him. Twisted into a knot at her nape, he wondered at its length. And imagined how it would look flowing loose down her back, its vibrant colour spread out against the bedsheets.

It was an evocative image, and one he banked down.

The breath caught in Francesca's throat at the primitive, almost electric awareness evident, and for endless seconds the room and its occupants faded into obscurity.

Crazy to feel so *absorbed* Francesca decided shakily as she forced herself to breathe normally.

She came into contact with attractive men almost every day of her life. There was nothing special about *this* particular man. Merely sexual chemistry, she rationalised, at its most magnetic.

Recognition was one thing. It was quite another to feel the tug of unbidden response.

She didn't like it, didn't want it.

And he knew. She could see it in the faint curve of that sensually moulded mouth, the slight darkening of those deep, almost black eyes. His smile deepened fractionally, and he inclined his head in silent acknowledgement as he released her arm.

Francesca kept her expression coolly aloof, and with a deliberately careless movement she slipped her wallet into the capacious shoulder bag, then turned with the intention of exiting the bank.

He was a few paces ahead of her, and it was difficult to ignore the animalistic grace of well-honed muscle and sinew. Leashed power and steel. Of body, and mind.

A man most women would find a challenge to explore, mentally as well as physically. To discover if the hinted knowledge in those dark eyes delivered the promise of sensual excitement beyond measure.

Ridiculous, she dismissed, more shaken than she was prepared to admit by the passage of wayward thought. It was merely a figment of an over-active imagination, stimulated by the effects of a long flight and the need to adjust to a different time-zone.

There was a slight tilt to her chin as she emerged onto the pavement. The sun was bright, and she lowered her sunglasses from their position atop her head, glad of the darkened lenses.

Head high, eyes front, faint smile, practised walk. Automatic reflex, she mused as she crossed the mall.

The foodhall was busy, and she took care selecting fresh fruit before adding a few groceries to the trolley. With various family members and friends to see, breakfast was likely to be the only consistent meal she'd eat in her apartment.

Family. A timely reminder that she should make the first of several calls, she determined wryly as she selected milk from the refrigerated section, added yoghurt and followed it with brie, her favourite cheese.

'No vices?' Low-pitched, male, the faintly accented drawl held a degree of mocking amusement.

Francesca was familiar with every ploy. And adept at dealing with them all. She turned slowly, and the light, dismissive words froze momentarily in her throat as she recognised the compelling dark-haired man she'd bumped into at the bank.

He possessed a fascinating mouth, white, even teeth, and a smile that would drive most women wild. Yet there was something about the eyes that condemned artifice. An assessing, almost analytical directness that was disturbing.

Had he followed her? She cast his trolley a cursory glance and noted a collection of the usual food staples. Perhaps not.

Humour was a useful weapon. The edges of her mouth tilted slightly. 'Ice cream,' she acknowledged with a trace of flippancy. 'Vanilla, with caramel and double chocolate chip.'

Dark eyes gleamed, and his deep husky laughter did strange things to her equilibrium.

'Ah, the lady has a sweet tooth.'

There was a ring on her left hand, and he wondered at his stab of disappointment. His cutting edge style of wheeling and dealing in the business arena hadn't stemmed from hesitation. He didn't hesitate now.

He reached forward and placed a light finger against the wide filigree gold band. 'Does this have any significance?'

Francesca snatched her hand from the trolley. 'Whether it does or not is none of your business.'

So she had a temper to go with that glorious dark auburn hair, Dominic mused, and wondered if her passion matched it. His interest intensified. 'Indulge me.'

She wanted to turn and walk away, but something made her stay. 'Give me one reason why I should?'

'Because I don't poach another man's possession.' The words held a lethal softness that bore no hint of apology, and his expression held a dispassionate watchfulness as she struggled to restrain her anger.

Dignity was the key, and she drew in a calming breath, then slowly raked her eyes over his tall frame from head to foot, and back again.

'Attractive packaging,' she accorded with silky detachment. She met his gaze squarely and held it. 'However, I have no interest in the contents.'

'Pity,' he drawled. 'The discovery could prove fascinating.' There was droll humour apparent, and something else she couldn't define. 'For both of us.'

'In your dreams,' she dismissed sweetly. The checkout lane was located at the far end of the aisle, and she had everything she needed.

He made no effort to stop her as she moved away, yet for one infinitesimal moment she'd had the feeling he'd seen into the depths of her soul, acknowledged her secrets, staked a claim and retreated, sure of his ability to conquer.

Insane, Francesca mentally chastised herself as she loaded carrybags into the boot and returned the trolley. Then she slid in behind the wheel of her car and switched on the ignition.

She was tired, wired. The first was the direct result of a long flight; she owed the second to a man she never wanted to meet again.

Re-entering the apartment, she stowed her purchases into the refrigerator and pantry. Rejecting coffee or tea, she filled a glass with iced water and drank half the contents before crossing to the telephone.

Fifteen minutes later she'd connected with each parent and made arrangements to see them. Next, she punched in the digits necessary to connect with Laraine, her agent.

Business. For the past three years it had been her salvation. Travelling the world, an elegant clothes-horse for the top fashion designers. She had the face, the figure, and the essential *élan.* But for how long would she remain one of the coveted few? More importantly, did she *want* to?

There were young waifs clamouring in the wings, eager for fame and fortune. Designers always had an eye for the look, and the excitement of a fresh new face.

Fashion was fickle. *Haute couture* a viperish nest of designer ego fed by prestigious clientele, the press, and the copy merchants.

Yet amongst the outrageousness, the hype and the glitter, there was pleasure in displaying the visual artistry of imaginative design. Satisfaction when it all came together to form something breathtakingly spectacular.

It made the long flights, living out of a suitcase in one hotel room or another, cramped backstage changing rooms, the *panic* that invariably abounded behind the scenes worthwhile. A cynic wouldn't fail to add that an astronomical modelling fee helped lessen the pain.

Financial security was something Francesca had enjoyed for as long as she could remember. As a child, there had been a beautiful home, live-in help, and expensive private schooling. Yet, while her mother had perpetuated the fairytale existence, her father had ensured his daughter's feet remained firmly on the ground.

There were investments, property, and an enviable

blue chip share portfolio, the income from which precluded a need to supplement it in any way.

Yet the thought of becoming a social butterfly with no clear purpose to the day had never appealed.

Perhaps it was her father's inherited Italian genes that kept the adrenalin flowing and provided the incentive to put every effort into a chosen project. 'Failure' didn't form part of her father's vocabulary.

Which brought Francesca back to the present. 'A week's grace,' she insisted, and listened to her agent's smooth plea to reconsider. 'Tomorrow morning we'll confer over coffee. Your office. Shall we say ten?'

She replaced the receiver, stretched her arms high, and felt the weariness descend. She'd make something light for dinner, then she'd undress and slip beneath the sheets of her comfortable bed.

CHAPTER TWO

FRANCESCA LEANED across the desk in her agent's elegantly appointed office and traced a list of proposed modelling assignments with a milk-opal-lacquered nail.

'Confirm the cancer charity luncheon, the Leukaemia Foundation dinner. I'll do Tony's photo shoot, and I'll judge the junior modelling award, attend the gala lunch on the Gold Coast.' She paused, considered three invitations and dismissed two. 'The invitation-only showing at Margo's Double Bay boutique.' She picked up her glass of iced water and took an appreciative sip. 'That's it.'

'Anique Sorensen is being persuasive and persistent,' Laraine relayed matter-of-factly.

The fact that Francesca was known to donate half her appearance fee whenever she flew home between seasons invariably resulted in numerous invitations requesting her presence at various functions, all in aid of one charity or another.

'When?'

'Monday, Marriott Hotel.'

'Tell me it's for a worthwhile cause, and I'll kill you.'

'Then I'm dead. It's for the Make-A-Wish Foundation® of Australia.'

'Damn,' Francesca accorded inelegantly, wrinkling her nose in silent admonition of Laraine's widening smile.

'But you'll do it,' the agent said with outward satisfaction.

'Yes.' Francesca stood to her feet, collected her bag and slid the strap over one shoulder. She had a particular sympathy for terminally ill children. 'Fax me the details.'

'What are your plans for the rest of the day?'

'A secluded beach,' she enlightened. 'A good book, and the mobile phone.'

'Don't forget the block-out sunscreen.'

Francesca's smile held a teasing quality. 'Got it.'

An hour later she sat munching an apple beneath a sun umbrella on a northern beach gazing over the shoreline to the distant horizon.

There was a faint breeze wafting in from the ocean, cooling the sun's heat. She could smell the salt-spray, and there was the occasional cry from a lonely seagull as it explored the damp sand at the edge of an outgoing tide.

The solitude soothed and relaxed her, smoothing the edges of mind and soul.

Reflections were often painful, and with a determined effort Francesca extracted her book and read for an hour, then she retrieved a banana and a peach from her bag and washed both down with a generous amount of bottled water.

Phone calls. The first of which was to a dear friend with whom she'd shared boarding school during emotionally turbulent years when each had battled a stepmother and the effects of a dysfunctional family relationship.

She punched in the number, got past Reception, then a secretary, and chuckled at Gabbi's enthusiastic greeting and a demand as to when they would get together.

'Tonight, if you and Benedict are attending Leon's exhibition.'

The flamboyant gallery owner was known for his soirées, invitations to which featured high on the social calendar among the city's fashionable élite.

'You are? That's great,' Francesca responded with enthusiasm. 'I'm meeting Mother for dinner first, so I could be late.'

'Have fun,' Gabbi issued lightly, and Francesca laughed outright at the unspoken nuance in those two words.

It *was* fun listening to Sophy's breathy gossip over chicken consommé, salad and fruit. Sophy's permanent diet involved minuscule portions of fat-free calorie-depleted food.

A gifted raconteur, she had a wicked way with words that was endearingly humorous, and it was little wonder her mother gathered men as some women collected jewellery. All of whom remained friends long after the relationship had ended. With the exception of Rick, her first husband and Francesca's father. He was the one who had remained impervious to Sophy's machinations.

It was after nine when the waiter brought the bill,

which Francesca paid, and she saw Sophy into a cab before crossing to her car.

Twenty minutes later she searched for an elusive parking space within walking distance of Leon's fashionable Double Bay gallery, located one, and made her way towards the brightly lit main entrance.

There were people everywhere, milling, drinking, and it was difficult to distinguish the muted baroque music beneath audible snatches of conversation.

'Francesca, *darling*!'

Leon—who else? She acknowledged his effusive greeting and allowed him to clasp her shoulders as he regarded her features with thoughtful contemplation.

'You must have a drink before you circulate.'

Her eyes assumed a humorous gleam. 'That bad, huh?'

'*Non*. But a glass in the hand—' He paused to effect a Gallic shrug. 'You can pretend, *oui*, that it is something other than mineral water.' He lifted a hand in imperious summons, and a waiter appeared out of nowhere, tray in hand.

Dutifully, she extracted a tall glass. 'Anything in particular you can recommend to add to my collection?'

'A sculpture,' Leon announced at once. 'It is a little raw, you understand, but the talent—' He touched fingers to his lips and blew a kiss into the air. '*Très magnifique*. In a few years it will be worth ten, twenty times what is being asked for it now.' He smiled, and brushed gentle knuckles to her cheek. 'Go, *cherie*, and examine. Exhibit Fourteen. It may not capture you immediately, but it grows, fascinates.'

An accurate description, Francesca accorded several minutes later, unsure of the sculpture's appeal. Yet there was something that drew her attention again and again.

Leon was an expert in the art world, she trusted his judgement, and owned, thanks to his advice, several items which had increased dramatically in value since their date of purchase. Therefore, she would browse among the other exhibits, then return and perhaps view it from a fresh angle. It was certainly different from anything she owned.

There were a few fellow guests whose features were familiar, and she smiled, greeted several by name, paused to exchange polite conversation, then moved on, only to divert from her intended path as she glimpsed the endearingly familiar features of an attractive blonde threading a path towards her.

'Francesca!'

'Gabbi.'

They embraced, and tumbled into speech. 'It's so good to see you.'

'And you. Where's Benedict?' It was unlike Gabbi's husband to be far from his wife's side.

'Eyes right, about ten feet distant.'

Francesca caught the dry tone and conducted a casual sweeping glance in the indicated direction. Benedict's tall, dark-haired frame came into view, together with that of a familiar female form. Annaliese Schubert, a model with whom she'd shared a few catwalks both home and abroad.

'Your dear stepsister is in town, and bent on creating her usual mayhem?' An attempt to seduce Benedict

Nicols appeared Annaliese's prime motivation. That she had been unsuccessful both before and after Benedict's marriage didn't appear to bother her in the slightest.

'Perceptive of you,' Gabbi replied wryly. 'How was Rome?'

Francesca hesitated fractionally, unaware of the fleeting darkness that momentarily clouded her eyes. 'The catwalks were exhausting.' Her shoulders lifted slightly, then fell. 'And Mario's mother lost a long battle with cancer.'

Empathetic understanding didn't require words, and Francesca was grateful Gabbi refrained from uttering more than the customary few.

'Let's do lunch,' Gabbi suggested gently. 'Is tomorrow too soon?'

'Done.'

'Good,' Gabbi said with satisfaction. She tucked a hand through Francesca's arm. 'Shall we examine the art exhibits for any hidden talent?'

They wandered companionably, slowly circling the room, and when Gabbi paused to speak to a friend Francesca moved forward to give closer scrutiny to a canvas that displayed a visual cacophony of bold colour.

She tilted her head in an attempt to fathom some form or symmetry that might make sense.

'It's an abstract,' a slightly accented male voice revealed with a degree of musing mockery.

Francesca's stomach muscles tightened, premonition providing an advance warning even as she turned slowly towards him.

The bank, the foodhall, and now the art gallery?

Dominic had witnessed her entrance, and noted her progress around the room with interest. And a degree of satisfaction when she was greeted with such enthusiasm by the wife of one of his business associates. It made it so much easier to initiate an introduction.

She regarded him silently. The deeply etched male features, the hard-muscled frame tamed somewhat beneath superb tailoring. Also apparent were the hand-stitched shoes, Hermes tie, and gold Rolex.

The smile reached his eyes, tingeing them with humour, yet there was a predatory alertness beneath the surface that was at variance with his portrayed persona.

A man who knew who he was, and didn't require any status symbols to emphasise his wealth or masculinity.

Power emanated from every pore, leashed and under control. Yet there was a hint of the primitive, a dramatic mesh of animalistic magnetism that stirred something within her, tripping the pulse and increasing her heartbeat.

'Francesca.'

The soft American drawl caught her attention, and she turned at once, her expression alive with delight.

'Benedict!' Her smile held genuine warmth as she leaned forward to accept his salutary kiss. 'It's been a while.'

'Indeed.' Gabbi's husband offered an affectionate smile in acknowledgement before shifting his attention to the man at her side. 'You've met Dominic?'

'It appears I'm about to.'

Something flickered in Benedict's eyes, then it was masked. 'Dominic Andrea. Francesca Angeletti.'

The mention of her surname provided the key to her identity, Dominic acknowledged, as details fell into place.

He was Greek, Francesca mused, not Italian. And the two men were sufficiently comfortable with each other to indicate an easy friendship.

'Francesca.'

Her name on his lips sounded—*different*. Sexy, evocative, alluring. And she didn't want to be any one of those things with any man. Especially not *this* man.

Dominic wondered if she was aware the fine gold flecks in her eyes intensified when she was defensive... and trying hard to hide it? He felt something stir deep inside, aside from the desire to touch his mouth to her own, to explore and possess it.

'Are you sufficiently brave to offer an opinion on my exhibit?'

He couldn't be serious? 'I'd prefer to opt out on the grounds that anything I say might damage your ego.'

His husky laughter sent a shivery sensation down the length of her spine. 'Benedict and Gabbi must bring you to dinner tomorrow night.'

If Dominic Andrea thought she'd calmly tag along he was mistaken! 'Why?'

'You intrigue me.' He saw her pupils dilate, sensed the uncertainty beneath her cool façade. And was curious to discover the reason.

'No. Thank you,' she added.

'Not curious to see my artist's attic?'

'Where you live doesn't interest me.' Nor do you, she wanted to add. And knew she lied. For there was an invisible pull of the senses, a powerful dynamism impossible to ignore.

A man who sought to forge his own destiny, she perceived, not at all fooled by the smile curving that generous mouth. The eyes were too dark and discerning, *dangerous*.

She had the strangest feeling she should be afraid of the knowledge evident in those depths. An instinctive sureness that he was intent on being a major force in her life.

'Six-thirty. Gabbi will give you the address.' His lips tilted slightly as he slanted her a mocking glance. 'If you'll excuse me?'

'Extraordinary man,' Francesca commented, silently adding lethal and persistent as she watched him thread his way to the opposite side of the gallery.

'A very successful one,' Benedict informed her mildly. 'Who dabbles in art and donates a lot of his work to charity.'

'Accept Dominic's invitation,' Gabbi added persuasively. 'If you don't, I'll be outnumbered, and the conversation will be confined to business.'

Francesca rolled her eyes. 'Not really a hardship. You excel in business.'

Gabbi's eyes sparkled with impish humour. 'Take a walk on the wild side and say *yes*. You might enjoy yourself.'

All Francesca's instincts shrieked a silent denial. She liked her life as it was, and didn't need nor want any complications that might upset its even tenure.

Although it might prove a challenge to play Dominic Andrea at his own game and win.

'What do you think of that sculpture in steel?' Benedict queried, successfully diverting their attention.

Ten minutes later Francesca chose to leave, indicating to Gabbi quietly, 'I'll see you at lunch tomorrow.'

Leon was effusive as she crossed to his side and thanked him for the invitation, and as she turned towards the door she saw Dominic Andrea deep in conversation with a stunning diminutive blonde.

Almost as if he sensed her gaze, his head lifted and dark eyes pierced hers with mesmerising awareness.

There was nothing overt in his expression, just an unwavering knowledge that had an electric effect on her equilibrium. It was almost as if he was staking a claim. Issuing a silent message that he would enjoy the fight, and the victory.

Fanciful imagination, Francesca dismissed as she gained the foyer, then she descended the short flight of steps and took the well-lit path to her car.

With the ignition engaged, she eased the vehicle forward and entered the busy thoroughfare.

Dominic Andrea had no part in her life, she assured herself silently as she headed towards her Double Bay apartment.

Francesca put the finishing touches to her make-up, examined the careless knot of hair she'd swept on top of her head, then stood back, pleased with the overall image.

Halter-necked black dress, sheer black tights, perilously high stiletto-heeled black pumps. Cosmetic artistry provided a natural look, and a brilliant red gloss coloured her lips. Jewellery comprised a diamond bracelet and matching ear-studs.

Without pausing to think, she collected a slim evening purse and car keys, walked out of the apartment and took the lift down to the basement car park.

Traffic was heavy as she drove through the city, and once clear of the Harbour Bridge she by-passed the expressway and headed towards Beauty Point.

Exclusive suburbs graced the city's northern shores, offering magnificent views over the inner harbour.

Dammit. *What was she doing?* Dressed to kill, on her way to attend a dinner she had no inclination to share with a man she hadn't wanted to see again.

She could turn back and go home, ring and apologise, using any one of several plausible excuses.

So why didn't she? Instead of turning between wrought-iron gates guarding an imposing concrete-textured Caribbean-style home situated at the crest of a semi-circular driveway?

All because of Gabbi's subtle challenge issued the previous evening, and endorsed and encouraged over lunch. Now it was a little late to have second thoughts.

Francesca parked behind Benedict's sporty Jaguar and cast a quick glance at the digital clock before she switched off the engine.

Perfect. By the time she emerged from the car and walked the few steps to the front door, she would be ten minutes late.

A silent statement that she was here on her own terms.

Subdued melodic chimes echoed as she depressed the doorbell, and seconds later the thick, panelled door swung open to reveal a middle-aged housekeeper.

'Miss Angeletti? Please come in.'

High ceilings and floor-to-ceiling glass created a sense of spaciousness and light, with folding white-painted wooden shutters. Expensive art adorned the walls, and there were several Oriental rugs adorning pale cream marble floors.

She was escorted into a large lounge where Dominic's tall frame drew her attention like a magnet.

Dark trousers and a casual blue shirt lent an elegance she knew to be deceiving, for beneath the sophisticated veneer there was strength, not only of body but of mind.

'Please accept my apologies.'

Dominic's dark eyes held hers, quiet, still. He wasn't fooled in the slightest, but his voice was smooth as silk as he moved forward to greet her. 'Accepted.' He swept an arm towards a soft-cushioned leather sofa. 'Come and sit down.'

She crossed to a single chair and sank into it with elegant economy of movement.

A further insistence on independence? 'What can I offer you to drink?'

Something with a kick in it would be nice. Instead, she offered him a singularly sweet smile. 'Chilled water, with ice.'

'Sparkling or still?'

She resisted the temptation to request a specific brand-name. 'Still. Thank you.'

There was that glance again, laser-sharp beneath dark lashes, the slight lift of one eyebrow before he crossed to the cabinet.

Benedict looked mildly amused, and Gabbi shook her head in silent remonstrance. Francesca merely smiled.

Dominic returned and placed a tall glass within her reach on the side table.

'Thank you.' So achingly polite. *Too* polite?

Within minutes the housekeeper appeared to announce the meal was served, and they made their way into a large dining room adjacent to the lounge.

The table was beautifully set with white damask, on which reposed fine china, silver cutlery and stemmed crystal glasswear.

Francesca's gaze idly skimmed the mahogany chiffonnier, the long buffet cabinet, the elegantly designed chairs, and silently applauded his taste in furniture. And in soft furnishings, for the drapes and carpet were uniform in colour, the contrast supplied by artwork and mirrors adorning the walls.

Dominic seated Francesca beside him, opposite Gabbi and Benedict.

The courses were varied, and many, and, while exquisitely presented, they were the antithesis of designer food. There was, however, an artistically displayed platter of salads decorated with avocado, mango, and a sprinkling of pine nuts.

A subtle concession to what Dominic suspected was a model's necessity to diet?

Francesca always ate wisely and well, with little need to watch her intake of food. Tonight, however, she forked dainty portions from each course.

'You have a beautiful home.' The compliment was deserved, and she cast a glance towards the original artwork gracing the walls. Not any of them bore the distinctive style of the abstract she'd sighted at Leon's gallery.

As if reading her mind, Dominic enlightened musingly, 'I keep my work in the studio.'

One eyebrow lifted, and her voice held a hint of mockery. 'Is that a subtle invitation to admire your etchings?'

His fingers brushed her wrist as he leaned forward to replenish her glass with water, and a chill shiver feathered its way over the surface of her skin in silent recognition of something deeply primitive.

The knowledge disturbed her, and her eyes were faintly wary as they met his.

'The expected cliché?' The drawled query held wry humour, and his eyes held a warmth she didn't care to define. 'At the risk of disappointing you, I paint in the studio and confine lovemaking to the bedroom.'

Something curled inside her stomach, and she lifted her glass and took a generous swallow before setting it down onto the table. 'How—prosaic.'

His husky chuckle held quizzical amusement, and an indolent smile broadened the sensual curve of his mouth. 'Indeed? You don't think comfort is a prime consideration?'

The image of a large bed, satin sheets, and leisurely

languorous foreplay sprang to mind…a damning and totally unwarranted vision she wanted no part of.

Francesca had a desire to give a stinging response, and probably would have if they'd been alone. Instead, she aimed for innocuous neutrality, and tempered it with a totally false smile that didn't fool anyone, least of all Dominic, in the slightest. 'Not always.'

'The chicken is delicious.' Dear sweet Gabbi, who sought to defuse the verbal direction of their exchange.

Francesca cast her a sweeping glance that issued a silent statement—*I'm having fun*. And saw her friend's eyes widen fractionally in answering warning.

'How was your trip to Italy, Francesca?' Benedict issued the bland query. 'Were you able to spend any time outside Rome?'

She decided to play the social conversational game. 'No,' she enlightened evenly. 'However, I'm due in Milan next month for the European spring collections.' Closely followed by Paris.

Her life was like riding a merry-go-round…big cities, bright lights, the adrenalin rush. Then, every so often, she stepped off and took time out in normality. A vacation abroad, or, more often than not, she flew home to spend time with family and friends. They were her rock, the one thing constant in her life she could rely on.

'You enjoy the international scene?'

Francesca turned slightly to the man seated at her side, glimpsed the remarkable steadiness in his gaze—and something else she was unable to interpret. 'Yes.'

'Would you care for more salad?'

A subtle reminder that she was scarcely doing the

sumptuous selection of food much justice? It hardly made sense that she was deliberately projecting the image of a diet fanatic, but there was a tiny gremlin urging her to travel a mildly outrageous path.

'Thank you.' She reached for the utensils and placed a modest serving onto her plate, then proceeded to fork small portions with delicate precision.

There was a dessert to die for reposing on the chiffonnier, and she spared the exquisitely decorated torte a regretful glance. A slice of mouthwatering ambrosia she'd have to forego the pleasure of savouring in order to continue the expected accepted image.

'Did Leon manage to sell your abstract?' She sounded facetious, and felt a momentary pang for the discourtesy.

'It wasn't for sale,' Dominic relayed with seemingly careless disregard, and smiled as her eyebrows arched in silent query.

'Really?' Francesca let her gaze encompass his rugged features and lingered on the strong bone structure before meeting the musing gleam in those dark eyes. 'You don't *look* like an artist.'

His mouth quirked slightly at the edges. 'How, precisely, is your impression of an artist supposed to look?'

Harmless words, but she was suddenly conscious of an elevated nervous tension that had no known basis except a strong, instinctive feeling that she was playing a dangerous game with a man well-versed in every aspect of the hunt.

Akin to a predator prepared to watch and wait as his

prey gambolled foolishly within sight, aware that the time was of his choosing, the kill a foregone conclusion.

Now you're being fanciful, she chided, suddenly angry with herself for lapsing into an idiotic mind game.

'Shall we move to the lounge for coffee?' Dominic suggested with deceptive mildness.

In a way it was a relief to shift location, and she breathed a silent sigh as the evening moved towards a close.

The impish gremlin was still in residence as she declined coffee and requested tea. 'Herbal, if you have it.' Long lashes gave an imperceptible flutter, then swept down to form a protective veil.

'Of course.' The request didn't faze him in the least. It was almost as if he'd been prepared for it, and within minutes she nursed a delicate cup filled with clear brown liquid she had no inclination to taste.

Terrible, she conceded as she studiously sipped the innocent brew. And smiled as Gabbi, Benedict and Dominic savoured dark, aromatic coffee she would have much preferred to drink.

Hoist by her own petard, Francesca acknowledged with rueful acceptance. It served her right.

'Another cup?'

Not if she could help it! 'Thank you, no. That was delicious.'

Benedict rose to his feet in one smooth movement, his eyes enigmatic as they met those of his wife. 'If you'll excuse us, Dominic?'

'It's been a lovely evening,' Gabbi said gently as she collected her purse.

Their imminent departure provided an excellent excuse for Francesca to leave. It was what Dominic expected. But she was damned if she'd give him the satisfaction.

Fool, she mentally chastised herself as he escorted Gabbi and Benedict to the front door. Pick up your evening bag and follow them.

Too late, she decided a few minutes later when he returned to the lounge.

Francesca watched as he folded his lengthy frame into a cushioned chair directly opposite.

'Your friendship with Gabbi is a long-standing one?'

'Are you going to express a need to explore my background?'

'Not particularly.'

'No request for an in-depth profile?' she queried drily.

Dominic was silent for several seemingly long seconds, wanting to tear down the barrier she'd erected but aware of the need for caution and a degree of patience. 'I'm aware of the professional one,' he drawled with assumed indolence. 'Tell me about your marriage.'

She stopped breathing, felt the pressure build, and sought to expel it slowly. She wanted to serve him a volley of angry words, throw something, *anything* that would release some of her pain. Instead, she resorted to stinging mockery.

'Gabbi failed to fill you in?'

His eyes were steady. 'Minimum details.'

'It can be encapsulated in one sentence: *champion racing car driver Mario Angeletti killed on the Monaco*

Grand Prix circuit within months of his marriage to international model Francesca Cardelli.'

Three years had passed since that fateful day. Yet the vivid horror remained. It didn't matter that she hadn't personally witnessed the tearing of metal, the disintegration of car and man as fuel ignited in catastrophic explosion. Television news cameras, newspaper photographs and graphic journalistic reports ensured no detail remained unrecorded.

Family and close friends had shielded her, protecting and nurturing during the emotional fall-out. And afterwards she had stepped back onto the catwalk, aware every move, every nuance of her expression was being carefully watched for visible signs of distress.

Some had even attempted to provoke it. Yet not once had she let down her guard. Only those who knew her well saw the smile didn't quite reach her eyes, and recognised the smooth social patter as a practised façade.

'It must have been a very painful time for you.'

Francesca was unable to verbally denounce his sympathy, for there was none. Merely an empathetic statement that ignored conventional platitudes.

'Would you like a drink? Some more tea, coffee?' The smile held musing warmth. 'Something stronger, perhaps?'

Francesca stood to her feet, her expression wary as he mirrored her action. 'I really must leave.'

'Do I frighten you?' The query was voiced in a soft drawl, and succeeded in halting her steps.

No doubt about it, his target aim was deadly.

'Fear' was a multi-faceted word that encompassed

many emotions. Slowly she turned towards him and met his gaze. Her chin tilted fractionally. A mental stiffening of her own resources? 'No.'

His eyes never left hers, but she felt as if he'd stripped every protective layer she'd swathed around her frozen heart and laid it bare and bleeding.

Oh, God, what was happening here? She'd known he was trouble the first time she saw him. *Walk away,* a tiny voice bade silently. *Now.*

A faint smile curved the edges of that sensual mouth, and there was a transitory gleam of humour apparent in the depth of those dark eyes. 'I'm relieved to hear it.'

'Why?' The demand seemed perfectly logical.

He looked at her carefully, weighing his words and assessing the damage they might do. And how he would deal with it. 'I want you,' he stated gently, lifting a hand to trace a gentle forefinger down the edge of her cheek.

His touch was like fire, and her pulse jumped, then raced to a quickened beat, almost as if in silent recognition of something she refused to acknowledge.

'Tangled sheets and an exchange of body fluids?' Inside, her emotions were shredding into pieces. Her eyes seared his, and her chin tilted fractionally as she took a step away from him. 'I don't *do* one-night stands.'

Courage. And passion. Banked, reserved. But there. He wanted it all. And knew she'd fight him every inch of the way.

'Neither do I.'

His words sent a shiver feathering down the length of her spine. What was it with this man? She found it annoying that just as she was about to categorise him, he shifted stance.

Dominic watched the play of emotions in her expressive eyes. No matter how much he wanted it to be different, he could wait. The temptation to pull her up against him and let her feel the effect she had on him was strong. To cover her mouth with his own, explore and vanquish.

He did neither. It would keep. Until the next time. And he'd ensure there was a next time.

Francesca felt the need to escape, and good manners instilled since childhood ensured she uttered a few polite words in thanks.

'Why, when you merely sampled a bird-like portion from each course, then picked at the salad?'

She experienced a momentary tinge of remorse for the manner in which she'd eaten the delectable food. Did he suspect it had been deliberate? Somehow she had the instinctive feeling he saw too much, *knew* too much of the human psyche.

'My loss of appetite bore no reflection on your housekeeper's culinary ability.'

'In that case, I'll refer the compliment.'

Francesca turned and walked from the room to the front door, acutely aware of his presence at her side. She paused as he reached forward to pull back one of the large, panelled doors.

'What were you doing shopping for food in a supermarket when you employ a housekeeper?'

He could have used any one of several glib excuses,

or employed a deliberately flattering remark. Instead he chose honesty. 'I wanted to see you again.'

Her stomach lurched, and an icy chill feathered her skin at the directness of his gaze.

'Goodnight.' She moved past him and stepped quickly down to her car, unlocked it and slid in behind the wheel.

The engine fired with a refined purr, and she resisted the temptation to speed down the driveway, choosing instead to ease the vehicle through the gates onto the road before quickly accelerating towards the main arterial road leading towards the Harbour Bridge.

Damn him. Francesca's fingers tightened on the steering wheel until her knuckles shone white. He was fast proving to be an intrusive force—one she didn't need in her life.

The sky was a deep indigo-blue sprinkled with stars, and beneath them lay the city, dark velvet laced by a tracery of electric lights that had no discernible pattern. Bright neon flashed, providing vivid colour as one advertisement vied with another. A commuter train slipped by in electronic silence, its carriages illuminated and partly empty.

It was still early, yet there was already action in the city streets. Professionals worked the pavements, hustling and touting and evading the law as they mingled with the tourists and the curious.

Francesca took the expressway through the Domain, bypassed Kings Cross and headed towards the main arterial road leading to Double Bay.

Her head felt heavy, and she would have given much

to be able to stop the car and walk in the clear night air. Instead she drove to her apartment building, garaged the car, then rode the lift to her designated floor.

A leisurely cool shower followed by an iced drink while she viewed television would have to suffice.

Yet nothing provided a distraction from the man who disturbed her thoughts.

Sleep didn't come easily, and even when it did, there were jagged dreams that made little sense. Except one, from which she awoke damp-skinned and damp-eyed. A vivid recall of Mario's laughing features as he stepped into his racing-car and donned his helmet prior to lining up for the last race of his life.

On the other side of the city Dominic stood looking out at the glittering lights across a darkened harbour as he reflected on the woman who had not long driven away from his home.

Sleep was elusive. At worst he could make do with six hours, five if he had to. Tonight he had the feeling he'd have to manage with less.

The fax machine shrilled in another room, and he ignored it.

What he needed was a carefully constructed strategy. A campaign that would leave nothing to chance.

Tomorrow he would make a call to Benedict Nicols in the hope that Gabbi might be persuaded to reveal details of Francesca's social calendar.

Subterfuge was permissible in the pursuit of an objective.

CHAPTER THREE

THE NEXT FEW days were relaxing as Francesca caught up with friends, did some shopping, and enjoyed a re-scheduled lunch with her father in an exclusive restaurant close to his office building.

The food was excellent, the ambience superb.

'How is Madeline?' Her stepmother was hardly the wicked kind, but Madeline viewed Francesca as a contestant for Rick's affections, and waged a subtle war to test her husband's priorities whenever Francesca was in town.

'Fine.' The warmth in his voice was unmistakable, and as long as Francesca continued to hear it she was prepared to forgive Madeline almost anything.

'And Katherine and John?' They were close, and Francesca regarded them as sister and brother rather than step-siblings. 'We must get together.'

'Is tonight too soon?' her father queried with a degree of wry humour. 'Katherine has, she assures me, an outfit to die for, and John seems convinced a new suit will elevate him in years to the enviable position of escorting his famed stepsister to an élite restaurant, where, God willing, some super-vigilant photographer will take a photo which will appear in tomorrow's newspaper, whereupon he'll be the most sought-after beau of the student ball.'

Francesca laughed. A glorious, warm, husky sound. 'I take it I should wear something incredibly glamorous?'

Rick Cardelli's smile held philosophical humour. 'Obscenely so, I imagine,' he said drily.

Concern clouded her features. 'I don't want to overshadow Katherine.' Or Madeline.

His dark eyes gleamed, and the edges of his mouth curved upward. 'My dear Francesca, Katherine wants you to shine—vividly.'

'Done.' Francesca lifted her glass and touched it to the rim of her father's wine glass. '*Salute*, Papà,' she said solemnly.

'*Ecco*. Health and happiness,' he added gently.

She picked up her cutlery and speared a succulent prawn from its bed of cos lettuce decorated with slices of avocado and mango. The dressing was divine, and she savoured every mouthful.

They were halfway through the main course when Francesca became aware of a strange prickling sensation at the back of her neck.

Almost as if she was being watched.

Recognition was an aspect of her profession that she had come to terms with several years ago, and she dealt with it with practised charm.

But this was different. Mild interest in her presence didn't usually elicit this heightened sense of awareness, an acute alertness, as if something deep inside was forcing her attention.

She turned slowly, allowing her gaze to idly skim the room. And came to a sudden halt as she caught sight of Dominic Andrea sharing a table with two men a few metres from her own.

At that moment he glanced up, and her eyes collided with his dark, piercing gaze. He offered a slow, musing smile, which merely earned him a brief nod before she returned her attention to the contents on her plate.

Her appetite diminished so as to be almost non-existent, and she declined dessert, choosing to settle for coffee.

'Francesca?'

She looked up at the sound of her name and realised she hadn't taken in a word her father had said. 'I'm sorry, what did you say?'

'Is there a reason for your distraction?' Rick queried, and she wrinkled her nose in wry humour.

'An unwanted one.'

Her father chuckled. 'Now that I have your attention… Madeline would like you to join us at home for dinner. Does Wednesday suit?'

'I'll look forward to it.'

The waiter cleared their table and brought coffee.

Francesca was conscious of every movement she made, aware as she had never been before of one man's veiled scrutiny.

No one would have guessed to what degree Dominic's presence bothered her, or how much she longed to escape.

'A refill?'

'No, thanks.' She cast her father a warm smile. 'This has been lovely.' She watched as he summoned the waiter to bring the bill.

'Rick. How are you?'

Even if the faint aroma of exclusive male cologne hadn't warned her, the slow curl in the pit of her stomach did.

Dominic Andrea. Dark eyes, inscrutable expression behind the warm smile.

'Francesca.' The intimate inflexion he gave her name made the hairs at her nape rise in protest. Something that irritated the hell out of her and lent a very polite edge to her voice as she acknowledged his presence.

Dominic leaned down and brushed his lips against her temple. The contact was brief, his touch light. But something ignited and flared through her veins, potent, alive—*electric*.

She wanted to kill him. In fact, she definitely would kill him the next time she saw him. *If* she saw him again. How *dare* he imply an intimacy that didn't exist? Would never exist.

'You know each other?' Rick queried, interested in the expressive play of emotions that chased fleetingly across his daughter's features.

'We dined together earlier in the week,' Dominic enlightened smoothly.

Damning. Francesca cursed, all too aware of his intended implication.

'Really?' Rick absorbed the information and wondered whether anything was to be made of it. 'You'll join us for coffee?'

'I'm with two colleagues. Another time, perhaps?' His eyes shifted to Francesca, who met his steady gaze with equanimity. 'If you'll excuse me?'

He reminded her of a sleeping tiger. All leashed power beneath the guise of relaxed ease.

Francesca watched as he turned and threaded his way back to his table.

'I didn't realise you were on such close terms with Dominic Andrea. I have one of his paintings.'

She couldn't imagine her father coveting anything resembling the colourful abstract resting in Leon's gallery. A mental run-through of the artwork gracing Rick and Madeline's walls brought a mental blank.

'The vase of roses in the dining room,' Rick enlightened. 'Madeline assures me it is perfect for the room.'

Francesca had to agree. She'd silently admired it numerous times. Such painstaking brushwork, a delicate blending of colours. Velvet curling petals, the perfection of leaf foliage, the drops of fresh dew. Displayed in a glazed ceramic bowl against a shadowy background. The work of a man, she conceded, who possessed infinite patience and skill. Did those same qualities extend to pleasuring a woman? Somehow she imagined that they did.

Sensation feathered the surface of her skin, and she consciously banked down the acute ache deep within. She experienced guilt, and mentally attempted to justify it.

'Shall we leave?' Rick suggested as he settled the

bill. Together they threaded their way towards the exit and parted with an affectionate kiss as they reached the pavement.

Shopping, a visit to the hairdresser and the beautician took care of the afternoon, then she drove home and dressed for the evening ahead.

Obscenely glamorous. Well, the gown was certainly that! Indigo lace over raw silk, form-fitting. A lace bolero, high-heeled pumps and evening purse. Her favourite perfume added a finishing touch.

Familial affection was in evidence during dinner, and Francesca relaxed in the warmth of it. There were gifts to distribute that she'd collected in Rome, and the photographer appeared at their table right on cue.

If Madeline knew it was a set-up, she didn't let on. It was enough that she and her children would appear on the social pages, their names in print.

Sunday brought abnormally high summer temperatures, and Francesca was glad she'd made arrangements to join her mother for a day cruising the harbour on a friend's boat. The breeze made for pleasant conditions, and for the first time in ages she slept the night through, rising later than usual the next morning at the start of what promised to be a hectic week.

Francesca drummed her fingers against the steering wheel in an increasingly agitated tattoo as it took two and sometimes three light changes to clear each computer-controlled intersection.

Traffic into the city was heavier than usual, and a

silent curse formed on her lips as green changed to amber, then red.

In less than five minutes she was due to check in backstage in readiness to appear on the catwalk for a charity fashion parade.

The first of many she'd agreed to do during her stay on Australian shores.

Damn. Another red light. Was everything conspiring against her?

Ten minutes later she swept into the main entrance of the hotel, handed her keys to the valet, took the parking stub, then hurriedly made her way into the foyer.

The Grand Ballroom was situated on the first level, and she tossed up whether to take the stairs or the lift.

The stairs won, and minutes later she threaded her way through milling guests to the main doors. Inside uniformed waiters were conducting a last-minute check of the tables, and harried committee members conferred, consulted and made small changes to existing seating arrangements.

'Francesca. *Darling!*' Six feet tall, Anique Sorensen, society doyenne and leading fundraiser, embraced her stature by clothing it as expensively and outrageously as possible. This year the focus appeared to be jewellery. Masses of gold chains round her neck and adorning each wrist. On anyone else it would have looked garish, even tacky. But Anique managed to make it appear a fashion statement. 'I'm so grateful you can be here today. You look fabulous. Just fabulous.' She paused to draw breath and clasped Francesca close in a bear-hug, then did the air-kiss thing before releasing her hold. 'How *are* you?'

Francesca said what she knew Anique expected to hear...in one syllable. 'Fine. And you?'

'Ask me after the show.' The smile was in place, but there was an edge to it. 'I'm waiting on two models.'

A fashion showing might *look* smooth and display professional co-ordination out front, but organised chaos ruled behind the scenes.

'Traffic's heavy,' Francesca offered, shifting her garment bag from one shoulder to the other. 'Who?'

'Annaliese and Cassandra.'

Cassandra was a doll, laid-back, easy to get along with and professional. Annaliese, on the other hand, was a sultry cat who played diva to the hilt both on and off the catwalk.

'They'll be here,' Francesca assured her, and caught Anique's wry smile.

'I know, darling. But *when*?' Her sharp gaze circled the room. 'The guests are due to be seated any minute, in ten the compère will announce the charity's chairwoman's introductory speech, and five after that we need to roll.'

'It'll all come together.'

'It always does,' Anique agreed. 'I'd kill for a cigarette and a double gin.' She gave a long-suffering sigh. 'I swear, next year I'm not going to be on *any* committee.'

'You will. They need you.' It was true. 'No one can pull in the people the way you do.'

The eyes softened, their expression sincere. 'You're a sweet girl, Francesca.'

The usual bedlam reigned backstage, with racks of clothes and accessories and fellow models in various stages of undress fixing their make-up. Designers' assistants, co-ordinators, were each running numerous preliminary checks in the countdown to showtime.

Always there were last-minute changes, alterations that had to be noted on everyone's list. Mostly, they got it right.

Francesca checked the clothes and accessories she was to wear, and their sequence, then she shed her outer clothes and got to work on her make-up.

'Fran, sweetie.' Cassandra, tall, willowy and a natural blonde squeezed in to grab some mirror space. 'I need someone to tell me I'm sane.'

'You're sane,' Francesca said obligingly. 'That bad, huh?'

Cassandra delved into her make-up bag and seconds later her fingers flew with lightning speed, a touch of blusher here, eyeshadow there, and an experienced twist with the mascara wand. 'My daughter has tonsillitis, I broke a nail on the car door latch, snagged a run in my tights, and got caught in traffic.' She outlined her mouth and applied brilliant red gloss. 'Annaliese has yet to put in an appearance out front, and Anique...' She paused, and rolled her eyes in a wonderfully expressive gesture.

'Is about to go into orbit?' Francesca completed drily.

'You got it in one.'

The compère's introduction could be heard in the background. 'Five minutes,' one of the co-ordinators warned, whirling as a figure dressed entirely in scarlet flew into the room. 'Annaliese. You're impossibly late.'

The leggy, dark-haired model gave a careless shrug, tried to look apologetic and failed. 'Blame the cab-driver.'

'We'll run you last in the first segment,' the co-ordinator improvised. 'Just *hurry*, will you?' She altered her list, and moved quickly to ensure the altera-tion was duplicated.

Francesca stepped into casual shorts, secured them, added a top, and slid her feet into heeled slingback white sandals. Then she picked up the wraparound skirt and hitched it over one shoulder.

The chairwoman's speech finished, the compère completed his spiel, and the music began.

'OK, girls,' the co-ordinator announced. 'This is it. Cassandra, you first. Then Francesca.'

Upbeat music, flashing lights, *showtime*.

It was a familiar scene, different catwalk, another city. Francesca waited for her cue, smile in place, then she emerged on stage. Each movement was perfectly co-ordinated as she walked to the centre, paused, and turned before taking the catwalk. Choreographed ac-tion that displayed the clothes to their best advantage.

Resortwear, swimwear, city and career wear, collec-tions, formal evening wear, bridal.

Designers fussed, assistants frowned, and the co-ordinators soothed and cajoled and kept everything moving smoothly.

Francesca effected one quick change after another, exchanging shoes, accessories. The bridalwear segment was the designers' *coup de grâce*, and each gown was

modelled solo to give specific impact. Slow music and
a slow pace down the length of the catwalk and back.

Then all the models appeared on stage together, the
guests gave a noisy ovation, the compère wound down
and the designers slipped out to stand beside the model
wearing their creation. Then it was all over.

Waiters began appearing, bearing trays laden with
plates of food, and drink waiters hovered unobtrusively
as they took and delivered orders.

Francesca emerged backstage and began discarding
the heavy satin beaded gown. Her own clothes felt comfortable by comparison, and she crossed to the mirror
to tone down her make-up.

On the agenda was something light to eat, then she'd
drive back to the apartment, change and swim a few
leisurely lengths of the pool.

'Will you be at Margo's tomorrow?'

She glanced up at the sound of Cassandra's voice.
'Yes. You too?'

'Uh-huh.'

'I don't do it for free,' Annaliese declared in bored
tones as she joined them.

'Really?' Cassandra queried sweetly, unable to let the
unintentional *double entendre* escape unmentioned. 'As
a matter of interest, how much do you charge?'

Francesca saw Annaliese's eyes narrow, glimpsed
the anger tighten that full mouth. 'Jealous, *sweetie*?'

'Why, *no*, honey. I don't relish the attached strings.'

'Pity you didn't consider *strings* when you opted to
travel the hard road as a single mother.'

Oh, my, Francesca accorded wryly. Much more of this and there would be a cat-fight.

'Annaliese, why don't you hush your mouth before I do it for you?' Cassandra queried silkily.

'One hopes that's an idle threat, darling. If not, let me warn that I wouldn't hesitate to lay assault charges.'

'Bitch,' Cassandra muttered as soon as Annaliese vacated the changing room. 'She likes to rattle my chain.'

'It's her favoured pastime,' Francesca enlightened as she collected her garment bag and slung it over one shoulder. 'I'm out of here.' Her lips curved into a generous smile. 'See you tomorrow.'

As she emerged from backstage Anique snagged her arm and heaped ebullient praise for a job well done.

Ever polite, Francesca paused to exchange a greeting with various women, some of whom she knew and others she did not. Consequently it seemed an age before she was able to escape into the main lobby and summon the valet to collect her car.

'A message for you, ma'am.'

Who? she queried silently as she took the envelope from the valet's hand. 'Thanks.' She switched on her mobile phone and checked her voicemail, then she lifted the envelope flap and extracted a business card.

Dominic Andrea's business card, with a message *Call me* penned on the back above a series of digits. Francesca didn't know whether to be annoyed or amused, and slipped the card into her bag as she stepped through the automatic sliding doors to wait for her car.

Within seconds it swept into the curved forecourt.

The valet jumped out and held open the door as she slid in behind the wheel.

It took longer than usual to reach her apartment, and once inside she tossed down her bag, slipped off her shoes, then padded barefoot into the kitchen for a cool drink.

Ten minutes later she took the lift down to the ground floor and made her way towards the indoor pool.

The soft, clear water relaxed her, easing the kinks from tired muscles as she stroked several laps, then she turned onto her back and allowed her body to drift with the movement of the water for a while before reversing her position.

Employing a slow breaststroke, she made her way to the side and levered herself up onto the tiled edge. Water streamed off her body as she stood to her feet, and she caught up her towel and dealt with the excess moisture.

It was almost five when she re-entered the apartment, and with automatic movements she crossed into the bedroom, entered the *en suite* bathroom and turned on the shower.

Ten minutes later she pulled on a towelling robe and began blowdrying her hair, then she moved into the kitchen to prepare something light to eat.

An omelette, she decided. Eaten in the lounge while watching television.

The phone rang twice during the evening. Her mother suggesting lunch, and Gabbi issuing an invitation to the theatre.

CHAPTER FOUR

MARGO'S BOUTIQUE was one of several in the exclusive Double Bay boulevard catering to the city's rich and famous.

An astute woman with a love of fashion, Margo had opened the boutique soon after her husband's death in a bid to channel her energies into something constructive. Adhering to instinct, she stocked expensive designer originals that were classically elegant. Her window display held one mannequin, whose apparel was changed every day. A selection of bags were offered to complement designer shoes.

Margo's quarterly invitation-only fashion showings were offered to a valued clientele, with the request that they each bring a guest. Champagne and orange juice flowed, catered refreshments were served with coffee and tea. Margo offered a ten per cent reduction in price on everything in the shop and donated a further ten per cent of the day's take to her favoured charity.

A fondness for using fledgling unknown models had boosted the careers of several, a few of whom had gone on to achieve international recognition.

Francesca had been one of them. Hence, if a visit home coincided with one of Margo's showings, Francesca donated her services *sans* fee, out of respect and affection for a woman who gave far more to charity than was generally known, and who insisted such philanthrophic gestures were never reported in the press.

Parking wasn't a problem, and Francesca crossed the square at a brisk pace, dodging small puddles accumulated from an early-morning rainfall. An elegantly clad vendeuse stood at the door, welcoming guests and checking their invitations. Outside there was hired uniformed security.

Collectively, the jewellery adorning fingers, wrists, necks and earlobes would amount to a small fortune.

Francesca counted two Rolls-Royces and a Bentley lining the kerb, and three chauffeurs engaged in transferring their employers from car to pavement.

The boutique's air-conditioned interior provided a welcome contrast to the high humidity that threatened, according to the day's forecast, to climb into the nineties.

'Francesca.' Margo's greeting held warmth and genuine enthusiasm. 'It's so good to see you. Cassandra arrived a minute ago, and the three novices are already quaking out back.'

A smile tugged the edges of her mouth. 'Quaking?'

Margo's eyes held a musing sparkle. 'Almost literally. And desperately in need of professional wisdom to help put them at ease.'

Francesca thought back nine years to the time she had stood consumed by nerves in one of Margo's changing rooms for the first time and doubted *any* words would make a difference.

'I'll do my best.'

'I'm counting on it.'

Francesca moved through the vestibule to the changing rooms, greeted Cassandra, the co-ordinator assigned to accessorise each outfit and detail their order of appearance, and smiled at the three girls whose expressions bore witness to a sense of awe and trepidation.

They were so *young*. Humour was the only way to go, and her eyes assumed a mischievous sparkle. 'You've forgotten everything Margo said, are convinced your limbs will freeze the instant you go out there, and, failing that, you'll trip and fall flat on your face.' Her mouth curved with impish wit. 'Right? None of which is going to happen. Trust me.'

Margo was an exemplary organiser, and with plenty of staff on hand the fashion showing began without a hitch. Champagne flowed, and the guests were receptive. Seating was arranged three deep in two opposing semi-circles.

Francesca was first out, and she paused, executed a slow turn, then completed a round of the inner circle.

It was as she turned back to the audience that she saw him. Dominic Andrea, attired in a formal business suit, blue shirt, navy tie. Looking, she noted wryly, very comfortable with his surroundings, and not at all daunted at being only one of three men present in a room filled with women.

What the hell was he doing here?

Francesca's smile encompassed everyone and her

eyes focused on no one in particular. Head held high, shoulders squared, she went through a familiar routine.

Yet she was acutely aware of the darkly attractive man whose attention she sensed rather than saw, and she had to actively steel herself against the faint shivering sensation that spiralled the length of her spine.

'What gives?'

Francesca cast Cassandra a harried glance as she slid down the zip fastening and stepped out of a tailored skirt. 'Be specific.' She unbuttoned the blouse and discarded it, then reached for an elegant trouser suit.

'There's a man seated third row, centre,' Cassandra declared as she donned tailored trousers and slid the zip in place, 'who seems to be showing an intense interest in your every move.'

As the morning progressed Francesca became increasingly aware of Dominic's presence. And his attention.

Why did she feel so *exposed* beneath his encompassing scrutiny? She hadn't felt this… 'Nervous' wasn't strictly accurate. She'd walked down too many catwalks, appeared at too many fashion showings to allow nerves to undermine professionalism.

Aware. That about summed it up. Attuned to one person to such an infinite degree that you were able to *sense* every glance without seeing it. The tingle that feathered down her spine, the slight heaviness of her breasts as each nipple tightened, and the slow, soft curling sensation deep within.

All this as a result of a few chance encounters with the man, a few shared hours in company of mutual friends over dinner, and the brush of his lips against her temple? It was crazy.

Even more absurd was the feeling that she'd entered a one-way street from which there was no return.

Wayward thoughts, she dismissed. Her life was pleasant, she had command of it, and memories of Mario filled her heart. What more did she need?

Shared passion. A warm body to hold onto in the long night hours.

Where had that come from?

Fleeting pain darkened her eyes as guilt, remorse, *anger* tore at something deep inside, and for one split second she wanted to run and hide.

Yet she did neither. Professionalism ensured she tilted her head a fraction higher, curved her lips to make her smile a little brighter, and she walked, turned, paused with the ease of long practice.

Intimate, classy, *successful*, Francesca dubbed the event as it came to a close. Everyone bought. Garments, shoes, bags. Each was folded reverently in tissue paper and deposited into one of Margo's stylish carrybags.

Francesca pulled on an elegant Armani trouser suit, slid her feet into high-heeled pumps, then caught up her capacious carry-all and slid the wide strap over one shoulder.

She entered the salon, saw the number of guests milling in groups, and took a steadying breath as she glimpsed Dominic deep in conversation with an attractive woman on the other side of the room.

Why was he still here?

Almost as if he sensed her glance, he raised his head

and cast her a penetrating look, then returned his attention to the woman beside him.

Shattering, Francesca perceived. The effect he had on her senses. She'd been supremely conscious of his scrutiny each time she'd circled the salon, and had managed to successfully ignore him.

'Francesca.'

He had the tread of a cat. Francesca turned slowly to face him. 'Dominic,' she acknowledged with due solemnity.

His smile was warm, and his eyes held amusement as he took hold of her hand and lifted it to his lips.

The touch was fleeting, yet she felt as if she'd been branded by fire. Heat flared through her veins, travelling a damning path. If he'd wanted to disconcert her, he'd succeeded.

Potent sexuality at its most lethal, she thought shakily. Wielded by an infinitely dangerous man who, unless she was mistaken, would play the game by his own rules.

He sensed the slight quiver of nervous awareness, felt the startled tightening of her fingers, and allowed her to pull free of him. For now.

During the past hour he'd watched her display a variety of clothes, admired her body's graceful movement, the tilt of her head, the warm generous smile.

Outwardly cool, she schooled her features into a polite mask, and knew that she hadn't fooled him in the slightest.

'If you'll excuse me?' She wanted, needed to get away.

'No.'

The refusal startled her. 'I beg your pardon?'

'No,' he repeated quietly.

Francesca pitched her voice sufficiently low so that no one else could hear. 'Just what the hell do you think you're doing?'

His gaze was steady. 'At this precise moment?'

She lifted one hand and let it fall to her side in angry resignation. 'OK, let's go with "this precise moment".'

A fleeting smile lightened his features, and she caught a glimpse of gleaming white teeth. 'Inviting you to lunch.'

Now it was her turn. 'No.'

His eyes gleamed with dark humour. 'I could add persuasion and kiss you in front of Margo's guests.'

Her voice lowered to a furious whisper. 'Do that, and I'll *hit* you.'

'It might be worth it to see you try.' He didn't give her time to think as he captured her face and lowered his head down to hers.

It wasn't a gentle touching of mouths, or a sensual tasting. Nor was it particularly brief.

This was claim-staking. Possession. Erotic, evocative, and intensely sexual.

Shock reverberated through her body, and she instinctively lifted her hands in an attempt to effect leverage against his chest.

He eased the pressure a little, and she tore her mouth away from his.

'You—'

He stilled the flow of angry words by placing a finger against her lips. 'Not here, unless you want to cause a scene.'

Her eyes sparked with fury, and her mouth shook as she sought to gain some measure of control. She became aware of her surroundings, the salon's occupants, and she wanted to verbally damn him as he took hold of her arm and led her outside.

'You arrogant, egotistical *fiend*,' Francesca accused the second they were alone.

'You didn't respond to my message, and with your telephone and mobile number ex-directory, your address unlisted, you left me no alternative.' He didn't add that he possessed sufficient influence to infiltrate the tight security screen she'd erected around her public and private persona.

'You inveigled an invitation to Margo's showing on that basis?' Anger was very much to the fore, sharpening the gold flecks in her eyes, accentuating the tilt of her head, stiffening her stance. She wanted to rage at him with a torrent of words that would singe the hair on his head.

He shrugged his shoulders. 'It was an interesting experience.'

'That's all you have to say?'

'It gave me the opportunity to watch you at work.'

Being one of few men in a room filled with avid women fashion-followers couldn't have held much appeal. 'I hope you suffered!'

Dark eyes gleamed, and his lips parted to form a quizzical smile. 'Oh, I did, believe me.'

Her chin lifted, and her eyes sparked furious fire.

'What is it with you? Do I present a challenge or something?'

Mockery was very much in evidence. 'Or something.'

It was a loaded statement, one that she refused to examine. 'Let me make it quite clear.' She drew in a deep breath. 'You're wasting your time.'

'That's a matter of opinion.'

Francesca closed her eyes, then opened them again. 'You know my father. Gabbi and Benedict Nicols are mutual friends.'

'What we share has nothing to do with your father, Gabbi or Benedict. Or anyone else for that matter.'

Emotion clouded her features, fleeting and pain-filled. 'We don't share *anything.*'

'Not yet,' Dominic said quietly. 'But we will.' He cupped her cheek in one hand and brushed his thumb along the length of her jaw. And didn't miss the movement in her throat as she compulsively swallowed.

Francesca glimpsed the deceptive indolence apparent in those deep eyes, the silent assurance of a man who knew what he wanted and would allow nothing to stand in his way. The knowledge tripped her pulse and made her heart beat faster. She had to put some distance between them.

'Please let me go.'

It was the 'please' that did it. He trailed his hand down her cheek, outlined her lips with the pad of one forefinger, then he dropped his hand down to his side as he offered a quizzical smile.

'I guess we don't get to eat together?'

'I have to be in the city in half an hour.' And lunch was going to be a salad sandwich and bottled water she'd pick up and eat along the way.

'Another modelling assignment?'

'A photographic shoot.' She took one step back, another to the side. 'I really must go.'

Francesca turned and crossed the road. She could feel a distinct prickle of awareness between her shoulderblades, and she was conscious of every step she took along the pavement.

It was only when she was safely behind the wheel of her car that the tension began to ease, and by the time she reached the city Dominic was firmly expelled from her mind.

The fashion shoot was exhausting, with the designer insisting the photographer do numerous takes from every conceivable angle. Accessories were changed countless times, her make-up touched and retouched, her hairstyle switched from loose and unruly to casually upswept, then confined in a sleek French pleat.

'Anything planned tonight, darling? I'd like to move outdoors, capture you on a lonely beach against the backdrop of a fading sunset.'

It was after six, and she was battling the onset of a headache. More than anything she wanted to step into her own clothes, climb into her car and drive back to her apartment. And sink into a spa and sip a long, cool drink, she added silently.

As a photographer, Tony was a perfectionist. And she was sufficiently professional to want to work *with* rather than against him.

'Are you going to allow me time to eat?' she queried with resignation.

'Of course, sweetie.' His smile was quick, and his eyes held a humorous gleam. 'I'm not an absolute monster.'

'Although you'll want me here early in the morning for dawn shots,' Francesca accorded with cynicism.

'How well you know me.' There was a certain wryness evident. 'But I'm the best.'

Knowledge, not vanity. He won awards every year for his photographic skill, and harboured a genuine love for the camera. Able to combine subject and background to maximum effect on celluloid, and an exceptional strategist, he loathed temperament, lauded professionalism and went to any length to achieve the look he wanted.

Together, they worked as a team, stowing clothes and equipment before adjourning to a nearby café for a meal eaten alfresco at a verandah table offering splendid views over a leafy green park.

Afterwards they headed north in a small convoy of vehicles to a designated cove where a makeshift tent was erected in which Francesca could change.

The cool breeze from the ocean whispered across her skin and lifted a few loose tendrils of hair as she moved at Tony's bidding, providing one pose after another as he clicked off rolls of film.

'Just a few more, Francesca. I want to do some black and white shots.'

Dusk began to dim the peripheral fringes, providing shadows that grew and lengthened, shading colour and merging lines.

'OK, that's it,' called Tony.

The equipment was dismantled, the clothes restored into individual garment bags and packed into the van. Lights along the boardwalk provided illumination, in direct contrast to the expanse of indigo sea.

Tony stowed his camera in the car, then turned towards her. 'Care to join me in a drink? There's a trendy little bar two blocks away.'

'Will you be offended if I say no?' Francesca countered.

'A date, darling?'

She smiled as they left the sand and stepped onto the bricked walk. 'With my bed. Solo,' she added as she anticipated his response. 'I imagine you'd prefer me bright-eyed and vivacious tomorrow?'

'As a photographer, yes,' he grinned. 'As a man, I'd derive pleasure from seeing you languorous and sated after a long night of loving.'

An arrow of pain lanced her body's core, and it cost a lot to inject a degree of humour into her voice and keep it light. 'You don't give up.'

'Maybe one of these days you'll say yes.'

He was a nice man. Personable, intelligent, and easy to talk to. She'd worked with him frequently in the past, and wanted to continue to work with him in the future.

'To a drink?'

His laughter brought a smile to her lips. 'Know all the angles, darling?'

'Almost every one,' she assured.

'So,' he concluded slowly, 'no shared nightcap, not even coffee?'

'I'm taking a raincheck, remember?' She leaned forward and placed a fleeting kiss to his cheek. '*Ciao*, Tony. I'll see you in the morning.'

CHAPTER FIVE

ELECTRONIC CHIMES brought Francesca into a state of wakefulness, and she uttered a faint groan as she rolled over to hit the 'stop' button.

Damn Tony and his photographic inspiration. Yet, even as she silently cursed him, she was sufficiently professional to recognise his vision. And doubtless she would applaud it when she sighted the finished prints.

A shower swept away any vestiges of the night's cobwebs, and a glass of fresh orange juice did much to revitalise her energy. It was too early for breakfast, so she merely extracted a banana from the bowl of fruit in the kitchen.

Attired in stylish loose-fitting cotton trousers and matching top, basic make-up complete, she slid her feet into low-heeled sandals, collected her bag, then took the lift down to the underground car park.

Within minutes she reached the main arterial road. Traffic at this early hour was minimal, and there was almost an eerie solitude in traversing darkened streets whose only illumination came from regulated electric lamps.

There was a tendency to be introspective and allow one's thoughts free passage.

Dominic Andrea. An intriguing man, with diverse interests and recognised as a skilled entrepreneur. There could be little doubt that that skill extended to the bedroom...or wherever else he chose to indulge in sex.

She drew the line at defining it as lovemaking. 'Love' was a definitive word that had little to do with a mutual slaking of the senses as two people took pleasure in each other's body without trust or commitment.

The thought of Dominic Andrea in the role of lover aroused feelings she found difficult to dispel. To tread such a path would be madness.

Dear heaven, what was the matter with her?

Francesca reached forward and switched on the car radio, grateful for the busy sound of rock music and the artificial brightness of an early morning DJ. It helped redirect her focus.

Which, she rationalised, was a dawn fashion shoot that needed to be set up in early-morning darkness with everything in readiness for the first sign of light on the horizon.

Three cars and a van hugged the kerb when she slid to a halt behind Tony's distinctive BMW. Lights were already set up on the beach, the tent was in position, and as she drew close she could hear the sound of muted voices.

'Morning, everyone.'

Tony gave her a weary smile as she entered the tent. 'Good girl, you're on time.' He cast his watch a quick glance. 'Ten minutes, OK? Same gown, hairstyle. Less make-up.'

The sky was just beginning to lighten as Francesca assumed position within a metre of the receding tide. Wet sand gleamed like well-oiled gunmetal, melding with a smooth liquid sea.

Before their eyes grey shadows melted beneath the emergence of soft colour, like the transforming brush from an artist's palette. And the air bore a freshness untouched by the sun's warmth.

'Let's get this show on the road. We won't have long,' Tony warned as he lifted his camera. 'Francesca?'

'Ready when you are.'

The camera clicked, shutter moving forward as he called for her to move this way, then that.

'Head up a little higher. That's it. Hold it. Now turn towards me and smile. Mona Lisa, darling.' Shot after shot was taken. 'OK, now we want happy. Not quite laughing. Got it.'

The shutter whirred at a fast pace. 'Movement, sweetie,' he directed. 'Let's see that skirt swirl, shall we? More. Again. And again.' He was moving rapidly, his hands and body co-ordinating perfectly as he talked. 'Damn. The light's coming up fast.'

Five minutes later he capped the lens. 'That should do it. Thanks, everyone.'

It was shaping up to be a hectic day, Francesca perceived a trifle ruefully as she shed the gown, then pulled on her trousers and top. At lunch she was booked to tread another catwalk, and this evening she was due to dine at her father's home. With deft movements she twisted her hair into a knot atop her head, then slid her feet into sandals.

'Care to share coffee before we each get on with the day?' Tony queried as she emerged from the tent.

'Love to,' Francesca accepted, grateful for their easy friendship as they trod a path across the sand to the parked cars.

They each stowed their bags, locked the boot, then crossed the road to the beachside café.

'I'll order,' Tony indicated as they slid into an empty booth. 'Short black?'

'Please,' she responded gratefully, and sipped the dark aromatic brew from the cup placed in front of her shortly afterwards.

'You're covering today's charity luncheon at the Hilton?'

''fraid so, darling.' He drained his cup and signalled for the waitress to refill it.

'All those dowagers dressed to kill, fawning over you in a bid to have their photo appear in the society pages, huh?' Francesca teased, and caught his faint grimace.

'They send me gifts. Champagne, expensive trinkets. One matron even went so far as to offer an unforgettable all-expenses-paid weekend on Hayman Island.'

'Tell me you declined.'

He offered a wry smile. 'I don't accept bribes, as tempting as some appear.'

It was almost eight when Francesca slid behind the wheel of her car and drove to the gym. An exercise routine was so much a part of her daily regime that she scarcely gave it a thought.

There was little time to spare when she returned to her apartment in order to shower, dress, and drive into the city.

The fundraising luncheon in aid of the Australian Cancer Society was a major event. The venue was prestigious, and the guest list read like an excerpt from the city's register of the city's rich and famous.

'Sell-out' was whispered from one to the other as the speeches progressed and lunch was served. Then the compère announced the start of the fashion parade and the music began.

The main lights dimmed and strategically aimed arc lights lit the catwalk. Showtime.

Afterwards, Francesca tidied her hair, retouched her make-up, then collected her bag. With luck she'd be able to slip out and make an exit without too much delay.

She was halfway across the room when she heard a familiar voice call her name.

'Francesca.'

Her stepmother, with Katherine at her side, seated at a nearby table. 'You'll join us for a coffee, won't you?'

Madeline was adept at making a query sound like a command, and there was little Francesca could do other than slip into the indicated seat.

Katherine offered a conspiratorial wink, well aware that her mother's main purpose in issuing the invitation was to bolster her own social prestige. Smart girl, Katherine.

It was thirty minutes before Francesca could orchestrate her escape, and a further half an hour before she joined the flow of traffic leaving the city. Consequently it was almost five when she re-entered her apartment.

After a day exchanging one elegant outfit for another, she would have preferred to slip on a robe, eat a light chicken salad, watch television, then settle for an early night.

Instead, she selected a stunning black silk trouser suit, added a touch of gold jewellery, applied minimum make-up, highlighted her eyes, and left her hair loose to cascade onto her shoulders.

Lights blazed in welcome as Francesca traversed the long, curved driveway leading to Rick and Madeline's elegant double-storeyed Tudor-style home situated high in suburban Vaucluse.

The interior reflected Madeline's exquisite taste, and Francesca greeted Katherine and John with affection, brushed cheeks with her stepmother and accepted Rick's warm bear-hug.

'Have a seat, Francesca,' Madeline bade. 'Rick will get you a drink.'

Diplomacy and an adeptness born of many years' experience in recognising Madeline's *modus operandi* ensured that Francesca kept within the unwritten boundaries. Once you knew the game, it was relatively easy to play.

'Orange juice? A wine spritzer?'

'A spritzer would be great,' she accepted warmly.

The sound of the door chimes provided an interruption, and Madeline turned towards Rick. 'That will be Dominic. Let him in, darling.' She turned to Francesca. 'You don't mind the inclusion of another guest?'

There was nothing she could do except smile. 'Of course not.'

Rick knew better than to matchmake. Madeline, however, had no such qualms, and was adept at assembling people together in order to create an interesting evening.

Dominic Andrea's motives for accepting the invitation were open to conjecture.

'He's really a hunk, isn't he?' Katherine enthused with teenage fervour, and Francesca was saved from making comment as her father ushered Dominic into the lounge.

In her line of business she came into contact with many visually attractive men, but few possessed this man's aura of power. It went beyond the physical, and meshed with a dangerous sexuality that threatened a woman's equilibrium. A potent combination, she conceded as she took in his expensive suit, silk tie, hand-stitched shoes, before allowing her gaze to settle on those broad, chiselled features.

Generous mouth, cleaved from a sensual mould. Eyes so dark, yet as expressive as he chose them to be. At this precise moment there was a tinge of humour beneath the projected warmth.

'Madeline.' He moved forward with fluid grace, took hold of his hostess's hand, then turned towards her stepdaughter.

'Francesca.'

'Dominic,' she acknowledged coolly. She felt on edge already, and he'd only just entered the room. What on earth would she be like at the end of the evening?

Unsettled, if he had anything to do with it.

'A drink, Dominic?' Rick was a considerate host who kept a well-stocked liquor cabinet designed to cater to the whim of any guest.

'Thanks. A soda.'

Madeline smiled. 'The need for a clear head?'

'Perhaps Dominic has an ulcer,' Francesca offered sweetly. 'I imagine an artistic temperament and the pressure of business play havoc with the stress levels.'

'Not an inclination to minimise alcohol to one glass of wine with the evening meal?'

She tilted her head and viewed him in silence for several long seconds. 'How.' She paused deliberately. 'Boring.'

His mouth curved slightly. 'You prefer a man whose mind and actions are clouded with alcohol?'

Oh, my. Was she the only one present who picked up on that *double entendre*?

Francesca silently willed the evening to pass quickly so that she could make her escape at the soonest possible moment without causing Madeline or her father offence.

She caught Dominic's faintly raised eyebrow, and realised that he'd accurately assessed her thoughts.

'I had no idea you were joining us tonight.' As a conversational gambit, it lacked inspiration.

His eyes held hidden warmth and a degree of cynical humour. 'Madeline issued an invitation to look at the positioning of two of my paintings in her home.'

Her head tilted fractionally. 'Do you make it a practice to approve where your paintings hang in all your buyers' homes?'

'Rarely,' he conceded.

'Rick and Madeline should feel duly honoured.'

His soft laughter was unexpected, the humour tilting the curve of his mouth and fanning tiny lines from each corner of his eyes. Eyes that were remarkably steady, even watchful as he caught each fleeting expression on her finely boned features.

'Perhaps.' Dominic lifted a hand and tucked a stray tendril of hair behind her ear in a gesture deliberately designed to startle. 'Although let there be no doubt that the main reason I'm here tonight is *you*.'

He glimpsed the faint widening of her eyes, the momentary shock, before she successfully masked her expression.

'Dinner is served, ma'am.' The cook's intrusion was a timely one, and Francesca expelled a relieved sigh as Madeline led the way.

Seating was arranged with Madeline and Rick facing each other at the head of the table, Katherine and John on one side, with Dominic and Francesca seated together.

Vichyssoise was followed by barbecued prawns on a bed of rice, with steamed fish, hollandaise sauce and salad as a main course. Crème caramel and fresh fruit sufficed as dessert.

A pleasant meal in what would have been relaxing company—if it hadn't been for Dominic's presence. Francesca was acutely aware of his every action, the smell of clean tailoring mingling with the subtle tones of his exclusive cologne.

He used his cutlery with precise, decisive movements, his enjoyment of the food evident, and he skil-fully drew Katherine and John into the conversation, transforming John into an amusing raconteur while Katherine bloomed beneath his attention.

Madeline was at her best. Fame or fortune in a guest was a bonus. To have two dine at her table who could lay claim to both was a considerable *coup*. Rick, sens-ing his wife's satisfaction, became more expansive as the evening progressed.

'Shall we adjourn to the lounge for coffee?' Mad-eline queried, signalling just that intention by stand-ing to her feet.

Everyone followed her directive, but Francesca was unprepared when Dominic moved behind her and drew out her chair.

She hadn't expected the courtesy, didn't want it, and had to consciously refrain from pulling her arm away as his fingers lightly clasped her elbow.

'Katherine, John,' Madeline invited graciously. 'If you choose, you can retire upstairs and view television.'

An exemplary mother, and a very shrewd one. Po-litical correctness and good manners were something Madeline insisted upon. It said much that neither of her children grasped the excuse to leave.

Fifteen minutes max, Francesca decided, then she would express her thanks and depart. She sank grace-fully into a lounge chair and accepted coffee.

It had been a long day, and tomorrow, after seeing her mother, she'd agreed to join a panel of judges assembled to select three junior models from twenty young hope-fuls parading their stuff on the catwalk.

Friday, Saturday and Sunday were free, and she'd designated them as *hers*. For pampering, a professional haircut, a massage. Sheer indulgence.

Unbidden, her eyes met those of Dominic, and she glimpsed the degree of sensual warmth evident in those dark depths. He presented a disturbing factor, and she was in no doubt of the steel-willed determination beneath the surface.

Francesca finished her coffee, declined a refill, and rose to her feet. 'If you'll excuse me, I really must leave.' Her warm smile encompassed Rick, Madeline, Katherine and John. 'It's been a lovely evening.'

'Likewise,' Dominic accorded with ease as he unwound his length from the chair. 'It's been very enjoyable.'

Why was he timing his departure to coincide with her own? Why shouldn't he? a silent voice demanded as she crossed the lounge at Rick's side, brushed a quick kiss to his cheek at the front door, then stepped quickly down the steps.

'Running away?' Dominic's voice held slight amusement as he matched his pace to her own.

She withdrew a keyring from her evening purse in readiness, and walked past a black Lexus to where her own car was parked. She selected a key and inserted it into the door.

His arm brushed hers as he reached forward and undid the latch, then drew open the door.

'How was your day?'

She slipped past him and slid into the driver's seat. 'You can't really want to know.'

He placed an arm on the roof and leaned in towards her. 'Yes. Humour me, Francesca.'

She slid the safety belt across and clipped it into position. She should have felt in control, yet somehow the advantage appeared to be his.

'A three-thirty a.m. start for a dawn photographic shoot, a fashion parade at the Hilton, dinner with family.'

'And guest.'

'Unexpected guest,' she amended.

'Whom you would have preferred not to be present.'

She tilted her head in order to meet his gaze. 'Perhaps you'll enlighten me as to how you came by the invitation.'

'I occasionally do business with your father.' His shoulders shifted in a slight shrugging gesture. 'Madeline appears to appreciate my paintings. It wasn't difficult to make a phone call.'

No, she supposed. Not difficult at all for a skilful manipulator to pose a few pertinent questions within a conversation in order to gain his objective.

She looked at him carefully, and his sloping smile had the strangest effect, causing sensation to unfurl deep inside and creep insidiously through her body.

'What should I expect next?' She kept her voice deliberately cool. 'The "Your place or mine?" spiel?'

Dominic regarded her steadily. 'Interpreted as, "Let's get between the sheets and I'll show you what you're missing"? I don't play that particular game.'

'With any woman?'

'With you,' he declared with soft emphasis. He

reached forward and caught hold of her chin between thumb and forefinger. 'Now, shall we begin again? To-morrow—'

'There isn't going to be a tomorrow.' Her voice sounded thick and vaguely husky.

'Yes,' he said quietly. 'There is. The day after, or the one after that. Next week. Whenever.'

Francesca looked at him long and hard, saw the calm awareness in his eyes, and felt *exposed* in a way she'd never experienced before. Fear, apprehension—both were prevalent. And a strange sense of recognition. Almost as if something deep inside her had sought and found the matching half of a whole.

She didn't want to deal with it, with *him*, and what he represented. She wanted time to think, to evaluate. Saying yes to this man, on any level, would lead her towards a path she was hesitant to tread.

'This is one situation where your persistence won't pay off,' she assured him.

'You don't think so?'

'I know so.'

'Then prove me wrong and share lunch with me. Nominate a day.' A challenge. Would she accept or refuse?

Fine, she accorded a trifle grimly. If that was what it took to convince him she wasn't interested, she'd agree. Besides, lunch sounded *safe*. Broad daylight, with the excuse of work as a legitimate escape route.

Francesca gave him a long, level look. 'Friday,' she capitulated. 'Name the restaurant, and I'll meet you there.'

'Claude's, Oxford Street, Woollahra. One,' he said without missing a beat.

A fashionably chic French eating place where advance bookings were a must. 'Fine.' She slid the key into the ignition and fired the engine, watching as he stood back and closed the door.

Seconds later she cleared the gates and entered the wide, tree-lined suburban street, following it down until it joined with New South Head Road.

Electric streetlights shared a pattern uniformity, vying with colourful flashing neon signs illuminating the city's centre. Ferries traversed the dark waters of Port Jackson, and a large cruise ship was ablaze with light and life as a tugboat led it slowly towards the inner harbour.

Magical, Francesca reflected silently, and felt a strange pull towards another harbour in another city on the opposite side of the world. Another car, a Ferrari Testarossa, driven by Mario through the steep winding hills above Rome. And how she'd delighted at the sight spread out before her, laughed with the joy of life, then gasped at the speed with which Mario had driven home in order to make love with her.

Mad, halcyon days that couldn't last. Even then she'd been afraid the candle that burned so brightly within him was destined for a short life.

It was almost eleven when she garaged her car and took the lift up to her apartment. With care she shed her clothes, removed her make-up, then she donned a slither of silk and slid in between cool percale sheets.

CHAPTER SIX

AN ELEGANT WOMAN, Sophy adored being *seen*. Consequently her choice of venue was one of the city's currently trendiest meeting places in town.

'*Drinks*, darling,' Sophy had specified the get-together, and Francesca slid into a reserved chair and ordered coffee.

Her mother would be late. After all these years it was accepted Sophy had no sense of time. Excuses, many and varied, were floated out with an airy wave of the hand, and her family and friends inevitably forgave her the lapse.

Thirty minutes wasn't too bad, Francesca conceded wryly as she glimpsed her mother making an entrance. There had been occasions when she'd waited for up to an hour.

Titian hair styled in a shoulder-length bob, exquisite features, and slim curves a woman half her age would die for. Add an exclusive designer outfit, and Sophy presented a visual image that drew appreciative admiration.

'Sorry, sweetheart.' Sophy effected a careless shrug as she slid into the seat opposite. 'Armand...' Her mouth tilted wickedly. 'You know how it is. The French—everything is *l'amour*.'

'I thought you were through with Frenchmen,' Francesca said equably.

'Ah, but they are so *gallant*.' Sophy cast her daughter an impish smile. 'Besides, darling, he is fantastic in bed.'

'How nice.'

'Yes,' her mother agreed, and her eyes gleamed with humour. 'It's a lovely bonus.'

Francesca wondered with philosophical resignation if Armand was even more unsuitable than his illustrious predecessor, who had squired her mother for a record ten months before Sophy discarded him.

'Now, sweetheart. Tell me what you think of your father. The last time I saw him I thought he was looking quite…' Sophy paused, then added delicately, 'Mature. A few more lines. I recommended my cosmetic surgeon, but you can imagine your father's response.'

Indeed. Voluble, to say the least.

'Madeline makes so many demands, and of course there's the children.'

An emotional minefield Francesca had no intention of entering. 'Would you like coffee?'

'Please.' Her eyes sharpened fractionally. 'You look—different.' Speculative interest was evident. 'Yes. Definitely.' Her mouth curved. 'It's a man, isn't it?'

A man. It seemed such a tame description for someone of Dominic Andrea's calibre.

'Now why would you think that?' Francesca countered evenly, and her mother smiled.

'Am I right?'

'Not really.'

'Ah,' Sophy declared with ambiguous satisfaction, and changed the subject. 'You have yet to mention Mario's mother. So sad. There was a nurse, of course?'

'Yes, round the clock.' Francesca didn't add that she'd shared each shift and snatched sleep as and when she could.

Frequenting the trendiest café ensured there were interruptions, as first one, then another of Sophy's friends stopped by. Introductions rarely identified Francesca as Sophy's *daughter*. Age was something her mother guarded jealously and refused to acknowledge to anyone—for how did a woman who *looked* thirty admit to a twenty-five-year-old progeny.

Armand duly arrived to collect his *amour*, and Francesca wondered how her mother could not see that the man was too attentive, too smooth, and too intent on feeding not only Sophy's ego but his own.

However, Francesca had long given up worrying about her mother's succession of paramours. Sophy was aware of all the angles.

The day after...next week...whenever. Dominic's words echoed inside Francesca's head as she considered calling him to say she'd changed her mind about meeting him.

Except she had the feeling all that would do was postpone the inevitable.

Perhaps it would be better to get it over and done with. They'd talk, eat, and discover whatever he thought they had in common didn't exist. And pigs might fly, she denounced disparagingly.

What existed between them was primeval chemistry, pure and simple. The question was, what was she going to do about it? More pertinently, what was she going to allow Dominic to do about it?

Oh, for heaven's sake. What are you afraid of? she silently berated herself.

Good question, Francesca noted wryly as she entered Claude's and was greeted by the *maître d'*.

'Ah, yes. Mr Andrea is already here.' His smile charmed, as it was meant to do. 'Please. Follow me.'

It was crazy to feel nervous. *Act*, a tiny voice prompted. You're good at it.

Dominic watched as she threaded her way through the room. He observed the number of heads turn in her direction, witnessed the speculation and admiration, and felt a certain empathy for their appreciation of Francesca's beauty.

Experience had taught him that the packaging didn't always reflect what existed in the heart, the mind, the soul, and that physical lust was an unsatisfactory entity without love. Consequently, he refused to settle for anything less.

As she drew close he sensed the imperceptible degree of nervousness beneath the sophisticated veneer, and discovered it pleased him.

He rose to his feet as she reached his table. 'Francesca.'

Her response was polite, and he smiled, aware of the

defence mechanism firmly in place…and wondered how long it would take to demolish it.

The *maître d'* held out a chair and she sank into it. 'Madame would prefer a few minutes before she orders a drink?'

'I'll have an orange juice.'

'I shall inform the drink steward,' he said gravely, and with a snap of his fingers a formally clad waiter appeared out of nowhere, took her order, then disappeared.

The lighting was low, the tables small. And Dominic seemed much too close.

Francesca looked at him carefully, and his features seemed more finely chiselled, the bone structure more pronounced in the dim illumination. Dark hair, dark eyes, dark suit. It accentuated his breadth of shoulder and emphasised a physical fitness most men would aspire to.

A complex man, she decided instinctively, who was capable of savagery and great tenderness. It was evident in his painting, for he possessed hands that could slash bold colour on a canvas yet brush strokes on another with such sensitivity the contrast was vast—too vast to imagine the artists were one and the same.

And as a man, a lover? Was he wild and untamed? Sensitive and loving? Were his emotions always under control? *Did she want them to be?*

Oh, God, where had that come from?

With a sense of desperation she picked up the menu and began to peruse it.

'If I say you look beautiful, will you hold it against me?'

His voice held mild amusement, and she lowered the

menu, cast him a level look, then offered him a singularly sweet smile.

'Probably.'

A soft chuckle escaped from his throat. 'Should we aim for polite conversation, or opt for companionable silence?'

'You could tell me what you did yesterday, then I'll tell you what I did,' she said with marked solemnity. 'That should take care of ten minutes or so.'

'Yesterday? I caught an early-morning flight to Melbourne, attended a meeting, lunched with a business associate, flew back mid-afternoon, and played squash.'

'You were meant to stretch that out a bit, not condense it into thirty seconds.'

He reached for his wine glass, lifted it, sipped from the contents, then replaced it onto the table. 'And you?'

'Sat on a panel judging junior models, caught up with my mother.'

'And thought of any number of reasons why you should cancel lunch today?'

It was a stab in the dark, but an accurate one. She opted to go with honesty. 'Yes.'

One eyebrow slanted. 'Do I pose such a threat?'

'You unnerve me.' The words slipped out without thought.

'That's a plus,' Dominic drawled.

She decided to set a few boundaries. 'We're sharing lunch. Nothing more.'

'For now,' he qualified. 'Shall we order? I can recommend the escargots.'

It was an acquired taste, but one she favoured.

The waiter appeared, noted their selection, and disappeared.

Francesca lifted her glass and took a long sip of iced water, then set the glass carefully on the table. Her eyes met his, their expression wary, faintly wry.

'Do you have anything planned for the weekend?' Dominic queried, and she rested the fork onto her plate then took time to dab her mouth with the napkin before answering.

'A quiet few days—no family, no social engagements.'

'Time out?'

Her fingers strayed to toy with the stem of her drinking glass. 'Yes.'

'There's a function in one of the major city hotels tomorrow evening for which I have tickets. Gabbi and Benedict suggest we join their table.'

Gabbi was a dear friend, whose company she enjoyed. Dominic was something else entirely. The thought that he had no willing partner he could call upon was ludicrous.

'I lend my support to a few charities, but rarely attend their social functions.'

Was her expression so easily readable? She wouldn't have thought so, yet this man possessed an uncanny ability to read her mind.

'Then why are you attending this particular one?'

He leaned back in his chair and regarded her with studied ease. 'Because it provides me with an opportunity to ask you out.'

'And no doubt you meant to sweeten the invitation by joining up with two of my best friends?'

The waiter cleared their plates, and inclined his head as they declined dessert and settled for coffee.

'A simple yes or no will do,' Dominic mocked, and she gave him a brilliant smile.

He always seemed to be one step ahead of her, and for once she felt inclined to reverse the process by doing the unexpected. 'Yes.'

He didn't display so much as a flicker of surprise, nor did he indicate satisfaction at her answer. 'Let me have your address and I'll collect you.'

She wanted to protest, acknowledged the foolishness of taking independence too far, then gave it, watching idly as he penned the apartment number and street on the back of a card.

It was after two when they emerged from the restaurant.

'Where are you parked?'

Francesca felt the touch of his hand on her arm and wanted to pull away, yet stay. A true contradiction in terms, she acknowledged wryly as she fought the deep, curling sensation that slowly unfurled and began spreading through her body.

'About fifty metres to the left.'

It was mid-afternoon and there were several people within close proximity. So why did she feel *threatened*? Fanciful thinking, she dismissed, and resisted the inclination to dismiss *him*, here, now, and walk quickly to her car.

Minutes later she paused at the kerb and withdrew her car keys.

He seemed to loom large, his height and breadth intimidating, and the breath caught in her throat as his head lowered down to hers.

A kiss, brief, in farewell. She would accept the firm brush of his lips, then step back and smile, slip into her car and drive away.

Francesca wasn't prepared for the warm softness of a mouth that seemed far too attuned to her own, its wants and needs.

Unbidden, her hands crept up to tangle together at his nape as he pulled her close, and a soft protest rose and died in her throat as he deepened the kiss to something so intimate, her whole body flamed with an answering fire.

An invasion of the senses, exploring, savouring. He conquered in a manner that made her forget who she was, and where.

When he lifted his head she felt lost, almost adrift, for the few seconds it took for her to regain a sense of reality.

Her eyes were wide and luminous, and she felt a sense of shock. And shame.

'Tomorrow,' Dominic reminded her gently. 'Six-thirty.' His smile was warm. 'Drive carefully.'

He wasn't even breathing quickly, whereas she felt as if she'd just been tossed high by an errant wave and carried breathless and choking into shore.

She didn't say a word. Couldn't, she rationalised as

she stepped from the kerb and crossed round the car to unlock her door.

With every semblance of calm, she started the engine, reversed the necessary metre to allow her clear passage into the flow of traffic, then moved the car out onto the road.

It wasn't until she was several kilometres distant that she began to breathe normally, and later that night, as she lay sleepless in bed, she could still feel the possession of his mouth on her own, the imprint of his body against hers, and the intoxication of her senses.

Francesca woke early, and after a leisurely breakfast she showered and dressed, then drove to a Double Bay clinic for her scheduled massage, facial and manicure.

Lunch was followed by a leisurely browse through several boutiques. One outfit really impressed her, together with shoes and matching bag. Her experienced eye put them all together and transposed them onto her stepsister's slender frame, and she smiled with pleasure as she anticipated Katherine's reaction when she received the gift.

There was time for a coffee with Margo, and it was after four when she slid into the car and headed home. The sun was strong, and she automatically reached for her sunglasses, only to discover they weren't atop her head. They weren't in her bag, either, and she cursed beneath her breath at the thought of having misplaced them.

Sensitivity to strong sunlight occasionally triggered

a migraine, particularly if she was under stress, and it was a situation she took precautions to avoid.

By the time she reached her apartment block the familiar ache had begun behind her right eye. If she was lucky, ordinary painkillers would arrest it, otherwise prescription pills and several hours' rest were the only source of relief.

Francesca gave it half an hour, then she rummaged in her bag for Dominic's card and reached for the phone.

He answered his mobile on the third ring. 'Andrea.'

The sound of his voice increased the splintering pain in her head. It hurt to talk, and she kept it as brief as possible.

'I'm in the vicinity of Double Bay. I'll be there within minutes.'

'No, don't—' It was too late, he'd already cut the call.

She didn't want him here. She didn't want anyone here. Even thinking hurt, so she didn't even try to qualify anything, she simply retrieved the packet of prescription pills and took the required dosage.

When the in-house phone buzzed she answered it, then pressed the release button as Dominic identified himself.

Francesca was waiting at the door when he came out of the lift, and he took one look at her pale face, the dark bruised eyes, then gently pushed her inside the lounge and closed the door.

'That bad, hmm?' He brushed his lips to her temple. 'You've taken medication? OK, let's get you into bed.'

She struggled between comfort and propriety. 'The couch.' Her protest was less than a whisper, for it would

be heaven to rest her head against his chest and close
her eyes.

Ignoring her, he put an arm beneath her knees, lifted
her into his arms, and took a calculated guess as to
which room was hers.

The bedroom was much as he had imagined it would
be. Feminine, but not overly so. There were no frills,
no clutter on flat surfaces, and the colour scheme was
pale peach and green.

Without a word he closed the drapes, folded back the
bedcovers, then, ignoring her protest, he carefully removed her outer clothes and gently deposited her onto
the bed.

'Comfortable?'

The medication was allowing her to sink into numb-
ing, almost pain-free oblivion. 'Yes.'

Dominic drew the sheet up to her shoulders then
sank into a nearby *chaise*, his expression enigmatic as
he watched her breathing deepen.

Unless he was mistaken, she'd sleep through until
the early-morning hours. He'd stay for a while, then
he'd leave.

She looked peaceful. Her features in repose bore a
classic beauty, the facial bone structure in perfect symmetry, alabaster skin as soft and smooth as silk. And a
generous mouth that could tilt with laughter and curve
with sensual promise.

Yet there was a vulnerability evident he knew she
would just hate anyone—him especially—to witness.
An inner fragility that tugged at something deep inside
him and made him feel immensely protective.

Dammit, he wanted the right to be part of her life. To earn her respect, her trust. And her love. The *forever* kind. Commitment. *Marriage*.

After one union that had ended tragically, it wasn't going to be an easy task to persuade her to marry again. Nor would she readily believe it was *love* he felt for her, not merely physical lust.

The temptation to cancel out of tonight and be here when she woke was strong. However, she'd resent such vigilance rather than thank him for it.

He left quietly, secured the door, then took the lift down to the lobby and drove home.

It was dark when Francesca stirred, and she opened her eyes long enough to determine she was in bed, then she closed them again, drifting easily back to sleep.

The sun was filtering through the drapes, lightening the room when she woke again, and she groaned as she glanced at the bedside clock.

Food. And something to drink. She tossed the sheet aside, slid to her feet, then padded into the kitchen.

A glass of fresh orange juice did much to begin the revitalising process, and she switched on the coffee-maker, slid bread into the toaster, and nibbled a banana while she waited. Cereal, a hardboiled egg, toast and an apple ought to do it, she mused as the coffee began to filter. Toast popped up, and when the coffee was ready she sank onto a high stool and took the first appreciative sip of caffeine. Bliss. Absolute bliss.

When she'd finished eating she'd take a leisurely shower, then dress and decide what to do with the day.

Meanwhile, she reflected on Dominic's ministrations, and his presence in her bedroom before the medication had taken its full effect. How long had he stayed? And *why*? She wasn't sure if she wanted to know the answer.

The phone rang twice while she was in the shower, and when she checked the answering machine the first call was from Dominic, the second from Gabbi.

She dialled Gabbi's number first, and apologised for her absence the previous night.

Gabbi's voice was full of concern. 'Are you sure you're OK?'

'Fully recovered and ready to face the day,' she reassured her. 'How were things last night?'

There was a momentary pause. 'It was a sell-out. Dinner was fine, and everyone declared the fashion parade to be a huge success.'

'You're hedging, Gabbi. I take it Annaliese played up?'

'You could say that.'

'Much as it goes against the grain, I think you're going to have to get down and dirty with that young lady.'

'Ah, now there's a thought. Any suggestions?'

'Yell? Throw something?'

'All out war, Francesca?' There was amusement evident. 'Think of the repercussions.'

Francesca wrinkled her nose. 'Benedict wouldn't give a damn.'

'Annaliese and her mother are a formidable pair,' Gabbi responded soberly.

Indeed. Francesca considered herself fortunate her own step-siblings were of the loving kind. And Madeline, although fiercely territorial, wasn't sufficiently vindictive to deliberately drive a wedge between Rick and his daughter.

'I suggest you sharpen your claws,' Francesca indicated with a touch of wry humour, and heard Gabbi's laugh echo down the line.

'Filed and ready.'

They ended the call on a light note, and Francesca was about to punch in the digits to connect with Dominic's mobile when the phone rang.

'Francesca.' Her pulse quickened and went into overdrive at the sound of Dominic's voice. 'You slept well?'

'Yes. Thank you,' she added politely.

'For what, precisely?'

His indolent query raised goosebumps where goosebumps had no right to be. Why was she thanking him? For caring enough to be there for her? Ensuring she was comfortably settled and waiting until the medication took effect? 'Just—thank you.'

She could almost see his features relaxing with a degree of humour, and that sensuously moulded mouth curve into a smile.

'Want to join me on a picnic?'

The question startled her, and she hesitated, torn by an image of finger food eaten alfresco.

'If I refuse, will you seclude yourself in the studio and paint?'

He gave a husky laugh. 'Something like that.'

There was a pull of the senses she found difficult to

ignore, and she aimed for a light response. 'How about a compromise?'

'Shoot.'

'I'll come watch you paint, *then* we go on a picnic.'

'You just want to see my etchings.'

She couldn't help the smile that curved the edges of her mouth. 'You've seen *me* at work.'

'Much more glamorous than a pile of blank canvas, numerous quantities of oil paint and mineral turps, I can assure you.'

'We have a deal?'

'Deal,' he responded easily.

'Give me five minutes and I'll be on my way.'

She retrieved a spare pair of sunglasses from the bedroom and slipped them into her bag. Should she contribute some food? Her refrigerator wasn't exactly a receptacle of gourmet treats. Fruit and frozen bread did not a feast make. OK, so she'd stop off somewhere *en route* and collect a few things.

Which was precisely what she did, arriving at Dominic's front door with no less than two carrybags held in each hand.

'I invited you to join me on a picnic, not provide one,' he remonstrated as he divested her of her purchases.

'I got carried away. Besides, I owe you a meal.'

'You don't owe me anything.'

She followed him through to the kitchen. 'Humour me. I have an independent streak.'

A friendly room with modern appliances, she decided as he unpacked the bags and stored a coldpack in the refrigerator.

She cast him an all-encompassing look, appraising the sleeveless shirt, the cut-off jeans, the trainers on his feet.

One eyebrow slanted. 'What did you expect? An enveloping artist's cape?' His eyes gleamed as he reached out a hand and touched one cheek, glimpsed the faint uncertainty evident and sought to alleviate it. 'Shall we go?'

She didn't resist as he led her to the glassed walkway, connecting the large studio above a multi-car garage to the house.

It was, she conceded, an artist's dream, with sections of floor-to-ceiling glass and sliding floor-to-ceiling cupboard doors closing storage areas. Even the roof held panels of glass to capture every angle of sunlight.

There were the tools of trade in evidence—pots and tubes of oil paint, three easels, canvas, frames—all tidily stored on racks.

Yet she saw splotches of paint on the bare wooden floor, denoting it as a functional room where work was achieved.

'Do you need to paint in silence? Or doesn't noise bother you?'

'Depends on the mood, and the creative muse,' Dominic answered, watching her closely. This was his sanctum, a room which revealed more of himself than he liked. Consequently he allowed very few people access.

'Tell me where you'd prefer me to sit or stand while you paint.'

'You don't want to explore?'

'I imagine if there's something you want to show me, you will,' Francesca said evenly.

'Take a seat, while I create a colourful abstract to be auctioned off for charity next week.'

She watched him turn a blank canvas into a visual work of art. First the block of colour, covered by bold strokes and strong slashes. It looked so easy, his movements sure as one hour passed, then another, and she sat there enthralled by his artistic ability to transfer image to canvas. It didn't seem to matter that she possessed little comprehension of the portrayed abstract or its symmetry. The creative process itself was inspiring.

His involvement was total, and interest, rather than curiosity, impelled a strong desire to see some of his completed works. She would have given much to examine the tiered rack where several canvases were stored. Maybe next time.

At last he stood back satisfied. 'That's enough for today.' He deftly deposited brushes, cleaned paint from his hands, then crossed to a nearby sink and washed.

'Let's get out of here.'

He left her in the kitchen. 'I'll go shower and change while you pack food into the cooler.'

He reappeared ten minutes later, dressed in casual trousers and a short-sleeved polo shirt.

They drove north to a delightful inlet that was relatively isolated.

'Hungry?' Dominic queried as he spread a rug on a grassy bank overlooking a curved half moon of sand and sea.

It was almost mid-afternoon. 'Famished.'

Francesca began unpacking the cooler while he unfurled a large beach umbrella and staked it firmly into the ground to provide essential shade.

She set out plates, fresh bread rolls, sliced ham, chicken and salads, brie, fruit.

'A soda?'

'Please,' she accepted gratefully, uncapping the bottle and taking a long swallow of iced liquid.

Dominic split the bread rolls in half and began filling them, then handed her one. 'OK?'

She took a bite, then grinned. 'Excellent.' She felt relaxed, despite the intimacy of their solitude. Carefree, she realized. Something she hadn't experienced in a long time.

Deep down she knew she should be wary, on guard against the mood between them taking a subtle shift. As it inevitably would. But not today. Today she needed some light-hearted fun, and the opportunity to get to know Dominic Andrea, the man beneath the projected persona.

'Tell me about yourself.'

He finished one bread roll and filled another. The look he directed her was piercing, steady. 'What do you want to know?'

'Where you were born, family.'

'The personal profile?' he mocked gently. 'Athens. My parents emigrated to Australia when I was seven. I have two younger sisters, one lives in America, the other in Santorini. My mother returned there five years ago when my father died from a heart attack.'

'Do you see them often?'

His smile held amusement. 'Every year.'

Somehow she'd pictured him as self-sufficient and a loner. 'I guess you have nieces, nephews?'

'Two of each, aged from three months to six years.'

It wasn't difficult to imagine him hoisting a squealing child astride his shoulders, or playing ball. Why hadn't he married and begun a family of his own?

'How about you?'

It was a fair question, and one she sought to answer with equal brevity. 'Sydney-born and educated. Two step-siblings on my father's side. Several from my mother's numerous marriages.'

She wasn't willing to provide him with any more facts than he already knew. 'Let's walk along the beach.'

She rose to her feet in one graceful movement and glanced at her watch, saw that it was four. 'What time do you want to leave?'

'There's no particular hurry to get back.' He stacked the remains of their picnic in the cooler, then stored it in the boot together with the umbrella and rug.

Together they traversed the grassy slope down onto the sand and walked to the water's edge. There was a slight breeze that teased the length of her hair and gently billowed the soft material of her blouse.

The inlet was small, with a rocky outcrop bordering each point as it curved into the sea. Dominic reached for her hand, and she didn't tug it away, nor did she protest when he indicated they walk the width of the inlet.

They exchanged anecdotes, enjoyed shared laughter, and Francesca was aware of a growing friendship that was quite separate from the sexual attraction simmering between them.

The awareness was always there, sometimes just hovering beneath the surface. And on other occasions, when she became conscious of every breath she took, every beat of her heart. Part of her wanted to relax and let her emotions go any which way, and be damned to the consequences. Then logic kicked in and persuaded her to take the cautious path.

It was almost five when they returned to the car, and Dominic deactivated the alarm then unlocked the passenger door.

Francesca reached for the latch, then caught her breath as he placed an arm either side of her, caging her in an inescapable trap.

She glimpsed the darkness in his eyes in the one brief second it took for his head to descend, then his mouth was on hers, seeking what she was too afraid to give.

His lips were warm, evocative, and his tongue slid between her teeth before she had the chance to think.

He was patient, when all he wanted to do was possess. Gentle, not willing to frighten. And coaxing, persuasive, waiting for her response.

Francesca felt the betrayal of her body, the rapid pulse-beat, the slight quiver that began deep inside and invaded her limbs. The ache of awareness throbbed, radiating until she felt *alive* with sensation, and she kissed him back, luxuriating in the brush of his tongue against her own in a light mating dance that soon began to imitate the sexual act itself.

She wanted him closer, much closer, and her arms lifted to encircle his neck as she leant against him.

His arousal was a potent force, and a silent gasp died in her throat as his hand slid down to cup her bottom, pressing her even closer.

Then he began to move, slowly, creating a barely perceptible friction that was so evocative it became almost unbearable to have the barrier of clothes between them.

A hand moved to her breast, outlined its shape, then slipped inside her blouse, beneath the lacy bra to tease the sensitised peak.

Her faint moan was all he needed, and his lips hardened as he took total possession of her mouth.

No one had kissed her with quite this degree of passion. Desire was there, raging almost out of control. His, hers. There was no sense of time or place, just total and complete absorption in each other.

It was a child's voice, pitched high and piercing, that succeeded in bringing a rapid return to sanity.

Dominic's breathing was no less heavy than her own as he buried his forehead in her hair. Her skin was warm and moist, as was his as she withdrew her arms and tried to gain leverage against the powerful body pressing far too close to her own.

'Dominic—' The protest left her lips and he lifted his head.

'I know.' With effort he straightened and unlatched the front passenger door, waited until she slid into the seat, then closed it before crossing to the driver's side.

Seconds later the engine fired and the car reversed in

a semi-circle, then purred towards the gravelled apron bordering the bitumen road.

Francesca reached for her sunglasses and slid them into place, grateful for the tinted lenses. Dear heaven, they'd behaved like unrestrained teenagers! Hard after that came the thought of what might have happened had they not been interrupted.

Dominic could feel her withdrawal, and sought to prevent it. With a skilled movement he pulled onto the side of the road and brought the car to a halt.

Her face was pale, her eyes far too large as she turned towards him. 'Why are you stopping?'

He leaned an arm on the steering wheel and shifted in the seat. 'Don't close up and go silent on me.'

'What do you want me to say? Shame about the timing?' Her eyes were clear, and there was a faint tilt to her chin. 'Or perhaps I should attempt to comment about the weather, the scenery, in a banal attempt at conversation.'

'I wanted you. You wanted me. If there's any blame, it falls on both of us. Equally. That's as basic as it gets,' he said hardily.

'We were like two animals in heat. In a public area, in full sight of anyone who happened by.'

'Fully clothed,' he reminded her. 'And in control.'

Her mouth opened, then closed again. That had been *control*? What the hell was he like without it? 'Let's forget it, shall we?'

'Nice try, Francesca.' His voice was satin-smooth with a hint of dry humour as he fired the engine and eased the car back onto the road.

She wanted to hit him, and would have if the car had been stationary. He should consider himself fortunate that it took thirty minutes to reach his home at Beauty Point. By then her temper had cooled down somewhat.

As soon as the car drew to a halt she slid from the seat, closed the door, and prepared to cross to where her own car was parked.

He took his fill of her set features, the straight back, and her defensive stance. 'Running away won't achieve a thing.'

Her eyes sparked with a mixture of residual temper and pride. 'Maybe not. But right now I'm going home.'

'I intend to see you again.'

He was right, she discovered shakily. Running away wouldn't achieve anything. But she needed space, and time to *think*.

She took the few steps necessary to her car, paused, then turned back to face him. 'I have a modelling assignment scheduled for Tuesday, and a reasonable night's sleep is a prerequisite to looking good.'

He followed her to the car, and stood within touching distance. The breath caught in her throat as he took hold of her shoulders and lowered his head down to hers.

She wanted to cry out a verbal negation, but it was too late as his mouth closed over hers in a kiss that tore at the very foundation of her being.

As he meant it to do.

The knowledge frightened her on a sensual level, and made her aware of a primitive alchemy that was shattering in its intensity.

'Tuesday night. Be here, Francesca,' Dominic commanded silkily.

She was incapable of uttering so much as a word, and her fingers shook as she unlocked her car. The engine fired seconds later and she cleared the gates, aware her breathing vied in raggedness with her fast-pulsing heartbeat.

CHAPTER SEVEN

THE LEUKAEMIA FOUNDATION luncheon was well patronised, the venue excellent, and the fashion parade succeeded without a visible hitch.

Behind the scenes it was a different story. Annaliese arrived late and in a dangerous mood, taking pleasure in denigrating a designer, which reduced him in a very short space of time to a quivering wreck. Nothing assigned from Wardrobe pleased her, and she insisted on making changes, which caused frayed tempers, handwringing, and mutterings among the ranks of fellow models, not to mention everyone else involved backstage. It wasn't the worst session Francesca had participated in, but it came close.

Choosing what to wear for the evening took considerable thought, and Francesca cursed as she riffled through the contents of her wardrobe. Relaxed and casual? Or should she aim for sophistication?

The tension knotted inside her stomach as she considered crossing to the phone and cancelling out.

Her fingers momentarily stilled as Dominic's image came vividly to mind. A curse fell from her lips and her eyes clouded with pensive introspection. *What was she doing?*

Why did she have the feeling that he would appear at *her* door within an hour of her failing to appear at *his*?

After much deliberation, she selected an elegant three-piece silk trouser suit in deep emerald-green. Jewellery was minimal, and she stepped into matching stiletto-heeled pumps.

It was a glorious evening. Clear sky, blue ocean, creating a perfect background for various harbour craft taking the benefit of a slight breeze drifting over the sea.

The worst of the traffic making a daily exodus from the city was over, and Francesca experienced no delays at computer-controlled intersections.

Consequently, it was six thirty when she turned into Dominic's drive, and within minutes she cleared the gates and drew to a halt close to the main door.

She hadn't suffered such a wealth of nervous tension since her early modelling days.

Dammit, get a grip, she counselled herself silently as she pressed the doorchimes. Seconds later the door opened, and she summoned a warm smile.

'Hello.'

Dominic's eyes narrowed slightly at the huskiness evident, the faint shadows clouding her expression.

Attired in dark tailored trousers and a cream cotton shirt unbuttoned at the neck, he looked relaxed and at ease.

It would be wonderful to move into those arms and lift her face for his kiss. For a wild moment she almost considered doing just that.

'Bad day?'

Francesca offered a faintly wry smile. 'I guess you could say that.'

'Want to tell me about it?'

'What part do you want to hear?'

'Let me guess. One of the models went ballistic, a designer threw a tantrum, and whoever was in charge of Wardrobe threatened to quit.' One eyebrow slanted in humour. 'Close?'

'Close enough.'

He took hold of her arm and led her into the lounge. 'Mineral water or wine?'

'It's sacrilege, but can I have half of each?'

She felt too restless to sit, and she crossed the room to examine a small painting that had caught her attention on a previous occasion.

It was beautiful in every detail, soft blues, pinks and lilacs, a garden scene. She glimpsed the signature in the lower right corner, and almost forgot to breathe. There was little doubt as to its originality.

'You admire Monet?'

Dominic had moved silently to stand behind her, and she felt his nearness, sensed the warmth of his body.

She turned slowly to face him. 'Who doesn't?'

He handed her a tall frosted glass, and Francesca gestured a silent toast. 'Salute.'

Dinner was a casual meal of barbecued prawns with a variety of salads, eaten informally on the terrace.

'Heavenly,' Francesca accorded as she selected slices of cantaloupe and plump red strawberries from a fruit

platter. There was also ice cream. Vanilla, with caramel and double chocolate chip.

She caught his teasing look, and laughed. 'You remembered.'

His eyes gleamed with latent humour. 'Will you eat
it? That's the thing.'

She wrinkled her nose at him and selected a spoon.
'Just watch me!'

The view out over the harbour was magnificent
as the sun began to fade towards the horizon and the
shadow of dusk cast a stealthy haze. Streetlights sprang
into life, regulated pin-pricks of white light spreading
out over suburbia as far as the eye could see. In the
distance was the heat and the beat of the city, flashing
neon, bright lights, action.

Yet here it was peaceful, almost secluded, with high
walls and cleverly planted shrubbery providing privacy
from neighbouring properties.

'Would you like to go indoors?'

Francesca wiped her fingers on a serviette, then let
her head rest back against the chair. 'I don't think I want
to move.' She sighed at the thought of checking in to
the airport at six the next morning.

A fashion parade at the Gold Coast Sheraton Mirage,
followed by a photographic shoot, then cocktails with a
public relations executive and his colleagues.

Soon she had to fly to Europe for the designer collections. After which she intended secluding herself for
a week of rest and relaxation. No phones, no contact
whatsoever with the outside world. Where the resort

staff were bound to secrecy and the guests paid a fortune for the privilege of total anonymity.

A few weeks ago she'd been sure of her future and its direction. Now she was beginning to query what she really wanted.

'Coffee?'

Francesca turned her head slightly to look at him. 'Please.'

Dominic stood to his feet and moved indoors, and she followed, suddenly restless for something constructive to do.

In the kitchen she watched as he filled the coffee-maker, added ground beans, opened cupboards, withdrew sugar, then set out cups and saucers on the servery counter.

His hands were sure, their movements economical, and her eyes travelled, encompassing the muscular forearms exposed by the turned-back cuffs, the breadth of shoulder, the expanse of chest covered in cream chambray, up to that defined jaw, sensuous mouth, sculpted cheekbones. Those eyes, so dark, so steady as they met hers.

The breath locked in her throat at what she saw there.

Desire. Raw and primitive.

Her pulse quickened to a thudding beat that was audible to her own ears. Visible, she felt sure, as her whole body began to reverberate with answering need.

'Come here.' The command was gently spoken, and she placed her fingers onto his outstretched palm and allowed herself to be pulled into his arms.

His mouth was firm as it settled over her own, shaping, exploring the soft contours, then nibbling at the lower fullness.

She felt his breath, warm and vaguely musky as he teased his tongue against her teeth, and she stifled a faint gasp as he began to invade the moist crevices, tasting, laving each ridge, each slight indentation, before creating a tantalising foray that deepened into total possession.

One hand slid down her spine and cupped her bottom, lifting her close up against him so that she could be in no doubt of his arousal.

She fitted as if she was meant to be there. *His.* All he had to do was convince her of that.

He could feel her acceptance of *now*, but he sensed her indecision and knew that afterwards she would feel she'd betrayed her dead husband's memory.

Francesca's hands clutched his forearms, then slipped up to his shoulders as his mouth left hers and trailed down to savour the fast-beating pulse at the base of her throat.

Her neck arched, allowing him free access, and she groaned out loud as his lips travelled down to the valley between her breasts and lingered there, caressing the soft fullness with his tongue as he edged the material down to reveal one burgeoning peak.

Dominic breathed in deeply as he tasted the wild honey that was her skin, and wanted more. Much more. He contented himself with the fact that a journey was made up of many steps. If he was to succeed, he'd have to exert patience and take one step at a time.

She wanted to feel his skin, and her fingers moved

to the buttons of his shirt, freeing each one, then, not content, she pulled it free of his waistband.

Dear God, he felt good. Tight-muscled midriff, taut chest, and a generous mat of dark hair that just begged to have her fingers curl into its length.

His mouth closed over the roseate peak and he suckled shamelessly, nibbled, then caught the nipple between his teeth and took her to the edge between pleasure and pain.

Her hand slid down over the fold of his zip-fastening, trailing the rigid length before seeking the tab and slowly releasing the nylon teeth.

Fingers feathered over silk briefs to explore what lay beneath, and she felt a momentary sense of panic at the size and thickness of him.

She needed gentle persuasion, reassurance, and above all he had to show her that this was more than just sex.

'Dominic—'

His mouth took possession of her own, cutting off her protest as he utilised every ounce of skill he possessed in showing her part of his heart.

She was vaguely aware of being swept into his arms and carried up a flight of stairs to a bedroom.

His, she decided dimly as he switched on a bedside lamp on a pedestal next to a large king-size bed. Slowly he let her slide down to her feet.

Oh, God—what was she doing? 'I don't think—' She halted as he took her face between his hands and lowered his mouth to hers.

'Don't think,' Dominic bade against her lips. 'Just feel.'

I'm not sure I can give what you want. How would he react if she said those words aloud?

His teeth nipped the tip of her tongue. 'Yes.' His tongue soothed hers and his hands gentled the agitated movements of her own. 'You can.'

He wanted her so badly, *needed* the advantage of joining his body with hers so that he could show her how much he cared. How *right* this was—for both of them.

He kissed her deeply, gently coaxing in a manner that made every bone in her body turn to jelly. Dominic uttered the two words he hoped would make the difference. 'Trust me.'

Dared she? She didn't have any choice as her body proved to be its own traitorous mistress by leaning in to his kiss, giving him access to her mouth so he could plunder at will.

Her clothes, his, were quickly, easily dispensed with, and she stood almost breathless at his male beauty.

Warm, sun-kissed skin sheathed strong muscle and sinew, defining superb musculature with a sculptor's precision. Tight flanks curved down from a narrow waist, his stomach taut with an arrow of dark hair that led down to the juncture at his thighs, thickening in growth as it couched his manhood.

He stood watching her appraisal, at ease with his nudity, and her eyes skimmed the potent thickness of his arousal, skittered to his chest, and came to rest at his chin.

'Look at me.'

I just have. She lifted her face fractionally and met his intense gaze.

He reached for her, closing his hands over her arms as he slid them up to capture her shoulders.

'Open your eyes, Francesca,' Dominic bade her as his breath feathered her cheek. 'I want you to see me. Only me.'

He pulled her forward and lowered his head down towards the soft hollow at the edge of her neck.

His mouth worked an evocative magic as he savoured each and every pleasure pulse until she quivered in his arms.

Heat shimmered through every vein as she went up in flames, and he hadn't even begun.

Beautiful, he thought reverently. The faint edge of shyness appealed, even as it appalled him. She didn't possess that fierce fervour of a woman well-versed in experiencing an explosive climax. Or of one who was fully aware of the pleasure her own body could give, not only to her partner but to herself.

Slow, he determined. Slow and easy. They had the night.

Francesca groaned softly as his fingers trailed low over her stomach, then tangled in the hair curling at the apex of her thighs.

His mouth suckled at one breast, tormenting its peak into a turgid arousal, and just as she thought his touch unbearable he crossed to render a similar assault on its twin.

Fire arrowed from the centre of her being, the flame

licking through her body until she felt every nerve, every cell overheating as his skilled fingers probed the moist folds, and she cried out as he stroked the small nubbin, caressing until her whole body shuddered and she sank against him.

A strangled gasp left her lips as he sank down onto his knees and traced the same path with his tongue, tasting the indentation of her navel before savouring the line of her hipbone.

Teasing, tantalising, until he reached the soft hair guarding entrance to her womanhood.

'Dominic—no—' The cry was one of stark disbelief, but he ignored the tug of her hands as she took hold of his head.

But it was too late, much too late as she began to experience the most intimate kiss of all. And as his tongue wrought havoc she went up in flames, unaware of the soft, guttural cries that emerged from her throat, the purring pleasure as he took her higher, or the subdued scream as he held her there before tipping her over the edge.

Dear God, she was sweet. An intoxicating mix of honey and musk. He suckled her moisture, savouring it like a fine wine, and held her firm when she would have fallen.

It was too much, Francesca thought dimly as she sought to retain a hold on her emotional sanity. Way too much. She wanted to beg him to stop, yet the words wouldn't formulate, let alone escape from her throat.

His lips began a slow path over her stomach, then travelled up to her breasts to caress each peak in turn, settled briefly on the rapidly beating pulse at the base of her throat, then took possession of her mouth.

She could taste herself, then only him as he encouraged her tongue to participate in a duelling dance with his own.

It was like nothing she'd ever experienced before. Total capitulation, complete possession, and she was hardly aware of the soft mattress beneath her back until he paused to extract a small foil package from the nearest pedestal drawer.

Quick, deft movements, then his hands moulded her slight frame, caressed, then gentled as he prepared her to accept his length.

She was slick with need, aching as she'd never ached for a man, and she gasped when her flesh stung slightly as he gained entrance. She could feel the expansion of muscles and tissue, the gradual acceptance as he buried himself to the hilt inside her.

Then he began to move, slowly, almost withdrawing before carefully plunging in again, angling his shaft slightly until he felt her muscles seize and grip him. Then, when she was ready, he gradually quickened his movements until she lifted her hips to take him even deeper.

Francesca had thought it couldn't get any better, but she was wrong. His oral onslaught had heightened her senses and stimulated desire to fever-pitch. Now he took her to a higher plane, where mind, body and soul reached perfect accord and transcended anything she'd ever experienced on a sensual level.

So much for control. She had none. Nor did she

want any, she decided dazedly as the spiral of sensation reached its zenith.

Perhaps she cried out as he shuddered in the throes of his own climax, for his mouth settled over hers, soothing, gentling, as he held her close.

For a while she didn't move. Couldn't. She felt warm, and wondrously lethargic. Later she'd feel the pull of unused muscles. But for now she was content just to lie here, and savour the tumultuous aftermath of passion.

She lifted a hand and let her fingers drift down the column of his back, lingering at the indentations of his spine as she explored each vertebra until she reached the strong splay of pelvic bone.

His buttocks flexed, and she felt him swell slightly inside her.

'Uncomfortable?' His voice sounded deep and faintly husky as he grazed the hollow at her neck.

'No.' She liked the closeness, the feel of his large body, the heat and the smell of it. 'Do you want to…?' She paused, suddenly hesitant, and she felt his mouth move to form a smile.

'Disengage? Not particularly.' He shifted his weight so that he rested the bulk of it on his elbows.

He could tell from her expression, the slightly dazed look in her eyes, the soft pink tingeing her cheeks and the glow of her skin that she felt good. Lord, she excited him as few women had in the past. He wanted to take her again, to feel the tightness as she sheathed him and experience the way she moved beneath him.

Yet perhaps not so soon. There was time to tease a little, to play.

Francesca felt him shift slightly as his hands curled beneath her shoulders, then he rolled onto his back, carrying her with him.

He lifted his hands and threaded his fingers through her hair, dislodging most of the pins which held its length in what had once been an elegant French twist.

'Hmm, that's better.' His smile was slightly crooked, his eyes deep and warm as he regarded the tumble of hair falling loose about her shoulders.

He traced the outline of her mouth with his forefinger, then probed the ridge of her lower teeth.

She bit him, not hard, but sufficiently firmly to see his pupils dilate. Then she suckled the tip of his finger, swirling it with her tongue, just once, before releasing it.

So, the ball wasn't entirely in his court after all, he mused.

There was a certain degree of power in sitting astride a man. Francesca felt in control and wholly sexual, exulting in the flare of passion evident as she used her knees to exert a little leverage, then began rocking, ever so gently, watching as his eyes darkened.

There was a faint line of sweat beading his upper lip, and she leaned forward and carefully removed it with her tongue.

He let his hand slip to her breast, caressing its peak as he cupped the fullness of its twin. Beautiful and firm, the slopes were as smooth as satin to his touch.

With care he urged one engorged peak into his mouth, laving its nipple into button-hardness, and heard her almost inaudible groan as sensation pooled deep within. He could feel her response in the faint tensing of internal muscles, and his own reaction in the burgeoning of his shaft.

For what seemed hours, he had commanded her body, her senses. Now she wanted to tip the scales a little in her favour.

And she did, tentatively at first, then as her confidence grew she took complete control, riding him as hard as she dared until he grasped hold of her hips and surged into her, again and again, lifting her as he arched his body higher and higher, so that his shoulders and his feet were the only parts of him anchored to the bed.

Afterwards he cradled her close, caging her to him as he smoothed his lips across her sweat-drenched brow, his hands soothing her shuddering body until she lay limp and spent.

She must have slept, for she remembered stirring a few times and being gently rocked in strong arms before slipping back into that blissful state that was neither true sleep nor part wakefulness.

'I must go,' she murmured, not once, but twice, only to succumb to the drift of his fingers, the persuasive touch of his mouth.

'Dominic,' she groaned in the early pre-dawn hours. 'I have an early flight to catch.'

He rolled out of bed and scooped her into his arms, then carried her, protesting, into the *en suite* shower.

He bathed her, then swathed her slim form in a voluminous towel. 'Why not come back to bed?' He kissed her nose, then gently savoured that soft mouth. 'To sleep. I promise.' He brushed her lips with his own. 'I'll set the alarm and cook you breakfast.'

It was tempting, oh, so tempting. 'I really have to go home.'

He dried her carefully, offered her a selection of toiletries, then watched as she quickly donned her clothes.

What did she say to him? *Thanks, it was great*?

Dominic saved her the trouble by placing a finger over her lips. 'Take care.'

There was a sense of unreality driving through almost empty streets. There were no stars, no moon. Just an eerie pre-dawn light lifting the greyness of night.

Precisely what time was it? The illuminated clock on the dashboard revealed it was almost four. Two hours from now she needed to front up at the airport check-in counter.

Hardly enough time to snatch little more than even an hour's sleep, she decided without a trace of weariness as she garaged the car and rode the lift up to her apartment. After the night's activity, she should have been almost dead on her feet. Yet she felt strangely exhilarated, *alive* as she hadn't been in the past three years.

Inside, she brewed a cup of strong coffee and drank it black with sugar, then she checked her bags, added a few last-minute items, and made herself breakfast. Fresh juice, fruit, muesli, toast. And more strong coffee.

Awake. And waiting wasn't such a good idea, for it provided time for thought.

Last night she'd slept with a man. A hollow laugh rose and died in her throat. Hell, *sleep* hadn't even been a consideration!

A complexity of emotions raced through her brain, clouding her perspective.

This relationship— Oh, who was she *kidding*? She groaned out loud. *What* relationship?

And what came next? Did she get to spend a night at his place, he at *hers*, escape for the occasional weekend together?

Good sex without emotional involvement. Responsible. A slightly hysterical bubble of laughter rose and died in her throat at the thought of blood tests, prophylactic protection.

Then she sobered as she became prone to introspection, and she succumbed to the inevitable feelings of guilt at having betrayed everything she held dear about Mario. The shared love, the laughter, her hopes and dreams, her fear for him. The stark replay of that fateful crash.

But tears were for the weak, and she'd shed them long ago.

With determined resolve she reset the answering machine, tidied the apartment, and at five-thirty she collected her bags, locked the door and rode the lift down to Reception, where a cab stood waiting to transport her to the airport.

CHAPTER EIGHT

THE ONE-HOUR flight to the Gold Coast was uneventful, and a friendly hostess escorted Francesca into the terminal and introduced her to a waiting chauffeur, who collected her bag and saw her seated into the rear of a luxury limousine.

There were some advantages in having acquired a degree of fame and recognition, Francesca acknowledged silently as she extracted sunglasses and slid them on.

The fact there were also many disadvantages couldn't be discounted, but this morning she was grateful for Laraine's organisational skills as the limousine headed towards Surfers Paradise.

Long, sandy beaches, gently rolling surf, deep blue ocean, and at this early morning hour a soft azure sky. The many highrise apartment buildings appeared like concrete sentinels in the distance, and as they drew close she could sense the pulse of a thriving industry dedicated to the tourist dollar.

The Sheraton Mirage was a luxury low-rise hotel,

with wonderful views and access to a uniquely designed shopping complex and marina.

Unpacking was achieved in minutes, and Francesca looked longingly at the large bed, then checked her watch. She had a few hours before she needed to present herself behind the scenes in the grand ballroom downstairs. Time she could kill by browsing the shopping complex, or, what was more sensible, catching up on some lost sleep.

No contest. The bed won. And she quickly slid out of her shoes, discarded her clothes, slipped on a wrap, set the alarm, then lay down.

Not such a good idea, she decided a short while later as she dwelt on the hours she'd spent in another bed.

The only precautions taken had been Dominic's use of prophylactic protection.

Dear heaven, it had been good. Better than good. She tried to come up with a superlative, and failed. Her body still ached from his invasion, and her skin burned as she vividly recalled every detail.

He had taken his time, seducing, making everything a feast of the senses.

To become involved with a man like Dominic Andrea was dangerous, for it would be all too easy to become addicted to his brand of lovemaking, to *him*.

She'd given her heart once, and had it broken. She never wanted to feel that bereft again.

Francesca must have dozed, for she woke to the sound of the alarm and was surprised that she'd managed to sleep at all. A shower would refresh her, then she'd tend to her make-up, her hair, dress, and present herself downstairs.

There was a bowl of fresh fruit in her room, and she selected a banana, peeled and bit into it *en route* to the bathroom.

The Gold Coast Mirage was built right on the beach, with an expanse of marble floor, a stunning indoor waterfall, and a massive pool with an island bar.

The ballroom was situated on the ground floor, and one glance was all it took to determine the social glitterati had turned out in force.

The luncheon was a tremendous success, with capacity seating. Backstage chaos was minimal. There were few mishaps, and none that gained public notice.

At last she was able to escape, albeit briefly, to nibble on some finger food before the scheduled photographic shoot was due to proceed.

The photographer was over-friendly—and, worse, a toucher. Whatever image the assistant instructed Francesca to present he wanted to change—personally.

After two hours of posing in various parts of the hotel and around the pool, Francesca was almost at screaming point. He was too much in her face, and she wanted to tell him so. Almost did, on one occasion, and only barely held her tongue.

At last the final shot was taken, and she could escape to her suite for a brief respite before it was time to change and show up for the cocktail party.

Classic black, long straight skirt split to mid-thigh, a black sequinned singlet top, black tights, high-heeled stiletto pumps, hair piled up on top of her head with a few loose tendrils falling beside each ear, a wide gold necklace and matching bracelet. Retouched make-up.

Francesca snatched up a slim black evening purse, slipped the long gold chain over one shoulder, collected her key, and made her way to the lounge bar.

One hour, tops, then she'd retire gracefully and return to her suite, where she'd order a room service meal, then shower and fall into bed.

Several more guests began to wander into the lounge, and there were introductions, polite small talk, as well as a few informal speeches while canapés were served.

The photographer gravitated to her side and made such a nuisance of himself that when he tried to get too close she aimed her stiletto heel and brought it down on his instep.

His face whitened, then flared blood red. 'Bitch.'

Without a word she turned away from him, located the hostess, then the organiser, and exited the lounge bar.

She reached her suite, and once inside put the safety chain in position. Then she leaned wearily against the door.

Damn. She hadn't needed aggravation at the end of a long and difficult day. Following a sexually active, sleepless night.

An audible groan escaped from her lips, and she levered herself away from the door and crossed the room to the bar fridge, where she selected cold bottled water, removed the cap, and poured the contents into a glass.

Francesca kicked off her shoes, removed her

earstuds, then carrying the glass into the bathroom, she began cleansing her face of make-up.

A sharp double knock on the outer door came as a surprise. She had yet to order room service, and it was way too early for the maid to turn down the bed.

She wiped her hands on the towel and crossed the room. 'Who is it?'

'Dominic.'

Dominic?

Francesca opened the door a few inches. 'What are you doing here?' The words slipped out before she could prevent them, and she saw one eyebrow lift.

'This is not the most ideal way to have a conversation,' he drawled, and she immediately freed the chain.

Attired in tailored dark trousers and an indigo cotton shirt unbuttoned at the neck, he exuded raw masculinity.

'I guess you just happened to be in the neighbourhood and decided to drop in.' As an attempt at flippancy, it failed miserably.

She didn't look as if she had weathered the day any better than he had. Fragile, definitely—and, if he wasn't mistaken, feeling acutely vulnerable.

He lowered his head and kissed her with gentle thoroughness, then pulled her into his arms and kissed her again.

When his mouth lifted fractionally from her own, she ventured, 'I should ask what you're doing here.'

He traced light kisses along her lower lip, then caught it between his teeth and bit gently. 'Should you?' His lips moved to one ear and trailed a path down her neck to one sensitive hollow, savoured it, and began exploring her throat. 'I didn't want to spend the night without you.'

Well, that certainly spelled it out. And momentarily rendered her speechless.

His soft laughter was almost her undoing. 'Did you manage to get any sleep at all?'

Francesca rolled her eyes expressively. 'I look that bad, huh?'

He lifted a hand and trailed fingers along the edge of her jaw. 'Slightly fragile.' He lowered his head and brushed his lips against her own.

'I think you can safely say that's an understatement.'

She felt rather than saw his faint smile. 'Then I think I should feed you.'

The sensual heat of his body was matched by the increasing desire in her own. If they remained in the suite they probably wouldn't get to eat at all.

'Let's walk across the road and choose one of the several restaurants overlooking the Broadwater,' she determined, and saw his lips curve with amusement.

'Safety among a crowd?'

She offered a witching grin. 'Yes.' She moved a few paces, slid her feet into heeled pumps, collected an evening bag, and tucked her hand in his.

They chose Saks, and within minutes they were seated at a window table. Soon the sky would darken and night would fall, but until it did they had a clear view of boats lining the marina and people strolling along the wooden boardwalk.

Francesca ordered a starter, a main course, and a delicious dessert.

It was an excellent meal, eaten leisurely, and afterwards they took their time over coffee. Then Dominic settled the bill and they took the overhead footbridge to the hotel.

No sooner had they entered the main lobby than a male voice announced, 'Well, well, look who's here.'

The photographer. Slightly inebriated, and, if Francesca wasn't mistaken, out for vengeance.

He positioned his camera and reeled off some film. 'Our famed ice maiden, and escort.' His smile was vaguely feral as he subjected Dominic to a raking appraisal before focusing his gaze on her. 'No wonder you skipped the party, darling.'

With camera in hand, he held a powerful weapon. Francesca pinned a smile in place and kept walking.

'Both staying here together?'

He followed them towards the guest wing, and ventured past the 'Private—Guests Only' glass sign.

Dominic paused, then turned so that Francesca was shielded behind him. 'One step further and I'll alert the management and have charges filed against you for harassment.'

'I'm only doing my job.'

'Then I suggest you go do it some place else.'

When they reached her suite Dominic held out his hand for her key. 'Is there any need to initiate damage control?'

Francesca preceded him into the room. 'A phone call to my agent.' She tossed her evening purse down onto the nightstand and lifted the handset. 'Help yourself to a drink.'

Five minutes later she replaced the receiver and turned to find Dominic watching her.

'You've encountered this sort of problem before?'

The stalker, the pervert, the fanatic. The nightmare no one wanted.

Only her father knew about the letters she'd received for months after Mario's death. Words cut from newspapers, magazines, pasted onto blank paper and sent through the post. Compiled by a sick but shrewd mind. It had taken six months for the police to pin him down, and in that time she'd learnt to defend herself. The down and dirty kind of fighting that wasn't taught in any dojo.

Dominic caught the fleeting shadows, calculated the reason, and decided not to pursue it. There would come a time when she trusted him enough to share, and he could wait.

Francesca met his dark, discerning gaze with equanimity. 'The photographer wasn't a problem, merely a nuisance.' She crossed to a single chair and sank into it.

Last night she'd shared every intimacy imaginable with this man. Now she didn't know how to proceed. Or even if she should. A hollow laugh rose and died in her throat.

She wasn't aware of him moving. Yet his hands rested on her shoulders, soothing, gently massaging the cricks, the stiffness out of tense muscles.

It felt like heaven. 'Don't stop,' she begged, and, closing her eyes, she gave herself up to the magic of his touch.

Minutes later she groaned in protest when he lifted her into his arms and deposited her on the bed. With deft movements he dispensed with her shoes, then her skirt. Next came her top.

'Dominic—'

He drew the bedcovers back, then pressed her forward to lie on her stomach. 'Just relax and enjoy.'

Francesca thought every muscle in her body would melt, and after the initial few seconds she simply pillowed her head on her arms.

It was impossible to fight against the tiredness as she reached a state of total relaxation and drifted to sleep.

She didn't feel the mattress depress slightly as Dominic carefully eased himself to his feet. Nor was she aware that he pulled the covers over her, or that he divested himself of his clothes, crossed round to the other side of the bed and slid between the sheets.

Francesca stirred, sensed the comfort of warm flesh and muscle, and in the depth of her subconscious mind she didn't question it. Merely shifted slightly to seek closer contact. And sighed with satisfaction as fingers lightly drifted the length of her spine.

It was a dream. A hazy, lazy vision she didn't want to lose. The faint musky male scent mingling with a subtle remnant of cologne merely added another dimension.

Lips grazed her cheek, then slipped to nuzzle the hollow at the edge of her neck. Mmm, that felt good. So good, she almost purred as the lips trailed to her breast, savoured, then suckled gently before sliding slowly to the curve of her waist where they traced a path to her navel, settled, succoured, and continued down over the soft concave of her belly.

Francesca moved restlessly with anticipatory pleasure, then groaned her disappointment when they began a caressing pattern close to her hip.

Fingers teased the short curls guarding her feminine core, then slid inward to stroke the sensitive clitoris.

This was one hell of an erotic dream, she mused as sensation built to a slow ache and began spiralling through her body. So acute that it seemed much too real to belong in anyone's subconscious mind.

The sweep of a hair-roughened leg against her own provided the catalyst that broke the dream and plunged her into reality.

There was a faint click, then the room flooded with light.

Francesca's lips parted, then closed, and her eyes felt incredibly large as she stared into masculine features mere inches from her own.

A dark shadow covered his jaw, a night's growth of beard that lent a raw sexuality to broad bone structure. His eyes were warm, dark, and incredibly sensual.

'Good morning,' Dominic said gently as he trailed a forefinger down the slope of her nose, then slipped down to trace the soft fullness of her mouth.

What followed was a sensual tasting—a prelude to slow and languorous loving when heightened senses flared to fever pitch, only to subside in a long sensuous aftermath.

'What time is it?'

Dominic angled his wrist in order to read the luminous dial on his watch. 'Ten past seven. Want me to order room service?'

She was hungry, and said so. At the sudden gleam in those dark eyes she quickly qualified, 'For food.'

His smile melted her bones, and he leaned forward to brush her lips with his own, then slid from the bed and stood to his feet. Unashamedly naked, his superbly muscled frame was sleek and potently male.

Far too potent, Francesca reflected as she watched him walk through to the *en suite* bathroom. Wide shoulders, a well-defined waist, tight buttocks, and long, muscular legs.

He moved with the natural ease of a physically fit man who was comfortable with his body. Assured, confident, and animalistically graceful, combining strength and power that was beautiful on an intensely male level.

As soon as the door closed behind him she pushed aside the bedclothes and reached for her robe.

Ten minutes later they walked through to the beach. White sandy foreshore and startlingly blue sea stretched as far as the eye could see to the south as the shoreline hugged the land mass.

At this hour of the morning the air held a clean freshness, warmed by the sun but without the intensity of heat that would follow as the day progressed.

'Is this going to be a brisk aerobic walk or do we stroll?' Dominic enquired as they cleared the perimeter of crunchy dry sand and gained the level, tightly packed variety fringing an outgoing tide.

Francesca cast him a considering look, taking in the casual shorts, the shirt slung carelessly across his shoulders and knotted at his chest, the peaked cap and the joggers. 'Aerobic,' she determined, and set the pace.

He shortened his stride to hers, and she shot him a winning smile.

'An attempt to expend any excess energy?'

'Mine or yours?'

His laughter was low and husky. 'Both, I imagine.' The dark, gleaming glance he threw her held more than humour, and she fought against the surge of heat flooding her veins.

He was getting too close. Much too close for her peace of mind. Invading her space, her time, and infiltrating her emotions. With a controlled determination set to destroy each and every one of her carefully erected defences.

She had a strong, instinctive feeling that with Dominic Andrea it would be all or nothing. And she wasn't anywhere near ready to examine *all*.

The beach was far from isolated. People walked, jogged, some casually, others with an intensity that spelled adherence to a fitness regime.

They reached Narrowneck, so named for the narrow strip of land separating river and ocean at that particular point, and followed the Esplanade into the heart of Surfers Paradise.

Tall, high-rise apartment buildings were positioned one after the other, and there were numerous outdoor cafés and ice cream parlours geared to attract the tourists.

'Want to stop for coffee?'

Francesca spared him a sweeping glance. 'And croissants?' she added, feeling ravenously hungry.

He smiled as he caught her hand in his and led her onto the boardwalk.

'A pre-breakfast snack?'

She wrinkled her nose at him and laughed. The day seemed suddenly brighter, and it had nothing to do with the sunshine.

They headed for the nearest café, took an outdoor table, and Dominic ordered from the waitress.

A large table umbrella protected them from the sun's encroaching heat, and Francesca sipped the ruinously strong brew as she idly viewed the ocean and the few people enjoying an early-morning swim.

He watched as she split open a croissant and spread each half with jam. She looked refreshed, alert. Yet he sensed the slight defensive edge beneath her smile. If he wasn't careful, she'd attempt to put him at arm's length.

'Want to do the return trip by sand or pavement?' Dominic queried when they had finished.

'Sand,' she said, without hesitation, and he directed her a lazy grin.

'Not afraid I might toss you into the ocean?'

'Chance would be a fine thing.'

They walked at a measured pace, and reached the hotel complex in good time. Francesca skirted the large outdoor pool, sank down on her haunches to remove her joggers, stripped down to a bikini, then slid into the cool water.

Heaven. For a few minutes she simply let her body cool, then she followed Dominic with a few leisurely laps before levering herself onto the ledge.

A towel was placed in her hand by a diligent hotel

employee, and she blotted the excess moisture from her skin, aware Dominic was mirroring her actions. She stopped to collect her outer clothes, wrapped a towel round her slender curves sarong-wise, then walked ahead of Dominic to her suite.

'You take the shower first. I'll pack.'

'We'll share.'

A droll reply rose to her lips, then died. It was OK to be sassy in a public place, but here in the confines of a private suite it was a different matter. 'There's breakfast, and a plane to catch,' she managed lightly. 'With not much time to spare.'

'Five minutes of sex in the shower isn't my idea of satisfaction.' He caught her close, sliding his hands up to cup her face as he lowered his head. 'And taking a later plane isn't an option.' His mouth hovered over hers. 'So this will have to do.'

Warm, and devastatingly sensual, his mouth plundered at will, taking, giving, until she sank in against him, wanting more, much more.

When he finally broke the kiss, she was incapable of moving, and he looked down at her slightly swollen lips, the glazed, almost dazed expression in those incredibly brown eyes, and smiled.

'The shower,' he insisted gently, urging her towards the bathroom.

I've slept with him, had sex with him. What's the big deal about sharing a shower? It isn't as if this is the first time you've shared a shower with a man.

With Mario, it had been fun and laughter.

But this was different. Way, way different.

There would be nothing humorous about sharing a shower with this man. Evocative heat pulsed through her body at the mere thought of standing a breath apart from his naked, virile frame.

She watched as he pushed down the knit boxer shorts, together with the thin black silk briefs beneath them.

Without a word she undid her bikini bra strap and discarded the scrap of Lycra, then stepped out of the matching briefs.

Water cascaded onto the tiled floor and she reached for the soap, studiously avoiding eye contact—*hell*, body contact—with Dominic.

Impossible, of course. His movements were vigorous, his use of the soap generous, and he made no attempt at modesty. Nor did his state of arousal appear to faze him.

Francesca liked to think she was adept at dealing with any situation, but this one left her fraught with nerves.

As soon as Dominic exited the shower cubicle Francesca reached for the shampoo, lathered and rinsed, then closed the water dial.

With a towel fastened round her slim form, she used the portable blowdrier on her hair, then quickly applied basic make-up and moved into the bedroom to scoop up fresh underwear and a change of clothes.

Ten minutes later she was ready, dressed in cream tailored trousers and matching top. A long silk scarf in brilliant shades of peacock-green and blue added a dash of colour.

'We'll leave our bags with the concierge while we have breakfast.' Dominic slid the zip fastener closed on

his, waiting while she added a few last minute items to
hers, then caught one in each hand.

The lagoon restaurant was almost empty, consequently service was swift. Fresh orange juice, coffee,
followed by cereal, fruit, toast, scrambled eggs and
mushrooms.

A limousine was waiting for them, their bags stowed
in the boot, as they emerged from the foyer.

Flashbulbs, one after the other in quick sequence,
took them unawares.

Francesca caught sight of yesterday's fashion shoot
photographer, and swore softly beneath cover of an artificial smile.

'*"Francesca Angeletti and prominent Sydney entrepreneur Dominic Andrea check out of Gold Coast
Sheraton Mirage Resort together. Society's hottest new
couple?"* Good caption, don't you think?'

So he'd done his homework. She'd suspected he
might make it a mission, simply to get back at her. She
didn't bother commenting, merely stepped into the rear
of the limousine ahead of Dominic, glad of tinted windows and the driver's skill as he cleared the resort's entrance in record time.

With no luggage to check in, they moved directly
through to the departure lounge and boarded the Boeing jet immediately prior to take-off.

'I'll pick you up at seven,' Dominic indicated as he
dropped her off outside her apartment building. At her
blank look, he prompted, 'We're joining Gabbi and
Benedict at the theatre, remember?'

The car slid away from the kerb before Francesca

had time to say a word. Minutes later she rode the lift up to her apartment, checked her answering machine for messages, collected three faxes and sorted through her mail.

Then she walked through to her bedroom and unpacked her bag, her expression pensive as she reflected on just how she was going to deal with Dominic.

She had the strangest feeling that the ball wasn't in her court at all, and that when it came to keeping score he was way ahead of her.

The thought stayed with her throughout the afternoon, bothered her as she showered and dressed for the evening ahead, and endorsed her decision to take control of the situation.

CHAPTER NINE

FRANCESCA SWEPT HER hair into a smooth knot above her head and secured it with pins, then she completed her make-up and crossed to the walk-in wardrobe where she removed a gown in deep ruby red velvet. Its style and cut gave credit to a little known designer who, in Francesca's opinion, would soon earn kudos in the international arena. There were matching heeled pumps and an evening purse, and she added a diamond pendant and attached diamond studs to each ear.

The intercom buzzed right on time, and she reached for the receiver. 'Dominic? I'm on my way down.'

He was waiting for her in the foyer, and the sight of him took her breath away. Attired in a black evening suit, with pin-pleated white cotton shirt, he looked every inch the sophisticated social dilettante.

Yet only a fool would fail to discern the leashed power beneath the surface. Or miss the faint ruthless edge that set him apart from most men.

A valuable ally, she acknowledged silently as she slid into the front passenger seat of the gleaming Lexus. And a feared enemy.

Gabbi's husband Benedict possessed similar qualities, she reflected as Dominic eased the car off the bricked apron and onto the road. Both were hardened by the vicariousness of a cut-throat business world and the men and women who inhabited it.

Traffic into the city flowed relatively smoothly, and Gabbi and Benedict joined them at a prearranged meeting place within minutes of their arrival.

'You look fantastic,' Francesca accorded softly as she brushed her cheek to Gabbi's.

'Same goes,' Gabbi responded with a quiet chuckle.

'Shall we mix and mingle, drink in hand?' Benedict queried. 'Or would you prefer to go directly into the auditorium?'

'Dominic—*darling*. How *are* you?'

Francesca heard the breathy feminine voice and turned, interested to see who would project such an intimate greeting.

Petite and blonde, it was the same woman Dominic had been deep in conversation with at Leon's gallery a few weeks ago.

Francesca, unprepared for the arrow of jealousy, watched as the blonde clung a few seconds too long as Dominic brushed his lips to her cheek. The beautifully lacquered pink nails lingered as they trailed down his jacket, and the smile, although brilliant, didn't quite mask the edge of sadness in her eyes.

'Simone,' Dominic said gently. 'You know Gabbi and Benedict. Have you met Francesca?'

'No. Although I've often admired you on the catwalk and in the glossies.'

The lights flickered, signalling patrons to enter the auditorium and take their seats.

'Perhaps we could have a drink together some time?' Simone ventured wistfully as they parted.

Francesca noted that although Dominic's smile held warmth, he didn't commit himself to an answer, and she wondered at the sudden spurt of anger that rose to the surface and made her want to demand what Simone meant to him.

Their seats were excellent, and, although Francesca had seen a stunning cast production in London some time ago, the Australian version was excellent, and as always the music, the theme, tugged at her emotions.

When the curtain came down on the first act it was Gabbi who suggested they move into the lobby for a drink.

There was an underlying hum of excitement evident among the mingling patrons, several of whom were society matrons determined to be seen by the few photographers commissioned to cover the night.

Francesca, well-used to the careless and frequent use of the 'darling' greetings, thought if she heard just one more in the next five minutes, she'd scream.

'Damn.'

Francesca heard the softly voiced curse and looked at Gabbi, raised one eyebrow, then lowered it in full comprehension as she saw Annaliese making her way towards them through the crowded lobby.

'Want to escape to the powder room?'

'And spoil her fun?'

'You mean we get to stay and watch?'

'Oh, yes,' Gabbi said firmly, slipping her hand into Benedict's large one.

Francesca watched as Gabbi's husband cast his wife a gleaming glance and lifted her hand to his lips.

'Benedict. Wonderful to see you,' Annaliese purred as she reached them. She turned towards Dominic and cast him a smile that would have melted most men into an ignominious puddle. 'Dominic. So kind of you to take pity on Francesca.'

Grrr. Kittens played. Cats fought. 'All alone, Annaliese?' Francesca queried smoothly.

'Of course not, darling.' The smile was saccharine sweet. 'How was the Gold Coast? I believe you became embroiled with a certain photographer at the Mirage? Word has it your reaction was...' She paused for maximum effect. 'Physical.'

Francesca sharpened metaphorical claws and aimed for the kill. 'Not nearly as physical as you were in Rome, or Paris. And then there was that much publicised débâcle in Milan, if I recall?' She arched one eyebrow and offered a slight smile that was totally lacking in humour. '*Touché*, Annaliese?'

'I think we've each run the media's gauntlet at one time or another,' Benedict indicated smoothly.

It was perhaps as well the next act was due to commence. Patrons were beginning to drift back into the auditorium, and anything she might have said was lost as the music started and the lights began to dim.

The finale gained enthusiastic and well-deserved audience applause, and at its close they rose to their feet and joined patrons exiting the auditorium.

'Let's go somewhere for supper,' Benedict suggested as they gained the car park. 'Dominic, Francesca? You'll join us, won't you?'

'Where?' Gabbi queried, and Francesca caught Benedict's faint smile as he responded.

'Double Bay.' The smile broadened. 'I doubt Annaliese will consider following us there.'

Or Simone, Francesca added silently, and admonished herself for being uncharitable.

It was almost midnight when Dominic brought the car to a halt in an allocated bay outside her apartment building.

Francesca reached for the door latch. 'Thanks for a pleasant evening.'

'We slept together last night, and made love the night before—not to mention this morning.' He caught hold of her chin and tilted it towards him. 'Tonight you want to dismiss me?'

A tiny shiver feathered through her body. 'I'm not sure I like where this is leading.'

'Define "this".'

She was afraid—of him, herself. 'You. Me.' Her eyes met his bravely. 'Soon I fly to Europe.' She felt his thumb trace her lower lip, and sensed its slight tremble at his touch. 'I won't be back in Australia for several months.'

'So...no strings?' Dominic queried in a dangerously silky voice. 'Just enjoy each other, responsibly. Alternate nights in your apartment or mine, as and when the mood takes us? Then we kiss each other goodbye and say, Hey, that was great, let's do it again some time?'

He was icily angry, so much so that he wanted to shake her, *hard.* 'Is that all it meant to you?'

She could end it now, she decided dully. Say the careless words that would ensure she walked away and never saw him again.

It was what she should do—if she wanted to retain her emotional sanity.

Acute pain pierced her body and punctured her soul at the thought of never experiencing the touch of his hands, his lips grazing over her skin, or the feel of his powerful body possessing her own.

'No.'

For a few mindless seconds he didn't say anything. He was content to brush gentle fingers across one satin-smooth cheek then thread them in her hair.

'Simone threw you off balance?'

Was she that transparent? 'It's obvious she cares deeply for you.'

'We were engaged briefly in our early twenties when I was a struggling artist hell-bent on resisting my father's efforts to join him in business. Simone disliked the idea of travelling around Europe for two years on a pittance.' He shrugged. 'We argued, I walked, and Simone married someone else.'

Francesca looked at him carefully in the dim light. 'So now you're simply good friends.'

Maybe there was something in her voice, the intonation she gave, for he smiled. 'Simone is aware it can never be anything else.'

Was that supposed to be reassurance? The thought of him arousing another woman to a state of mindless abandon, his strong body urging her towards ecstasy, caused pain of a kind that made her feel ill.

'It's late.' She released the latch and opened the door. He slid out from behind the wheel and crossed round to clasp her arm. 'Dominic—'

A finger touched her lips. 'Tell me you want to be alone, and I'll go.'

She almost said yes. Then she thought how darned *good* it felt to be held in his arms, to go to sleep knowing he would be there whenever she woke through the night.

It was a tantalising vision. Part of her wanted to accept what they had together without questioning where it might lead or how it would end. Simply live for the *now*, without pondering what the future might bring.

She wanted the sweet sorcery of his touch, the sensual magic no other man had been able to evoke.

'You get to make breakfast,' Francesca capitulated lightly.

He extended a hand for her keys, and once through security they rode the lift together in silence.

Why did she feel so nervous, for heaven's sake? And alive, so gloriously wonderfully *alive*.

Such a complex mix of emotions, she acknowledged on entering the apartment.

Out of habit she slipped off her shoes, then crossed the lounge to the kitchen. 'Coffee?'

He shrugged off his jacket, folded it over a chair and followed her. 'Please. Black, one sugar.'

She took down two cups and set them on saucers. She shouldn't feel awkward, but she did. Maybe because it was her apartment, her territory, and not the neutrality of a hotel suite.

Theatre seemed a safe topic, and they discussed other shows they'd each enjoyed, and a few dramatic productions.

Dominic replaced his empty cup, removed her own, and held out his hand. 'Turn off the lights and come admire the view with me.'

He looped his arm over her shoulders as they reached the wide expanse of floor-to-ceiling glass. A touch on the remote control module and the drapes slid back to reveal a panoramic vista. Pinpricks of electric light formed a magical pattern that extended as far as the eye could see.

Francesca made no protest when he turned her towards him, and her arms lifted, encircling his neck as his head lowered down to hers.

Mesmeric, gentle, he made kissing a sensual feast, building up a slow heat until she burned with need. Then he swept her into his arms and carried her through to the bedroom.

Her fingers were feverish as she sought to free the buttons on his shirt, and she dragged the material free from his trousers, then reached for his belt. She didn't want any barrier restricting access to his naked flesh. Or her own. And seconds later the velvet gown slid to the floor, followed by a gossamer-fine lace teddy.

They tumbled down onto the bed, and she voiced a faint protest as Dominic reached out and snapped on the bedside lamp.

'I want to see you,' he growled. 'I want you to see me.'

Francesca was past caring whether there was light or the comfort of darkness. His fingers brushed a path up her inner thigh and traced a fiery pattern before sinking into the moist tunnel in a simulation of the act itself.

Her body arched beneath him, seeking the solace he offered, then she cried out when blind need drove her over the edge.

Dominic slid into her with one powerful movement, matching each thrust to a timeless rhythm as she urged him harder and faster until they reached the pinnacle, poised there for seemingly long seconds before soaring towards a shattering climax that left them both labouring for breath.

Francesca lay limp and totally enervated, her skin moist with sweat. In her mind she'd cried out, soft, guttural sounds that had built in frequency and pitch until she was no longer conscious of where or who she was.

Dear heaven, she hadn't realised, hadn't known it was possible to lose oneself so totally in the sexual act.

To know your emotional sanity, your very existence was dependent on another caused fear of a kind she wasn't sure she wanted to deal with.

'Open your eyes,' Dominic commanded softly.

Francesca felt the drift of his fingers as they brushed her cheek, and wasn't sure she wanted to obey. For then she would have to face him, visually, physically, and acknowledge what they'd shared together.

'Tell me how you feel.'

She couldn't find the words even to begin to describe the magic euphoric state of her body and mind. Where did she start? What did she say? That her skin was a mass of acutely sensitised nerve-endings so highly attuned to *him* that it reacted to his touch as if it had received an electrical charge? Radiating heat through veins and nerve fibres to the centre of her sensual being until her entire body *sang* like a piano tuning fork?

Or perhaps she could attempt to explain the incredible meshing of mind with body? How on some deep mental level there was recognition of a kind that was like some incredible discovery, almost as if they'd known each other in another era, a former age.

The thought it could even be a possibility tore at everything she knew. It made her question *love*, and what it meant. Worse, she was forced to accept that love could assume many guises and with Mario she had experienced only one of them. And that wasn't something she wanted to examine right now.

If Dominic wanted an insight into her mind at this precise point, she would allow him to see anger. The confusion, the self-doubt. The glimmering of an enlightening revelation was hers alone.

Francesca's eyelashes fluttered upwards. 'You want assurance on how you scored?'

Something dark moved in his eyes, creating a shadow that made her feel suddenly afraid.

He had watched every fleeting expression, divined each one of them, and felt a growing frustration at being almost completely powerless to exorcise them. There was only one path to travel, that of total honesty, even if it was accorded confrontational.

'This isn't about "Was it as good for you as it was

for me?" You were with me every step of the way, and we both went up in flames.'

The heat began to diminish, chilled by her own hand. A part of her bled for that loss, while another urged her towards re-establishing emotional self-preservation.

'You're a skilled lover.' Dear heaven. An understatement if ever there was one.

He was silent for a few heartstopping seconds, then he spoke in a chillingly soft voice that sent icy shivers down her spine. 'Is that all you thought it was?' His breath feathered against her cheek. *'Technique?'*

It was impossible to read his expression, and she didn't offer a word as he caught her face between both hands and tipped it so she was forced to meet his gaze.

'Francesca?' His eyes raked her features, glimpsing the defensiveness apparent in her eyes, and he swore softly beneath his breath.

'What *is* this?' Her eyes were dark and furious. 'Twenty questions?' She wanted to vent some of her anger, verbally, physically. 'What do you want to hear, Dominic? That you're the first man I've had sex with in three years?' She was like a runaway train, unable to stop. 'That having had sex with you, I'm going to allow you to be part of my life?'

He fastened his mouth on hers, effectively halting the flow of words in a plundering possession that ravaged each and every layer guarding her soul.

It went on for what seemed an age, and when at last he lifted his head she had to struggle to regain her breath.

'I'm not giving you a choice.' His voice was deep, smoky, and filled with intent.

With an anguished cry Francesca launched herself at him, hands bunched into fists as she sought to inflict damage wherever she could connect. 'The *hell* you're not.'

She heard him grunt as she landed a blow to his ribs, and experienced a short-lived surge of satisfaction before he caught hold of one wrist, then the other and forced them behind her back.

He soon rendered her legs ineffectual by trapping them between his own, and she struggled against him, unable to gain any purchase except with her mouth, which she used without thought or aim, sinking her teeth into a hard muscled shoulder.

His retaliation was swift as he shifted slightly and took hard succour from her breast before leaving his mark on its sensitive curve.

Francesca renewed her struggle and gained nothing except a knowledge of his strength.

'Enough. You'll hurt yourself.'

She was breathing hard, her eyes molten with self-rage as she was forced to concede defeat. While he didn't look as if he was doing more than restraining a recalcitrant child.

'I hate you.' It was said almost matter-of-factly, without venom, and a muscle tensed along his jaw.

'No, you don't.'

The anger was beginning to fade a little, yet it was still there, waiting to flare given the smallest opportunity.

'Damn you.' Her eyes hurt with angry tears she refused to let fall. 'For three years I've been able to convince myself I'm doing fine.' Her vision misted. 'And I was. Until you swept into my life.' And tore it apart.

Dominic lifted a hand and traced the fullness of her lower lip with his thumb. 'I don't drive fast cars or take any unnecessary risks.'

Francesca froze with pain, then reaction set in and she reared back from him, scrambling to the edge of the bed.

'That was uncalled for, and unfair.'

'It's the truth.'

'I'd like you to leave.' Cool clear words, as cool as the ice beginning to form round her heart. She stood to her feet and snatched up a robe, then pulled it on and tied the belt.

He didn't move, and her eyes were stormy with anger as she turned to face him. 'Get dressed, and get out of here.'

Had anyone told her how beautiful she was when she was mad? With her hair tumbling onto her shoulders in disarray, her skin flushed and her eyes sparking anger, she resembled a tigress.

He slid to his feet, collected briefs and trousers and pulled them on, then stood facing her across the width of the bed.

'I'm alive,' Dominic said quietly. 'Remember that before I walk out of here.' His eyes held hers, equally as dark as her own. 'And we both lose something we could have had for the rest of our lives.'

She watched as he reached for his shirt and shrugged

into it. Then he retrieved his shoes and socks and put them on.

'That's emotional blackmail.'

He paused in tying his shoelaces and cast her a long, steady look. 'It's a statement of fact.'

'A manipulative one,' Francesca corrected heatedly.

'You think I don't know how difficult it is for you to let go of the past?' There was something primitive in his expression, a ruthlessness that was harnessed, yet exigent beneath the surface. 'Or how afraid you are to let any man too close in case you get hurt?'

Her eyes were still stormy. 'It's called self-preservation. Emotional survival.'

'You think so? Destruction might be more apt.' He paused, collected his jacket and hooked it over one shoulder, aware as he said the words that he was taking the biggest gamble of his life. 'Be happy enclosed in your glass house, Francesca.'

The image was vivid, almost frightening. Inaccessible, destined always to be alone, leading an empty, shallow existence devoid of emotion. An observer, never a player. Was that what she wanted?

'Every time I take one step forward, you force me to take another,' she cried in anguish. She lifted one hand and let it fall helplessly to her side. 'I don't even know the direction, let alone the destination.'

Dominic skirted the bed and moved to stand within touching distance. 'I want it all. My ring on your finger. *Marriage.* And the right to share the rest of your life.'

Francesca felt the blood drain from her face. 'You can't mean that.'

'Can't I?' The demand was dangerously soft, and she shivered at its silent force. 'No other woman has taken control of my emotions the way you do. I doubt anyone else could.'

She was hesitant in her need to choose the right words. 'That's not a good enough reason.'

Something flared in his eyes, a flame that was quickly masked. 'What about love?'

The breath locked in her throat. *Love?* The everlasting kind? 'I had that once. It nearly killed me when I lost it.'

Dominic tossed his jacket onto a chair, and she was powerless to evade his fingers as he caught hold of her chin and tilted it so she had no recourse but to look at him.

'Life doesn't come with a guarantee, Francesca.' His hands slid to cup her face, his eyes dark with latent emotion. 'You make the most of what you have for as long as it's there.'

His mouth settled on her with a wild, sweet eroticism, seeking, soothing, seducing in a manner that sent the blood coursing through her veins, heating her body almost to fever-pitch.

Francesca lost all trace of time or place as she became caught up in the magic of his touch, the feel of his body as his arms shifted to bind her more closely against him.

She kissed him back, hungrily wanting as much as he could give, meeting and matching him every step of the way.

He broke free slowly, easing the pressure, the intensity, as he trailed his mouth gently over the swollen contours of her own, then he placed light, open-mouthed kisses along the edge of her jaw, traversed the column at her neck, then settled in the hollow beneath her throat.

'Will you tell me about Mario?' Dominic queried gently. 'I think I deserve to know.'

She moved back a pace, putting minimal distance between them.

Oh, God. Where did she start? Much of their lifestyle had been portrayed by media hype, some of it fact, mostly fiction. Dominic could access that any way he chose. No, it was the private story, the personal details he wanted.

'We met at a party in Rome,' she began slowly. 'We were both celebrating a personal victory. He'd won on the race circuit and I'd signed a modelling contract with a famed Italian designer.' She struggled to keep it light. 'Mario was...outgoing, gregarious.' How did you explain one man to another? Simple things, like the way he drew people, women especially, like a magnet?

'We had a whirlwind romance, and married three weeks later.' She hugged her arms tightly over her midriff in a protective gesture, and stared sightlessly ahead. 'He lived and breathed the race circuit. There was the constant adrenalin rush of the practice sessions, improving lap times, always needing to go faster, be better than anyone else. Each time he went out on the track I mentally prepared myself for the fact he mightn't come back in one piece.'

Dominic pulled her close and she wound her arms around his waist as she absorbed his strength.

They stood together like that for an age, then she felt his fingers drift up and down her spine in a soothing gesture, and there was the touch of his lips on her hair, at her temple.

'I love you.'

His hands captured her face, and she almost died at the expression in his eyes before his head descended and his mouth closed over her own.

A slight tremor shook her slim form, at what he sought to give and what she was almost afraid to take. Then she let herself go with the magic of his touch, matching his passion with such a wealth of feeling she had no recollection of anything other than the moment and the need for total fulfilment.

Their loving held a primitive quality, wild and so incredibly intense that it surpassed anything they had previously shared together. It was a long time before their breathing slowed and they lay sated, completely enervated by the depth of their emotions.

They must have slept, for Francesca stirred at the drift of fingers tracing a lazy pattern across the soft curve of her hip. Then she murmured a faint protest as the hand slipped lower and began an intimate exploration that warmed her blood and turned her body into a molten mass of malleable sensuality.

This time there was none of the heat and hunger of the night before, only a slow, leisurely loving that displayed exquisite care.

Francesca's eyes met his and held them, witnessed the strength, the purpose, and she knew she didn't want to lose him. Whatever it was they shared, she wanted the opportunity to explore it.

He saw the subtle change, felt the tension in her body begin to ebb, and sought to provide the reassurance she needed.

His mouth was gentle yet possessive as he loosened his hold and traced the indentations of her spine.

Heaven was the mutual giving and taking of pleasure, discovering, wanting to test his restraint as he tested hers until nothing else mattered but the moment. Each time they came together it seemed as if she gifted him a little bit of herself.

They slept a little, then made love whenever one or the other stirred into a dreamy state of half-sleep, part-wakefulness.

Something which happened often, Francesca acknowledged as she felt the soft passage of Dominic's lips across one cheek.

'I have an exhibition in Cairns on Saturday,' Dominic imparted close to her ear. 'Cancel any plans you have and come with me for the weekend. We'll fly up tomorrow and have a day in Port Douglas.'

From the soft dawn light filtering through the drapes, 'tomorrow' had already arrived.

She gave in to the temptation to tease him a little. 'I'll give it some consideration.'

'Minx,' he accorded huskily. 'Do you have to think about it?'

'The exhibition sounds fun. It means I get to view some of your work. Not to mention being able to observe you in the role of artist.' She was on a roll. 'And the far north holds special childhood memories for me.'

'Is that a yes or a no?'

She smiled in the semi-darkness. 'What time do you want to leave?'

'Eight. I need to collect my bag from the house.'

She'd call her parents to let them know she'd be out of town.

His lips traced a path to the corner of her mouth. 'Hungry?'

'For you, or food?' she teased, and felt his smile.

'Both.'

She ached in places she hadn't thought it was possible to ache. 'I guess that means I don't get to snatch an hour's sleep before we need to shower, change and have breakfast?'

'Do you *want* to sleep?'

'You're offering something better?'

He didn't answer, merely showed her. It took quite a while. And afterwards he tested the speed limit, and they were last to board the flight north.

CHAPTER TEN

IT WAS HOT and sultry in Cairns, with high humidity, dull skies and the threat of an imminent tropical Wet Season.

Soaring outdoor temperatures hit them like a wall of heat as they left the comfort of the air-conditioned terminal and walked the short distance to their hire car.

Francesca stripped off her cotton jacket and tossed it onto the rear seat, and Dominic loosened the top few buttons of his shirt.

The air was different up here, the pace of life less frenetic than the southern cities, and the foliage covering the ranges bordering the coastline was a lush dark green.

Port Douglas lay approximately seventy kilometres further north, with wide sweeping beaches bounding the eastern fringes and an inner harbour to the west of a narrow promontory.

Sugar cane country, Francesca mused as they passed acres of freshly farrowed paddocks. Mechanical planting and cutting now. Only firing the cane remained the same as it had in years gone by. Small rail tracks crossed the road at intervals, connecting one farm to another, so that cut cane could be loaded and transported to the mill.

She remembered holidaying in this region as a child, visiting Italian grandparents who'd owned vast cane holdings and a farmhouse that was filled with exotic cooking smells, much love and laughter. Now her grandparents lay buried side by side, and the land had been divided and sold off in part to developers.

There were several resorts bordering each side of the four-kilometre stretch leading into Port Douglas, and Dominic took the long, curved driveway that led to the exclusive Sheraton Mirage.

Their suite was luxurious, with sweeping views of the ocean. 'I need to make a couple of calls,' Dominic relayed as he stowed their bags. 'Then we can swim, explore, drive up onto the Tableland. Or,' he suggested, closing the space between them, 'stay here and order in as the mood takes us.'

Francesca moved into his arms and lifted her face for his kiss, loving the feel of his mouth on hers, the gentle possession that rapidly led to hunger of a kind neither of them wanted to deny.

He was a caring lover, pacing his needs to her own, then, when he'd driven her to the point of wildness, he tipped her over the edge and held her as she fell.

There was no sense of time or place in the long afterplay. The drift of fingers, the exploration by lips and the slow sensual tasting that teased and lingered, incited, until only total fulfilment would suffice.

It was dark when they rose from the bed, showered and dressed.

Dominic regarded her quizzically as she applied minimum make-up and stepped into heeled sandals.

'Does this mean you'd prefer to eat dinner in the dining room?'

Francesca's eyes held a devilish gleam, and her smile was almost wicked. 'I need food as an energy boost to last me through the night.' She touched her lips with the tips of her fingers and blew him a kiss. 'Besides, it would be nice to enjoy the ambience, don't you think?' The corners of her mouth lifted with delicious humour. 'A light white wine, seafood. The local barramundi is superb, and when we've had coffee we can stroll through the grounds.'

Dominic pulled on trousers, added a polo shirt, and slid his feet into loafers. 'Just remember this was your idea.'

A soft bubble of laughter emerged from her throat. 'Think of the anticipation element.'

He bestowed upon her a brief, hard kiss, then caught hold of her hand. 'I'll bear that in mind.'

The dining room was well patronised, the food excellent and the wine superb. They lingered over coffee, then elected to traverse the extensive pool perimeter before retreating to the covered walkways linking the resort's various guest villas together.

Dominic's arm curved round her shoulders, pulling her close, and she smiled in the semi-darkness. It felt good. Better than good. It felt *right*.

Their air-conditioned suite was blessedly cool after the heat of the night, and it was she who moved into his arms, pulling him close for a long, hungry kiss.

Clothes soon became an impossible barrier, and they took pleasure in the process of discarding them before tumbling down onto the bed.

This time there was no feeling of guilt, no sense of shame. It was Dominic's features she saw, the passion she experienced solely for him.

In the morning they woke late, enjoyed a leisurely breakfast, then checked out of the resort and took the inland highway through Julatten and Mount Molloy to Mareeba, before heading east via the Kuranda range to Cairns.

A late lunch, a check of the gallery, then they returned to their hotel for dinner. Invited guests were scheduled to arrive at the gallery at eight, and a limousine was to be despatched to the hotel to transport them the two blocks distant.

Francesca had selected black Armani evening trousers and matching jacket, high-heeled pumps and discreet gold jewellery. Her make-up was understated, with emphasis on her eyes.

'Sensational,' Dominic commended with a slow sweeping appraisal that made her heart beat faster. He fixed his black bow tie, adjusted cufflinks, then shrugged into his suit jacket. The look was that of a high-powered business executive, sophisticated, at ease and in total control.

Dominic reached into his pocket and withdrew a slim jeweller's case. Inside was an exquisite gold chain, and she watched as he extracted it and fastened it around her neck.

His eyes met hers and held them as he lifted her left hand and pressed the intricate gold band to his lips.

The gesture shocked her, and a sensation akin to pain settled deep in her heart. She could only look at him in silence, incapable of uttering so much as a word, and she made no protest as he caught hold of her hand and led her from the suite.

The gallery was in a converted old Queenslander-style home, with wide covered verandahs bordering each of the four external walls. Double French doors led onto the verandah from every room, and the effect was one of rambling spaciousness.

Dominic was greeted effusively, Francesca recognised, and accorded equal reverence.

There was little opportunity to wander at will and admire the exhibited paintings before the first of the guests began to arrive.

'You're a hit,' Francesca murmured later as the gallery filled and the erudite examined and essayed an opinion as they conferred with apparent knowledge on style and form. A 'Sold' sticker appeared on one painting after another.

'Me, or my art?' Dominic teased, and saw her eyes gleam with hidden laughter.

'Both,' she said succinctly. 'Think you can hold things together for a while?' There was no doubt he could. 'I intend to appraise the exhibits.'

'Why is it that your opinion makes me nervous?'

She cast him a musing smile, then saw that he meant it. 'Afraid I might get a glimpse of your soul, Dominic?'

'Perhaps.'

How did one judge the complexities of a man who was capable of such artistic expression? Was any part of it an extension of the man himself, or merely a practised style?

'He's very talented, don't you think?'

Francesca turned at the sound of a male voice, and smiled at the elderly silver-haired gentleman. 'Yes. Yes, he is.'

He indicated the abstract. 'What do you see in this?'

'It intrigues me,' she said honestly. 'I look for hidden meanings, and find none.'

'Precisely. But one cannot easily give up the search for a key which could unlock the puzzle, hmm?'

'You're right,' she conceded slowly, and he lifted an imperious hand.

'I shall buy it. As an investment it will increase three-fold in value over the next few years. It will also provide my guests with a conversation piece.' He lowered his hand as an assistant hurried forward. 'Now, my dear, what takes your eye?'

He accompanied her from one room to another, his interest keen, his charm and wit entertaining. It was more than an hour before Francesca rejoined Dominic, and she met his faintly raised eyebrow with a smile.

'I've been conversing with a very interesting gentleman.'

'Samuel Maxwell, art critic and collector,' Dominic acknowledged.

'He thinks you're very talented.'

His eyes gleamed with mocking humour. 'I'm honoured.'

'He bought an abstract.'

'And flattered,' he said steadily. 'Maxwell is selective.'

'There you go,' she said lightly. 'Another fan.'

'And you, Francesca. Are you a fan?'

'Of the art, or the man?'

She was saved from answering when his attention was caught by a dowager of generous proportion who flirted outrageously. Francesca cast him a faintly wicked smile, and moved to the far side of the room.

It was a further hour before they could slip away. The evening was, according to the ecstatically fulsome gallery owner, a tremendous success.

A limousine returned them to their hotel, and they took the lift to their floor.

'Tired?' Dominic queried as they entered their suite.

'A little.' She slipped off her shoes and loosened her jacket.

He lifted a hand and lightly traced the gold chain to where it nestled in the valley between her breasts. 'You have beautiful skin.'

Her eyes lightened with humour. 'Are you seducing me?'

'Am I succeeding?'

Every time. She had only to look at him and her body went into sensual overdrive. All evening she'd been supremely conscious of him, part of the scene yet apart from it. And knew that he was equally as aware of her as she was of him. It had been evident in every glance, the touch of his hand whenever she drifted into his orbit, the warmth of his smile.

He made her feel so incredibly alive. A warm, sensual woman in tune with her own sexuality and aware of its power.

It was an awakening, a knowledge that heightened the senses and brought another dimension to the physical expression of shared sex. The body and mind in perfect accord with that of another. Mutual pleasuring gifted freely without self-thought.

Francesca lifted her arms and pulled his head down to hers, loving the feel of his lips as they grazed across her cheekbone, traversed her jaw, then settled with unerring accuracy on her mouth.

They had the night. Tomorrow they'd board a flight south and resume the hectic tenure of their individual lives. But for now it was enough to savour the loving.

Francesca awoke slowly to the light trail of fingers creating a pattern over the concave of her stomach, and she felt the rekindling of desire as lips settled fleetingly on one shoulder and trailed a path to her breast.

She could feel the faint rasp of his night's beard as it grazed lightly over her skin, and she gave a soft, exultant laugh as he caught her close and rolled onto his back.

There was a feeling of power in taking control, and he allowed her free rein as she tantalised and teased, then it was he who set the pace and she who clung to him in a ride that tossed her high, so high she had no recollection of anything except acute sensual pleasure, and the knowledge he shared it with her.

Long afterwards she lay cradled against his chest,

his arms caging her close as he smoothed her tumbled hair and stroked fingers over her silken skin.

It was late when she woke, and they showered together, ordered in breakfast, then dressed and checked out in time to connect with the Sydney flight.

Several hours later they disembarked, exited the airport terminal, and entered into the stream of traffic heading towards the city.

'I have to be in Melbourne tomorrow,' Dominic informed her as he negotiated a busy intersection, and Francesca felt a sense of loss.

'When will you be back?'

'Wednesday at the earliest. Probably Thursday.'

She'd miss him. 'I have a photographic session Wednesday, another scheduled for Thursday.'

They were traversing the Harbour Bridge before she realised he hadn't taken the Double Bay turn-off.

'Dominic—'

'Stay with me tonight.'

She didn't need to think, didn't *want* to think. She'd have enough time to do that while he was away.

It was after eight the next morning when Dominic deposited Francesca outside her apartment building on his way to the airport.

She rang Rick, then Sophy, caught up with Gabbi, and had a long conversation with her agent. An international fax from her mother-in-law's Italian solicitor needed an immediate response, which entailed a search through copies of legal correspondence.

Lunch comprised a salad sandwich followed by fruit, and she cooked pasta for dinner.

Dominic called her at nine, and the sound of his voice produced an unbearable longing. 'Missing me already?'

You don't know how much. 'A little.'

'It'll keep, Francesca.'

She hadn't fooled him in the slightest. 'Sleep well,' she lightly mocked, and she heard his soft chuckle.

'Promises?'

'Maybe.'

It was late when she slipped into bed, and she lay awake for an age, damning her inability to fall asleep. After an hour she switched on the television and changed channels for a while. Her head felt heavy with tiredness, and she lifted the weight of hair from her nape in an effort to ease the kinks.

Her fingers touched on the gold chain at her neck, and she absently traced its length as she thought of the man who had put it there, and why.

What she'd had with Mario had been special. No one could take it away. But would he have wanted her to live the rest of her life alone? To deny herself happiness and love—a different kind of love perhaps—and children, with another man? Somehow she didn't think so.

Without questioning her actions she drew off Mario's wedding ring and attached it to the chain, feeling the weight nestle in the valley between her breasts.

There were roses waiting for her in Reception when she entered her apartment building late the following afternoon, and she rang Dominic on his cellphone, only to discover he was in a meeting and unable to talk freely.

'I can say anything, and you'll be hampered in your response?' Francesca teased.

'I can always reschedule.'

She laughed. 'For something terribly decadent, with fresh strawberries and expensive champagne?'

'Is that a definite?'

'Would you prefer yoghurt or whipped cream?'

'Count me in.'

'I'm offering seconds.'

'That, too.'

'What would your associates think if they knew you were indulging in mild phone sex?'

His voice deepened. 'I'll look forward to settling with you in a day or two.'

She gave an irrepressible chuckle. 'I'll hold that thought.'

It was no easier to summon sleep than it had been the night before, and Francesca lay awake in the darkness caught up in a web of reflective thought.

Love. Was *this* what it was? An inability to *think*, to function without him? To want, *need* with such intensity it became difficult to focus on anything else?

Wednesday's fashion shoot went way over time, and an unexpected summer shower saw Tony transfer the shoot indoors, to his studio, before moving on as scheduled to a major city department store.

It was almost closing time when the final shot was taken. Staff were packing up, and only a few last-minute shoppers remained.

In the changing room Francesca stepped into cotton trousers, fastened the zip, then pulled a skinny-rib top over her head.

The store's background piped music clicked off as she stepped into heeled sandals and gathered up her bag.

'Who the hell are you, and what are you doing here?'

'Waiting for Francesca,' a deep male voice drawled in response.

Dominic.

She smoothed nervous fingers over the length of her hair, then emerged from the changing room to see Tony regarding Dominic with hard-eyed suspicion.

He turned towards Francesca as she moved forward. 'You know this man?'

Her eyes met Dominic's, and what she saw there made her catch her breath. Then she smiled. 'Yes.' She didn't hesitate, just walked straight into his arms and raised her face for his kiss.

Dominic was very thorough, and it was several minutes before he lifted his head. 'The lady is with me,' he said with deadly softness, for the benefit of anyone who might have held the slightest doubt. Then he looked down at her. 'Isn't that so?'

He was asking much more than that, and she gave him his answer. 'Yes.'

Later, much later, they lay entwined in the shadowy dark hours of night, sated and deliciously drowsy after a long loving.

'You are going to marry me?'

Francesca lifted a hand and gently traced a finger over the length of his jaw. 'Am I?'

Dominic let his teeth nip at a delicate swell of flesh, felt her shudder, and sought to soothe the tiny bruise with a gentle open-mouthed kiss.

'That was meant to be a statement, not a question.'

'Ah.' She smiled in the darkness. 'Being masterful, are we?'

'Soon.' The insistent undertone made her want to tease him a little.

'Next year?' The query earned her an evocative kiss that made her forget everything.

'Next week.'

'That could be difficult.'

She felt rather than heard his soft laughter as he trailed his mouth down the edge of her neck. 'Nothing is difficult.'

No, it wasn't, if you had the money to pay a horde of people to organise everything.

'Like to hear what I have in mind?'

She let her fingers traverse the indentations of his back, then conducted a slow sweep to one hip. 'Why is it I get the feeling you've already set a plan in motion?'

'A ceremony in the gardens at my home, a celebrant, family and immediate friends.'

It sounded remarkably simple. And romantic. Francesca could almost see it. A red carpet rolled out on the spacious lawn, glorious stands of trailing roses framing the gazebo. She even had a dress she'd never worn that would be perfect.

She sensed the faint tightening of muscles beneath

her straying fingers, felt the increased beat of his heart and was unable to continue teasing him. 'OK.'

'OK? That's it?'

'Yes,' she said gently. 'There's just one consideration.'

'Tell me.'

'I'm due in Milan, remember? Then Paris.'

'My darling Francesca,' Dominic declared with deceptive indolence, 'I'll not only be sharing your flight—' he placed his lips against a particularly vulnerable part of her anatomy and felt her indrawn breath '—I'll be standing at the rear of every function room wherever you appear on the catwalk.' He suckled gently and felt her fingers rake through his hair. 'And occupying your bed every night.'

'Mmm,' she murmured with satisfaction. 'I was hoping for that.'

His laugh was low and smoky. 'Should I be brave and ask which has priority?'

As if he needed to ask! Her lips curved to form a winsome smile. 'It's nice to share travel with a companion.'

'Really?'

'Uh-huh. And of course it will be reassuring to know you're in the audience.' The smile widened. 'Although you should be warned that designers are temperamental creatures who won't tolerate distractions.'

'Guess I don't get to go backstage.'

'Not if you value your life.'

'They're likely to get physical?' He was deliberately baiting her, and she responded in kind.

'No, but I might.' Too many women in various stages

of undress wasn't something she felt inclined to share with him.

'You've left out something.'

'I have?' She gave a tiny yelp as he rolled onto his back and carried her with him. A slow, sweet smile lightened her features and she lifted her arms high in a graceful cat-like stretch. 'Oh, yes. You get to share my hotel suite each night.'

'Witch,' Dominic accorded lazily.

It was a while before Francesca could summon sufficient energy to talk.

'A rooftop apartment in Paris, and a delayed honeymoon would be a nice way to bring my career to a close.'

Something jerked at his insides, and he carefully controlled it. 'You're thinking of giving up modelling?'

She hadn't needed to give it much thought. 'Professionally.'

There was silence for a few seemingly long seconds. 'Don't you want to ask me why?' Francesca queried gently.

This was one time he found it difficult to co-ordinate the right words. 'Tell me.'

'I want to have your child. Children,' she corrected. 'That is, if you—'

Dominic didn't allow her to finish as he brought her head down to his, and his mouth was an evocative instrument as he kissed her with such passionate intensity it melted her bones.

When at last he lifted his head, she could only press her cheek into the curve of his neck, and a slight tremor shook her slender frame as he cupped her face and shifted it so that he could see her expression in the slim stream of moonlight arcing across the room.

'You'll make a beautiful mother,' he said gently.

She felt the prick of tears, and consciously banked them down, but not before he'd glimpsed the faint diamond-glitter drops on the edge of her lashes.

His mouth possessed hers with a soft, evocative hunger that was so incredibly tender she could almost feel her whole body sigh in silent acceptance of a joy so tumultuous it transcended any rationale.

CHAPTER ELEVEN

THE LIMOUSINE CARRYING Francesca, Gabbi and Katherine swept smoothly across the Harbour Bridge, then headed towards Beauty Point.

It was a glorious summer afternoon, the sky a clear azure with only a nebulous drift of cloud to mar its perfection.

Francesca lifted a hand and absently fingered the single strand of pearls at her neck. It held a pendant, a pearl teardrop surrounded by diamonds. There were earstuds to match. Dominic's gift to his prospective bride.

Her gift to him was simplistic, but meaningful. A secret smile curved her lips, and her eyes softened as she imagined his reaction.

Her fingers sought the slim gold chain, and failed to find it. A slight frown creased her forehead. It must be directly beneath the pearls. She remembered taking it off before she showered...and had a mental image of lifting the pearls from their flat jeweller's box.

She'd left the chain on the bedside pedestal.

'We have to go back.' The words slipped out before she was even aware she'd voiced them.

'But we're almost there,' Gabbi protested. And at

the same time Katherine expressed in consternation, 'Francesca, we'll be late.'

Somehow she didn't think Dominic would mind. Although first she needed to instruct the driver, then she had to make a call from the car phone. When both were achieved, she sank back against the cushioned seat.

'Are you going to tell us what this is all about?' Gabbi asked curiously.

'I left Dominic's gift at my apartment.'

'You could have given it to him later,' Gabbi rationalised.

'Yes,' Francesca agreed, 'I could. Except it wouldn't be the same.'

Thirty minutes later the limousine drew to a halt at the apex of Dominic's driveway, and Francesca slid out from the rear seat to stand still as Gabbi and Katherine ran a last-minute check on the exquisitely pale champagne gold sheath dress with its cream antique lace overlay Francesca had chosen to wear for her wedding.

Gabbi grinned and gave her approval. 'Let's get this show on the road.'

Rick was waiting inside the house, and he came forward the instant they entered the lobby.

'Francesca.' He caught hold of her shoulders and held her at arm's length. 'Everything OK?'

'Very much OK,' she assured gently as she leaned forward and brushed his cheek with her own. She made an attempt to lighten the situation. 'That is, if Dominic is still waiting out there for me.'

'With considerably more patience than most men would be able to summon in similar circumstances,' Rick accorded drily.

'Then let's not keep him waiting any longer, shall we?' Francesca suggested lightly.

The gardens were beautiful, the flowers and shrubs clipped to perfection, and the lawn a carpet of green.

There were a few guests seated behind members of her immediate family, but she hardly saw them. Her focus was centred on the white-painted gazebo and the tall, dark-suited figure who stood watching her progress as she walked the length of red carpet with Rick at her side.

Francesca looked into Dominic's eyes and saw everything she needed to know laid bare. Her own eyes misted, and there was a slight quiver to her lips as she summoned a slow, sweet smile.

A few more steps and she'd be able to place her hand in his, feel its warm strength and accept what he offered for the rest of her life. There was no lingering doubt or apprehension, only love.

Dominic gathered her in close and kissed her with such passion it was all she could do to keep a hold on her sanity.

It could have lasted seconds or minutes, she had no recollection of the passage of time.

Minutes, she decided, as she heard the sound of faint amusement from those assembled behind her.

'Mr Andrea, it's usual to kiss the bride *after* the ceremony.'

'Believe me, I intend to do it then, too,' Dominic drawled with musing indolence.

The celebrant chuckled, then cleared his throat. 'Shall we begin?'

'Could you wait just a moment?' Francesca requested. 'There's something I need to do first.'

She turned towards Dominic, caught his faintly raised eyebrow, and smiled as she lifted both hands to her neck. Seconds later she placed the long thin gold chain holding Mario's wedding ring in the palm of his hand.

Would he realise the significance of her action? *Know* that by gifting him Mario's ring she was willingly giving Dominic her heart? All of it.

Francesca wasn't aware she was holding her breath until his mouth curved into a warm smile, his eyes liquid with comprehension, and she released it shakily, only to catch it again as he lifted her left hand to his lips and kissed the bare finger awaiting the placement of *his* wedding band.

'Thank you,' he said gently.

'I thought it would mean more to you than anything else I could gift you,' she responded softly, adding with a faintly wicked smile, 'At this moment.'

His eyes flared, then became incredibly dark.

Francesca turned a radiant face towards the celebrant. 'We're ready.'

It was a simple ceremony, and afterwards Dominic kissed his wife with such incredible gentleness the men among the guests shifted uncomfortably and the women were seen to blink rather rapidly.

The food was superb, with catering staff serving at tables set out on the wide terrace with its panoramic view of the harbour. The cake was cut and photographs were taken.

Francesca barely remembered tasting a morsel, and she merely sipped from a flute of champagne.

She was supremely conscious of Dominic seated at her side, the touch of his hand, the way his body brushed against her own. His eyes, those dark, almost black depths, liquid with emotion whenever she caught his gaze, tugged at an answering need deep inside her.

A musing smile curved her lips as he leaned his head close to her own.

'I guess it wouldn't do to leave early.'

She turned her head slightly and brushed her lips against his. 'I don't think so.'

'Damn,' he cursed lightly.

Her lashes curled upwards, revealing a wicked gleam in those stunning liquid brown eyes. 'Another hour won't kill you.'

His mouth curved in answering humour. 'It might.' His lips feathered close to her ear. 'I have this pressing need to…' In a voice as soft as the finest silk he proceeded to explain what he meant to do the instant they were alone.

Her body began to melt, curving into his like warm wax. 'I think we should mingle,' she said unsteadily. 'Otherwise we're in danger of shocking the guests.'

His mouth drifted over hers, savoured briefly, then he caught hold of her hand.

Together they circled the tables, lingering, laughing, until it was time to change, collect their bags and slip into the limousine that would transport them to a city centre hotel.

'This is…' Francesca paused in the centre of a sumptuous penthouse suite. 'Overwhelming.'

Dominic closed the door, then walked to where she stood. '*You* overwhelm me.' He lifted a hand and brushed his fingers against her cheek. He didn't care that they were slightly unsteady as he glimpsed the emotion evident in her wonderfully luminous eyes. For him. Only him.

'I love you,' he said gently. 'Today. All the tomorrows.' He traced the curve of her mouth with his thumb, felt its soft fullness, and wanted the sweetness inside. 'I can promise never to willingly hurt you. You have my heart, my soul.'

She ached so much, so deeply, that her eyes hurt with the strength of her emotions. 'I didn't think love could happen twice.' She had to blink to keep the prickle of threatening tears at bay.

He smiled and drew her close, his breath catching as her arms lifted to his shoulders then crept to encircle his neck.

Her lips touched his, opening like the petals of a rose as he took possession, deepening the kiss until she lost recognition of everything except the man.

He filled her senses and made her *want* as he offered the promise of heaven on earth. More. He delivered. And then some.

But then, so did she. Willingly, wantonly. Gifting him more than her body. Everything.

Tonight there was none of the urgency, little of a driven need. Just a long, slow loving that took them to the heights several times and beyond. They slept a little, then woke to exult in each other again until the sunlight chased away the shadows of night.

Francesca lifted a hand, pushed back her tangled hair, then she met his eyes and smiled. 'I love you.'

Her pulse-beat had returned to normal after a passion so incredibly tumultuous every nerve-end still hummed with acute sensation.

'Do you know how much it means to me to have you say that?' Dominic queried huskily.

His hand began to drift as his fingers traced a lazy pattern across her stomach, explored her navel, then moved to tease the whorls of hair at the apex between her thighs.

The scent of her drove him crazy. Her skin was so delicate, so fragile, he almost felt afraid to touch her. Yet she shared his hunger, and exulted in his possession, until he forgot who he was in the need to gift her not only his body but his mind. It was frightening to give up so much power, to lay oneself so open and bare. Yet he doubted she would ever use the advantage against him.

His head lowered to her breast and he began grazing a tender nipple with the edge of his teeth.

The tug of renewed desire arrowed through her body, and she trailed her fingers across his back, exploring the muscular ridges, aware of the strength and the power, and wondered for the nth time how she had existed, believed she'd lived, before meeting this man who was now her husband.

Almost as if he read her mind his head lifted and he settled his mouth over hers, soothing, gentling, marking her as his own as surely as if he'd branded her flesh with fire.

The strident peal of the telephone sounded loud in the silence of the room, and Dominic shifted, then reached for the receiver.

'Our wake-up call?' Francesca hazarded as Dominic replaced the handset.

'We have fifteen minutes to shower and dress before room service deliver our breakfast.'

She looked at him with mock solemnity. 'It was your idea to book an early-morning flight to Athens.'

His eyes held a wicked gleam. 'Ah, but I had the foresight to organise a stop-over *en route*.'

A smile tugged the edge of her mouth. 'How thoughtful.' The temptation to tease him a little was irresistible. 'Shall we hit the shower separately or together?'

'You really want me to answer that?'

She slid out from the bed and walked unselfconsciously towards the adjoining bathroom. When she reached the door she turned and shot him a tantalising smile. 'Can't stand the heat, huh?'

She'd barely made it to the shower cubicle when firm hands fastened around her waist, lifting, turning her until she was positioned astride his hips.

A laugh bubbled up in her throat, then died as he bestowed upon her a brief, hard kiss before lowering his mouth to settle at the acutely sensitive pulse at the base of her throat.

She shuddered as sensation spiralled through her body, and she arched up against him, groaning out loud as his teeth closed over one swollen nipple, teasing, suckling, until she was almost driven to the brink of sanity.

Francesca cried out when he shifted his head and rendered a similar salutation to the twin peak.

His eyes were impossibly dark when they finally met hers, and she felt herself drowning in those dark depths, seriously adrift as his mouth lowered to possess hers in a kiss that echoed the deep, pulsing thrust of his powerful body.

She rose with him, wrapping her arms round his neck as she held on and gloried in their shared passion.

And afterwards she buried her lips in the hollow of his neck, too enervated to move as her racing heart slowed and steadied to its normal beat.

His hand travelled slowly up and down her spine, soothing as he pressed his lips to her hair.

It was heaven to rest against him like this, to feel that what they shared meshed the physical and spiritual in a rare coupling that few were fortunate to attain.

She felt him burgeon inside her, sensed the increased urgency, and rode with him one more time, slowly, gently, as if they had all the time in the world.

A hard double knock on the outer door brought them both back to the reality of the day, and a faint curse escaped Dominic's lips as he carefully lifted her down onto her feet.

'Breakfast.' He reached for a towelling robe and tugged it on, then he leaned forward and pressed a gentle kiss to her faintly swollen mouth. 'Stay there. I'll be back in a minute.'

She could imagine him crossing the suite, opening the door, signalling for the waiter to deposit the tray.

The thought of cereal and fruit, scrambled eggs and toast gave her an appetite, and she reached for the dial, set it to warm and released the lever.

Seconds later the glass door slid open and Dominic stepped into the stall, removing the soap from her fingers as he lathered every inch of her skin. Then he held out the soap. 'Your turn.'

'Oh, no,' Francesca denied, laughing softly. 'You're on your own.' She reached up and pulled down his head for one brief, soft kiss. 'Too many challenges and we'll not only miss breakfast, we'll miss the plane.' She shot him a dazzling smile. 'Besides, I'm *food* hungry.'

He let her go, with a devilish smile that hinted her escape was only temporary.

As the giant jet taxied down the runway Dominic reached for her hand and lifted it to his lips.

'No regrets?'

Francesca looked at those strong features, the raw emotion evident in his eyes. She lifted shaky fingers to his cheek, then trailed them to the edge of his mouth, and stifled a gasp as he drew the tips in between his teeth. 'Not one.'

He reached for her, uncaring of the fellow passengers sharing the first-class cabin, or the hostess who was waiting to serve them.

His mouth on hers was incredibly gentle, and when he lifted his head he glimpsed the faint shimmer of tears.

'We have a lifetime.'

Her bones liquefied at the warmth evident in those dark eyes. 'Yes,' she affirmed simply.

Carpe diem. Seize the day. And she would, with both hands, and rejoice in every one of them.

* * * * *

THE MARRIAGE
CAMPAIGN
HELEN BIANCHIN

CHAPTER ONE

IT SHOULD BE Friday the thirteenth, Suzanne determined as she perused the perfectly printed legal document on her desk and noted yet another clause she knew wasn't worded to her client's best interest.

Midwinter had delivered metropolitan Sydney with a shocking day, and she'd woken to howling winds and heavy rain. Consequently she'd got wet traversing the external stairs leading from her tiny Manly flat down to the garage beneath.

Her car, which had up until now behaved impeccably, had decided not to start. A telephone call to the automobile association had elicited there was a backlog of calls, and it would be at least an hour before someone could come to her rescue. Two hours later the diagnosis had been a dead battery, and it had taken a further hour to organise a replacement and drive into the city.

Consequently she'd been late, very late arriving at the inner-city legal office where she worked as one of several junior solicitors. A fact that hadn't sat well with two waiting clients who had been virtuously punctual.

Nor had the senior partner been very happy that she'd missed an important staff meeting.

There had been files piled up on her desk, messages that required attention, and three rescheduled appointments lined up one after the other. Lunch hadn't even been an option.

Mid-afternoon came and went as she struggled to catch up on a workload that threatened to spill over into work she would have to take home.

'Suzanne, urgent call on line three.' The receptionist's voice sounded hesitant, diffident, and vaguely apologetic for breaching a 'hold all calls' instruction. 'It's your mother.'

Her mother *never* rang her at work. An icy hand clutched Suzanne's heart as she snatched up the receiver. 'Georgia? Is something wrong?'

A light, husky laugh echoed down the line. 'Darling, everything's fine. It's just that I wanted you to be the first to hear my news.'

'*News*, Mama?' She kept her voice deliberately light. 'You've won a fabulous prize? Bought a new car? Booked an overseas trip?'

There was a breathless pause. 'Right on two counts.'

'Which two?'

'Well, sweetheart,' Georgia began with a delicious chuckle, 'the overseas trip is booked... *Paris*, would you believe? And I *have* won a fabulous prize.'

'That's wonderful.' Really wonderful. Suzanne shook her head in silent amazement. Georgia was always taking lottery and raffle tickets, but had never won anything other than the most minor of prizes until now.

'It's not exactly a *prize* prize.'

The faintly cautious tone had Suzanne sinking back in her chair. 'You're talking in riddles, Mama. Is there a catch to any of this?'

'No catch. At least, not the kind you mean.'

What had her cautious mother got herself into? 'I'm listening.'

'Bear with me, darling.' Georgia's voice hitched, then raced on in an excited rush. 'It's all so new, I still have a hard time believing it. And I wouldn't have rung you at work, except I really couldn't wait a minute longer.'

'Tell me.'

There was silence for a few seconds. 'I'm getting married.'

Initial joy was quickly followed by concern, and it was a frightening mix. Her mother didn't *date*. There was a collection of friends, but no *one* man. 'I didn't know you were seeing anyone,' Suzanne said slowly, and heard her mother's light laughter in response. 'Who is he, and where did you meet him?'

'We met at your engagement party, darling.'

Three months. They'd only known each other three months. 'Who, Mama?'

'Trenton Wilson-Willoughby. Sloane's father.'

Oh, my God. Heat rushed through her veins, then chilled to ice. 'You're not serious?' Tell me you're not serious, she pleaded silently.

'You sound—shocked,' Georgia responded slowly, and Suzanne quickly gathered her wits.

Recoup, regroup, *fast*. 'Surprised,' she amended. 'It seems so sudden.'

'Sometimes love happens that way. Sloane swept you off your feet in a matter of weeks.'

Like father, like son. 'Yes,' she agreed cautiously. Sloane had gifted her a sparkling diamond, whisked her down to Sydney from Brisbane, and moved her into his Rose Bay penthouse apartment before she'd had time to think, let alone catch her breath. Blinded by a riveting attraction and primitive alchemy.

'When is the wedding taking place?' A few months from now would give her plenty of time to—what? Explain that she was no longer living with Sloane?

'This weekend, darling.' Georgia sounded vaguely breathless and tremendously excited.

This weekend. Today was *Wednesday*, for heaven's sake. 'Don't you think—?'

'It's a bit sudden?' her mother finished. 'Yes, darling, I do. But Trenton is a very convincing man.'

Suzanne took a deep breath, then released it slowly. 'You're quite sure about this?'

'As sure as I can be.' There was a funny catch in her voice. 'Aren't you going to congratulate me?'

Oh, *hell*. She had to collect her thoughts together. 'Of course I am. And give you my blessing. I'm just so happy *you* are happy.' She was babbling, she knew, but she couldn't stop. 'Where is the wedding taking place? Have you chosen what you'll wear?'

Georgia began to laugh, and, Suzanne suspected, to cry. 'Bedarra Island, Saturday afternoon. Would you believe Trenton has booked all the accommodation on the island to ensure total privacy? I'm wearing a cream silk suit, with matching shoes and hat. We want you and Sloane to be witnesses.'

Bedarra Island was a privately owned resort situated high in North Queensland's Whitsunday group of tropical islands. A minimum three-hour flight, followed by a launch trip to Bedarra.

'Trenton has organised for you both to fly up on Friday morning and stay until Monday.'

Oh, my. Trenton's organisation would include the family jet, the charter of a private launch.

Sloane.

It was three weeks since she'd walked out of his apartment, leaving a penned note briefly spelling out her need for some time alone. It attributed nothing to the reality of an anonymous threat if she didn't end the engagement.

A threat she hadn't taken seriously until the young socialite who'd initiated it had almost run Suzanne's car off the road to emphasise her intent, then identified herself and promised grievous bodily harm if Suzanne failed to comply.

The sequence of events had been very carefully planned, she reflected, to coincide with Sloane's absence overseas. Bitter, vitriolic invective had merely added doubt as to the socialite's mental stability, and extreme caution had motivated Suzanne to leave Sloane's apartment and move all her clothes into a flat on the other side of the city.

However, she had underestimated Sloane. When she'd refused to take his calls on his return, he'd pulled rank and walked unannounced into her office. His icy anger when she had refused to elaborate on the contents of her note had been so chilling, it had been all she could do not to fall in a heap the second the door had closed behind him.

Now it appeared she had little option but to see him again.

Suzanne slowly replaced the receiver, then stared sightlessly at the wall in front of her. Georgia and Trenton. Could her mother possibly guess at the complications she'd created?

Allowing no time for hesitation, Suzanne punched in the digit to access an outside line, then completed the set of numbers that would connect with Sloane's law chambers.

Not that the call did much good. All she received was a relayed message stating that Sloane Wilson-Willoughby was in court and wasn't expected back until late afternoon. Suzanne logged in her name and phone number on his message bank.

Damn. The silent curse did little to ease her frustration as she turned her attention to the documents requiring her perusal. She made a note of two clauses she felt were not entirely to her client's advantage, pencilled in a notation to delete one, and re phrase another. Then she had her secretary lodge the necessary call in order to apprise the client of her suggested alterations.

The afternoon was hectic, and the nerves inside her stomach became increasingly tense as the minutes ticked by. Each time the phone rang, she mentally prepared herself for it to be Sloane, only to have her secretary announce someone else.

Was he deliberately delaying the call? Just to make her sweat a little? Whatever, it was playing havoc with her nervous system.

At five her phone buzzed just as she ushered a client from her office, and she crossed to her desk and picked up the receiver.

'Sloane Wilson-Willoughby on line two.' The information was imparted in a faintly breathless voice, and Suzanne momentarily raised her eyes towards the ceiling.

Sloane tended to have that effect on people. Women, especially, responded to something in his deep, smoky voice. Once they sighted him in the flesh, the response went into overdrive and tended to make vamps and vixens out of the most sensible of females.

She should know. She'd been there herself. Part of her ached for the promise, the dream of what they might have had together.

Then she drew in a deep breath, released it, and picked up the receiver. 'Sloane.' To ask 'how are you?' seemed incredibly banal.

'Suzanne.' The polite acknowledgement seared something deep inside, and she resolutely kept her voice even as she sank back in her chair. 'Georgia rang me. I believe Trenton has relayed their news?'

'Yes.' Brief, succinct, and unforthcoming.

He wasn't making it easy for her. There was no way out of this, and it was best if she just got on with it.

'We need to talk.'

'I agree,' Sloane indicated silkily. 'Make it dinner tonight.' He named a restaurant in a city hotel. 'Seven.'

She needed to put in another hour in order to appease her employer. 'I don't think—'

'It's the restaurant or your flat.' His voice acquired the sound of silk being razed by steel. 'Choose.'

She didn't hesitate. 'Seven-thirty.' A public place where there were people was the lesser of two evils. The thought of Sloane appearing at her flat, demanding entry...

'Wise.'

No, it was most *un*wise, but she didn't appear to have much option.

Suzanne replaced the receiver and attempted to concentrate on notations she needed to finalise.

Consequently it was well after six when she left the office, and almost seven before she reached home.

Within half an hour she'd showered, dressed, swept her damp hair into a sleek twist, applied make-up with practised precision, and she was on her way out of the door, retracing a familiar route into the city.

Except this time the traffic was more civilised. And there was the advantage of valet parking. Even so, she was fifteen minutes late.

Suzanne pushed open the heavy glass door and entered the hotel lobby. It took only seconds to locate a familiar dark-suited figure standing several metres distant.

Her pulse tripped its beat and accelerated to a faster pace as she watched him unfold his lengthy frame from a deep-cushioned lounge chair.

Sloane Wilson-Willoughby stood four inches over six feet, with the broad shoulders and muscled frame of a superbly trained athlete. Inherited genes had bestowed ruggedly attractive facial features, piercing brown eyes, and thick dark brown hair. Evident was an aura of power, and the ease of a man well versed in the strengths and weaknesses of his fellow men.

He watched as she moved towards him, his appraisal swift, taking in the red power suit adorning her petite frame, the upswept hairstyle and the stiletto heels she invariably wore to add inches to her height. She possessed an innate femininity that was at variance with the professional image she tried so hard to maintain. Slight but very feminine curves, slender, shapely legs, silken-smooth honey-gold skin, deep blue eyes, and a mouth to die for.

He'd tasted its delights, savoured the pleasures of her body, and put an engagement ring on her finger. It had stayed there precisely ten weeks before she'd taken it off with an excuse he'd no more believed then than he did now.

'Sloane.' She moved forward and accepted the touch of his hand at her elbow. And told herself she was impervious to the clean male smell of him mingling with the faint aroma of his exclusive brand of cologne. Immune to the latent sensuality that seemed to emanate from every pore.

He searched her pale features, and noted the faint smudges beneath eyes that seemed too large for her face. 'Working hard?'

The deceptive mildness of his voice didn't fool her in the slightest. She effected a light shrug and opted for flippancy. 'Next you'll tell me I've dropped weight.'

He lifted a hand and traced her jawline with his thumb. And saw her eyes dilate. 'Two or three essential kilos, at a guess.'

His touch was like fire, and a muscle flickered in involuntary reaction. 'Judge, advocate and jury rolled into one?'

'Lover,' Sloane amended.

'Ex-lover,' she corrected him, and saw the sensual curve of his lower lip.

'Your choice, not mine.'

She deliberately moved back a pace, and met his gaze squarely. 'Shall we go in to dinner?'

'You wouldn't prefer a drink first?'

She really wanted to keep this as short as possible. 'No.' She sought to qualify her decision. 'I really can't stay long.'

There was a tinge of wry humour evident in his voice as they walked towards the bank of lifts. 'Dedication to duty, Suzanne?'

The humour stung. 'Suffice it to say it's been one of those days, and I have work to catch up on.'

A set of doors slid open and she preceded him into the lift. They were the only occupants, and he leaned forward to depress the button for the appropriate floor.

His suit sleeve brushed against her arm, and she tried to ignore the shivery sensation feathering over her skin. Her fine body hairs rose in protective self-defence, and she felt her pulse trip and surge to a faster beat.

Did he realise he still had this effect on her? Probably not, she reassured herself silently, for she strove very hard to project detached disinterest.

The restaurant was well patronised, and the *maître d'* led them to a reserved table, saw them seated, and summoned the drinks waiter.

Suzanne viewed the menu with interest, and she ordered soup *du jour*, a seafood starter, and grilled fish as a main course.

'Do we attempt to engage in polite conversation,' Sloane drawled as soon as the waiter disappeared, 'or shall we cut straight to the chase?'

Suzanne forced herself to hold his gaze. 'Dinner was your idea.'

Evident was the leashed anger beneath his control. 'What did you expect? A curt directive to meet me at the airport Friday morning?'

'Yes.'

His smile was totally without humour. 'Ah, *honesty*.'

'It's one of my more admirable traits.'

Their drinks were delivered, and Suzanne sipped the iced water, almost wishing it were something stronger. Alcohol might soothe her fractured nerves.

She watched as Sloane took an appreciative swallow of his customary spritzer before setting the glass onto the table, then leaning back in his chair.

'You haven't responded to any of my messages.'

It was difficult to retain his gaze, but she managed. 'There didn't seem much point.'

'I beg to differ.'

He was a skilled wordsmith and a brilliant strategist. He was also icy calm. When all he wanted to do was reach forward and *shake* her.

'We're here to discuss our respective parents' marriage to each other,' she managed civilly. 'Not conduct a post-mortem on our affair.'

'Post-mortem?' His voice was a sibilant threat. *'Affair?'*

He was playing with her, much as a predatory animal played with its prey. Waiting, watching, assessing each and every move, in no doubt of the kill. It was just a matter of *when*.

Suzanne rose to her feet and reached for her bag. 'I've had one hell of a day. I have work to get through when I get home.' Her eyes flashed angrily. 'I don't need you playing cat-and-mouse with me.'

A hand closed over her arm, and it took all her control not to shake it free.

'Sit down.'

She would have liked nothing better than to turn and walk out of the door. But there was Georgia to consider. No matter how difficult the weekend might prove to be, she *had* to be present at her mother's wedding. Anything else was unthinkable.

'Please,' Sloane added, and without a word she sank down into her chair.

Almost on cue the waiter delivered their soup, and she spooned it slowly, grateful for the ensuing silence.

When their plates were removed she picked up her glass and sipped the contents.

'Tell me about your day,' Sloane commanded with studied ease.

Suzanne looked at him carefully. 'Genuine interest, or an adept attempt to keep our conversation on an even keel?'

'Both.'

His faint, mocking smile was almost her undoing, and she felt like screaming with vexation. 'I'd prefer to discuss the weekend.'

'Indulge me. We have yet to begin the main course.'

At this rate she'd suffer indigestion. As it was, her stomach seemed to be tied in numerous knots.

'The car refused to start, the automobile club took ages to send someone out, I was late in to work, and I got soaked in the rain.' She effected a light shrug. 'That about encapsulates it.'

'I'll organise for you to have the use of one of my cars while yours is being checked out.'

A surge of anger rose to the surface. 'No. You won't.'

'Now you're being stubborn,' he drawled hatefully.

'Practical.' And wary of being seen driving his Porsche or Jaguar.

'Stubborn,' Sloane reiterated.

'You sound like my mother,' Suzanne responded with a deliberately slow, sweet smile.

'Heaven forbid.'

Anger rose once more, and her eyes assumed a fiery sparkle. 'You disapprove of Georgia?'

'Of being compared to anything vaguely *parental* where you're concerned,' Sloane corrected her with ill-concealed mockery.

Suzanne looked at him carefully, then honed a verbal dart. 'I doubt you've ever lacked a solitary thing in your privileged life.'

One eyebrow rose, and there was a certain wryness apparent. 'Except for the love of a good woman?'

'Most women fall over themselves to get to you,' she stated with marked cynicism.

'To the social prestige the Wilson-Willoughby name carries,' Sloane amended drily. 'And let's not forget the family wealth.'

The multi-million-dollar family home with its incredible views over Sydney harbour, the fleet of luxurious cars, servants. Not to mention Sloane's penthouse apartment, *his* cars. Homes, apartments in major European cities. The family cruiser, the family jet.

And then there was Wilson-Willoughby, headed by Trenton and notably one of Sydney's leading law firms. One had only to enter its exclusive portals, see the expensive antique furniture gracing every office, the original artwork on the walls, to appreciate the elegance of limitless wealth.

'You're a cynic.'

His expression didn't change. 'A realist.'

Their starter arrived, and Suzanne took her time savouring the delicate texture of the prawns in a superb sauce many a chef would kill to reproduce.

'Now that you've had some food, perhaps you'd like a glass of wine?'

And have it go straight to her head? 'Half a glass,' she qualified, and determined to sip it slowly during the main course.

'I hear you've taken on a very challenging brief,' she said.

Sloane pressed the napkin to the edge of his mouth, then discarded it down onto the damask-covered table. 'News travels fast.'

As did anything attached to Sloane Wilson-Willoughby. In or out of the courtroom.

He part-filled her glass with wine, then set it back in the ice bucket, dismissing the wine steward who appeared with apologetic deference.

Their main course arrived, and Suzanne admired the superbly presented fish and artistically displayed vegetable portions. It seemed almost a sacrilege to disturb the arrangement, and she forked delicate mouthfuls with enjoyment.

'Am I to understand Georgia meets with your approval as a prospective stepmother?'

Sloane viewed her with studied ease. She looked more relaxed, and her cheeks bore a slight colour. 'Georgia is a charming woman. I'm sure she and my father will be very happy together.'

The deceptive mildness of his tone brought forth a musing smile. 'I would have to say the same about Trenton.'

Sloane lifted his glass and took a sip of wine, then regarded her thoughtfully over the rim. 'The question remains... What do you want to do about us?'

Her stomach executed a painful backflip. 'What do you mean, what do I want to do about *us*?'

The waiter arrived to remove their plates, then delivered a platter of fresh fruit, added a bowl of freshly whipped cream, and withdrew.

'Unless you've told Georgia differently, our respective parents believe we're living in pre-nuptial bliss,' Sloane relayed with deliberate patience. 'Do we spend the weekend pretending we're still together? Or do you want to spoil their day by telling them we're living apart?'

She didn't want to think about *together*. It merely heightened memories she longed to forget. Fat chance, a tiny voice taunted.

Fine clothes did little to tame a body honed to the height of physical fitness, or lessen his brooding sensuality. Too many nights she'd lain awake remembering just how it felt to be held in those arms, kissed in places she'd never thought to grant a licence to, and taught to scale unbelievable heights with a man who knew every path, every journey.

'Your choice, Suzanne.'

She looked at him and glimpsed the implacability beneath the charming façade, the velvet-encased steel.

As a barrister in a court of law he was skilled with the command of words and their delivery. She'd seen him in action, and been enthralled. Mesmerised. And had known, even then, that she'd have reason to quake if ever he became her enemy.

A game of pretence, and she wondered why she was even considering it. Yet would it be so bad?

There wasn't much choice if she didn't want to spoil her mother's happiness. The truth was something she intended to keep to herself.

'I imagine it isn't possible to fly in and out of Bedarra on the same day?'

'No.'

It was a slim hope, given the distance and the time of the wedding. 'There are no strings you can pull?'

'Afraid to spend time with me, Suzanne?' Sloane queried smoothly.

'I'd prefer to keep it to a minimum,' she said with innate honesty. 'And you didn't answer the question.'

'What strings would you have me pull?'

'It would be more suitable to arrive on Bedarra Saturday morning, and return Sunday.'

'And disappoint Trenton and Georgia?' He lifted his glass and took an appreciative swallow of excellent vintage wine. 'Did it occur to you that perhaps Georgia might need your help and moral support *before* the wedding?'

It made sense, Suzanne conceded. 'Surely we could return on Sunday?'

'I think not.'

'Why?'

He set the glass down onto the table with the utmost care. 'Because *I* won't be returning until Monday.'

She looked at him with a feeling of helpless anger. 'You're deliberately making this as difficult as possible, aren't you?'

'Trenton has organised to leave Sydney on Friday and return on Monday. I see no reason to disrupt those arrangements.'

A tiny shiver feathered its way down her spine.

Three days. Well, four if you wanted to be precise. Could she go through with it?

'Do you want to renege, Suzanne?'

The silkily voiced query strengthened her resolve, and her eyes speared his. 'No.'

'Can I interest you in the dessert trolley?'

The waiter's appearance was timely, and Suzanne turned her attention to the collection of delicious confections presented, and selected an utterly sinful slice of chocolate cake decorated with fresh cream and strawberries.

'Decadent,' she commented for the waiter's benefit. 'I'll need to run an extra kilometre and do twenty more sit-ups in the morning to combat the extra kilojoules.'

Even when she'd lived with Sloane, she'd preferred the suburban footpaths and fresh air to the professional gym housed in his apartment.

'I can think of something infinitely more enjoyable by way of exercise.'

'Sex?' Was it the wine that had made her suddenly brave? With ladylike delicacy, she indicated his selection of *crème caramel*. 'You should live a little, walk on the wild side.'

'Wild, Suzanne?' His voice was pure silk with the honeyed intonation he used to great effect in the courtroom.

Knowing she would probably lose didn't prevent her from enjoying a verbal sparring. 'Figuratively speaking.'

'Perhaps you'd care to elaborate?'

Her eyes were wide, luminous, and tinged with wicked humour. 'Do the unexpected.'

Very few women sought to challenge him on any level, and none had in quite the same manner this petite, independent blonde employed. 'Define unexpected.'

Her head tilted to one side. 'Be less—conventional.'

'You think I should play more?' The subtle emphasis

was intended, and he watched the slight flicker of her lashes, the faint pink that coloured her cheeks. Glimpsed the way her throat moved as she swallowed. And felt a sense of satisfaction. With innate skill, he honed the blade and pierced her vulnerable heart. 'I have a vivid memory of just how well we *played* together.'

So did she, damn him. Very carefully she replaced her spoon on the plate. 'Perhaps you'd care to tell me what arrangements you've made for Friday morning.'

'I've instructed the pilot we'll be leaving at eight.'

'I'll meet you at the airport.'

'Isn't that carrying independence a little too far?'

'Why should you drive to the North Shore, only to have to double back again?' Suzanne countered.

Something shifted in his eyes, then it was successfully masked. 'It isn't a problem.'

Of course it wasn't. *She* was making a problem out of sheer perversity. 'I'll drive to your apartment and garage my car there for the weekend,' she conceded.

Sloane inclined his head in mocking acquiescence. 'If you insist.'

It was a minor victory, one she had the instinctive feeling wasn't a victory at all.

Sloane ordered coffee, then settled the bill. She didn't linger, and he escorted her to the lobby, instructed the concierge to organise her car, and waited until it was brought to the main entrance.

'Goodnight, Suzanne.'

His features appeared extraordinarily dark in the

angled shadows, his tone vaguely cynical. An image of sight and sound that remained with her long after she slid wearily into bed.

CHAPTER TWO

THURSDAY PROVED TO be a fraught day as Suzanne applied for and was granted two days' leave, then she rescheduled appointments and consultations, attended to the most pressing work, delegated the remainder, *and* donated her entire lunch hour to selecting something suitable to wear to Georgia's wedding.

Dedication to duty ensured she stayed back an extra few hours, and she arrived home shortly after eight, hungry and not a little disgruntled at having to eat on the run while she sorted through clothes and packed.

Elegant, casual, and beachwear, she determined as she riffled through her wardrobe, grateful she had sufficient knowledge of the Wilson-Willoughby lifestyle to know she need select the best of her best.

Comfortable baggy shorts and sweat-tops were out. *In* were tailored trousers, smart shirts, silk dresses, tennis gear. And the obligatory swimwear essential in the tropical north's Midwinter temperatures.

Some of Trenton Wilson-Willoughby's guests would arrive with large Louis Vuitton travelling cases containing what they considered the minimum essentials for a weekend sojourn.

Suzanne managed to confine all she needed into one cabin bag, which she stored on the floor at the foot of her bed in readiness for last-minute essentials in the morning, then she returned to the kitchen and took a can of Diet Coke from the refrigerator.

She crossed into the lounge, switched on the television and flicked through the channels in the hope of finding something that might hold her interest. A legal drama, a medical ditto, sport, a foreign movie, and something dire relating to the occult. She switched off the set, collected a magazine and sank into a nearby chair to leaf through the pages.

She felt too restless to settle for long, and after ten minutes she tossed the magazine aside, carried the empty can into the kitchen, then undressed and took a shower.

It wasn't late *late*, but she felt tired and edgy, and knew she should go to bed given the early hour she'd need to rise in the morning.

Except when she did she was unable to sleep, and she tossed and turned, then lay staring at the ceiling for an age.

With a low growl of frustration she slid out of bed and padded into the lounge. If she was going to stare at something, she might as well curl up in a chair and stare at the television.

It was there that she woke, with a stiff neck and the television screen fizzing from a closed channel.

Suzanne peered at her watch in the semi-darkness,

saw that it was almost dawn, and groaned. There was no point in crawling back to bed for such a short time. Instead she stretched her legs and wandered into the kitchen to make coffee.

Casual elegance denoted her apparel for the day, and after a quick shower and something to eat she stepped into linen trousers and a matching silk sleeveless top. Make-up was minimal, a little colour to her cheeks, mascara to give emphasis to her eyes, and a touch of rose-pink to her lips. An upswept hairstyle was likely to come adrift, so she left her hair loose.

At seven she added a trendy black jacket, checked the flat, then she fastened her cabin bag, took it downstairs and secured it in the boot. Then she slid in behind the wheel and reversed her car out onto the road.

At this relatively early hour the traffic flowed freely, and she enjoyed a smooth run through the northern suburbs.

The city skyline was visible as she drew close to the harbour bridge, the tall buildings bathed in a faint post-dawn mist that merged with the greyness of a midwinter morning and hinted at rain.

Even the harbour waters appeared dull and grey, and the ferries traversing its depths seemed to move heavily towards their respective berths.

Once clear of the bridge, it took minimum time to reach the attractive eastern suburb of Rose Bay. Sloane's penthouse apartment was housed in a modern structure only metres from the edge of the wide, curving bay.

A number of large, beautiful old homes graced the tree-lined street and Suzanne admired the elegant two-

and three-storeyd structures in brick and paint-washed stucco, situated in attractive landscaped grounds, as she turned into the brick-tiled apron adjoining Sloane's apartment building.

He was waiting for her, his tall frame propped against the driver's side of his sleek, top-of-the-range Jaguar. Casual trousers, an open-necked shirt and jacket had replaced his usual three-piece business suit, and he looked the epitome of the wealthy professional.

The trousers, shirt and jacket were beautifully cut, the shoes hand-stitched Italian. He didn't favour male jewellery, and the only accessory he chose to wear was a thin gold watch whose make was undoubtedly exorbitantly expensive. His wardrobe contained a superb collection, yet none had been acquired as a status symbol.

Suzanne shifted the gear lever into neutral, then she slid out from behind the wheel and turned to greet him. 'Good morning. I'm not late, am I?' She knew she wasn't, but she couldn't resist the query.

Independence was a fine thing in a woman, but Suzanne's strict adherence to it was something Sloane found mildly irritating. His eyes were cool as they swept her slim form. Cream tailored trousers, cream top and black jacket emphasised her slender curves, and lent a heightened sense of fragility to her features. Clever make-up had almost dealt with the shadows beneath her eyes. He derived a certain satisfaction from the knowledge. She obviously hadn't slept any better than he had.

'I'll take your car down into the car park,' Sloane indicated as he removed the cabin bag from her grasp and stowed it in the open boot of his car.

Within minutes he'd transferred her vehicle, then returned to slide in behind the wheel of his own car. The engine fired, and he eased the Jaguar out onto the road.

'The jet will touch down in Brisbane to collect Trenton and Georgia,' Sloane drawled as the car picked up speed.

Suzanne endeavoured not to show her surprise. 'I thought Trenton would travel with us from Sydney.'

'My father has been in Brisbane for the past week.' He paused to spare her a quick glance, then added with perfect timing, 'Ensuring, so he said, that Georgia didn't have the opportunity to get cold feet.'

Georgia had rarely, if ever, dated. There had been no male friends visiting the house, no succession of temporary 'uncles'. Georgia had been a devoted mother first and foremost, and a dedicated dressmaker who worked from the privacy of her own home.

For as long as Suzanne could remember they'd shared a close bond that was based on affectionate friendship. Genuine equals, rather than simply mother and daughter.

At forty-seven, Georgia was an attractive woman with a slim, petite frame, carefully tended blonde hair, blue eyes, and a wonderfully caring nature. She *deserved* happiness with an equally caring partner.

'From Brisbane we'll fly direct to Dunk Island, then take the launch to Bedarra,' said Sloane.

Suzanne turned her head and took in the moving scenery, the houses where everyone inside them was stirring to begin a new day. Mothers cooking breakfast, sleepy-eyed children preparing to wash and dress before eating and taking public transport to school.

The traffic was beginning to build up, and it was almost eight when Sloane took the turn-off to the airport, then bypassed the main terminal and headed for the area where private aircraft were housed. He gained clearance, and drove onto the apron of bitumen.

Suzanne undid her seat belt and reached for the doorhandle, only to pause as he leaned towards her.

'You forgot something.'

Her breath caught as Sloane took hold of her left hand and slid her engagement ring onto her finger.

She looked at the sparkling solitaire diamond, then lifted her head to meet his gaze.

'Trenton and Georgia will think it a little strange if you're not wearing it,' he drawled with hateful cynicism.

The charade was about to begin. A slightly hysterical laugh rose and died in her throat. Who was she kidding? 'This is going to be some weekend.'

'Indeed.'

'Sloane—' She paused, hesitant to say the words, but needing quite desperately to set a few ground rules. 'You won't—'

Dammit, his eyes were too dark, too discerning.

'Won't *what*, Suzanne?'

'Overact.'

His expression remained unchanged. 'Define overacting.'

She should have kept her mouth shut. Parrying words with him was a futile battle, for he always won. 'I'd prefer it if you kept any body contact to a minimum.'

His eyes gleamed with latent humour. 'Afraid, Suzanne?'

'Of you? No, of course not.'

His gaze didn't falter, and she felt the breath hitch in her chest. 'Perhaps you should be,' he intimated softly.

A chill settled over the surface of her skin, and she controlled a desire to shiver. She should call this off *now*. Insist on using his mobile phone so she could ring Georgia and explain.

'No,' Sloane said quietly. 'We'll see it through.'

'You read minds?'

'Yours is particularly transparent.'

It irked her unbearably that he was able to determine her thoughts. With anyone else it was possible to present an impenetrable façade. Sloane dispensed with each and every barrier she erected as if it didn't exist.

Suzanne fervently wished it were Monday, and they were making the return trip. Then the weekend would be over.

A sleek Lear jet bearing the W-W insignia stood waiting for them, its baggage hold open. Sloane transferred their bags, then spoke to the pilot before they boarded.

The interior portrayed the ultimate in luxury. Plush carpets, superior fittings—the jet was a wealthy man's expensive possession.

A slim, attractive stewardess greeted them inside the cabin. 'If you'd each care to be seated and fasten your seat belts, we'll be ready for immediate take-off.' She moved to close the door and secure it, checked her two passengers were comfortable, then she acknowledged internal clearance via intercom with the pilot.

The jet's engines increased their whining pitch, then the sleek silver plane eased off the bitumen apron and cruised a path to the runway.

Within minutes they were in the air, climbing high in a northerly flight pattern that hugged the coastline.

'Juice, tea or coffee?'

Suzanne opted for juice while Sloane settled for coffee, and when it was served the stewardess retreated into the rear section.

'No laptop?' Suzanne queried as Sloane made no attempt to take optimum advantage of the ensuing few hours. 'No documents to peruse?'

He regarded her thoughtfully. 'The laptop and my briefcase are stowed in the baggage compartment. However, I thought I'd take a break,' he revealed with indolent amusement.

'I have no objection if you want to work.'

'Thereby negating the need for conversation, Suzanne?'

She aimed a slow, sweet smile at him. 'How did you guess?'

Sloane's eyes narrowed fractionally. 'We should, don't you think, ensure our stories match on events during the past three weeks?' He leant back in his chair. 'Minor details like movies we might have seen, the theatre, dinner with friends.'

Separate residences, separate lives. Hectic work-filled days, empty lonely nights.

A particularly lacklustre social calendar, Suzanne

conceded on reflection, and was unable to prevent a comparison to the halcyon days when she'd shared Sloane's apartment and his life. Then there had been a succession of dinners, parties, and few evenings together alone at home. Long nights of loving, a wonderfully warm male body to curl into, and being awakened each morning by the stroke of his fingers, his lips.

Something clenched deep inside her, and she closed her eyes, then opened them again in an effort to clear the image.

'Suzanne?'

Clarity of mind was essential, and she met his gaze, acknowledged the enigmatic expression, and managed a slight smile. 'Of course.' Her attendance at the cinema had been her only social excursion. She named the movie, and provided him with a brief plot line. 'And you? I imagine you maintained a fairly hectic social schedule?'

'Reasonably quiet,' Sloane relayed. 'I declined a dinner invitation with the Parkinsons.' His level gaze held hers. 'You supposedly had a migraine.'

'And the rest of the time?'

His expression held a degree of cynical humour. 'We dined *à deux*, or stayed home.'

Suzanne remembered too well what had inevitably transpired during the evenings they'd stayed in. The long, slow foreplay that had begun when they'd entered the apartment. Sipping from each other's glass, offering morsels of food as they'd eaten a leisurely meal. A liqueur coffee, and the deliberate choice of viewing cable television or a video. The drift of fingers over

sensitised skin, the soft touch of lips savouring delicate
hollows, a sensual awakening that had held the promise
of continued arousal and the ultimate coupling of two
people who had delighted in each other on every plane.

Sometimes there had been no foreplay at all. Just
compelling passion, the melding of mouths as urgent
fingers had freed buttons and dispensed with clothes.
Occasionally they hadn't even made it to the bedroom.

Suzanne met his gaze and held it, fought against a
compulsive movement in her throat as she contained the
lump lodged there, and chose not to comment.

A hollow laugh died before it was born. Who was she
kidding? There was no choice at all. If she opened her
mouth, only the most strangled of sounds would emerge.

She saw the darkness reflected in his eyes, glimpsed
the flare of passion and his banking of it, then wanted
to die as his lips curved into a slow, sensual smile.

'Memories, Suzanne?'

Try for lightness, a touch of humour. Then he'd never
know just how much she ached inside. 'Some of them
were good, very good.' He deserved that, if nothing
else. Others were particularly forgettable. Such as the
bitchiness of some of his social equals.

Oh, damn. She was treading into deeper water with
every step she took. And she'd only been in his company an hour. What state would she be in at the end of
the weekend, for heaven's sake?

She fished a magazine from a strategically placed
pocket, and began flipping through the glossy pages
until she discovered an article that held her interest. Or

at least she could feign that it did for the duration of the short flight to Brisbane.

It was a relief when the jet landed and cruised to a halt on the far side of the terminal. Suzanne glimpsed a limousine parked close to the hangar, and Sloane's father boarded as soon as the jet's door opened and the steps were unfolded.

'Good morning.'

Trenton moved lithely down the aisle and closed the distance to greet them.

The family resemblance between father and son was clearly evident, the frame almost identical, although Trenton was a little heavier through the chest, slightly thicker in the waist, and his hair was streaked with grey.

He was a kind man, possessed of a gentle wit, beneath which was a shrewd and knowledgeable business mind.

Suzanne rose to her feet and allowed herself to be enveloped in a bear-hug.

'Suzanne. Lovely to see you, my dear.' He released her, and acknowledged his son with a warm smile. 'Sloane.' He indicated the limousine. 'Georgia is making a call from the car.' The smile broadened, and his eyes twinkled with humour as he placed a hand on Suzanne's shoulder. 'A last-minute confirmation of floral arrangements for the wedding. Go down and talk to her while I check the luggage being loaded on board.'

Georgia was fixing her lipstick, a slight pink colouring her cheeks as Suzanne slid into the rear seat, and she leaned forward and brushed her mother's cheek with her own. 'Nervous?'

'No,' her mother denied. 'Just needing someone to tell me I'm not being foolish.'

Georgia had been widowed at a young age, left to rear a child who retained little memory of the father who had been killed on a dark road in the depth of night by a joyriding, unlicensed lout high on drugs and alcohol. Life thereafter hadn't exactly been a struggle, as circumspect saving and a relatively strict budget had ensured there were holidays and a few of life's pleasures.

'You're not being foolish,' Suzanne said gently.

Georgia appeared anxious as she lifted a hand and pressed fingers to Suzanne's cheek. 'I would have preferred to put my plans on hold until after your wedding to Sloane. You don't mind, do you?'

It was difficult to maintain her existing expression beneath the degree of guilt and remorse she experienced for embarking on a deliberately deceitful course.

'Don't be silly, Mama,' she said gently. 'Sloane has briefs stacked back to back. We can't plan anything until he's free to take a few weeks' break.' She tried for levity, and won. 'Besides, I doubt Trenton would hear of any delay.'

'No,' a deep voice drawled. 'He wouldn't.'

Trenton held out his hand and Suzanne took it, then stepped out of the car, watching as he gave Georgia a teasing look. 'Time to fly, sweetheart.'

Suzanne boarded the jet, closely followed by her mother and Trenton, and within minutes the jet cruised a path to a distant runway, paused for clearance, then accelerated for take-off.

An intimate cabin, intimate company, with the emphasis on *intimacy*. It took only one look to see that Trenton was equally enamoured of Georgia as she was of him.

Any doubts Suzanne might have had were soon dispensed with, for there was a magical chemistry existent that tore the breath from her throat.

You shared a similar alchemy with Sloane, an inner voice taunted.

Almost as soon as the 'fasten seat belts' sign flashed off Trenton rose to his feet and extracted a bottle of champagne and four flutes from the bar fridge.

'A toast is fitting, don't you agree?' He removed the cork and proceeded to fill each flute with vintage Dom Perignon, handed them round, then raised his own. 'To health, happiness—' his eyes met and held Georgia's, then he turned to spare Sloane and Suzanne a carefree smile '—and love.'

Sloane touched the rim of his flute to that of Suzanne's, and his gaze held a warmth that almost stole her breath away.

Careful, she cautioned. It's only an act. And, because of it, she was able to direct him a stunning smile before turning towards her mother and Trenton. 'To you both.'

Alcohol before lunch was something she usually chose to avoid, and champagne on a near-empty stomach wasn't the wisest way to proceed with the day.

Thankfully there was a selection of wafer-thin sandwiches set out on a platter, and she ate one before sipping more champagne.

Sloane lifted a hand and tucked a stray tendril of hair back behind her ear in a deliberately evocative gesture.

It pleased him to see her eyelashes sweep wide, feel the faint quiver beneath his touch, and glimpse the increased pulse-beat at the base of her throat.

It would prove to be an interesting four days. And three nights, he perceived with a degree of cynical amusement.

Suzanne felt the breath hitch in her throat. *Was she out of her mind?* What had seemed a logical, commonsense option now loomed as an emotional minefield.

CHAPTER THREE

BEDARRA ISLAND resembled a lush green jewel in a sapphire sea. Secluded, reclusive, a haven of natural beauty, and reached only by launch from nearby Dunk Island.

Bedarra Island at first sight appeared covered entirely by rainforest. It wasn't until the launch drew closer that Suzanne glimpsed a high-domed terracotta-tiled villa roof peeping through dense foliage, then another and another.

There were sixteen private villas, walking was the only form of transport, and children under fifteen were not catered for, she mused idly, having studied the brochure she'd collected the day after she'd become aware of their destination.

She stood admiring the translucent sea as the launch cleaved through the water. It looked such a peaceful haven, the ideal place to get away from the rush and bustle of city life.

Acute sensory perception alerted her to Sloane's presence, and she contained a faint shivery sensation as he moved in close behind her, successfully forming a casual cage as he placed a hand at either side of her on the railing.

No part of his body touched hers, but she was intensely aware of the few inches separating them and how easy it would be to lean back into that hard-muscled frame.

She closed her eyes against the painful image of memory of when they had stood together just like this. Looking out over a sleeping city from any one of several floor-to-ceiling windows in his penthouse; in the kitchen, where she'd adored taking the domestic role; the large *en suite*. On any one of many occasions when he'd enfolded her close and nuzzled the sensitive slope of her neck, her nape, the hollow behind each earlobe.

Times when she had exulted in his touch and turned into the circle of his arms to lift her face to his for a kiss that was alternately slow and gentle, or hard and hungry. Inevitably, it had led them to the bedroom and long hours of passion.

Suzanne's fingers tightened on the railing as the launch decreased speed and began to ease in against the small jetty. Was Sloane's memory as vivid as her own? Or was he unmoved, and merely playing an expected role?

Damn. She'd have to get a grip on such wayward emotions, or she'd become a nervous wreck!

'Time to disembark.'

She felt rather than heard him move, and the spell was broken as Georgia's voice intruded, mingling with that of Trenton.

'It's beautiful,' Georgia remarked simply as they trod the path through to the main complex and reception.

'Secluded,' Trenton concurred. 'With guaranteed privacy, and no unwanted intrusion by the media.'

For which he was prepared to pay any price, Suzanne concluded, knowing only too well how difficult it was at times to enjoy a private dinner out without being interrupted by some society photographer bent on capturing a scoop for the tabloid social pages.

Exotic native timbers provided a background for the merging colour and tone of furnishings adorning the reception area.

The reception manager greeted them warmly, processed their check-in with practised speed, indicated their luggage would be taken to their individual villas and placed two keys on the counter.

Suzanne felt as if she'd been hit in the solar plexus by a sledgehammer. *Fool.* Of course she and Sloane were to share a villa. Why on earth not, given they were supposedly still engaged and living together?

'We'll meet in the dinin groom for lunch.' Trenton collected one key and spared his watch a glance. 'Say— half an hour?'

Together they traversed a curving path and reached Trenton and Georgia's villa first, leaving Sloane and Suzanne to continue to their own.

Suzanne could hear the faint screech of birds high in the trees, and she wondered at their breed, whether they were red-crested parrots with their brilliant blue and green plumage, or perhaps the white cockatoo, or pink-breasted galah.

Sloane unlocked the door and she preceded him inside, waiting only until he closed the door behind him before turning towards him.

'You knew, didn't you?' she demanded with suppressed anger.

'That we'd share? Yes.' He regarded her steadily. 'You surely didn't imagine we'd have separate accommodation?'

She watched as he moved into the room, and wanted to throw something—preferably at him. 'And, of course, as Trenton has booked out the entire island there are no free villas.'

He turned and directed her a level look. 'That's true. Although even if there were we'd still share.'

'The projected image of togetherness,' Suzanne said with heavy cynicism, and glimpsed one eyebrow slant in silent query.

'Something we agreed as being the favoured option, I believe?'

A temporary moment of insanity when she'd put her mother's feelings to the forefront with very little thought for her own, she decided disparagingly. Then felt bad, for she'd do anything rather than upset Georgia.

The villa was spacious, open-plan living on two levels. And it was remarkably easy to determine via an open staircase that the upper level was given over to one bedroom, albeit that it was large and housed a queen and single bed, as well as an adjoining *en suite* bathroom.

Suzanne followed him upstairs, and discovered the bedroom was larger than she'd expected, with glossy timber floors and a high ceiling. A central fan stirred recycled air-conditioned air, and dense external foliage provided an almost jungle-like atmosphere that heightened the sensation of secluded tra nquillity.

Her eyes skimmed over both beds, and quickly skittered towards the functional *en suite*. Four days of enforced sharing. It had hardly begun, and already she could feel several nerve-ends curling in protective self-defence.

'Which bed would you prefer?' she asked in civil tones, wanting, needing to set down a few ground rules. Rules were good, they imposed boundaries, and if they adhered to them they should be able to get through the weekend with minimum conflict.

He regarded her thoughtfully. 'You don't want to share?'

'No.' She didn't want to think about it, didn't *dare*. It was bad enough having to share the same villa, the same bedroom.

To share the same bed was definitely impossible. Unless she was into casual sex, for the sake of sex. And she wasn't. To her, sex meant intimacy, sensuality, *love*. Not a physical exercise to be indulged in simply to satisfy a basic urge.

Sloane watched her expressive features, perceived each deliberation and recognised every one of them. 'Pity.'

Suzanne's lashes swept upwards, and her eyes sparked with anger. 'You surely didn't expect me to agree?'

'No.' His smile held wry humour, and there was a musing gleam evident in the depth of his appraisal.

He reached out an idle finger and touched its tip to the end of her nose. The smile broadened. 'But you rise so beautifully to the bait.'

Of all the… She drew in a deep breath, and expelled it slowly in an effort to defuse the simmering heat of her rage. 'I think,' she vouchsafed with the utmost care, 'we had better agree not to ruffle each other's feathers. Or we're likely to come to blows.'

'Verbal, of course.'

His faint mockery further incensed her. '*Physical*, if you don't watch your step!'

'Now there's an interesting image.' He gave a silent laugh, and his eyes were as dark as she imagined the devil's own to be. 'A word of warning, Suzanne,' he said softly. 'Don't expect me to behave like a gentleman.'

This conversation had veered way off course, and she attempted to get back on it. With deliberate calm she turned her attention to one bed, then the other, entertained a brief image of Sloane attempting to fold his lengthy frame into the single one, and made a decision. 'You can have the larger bed.'

'Generous of you.'

'Half the wardrobe is mine,' she managed firmly. 'With equal time and space in the bathroom.'

A lazy smile curved the edges of his mouth. 'Done.'

She looked at him warily. His calm acceptance of her suggested sleeping arrangement was…unexpected.

There was a loud knock on the door, and Sloane moved indolently downstairs to allow the porter to deposit their bags, then, taking hold of one in each hand, he ascended the short flight of stairs.

'I'll unpack.' A prosaic task that would take only minutes.

She was all too aware of Sloane's matching actions as she hung a few changes of clothes on hangers in the wardrobe, lay underclothes into a drawer, and set out toiletries and make-up on one half of the vanity unit.

'Anything for valet pressing?'

'No.' She watched as he extracted the appropriate bag, added two shirts, then filled in the slip and slung it down onto the bed.

'When you're ready, we'll go join Georgia and Trenton in the dining room.'

She needed to run a quick brush through her hair and retouch her lipstick. 'Give me a few minutes.'

In the *en suite* she regarded her mirror image with critical appraisal. Her eyes were too darkly pensive, her features too pale.

A few swift strokes of eyeshadow, blusher and lipstick added essential colour, and she made a split-second decision to twist the length of her hair into a careless knot atop her head.

Her hand automatically reached for the light *parfum* spray Sloane had gifted her. Her fingers hesitated, then retreated.

Oh, to hell with it. She wore perfume because she liked the fragrance, not because of any attempt to tantalise a man. If Sloane chose to think the fresh application was attributed to *him*, he was mistaken.

A quick spray to the delicate veins crossing each wrist, the valley between each breast. Better, much better, she determined as she emerged into the bedroom.

Sloane regarded her with one swift encompassing glance, then caught up his sunglasses and held out her own before standing to one side to allow her to precede him down onto the lower level.

Suzanne was supremely conscious of the intense maleness emanating from his broad frame as they stepped outside their villa. It was like a magnet, pulling at something deep inside her, heightening emotions to a level she didn't want to acknowledge.

'Hungry?'

The sun's warmth caressed her skin, the slight breeze teasing free a few tendrils of her hair as she offered him a brilliant smile. 'Yes.'

A gleam lit his expressive eyes, and he gave a soft laugh as he caught hold of her hand and lifted it to his lips.

Her stomach curled at the implied intimacy, and she silently damned the way each and every one of her nerve-ends sprang into acutely sensitised life.

She attempted to pull her hand free without success. 'The act is a little premature, don't you think?'

'Not really, given we're in a public place and unsure who can see and hear us.'

The tinge of humour in his voice brought forth a rueful smile. 'You're enjoying this, aren't you?'

One eyebrow slanted upwards. 'It's a rare opportunity for me to gain an upper hand.'

'Don't overdo it, Sloane,' she warned in a low voice, and glimpsed his mocking smile.

'What a vivid imagination you have.'

Much too vivid. That was the problem.

The restaurant was spacious, with tables set wide apart indoors and beneath the covered terrace. It was a peaceful setting overlooking the wide sweep of the bay as it curved out into the ocean, the bush-clad undulations of the island providing a tranquil remoteness.

'Would you prefer to sit indoors or out on the terrace?'

'The terrace,' Suzanne said without hesitation.

Georgia and Trenton had yet to arrive, and she selected a table protected from the sun's warm rays.

She watched as Sloane folded his length into an adjoining seat, and was grateful for the tinted lenses shading her eyes. They provided a barrier that made it a fraction more comfortable to deal with him.

A silent laugh stuck in her throat. Who was she kidding? No one *dealt* with Sloane. That was his prerogative. Control, which some would call manipulative strategy, was a skill he'd honed to an enviable degree in the business arena. In his private life, he added charm and seductive warmth with dangerous effect.

'Mineral water?'

She met his gaze, partly masked by tinted lenses, and offered a slight smile. 'Orange juice.'

The generous curve of his mouth relaxed and humour tugged its edge. 'Preference, Suzanne? Or a determined effort to thwart me?'

'Why would I want to do that, Sloane,' she queried evenly, 'when the next three days are supposed to project peace, harmony and celebration?'

'Why, indeed?'

His tone was pure silk, with the merest hint of caution should she attempt to try his patience too far in this game they'd each agreed to play.

A young waitress crossed to the table to take their order, her smile bright, her expression faintly envious as her eyes lingered fractionally longer than necessary on Sloane's attractive features.

Suzanne felt a slight stab of something she refused to accept as jealousy. Dammit, *why* was her body so attuned to this man, when she'd determinedly dismissed him from her mind?

It was one thing to uphold when she had the distance and protection of a telephone conversation. It was something else entirely when confronted with his presence, for then the barriers she'd erected seemed in danger of disintegrating into a heap at her feet.

Conversation seemed safer than silence. 'Tell me about the case you're currently involved in.'

'Genuine interest, Suzanne?'

His amused drawl touched a raw nerve. 'What would you prefer? A polite dissertation about the weather?'

'You could try for an unexpurgated version of what motivated you to walk out on me.'

Straight for the jugular. She aimed for levity. Anything else was impossible. 'And risk the possibility of having Georgia and Trenton appear in the middle of a heated discussion?'

He sank back in the chair and folded his hands together behind his head. 'My dear Suzanne, I rarely have the need to raise my voice.'

Why should he resort to anger when he could employ a wealth of words with such innate skill, their delivery sliced with the deadliness of an expertly wielded scal-pel? Anger had been *her* emotional defence.

'This isn't the time, or the place.'

The waitress's reappearance bearing a tray contain-ing two tall glasses filled with orange juice and chink-ing ice cubes brought a halt to the conversation, and Suzanne watched as the young girl made a production of placing decorative coasters down onto the table, fol-lowed by each individual glass.

'If there's anything else you need, just call.' The smile was pure female and aimed at Sloane before she turned and retreated to the bar.

'Oh, my,' Suzanne said with saccharine sweetness. 'You don't even have to try.'

His smile held wry cynicism. 'I suppose I should be grateful you noticed it was entirely one-sided.'

I notice, she silently assured him. Everything about you. She reached for her glass, lifted it, and took an ap-preciative sip of the iced liquid. 'She looks—available.'

His eyes narrowed. 'You forget,' he remarked in a silky drawl. 'I'm with you.' The words alone were sim-ple. His delivery of them was not.

It cost her to lift one eyebrow in a gesture of ill-concealed mockery. 'It's only day one, and already we're into verbal sparring. What will we both be like at the end of day four?'

There was warm humour evident in his smile, and she felt her stomach clench with something she refused to acknowledge as pain.

'Oh, I don't know,' he replied indolently. 'I'm rather

looking forward to the progression.' He lifted his glass and touched its rim to her own. 'Here's to us.'

'There is no *us*,' Suzanne declared adamantly.

'Isn't there?'

She shot him a baleful glare. 'Get too close, Sloane, and you'll discover I bite.'

'Be warned I'll retaliate.'

Yes, he'd do that, and ensure that, while he might permit her to win a battle, he had every intention of winning the war.

It was a chilling thought, and one which had her poised for a stinging response.

'Georgia and Trenton have just entered the restaurant,' he warned, and she changed a glare to a slow, sweet smile, glad of the tinted shield shading her eyes as he leaned forward and brushed his fingers against her cheek.

A blatant action if ever there was one, signalling his intention to take advantage of each and every situation during their island sojourn. If he was intent on playing a game, then it shouldn't be uneven, she decided with a touch of vengeance.

With deliberate calm she captured his hand with her own and brought it to her lips, then used her teeth to nip the soft pad of one finger...*hard*.

Triumph, albeit temporary, was very sweet. Despite the faint warning flare that promised retribution.

'Isn't this an idyllic place?' Georgia enthused as she sank into the chair Trenton held out for her.

'Wonderful,' Suzanne agreed lightly. Almost anything was worth it to see her mother so blissfully happy. Even wielding emotional and verbal swords with Sloane.

'I've checked arrangements with the hotel staff,' Trenton disclosed as he settled into the remaining chair.

The waitress appeared at his side, took an order, then retreated to the bar to fill it.

'Everything's under control.'

Why wouldn't it be? Suzanne questioned silently. The Wilson-Willoughby name was sufficient to ensure assistants scrambled over one another in the need to please.

Success wasn't born of those who were faint-hearted, insecure, or inept. And no one in their right mind could accuse Trenton or Sloane of possessing any one of those character flaws.

Power was the keynote, and with it came a certain ruthlessness Suzanne found difficult to condone. A paradox, for it was a quality she could also admire.

'When do the guests arrive?'

'Tomorrow morning. The launch will make an unscheduled run from Dunk Island.'

Lunch comprised a superb seafood starter, followed by freshly caught grilled fish and salad, and they each chose a selection of succulent fresh fruit for dessert.

'Have I met each of the invited guests?' Suzanne voiced the query with what she hoped was casual interest, and tried to ignore the faint knot twisting in her stomach as she waited for Trenton's response.

Sloane's eyes sharpened, although his expression remained unchanged.

'I'm almost certain of it,' Trenton concurred with a

relaxed smile. He named them, and Suzanne endeavoured to breathe normally as she waited for one specific name, and felt the easing of tension when it wasn't mentioned.

Sloane was aware of every nuance, every gesture, no matter how slight. His suspicions, laser-sharp, moved up a notch.

'Shall we leave?' Georgia broached with a sunny smile. 'I haven't finished unpacking, and there are a few things I want to check on.'

Sloane rose to his feet, and held Suzanne's chair as she followed his actions. His hand brushed her arm, and she felt warmth flood her veins in an instantaneous reaction to his touch. There was little she could do to prevent the casual arm he placed around her waist as he led her from the restaurant. Nor could she give in to temptation and shrug it off as they lingered outside.

With a hint of desperation she turned towards her mother. 'Do you need help with anything this afternoon?' Say *yes. Please*, she begged silently, doubtful anyone, least of all her radiant mother, would take heed. Murphy's law had prevailed from the moment she'd picked up the phone the day before yesterday to take Georgia's call.

'Oh, darling, thank you. But no, there's nothing.'

Of course not. Anything that needed to be done had been taken care of before Georgia had boarded the plane in Brisbane. And here on this idyllic island there were ample staff to cater to a guest's slightest whim.

'The past few days have been so hectic,' Georgia continued, sparing Trenton a warm glance. 'Now that we're here, I just want to relax.' The warmth heated, and was diffused with a generous, faintly humorous smile. 'You and Sloane take time out to explore. We'll join you for a drink before dinner. Shall we say six?'

There was little to do except agree, and Suzanne suffered Sloane's loose hold as he led the way back to their villa, pulling free as soon as they were safely inside with the door closed behind them.

Suzanne glanced around the elegant tropical-designed furnishings, the four spacious walls, and felt the need to escape.

'I think I'll go for a walk.' She moved towards the stairs leading to the bedroom. She'd change into cotton shorts and sleeveless top, and exchange her shoes for light trainers.

'I'll come with you.'

His drawling tone halted her steps and she turned to face him. 'What if I don't want you to?'

'Tough.'

Anger rose to the surface, tingeing her cheeks with colour, and adding a dangerous sparkle to her eyes. 'You're determined to make this as difficult as possible, aren't you?'

He closed the distance between them. 'Everything we do this weekend, we do together. Understood?'

'*Everything*, Sloane?' Her chin tilted. 'Isn't that a bit too *literal*?'

Those dark eyes above her own hardened fractionally, and she forced herself not to blink as he lifted a hand and cupped her cheek. 'We agreed to a temporary truce. Let's try to keep it, shall we?'

She'd never seen him lose his temper, only witnessed a chilled expression turn his eyes almost black, detected the ice in his voice more than once in the courtroom, and on a few occasions when dealing with an adversary over the phone. But never with her.

A faint shiver shimmied across the surface of her skin, and she fought to diffuse the intense, potentially dangerous air that swirled between them.

'I hope you packed trainers,' she said lightly. 'Those hand-stitched Italian shoes you wear weren't made for trekking through sand and bush.'

The edges of his mouth quirked, then relaxed into a musing smile. 'A temporary escape, Suzanne?'

'Got it in one.'

His thumb brushed across her lower lip, then he let his hand fall to his side. 'Give me a few minutes to change, then let's go try to enjoy it.'

She ascended the stairs and quickly changed, deciding on the spur of the moment to don a bikini beneath shorts and top. With a deft movement she pulled on a peaked cap, slid her sunglasses into place, caught up a towel and turned to face him.

'Ready?'

Shorts had replaced tailored trousers, and the hand-stitched shoes had been exchanged for trainers. He looked, Suzanne decided, relaxed and at ease. A projected persona that could be infinitely deceiving.

She followed in his wake, aware of the broad set of his shoulders, the powerful back beneath the cotton polo shirt. The exclusive tones of his cologne teased her senses, heightening them to a degree that made her want to scream.

Elusive scents, the movement of honed muscle and sinew, *knowing* their power, the sensual magic this one man could create within her—it was torture.

It had taken her every hour of every day since she'd left him to build up invisible walls from within which she could protect and defend herself against his powerful alchemy. Night after night she'd lain awake rationalising her motives for leaving him; applied logic, indulged in amateur psychology, and resolved that she'd reached a satisfactory and sane decision.

Yet somehow instinct continued to war with rationale, and she disliked the contrariness of her ambivalence.

'OK, where shall we begin?' Determination was the key. 'The beach?'

'Why not?'

Sloane's voice held a tinge of amusement, and she spared him a searching glance for evidence of cynical humour. However, it was impossible to detect anything behind the dark lenses of his sunglasses.

CHAPTER FOUR

THE SAND RESEMBLED light honey, marked high by a thin line of shells, most broken, some whole, and scraps of seaweed: the flotsam of an outgoing tide.

Suzanne paused every now and then to select a few, only to send them skimming out into the translucent blue-green water.

It was quiet, so quiet as to imagine there was no one else on the island. The sun was pleasantly warm in a tropical climate known as the winterless north, and tempered only by a slight breeze drifting in from the sea.

She was supremely conscious of the man at her side; how, now she was in casual trainers, her height seemed diminished in comparison to his. It made her feel fragile and vaguely vulnerable, which was crazy.

'Do you want to clamber over those rocks and discover what's on the other side?'

They had followed the beach's gentle curve to a wide outcrop of boulders that separated land and sea.

Anything was better than going back to their villa. 'OK.'

They came to a small cove, the shallows bounded

by an irregular scatter of huge boulders, and patches of soft crunchy sand above the shoreline. Isolated, and quite breathtakingly beautiful.

'Want to continue on?'

'Swim,' Suzanne said without hesitation, and she spared him a quick glance.

His warm smile caused the breath to catch in her throat. 'I'll join you.'

Was he wearing briefs? This was a sufficiently isolated spot for it not to matter. So why should it bother her? Except it did, of course. Badly.

'You object?' His soft drawl made her stomach dip and execute a series of slow somersaults.

'No, of course not.' How come a decision to swim suddenly seemed dangerous? *Fool*, she silently castigated herself as she quickly stripped down to her bikini.

Suzanne was conscious of Sloane matching her actions, and a surreptitious glance beneath her lashes was sufficient to determine that thin black silk provided an adequate covering.

Although *adequate* hardly equated with a hard-muscled masculine frame at the peak of physical fitness. A visual attestation of powerful male destined to cause the female heart to leap into a quickened beat.

Yet it was more than that, much more.

Sloane possessed a primitive magnetism, an animalistic sense of power which, combined with an intimate knowledge of the human psyche, set him apart from other men. It was evident in his eyes, an essential hardness that alluded to an old soul, one that had seen much, dealt with it and triumphed. Equally, those dark, almost black depths could soften and warm for a woman, give hint to sensual delight, the promise of devastating sexual pleasure.

Remembering just how devastating had kept her awake nights, tossing and turning in an attempt to forget.

In the daylight hours she could convince herself she was fine, really fine.

Now, she was faced with his constant company for three, almost four days. Mistake; big mistake. Seven hours into this farcical misadventure, and she was already a bundle of nerves, almost jumping out of her skin whenever he came within touching distance.

Why, why, *why* had she put herself in such jeopardy?

For Georgia. Dear sweet Georgia, who *deserved* happiness during her wedding celebration unclouded by an edge of anxiety for her only beloved daughter.

It wasn't so much to ask, was it?

'Do you want to swim, or simply gaze at the ocean?'

Sloane's drawling voice snapped Suzanne's introspection, and she summoned a faint smile.

'Race you in.'

She sprinted into the cool blue-green water until it reached waist-level, then she broke into long, strong strokes that took her a few metres out from the shore.

Seconds later a sleek dark head broke the surface beside her, and she regarded him a trifle warily as she trod water.

'You look,' Sloane said softly, 'as if you're waiting for me to pounce.'

She should never play poker, he decided silently. Her

eyes were too expressive. He knew every nuance in her voice, could read each movement of that wide, mobile mouth.

'Why would you do that?' Suzanne queried evenly. 'There's not a soul in sight.'

'No need for you to be under any illusion, hmm?'

He moved close, much too close, and his legs curled around hers before she could attempt to put some distance between them. A hand curved round her waist, while the other held fast her nape, and she didn't have a chance to utter a sound before his mouth closed over hers in a kiss that was incredibly gentle in its possessiveness.

She felt as if she was drowning, sinking, and entirely at his mercy as he took her down beneath the water's surface. He held her so close she was aware of the pressure of his body, the strength of his arousal, the absorption of his mouth on hers, then the power of his thighs as he kicked to bring them up for air.

The breath tore at her throat, and she gasped deeply as he released her mouth and slowly eased his hold. Her eyes were wide with a mixture of shocked surprise and anger, and her lips moved soundlessly for an instant before she broke into spluttering speech, only to lapse into an inaudible murmur as he pressed a forefinger over her mouth.

'Just so you're not in any doubt,' Sloane murmured in a husky undertone, and covered her mouth with his own.

This time there was nothing gentle about his possession, and her head whirled as his tongue mated with hers, sweeping deeply and in total control. She whimpered as he took his fill, his jaw powerful in its demanding onslaught until compliance was her only option.

She had no idea how long it lasted, only that it seemed an age before the pressure began to ease. She felt the light brush of his lips as he explored the bruised softness of her mouth before he lifted his head.

His eyes were incredibly dark, almost black as he regarded her pale features, and for one infinitesimal second he experienced a tinge of regret.

She wanted to hit him. Would have, if she thought she could connect and physically *hurt* him. Instead, she resorted to words.

'If you've quite finished playing the masterful macho *male*, I'd like to go ashore and dry out.' Nothing would allow her to admit how *shaken* she felt. Or how ravaged.

His soft laughter almost unleashed her control, and she kicked out at him, then swore when she failed to connect.

'Most unladylike,' Sloane chided with an indolence that set her teeth on edge.

'I don't *feel* ladylike,' she assured him, hating him for tearing her emotions to shreds. Claim-staking. A reminder of how it had been between them; a promise of how it could be again.

Without another word she turned and swam back to shore, uncaring whether he followed her or not.

The sun's rays warmed her body as she emerged onto the sand, and she lifted her hands to squeeze excess water from her hair, then combed her fingers through its length so that it would dry more quickly, before tending to the moisture beading her body with a towel.

She possessed naturally fair skin which she took care to protect with sunscreen, and she applied coverage from the slim tube she'd brought with her.

By the time she finished the Lycra bikini was almost dry, and she pulled on shorts and top, slid her feet into trainers, then made her way towards the rocky outcrop to explore…in solitude.

Breathing space, she qualified, uncaring how Sloane chose to occupy himself. As long as it wasn't with her.

There were pools of water trapped in several natural rock hollows, tiny lizards the length of her finger which scattered out of sight, and the occasional shell of a dead crustacean.

She could hear the faint lap of water against the rocks, and every now and then there came the screeching call from parrots disturbed in their natural habitat.

Suzanne rounded the corner, and paused to admire the long curve of clean golden sand stretching to the northern point of the island. Beautiful, she thought, stepping from one rock to another.

Was it some form of sensory perception that made her pause and glance to her rear? Or simply an elusive connection she shared with the one man from whom she'd sought a temporary escape?

Sloane stood highlighted against the sky as he closed the distance between them, and she turned back, quickening her steps.

Foolishly, for she misjudged, slipped, and cushioned her fall with an outstretched hand.

Nothing, she determined within seconds, was twisted or broken. Tomorrow she might have a bruised hip, but she could bear with it. There wasn't even a graze on either leg, and her ankles were both fine.

'What in sweet *hell* were you thinking of?'

Sloane's anger was palpable as he crouched down beside her, and she directed him a dark look as she aimed for brutal honesty.

'Aiming to get down onto the sand before you caught up with me.'

His hands skimmed her arms, her legs with professional ease. 'Are you hurt?'

Now there was a question. If she said her emotions were, what good would it do?

He caught hold of her hands, examined the fine bones, then extended his attention to each palm.

Blood seeped from a deep graze on the fleshy mound beneath her left thumb, and she regarded it with a degree of fascination, wondering why it should sting quite badly when at the time she hadn't been conscious of it at all.

'I'll go wash it in the sea.'

'It needs antiseptic.'

She gave a slight shrug. 'So I'll put some on when I get back to the villa.'

Sloane gave her a penetrating look. 'Are your tetanus shots up to date?'

'Oh, for heaven's sake. *Yes*.' She tried to wrench her hand from his grasp. Unsuccessfully, which only served to increase her exasperation.

His eyes were steady, their depths too intensely dark

for her to mistake the implacability evident, then without a further word he lifted her hand to his lips, took the fleshy mound into his mouth, and began cleansing the wound with his tongue.

The provocative action caused sensation to feather the length of her spine, and she suppressed a faint shiver at the sheer power of her emotions.

Everything faded beyond the periphery of her vision. There was only the man as she became caught up in the spell of him. Acute sensuality, so potent it robbed the strength from her limbs.

She was aware of the soft body hair that curled darkly, visible in the deep V of his polo shirt, and the faint musky aroma of cologne and salt emanating from his skin.

Her heart began to race, and she became supremely conscious of the need to regulate her breathing in an effort to portray a dispassionate calmness.

Fire coursed through her veins, heating pleasure that pooled in each erogenous zone and became evident with every pulsing beat.

This close, it was possible to detect the dark shadow of almost a day's growth of beard he deemed necessary to dispense with night and morning. It was an intensely masculine feature, and one she found attractive.

Dear heaven, she had to get a grip, otherwise she'd never survive the next few days with any semblance of emotional sanity.

'Don't.' The single negation sounded vaguely husky, and she swallowed compulsively as he raised his head.

'Don't—what?' His eyes pierced hers. 'Take care of you?' His voice dropped a tone. '*Love* you?'

It felt as if a fist slammed into her chest at the last two words, and she held her breath in silent pain. 'Sloane—'

'Another *don't*, Suzanne?' His voice was too quiet, too controlled as he released her hand. 'You think ignoring what we share together will make it go away?'

Her eyes were remarkably clear as they met and held his. 'No. But I plan to work on it.'

'Why?'

The silky tone aroused a dormant rage that coloured her fine-textured skin and turned her eyes to pure crystalline sapphire.

'You don't get it, do you?' The heat emanated from the pores of her skin. '*Love*—' she paused, drew in a deep breath, then expelled it '—doesn't provide a security blanket against reality.' She rose to her feet in one fluid movement, and immediately lost the momentary advantage as he followed her actions.

'You demean my intelligence.'

'Really?' Her chin tilted in open contempt. 'Then perhaps you should consider re-evaluating it.'

She turned away and traversed the few remaining rocks to the sandy stretch below, aware that he followed close behind.

'Suzanne.'

She swung round to face him. *Fine*. If a confrontation was what he wanted, then so be it!

'What do you want, Sloane? A pound of my flesh because I dared assess a situation, and decided retreat was the wisest course of action?' She was defiant, determined to hide the utter defencelessness she hadn't been able to deal with then, any more than she could now.

His eyes darkened into a deep flaming brilliance. 'Dammit, were you so emotionally unsure of yourself— of *me*, that you felt the only option you had was to throw in the towel?'

Anger flashed in her clear blue eyes. 'I didn't throw in the towel!'

A slight smile curved his mouth, lending it a cynical edge. 'Yes, you did.'

'No, I didn't!'

One eyebrow rose slightly. 'What would you call it?'

'A tactical withdrawal.'

He was silent for several long minutes, his regard unwavering. 'You possess a high degree of common sense.' His gaze intensified, and his eyes became incredibly dark. 'Sufficient, I would have thought, to judge me for the man I am beneath the superficiality of material possessions.'

It hurt to enunciate the words without allowing a slight catch to affect her voice. 'Oh, I did, Sloane. I fell in love with the man.' Her expression became pensive, her eyes incredibly sad. 'Then I discovered it was impossible to separate the man from everything that comes with the Wilson-Willoughby tag.'

'On that basis, you took the easy route and threw what we had together away?'

She felt like a laboratory specimen being examined beneath a microscope, and at that precise moment she hated him. 'Damn you, Sloane! What was I supposed to do?'

'Stay.'

One word. Yet it conveyed so much. 'I'm not into masochism.'

His eyes narrowed. 'What in hell are you talking about?'

'*You* are regarded as the ultimate prize in a field of wealthy, well-connected men.' A tight smile momentarily widened her mouth. 'And I, heaven forgive me, am merely a nonentity who dared to usurp each and every one of the women aspiring to share your life.'

The hurt, some of the pain clouded her eyes, and her lashes lowered to form a protective veil. 'I chose not to compete.' There was more, much more she could have said. Repeated the bitchy comments, relayed one very real threat.

'Unnecessary, when there was no contest.' Sloane enunciated the words with quiet emphasis, and felt a wrench of pain at the momentary sadness reflected in her expression.

'No?'

'You hold me responsible for other women's aspirations?'

Her hands clenched until the knuckles showed white, although she managed to keep her voice remarkably calm. 'No more than I hold you responsible for being who you are.'

He wanted to shake her. 'And, being *who I am*, I should select any one of several society princesses from the requisite gene pool, have her grace my arm, my bed, and produce the expected two children?'

The image hurt. So much, it was all she could do not to close her eyes in an attempt to shut it out.

'Be content with a marriage devoid of passion?' Sloane persisted ruthlessly. 'Based on duty and a degree of affection?' His voice lowered and became almost brutally merciless. 'Is that what you're saying?'

Her eyes flashed with latent anger at his analytical and persistent questioning. 'Damn you! I'm not on the witness stand.'

He didn't touch her, but she felt as if he had. 'Humour me. Pretend that you are.'

'And play the truth deal, entirely for your benefit? Sorry, Sloane. I'm not in favour of game-playing.'

His eyes held hers, and she was unable to look away. 'Neither am I.'

'Yet you do it every day in the courtroom,' Suzanne retaliated, and saw his mouth form a cynical twist.

'I don't allow my profession to intrude into my personal life.'

His compelling scrutiny was unsettling, and her eyes gleamed with hidden anger. 'You're so skilled with word play, I doubt it's possible to separate one from the other.'

'You think so?' He moved forward, and she had to forcibly refrain from taking a step backwards. His action wasn't intimidating, but nevertheless she felt threatened.

'Sloane—'

He lifted a hand and brushed a thumb along her jawline. 'Tell me the love changed.'

Oh, God. She closed her eyes, then opened them again, stricken by the tearing pain deep inside. She was powerless to move as he lowered his mouth to capture hers in a kiss that made her ache for more.

She physically had to prevent her body from leaning into his as she tried to stem the hunger that activated every nerve-ending. It would be so easy to wind her arms up around his neck and hold on as he took her on an emotional ride, the equal of which she'd never experienced with anyone else. Yet eventually the ride would be over, and she'd be left with only battered pride.

The sensual magic that was his alone tore at the very foundation of her being, tugging her free until she had no concept of anything but the heat of his mouth and the wild, sweet promise of heavy, satiated senses as they merged as one entity, meshing mind and soul.

A hollow groan rose and died in her throat at the need for *more*, much more than this. She wanted to dispense with the restriction of their clothes, to feel the texture of his skin, the flex of muscle beneath her hands, and have his lips, his mouth savour every inch of her body as they urged each other from one sensual plane to another.

What are you doing? The insidious query rose silently to taunt her. For a few long seconds she ignored it, then reality intervened as the magnitude of what she was inciting doused the heat and began cooling the warm blood in her veins.

Sloane sensed the moment it happened and mentally cursed the swing of her emotions. For the space of a few seconds he considered conquering the subtle change, then discarded the urge, aware that she would hold it against him.

Instead, he lightened the depth of emotion. Slowly easing the pressure of his mouth as he withdrew his possession, he allowed his lips to linger against her own as he pressed a number of light kisses over the full, slightly swollen contours.

At the same time his hands soothed her body, sliding gently over her slim curves, subtly massaging her nape, the delicate bones at the base of her scalp, the fine slope of her back, the firm waist.

Then his mouth left hers and trailed down the edge of her neck to savour the faint hollows at the base of her throat.

He wanted to lift her into his arms and take her here, *now*, remove what remained of her clothes, his, and make love until there could be no vestige of doubt in her mind as to how he felt.

Except she would equate that with sexual satisfaction. And while it would certainly ease the ache it wasn't enough while there were doubts to appease. He wanted her mind, her soul. *Everything.*

Who had poisoned the verbal darts and aimed them with careful precision, sufficient to undermine her confidence to such a level that she felt the only option she had was to leave?

Any one of many, came the cynical knowledge as he ran a mental gamut of numerous female acquaintances capable of sowing the seeds of doubt…and revelling in the byplay.

Sloane trailed his lips to her mouth, pressed a warm kiss to its edge, then withdrew to within touching distance, his smile tinged with a certain wry humour as he surveyed her bemused expression.

'There's a path leading off from the beach. Shall we see if it leads back to the villa?'

He was letting her off the hook…for now. She told herself she was relieved, and made a valiant effort to ignore the vague stirrings of disappointment.

'Let's go,' Suzanne declared decisively. 'Maybe we can fit in a set of tennis before dinner.'

His gaze was far too discerning. 'With the intention of wearing yourself out?'

How could she say she wanted to collapse into bed, too tired to do anything but sleep, instead of lying awake for most of the night cautioning herself not to toss or turn in case the movement disturbed the man occupying the large bed a short distance from her own?

'I might even permit you to win,' she said lightly. Some chance. He had the height, the strength, the experience to trounce her off the court!

Sloane's husky chuckle set the nerves in her stomach into action, and he slid on his sunglasses, then extended his hand.

Suzanne hesitated fractionally, then threaded slender fingers through his own.

They crossed to a sandy path that curved through increasingly dense rainforest, and initiated a leisurely pace. Sunlight filtered between wide-branched trees, lowering the warm temperature by several degrees.

There had to be a variety of tropical insects, but none was immediately evident. It was so quiet. Peaceful. Almost idyllic. A wonderful place to get away from it all.

If only... She stopped the traitorous thought right there. Life was crowded with 'if only's and 'what if?'s. And in the weeks since she'd moved out of Sloane's apartment she'd covered a plethora of each.

Silence allowed for too much introspection, and she sought a temporary distraction.

'Word has it you'll win a large settlement in the Allenberg trial.'

Sloane had a reputation for scrupulous research and meticulous attention to detail. He enjoyed pitting his skill in the court arena, and was known to accept difficult and complex cases for the mental challenge rather than his barrister's fee.

'Interesting.'

Now there was an ambiguous statement if ever there was one. Interesting that she'd mentioned the brief? Or interesting that she'd opted to veer away from anything personal by way of conversation?

She looked at him carefully. 'You have doubts?'

The path levelled out and began following the shoreline. Leading, she suspected, in a meandering fashion back to the main complex.

'I never discount the element of surprise.'

Suzanne had the strangest feeling he wasn't referring to the brief. 'I imagine you've covered all the angles.' Impossible that he hadn't.

He spared her a penetrating glance, then lightened it with a faint smile. 'It's to be hoped so.'

There was a sense of isolation in the stillness surrounding them. Possible almost to believe they were the only inhabitants on the island.

It was comforting to know that staff and civilisation lay within a short distance. Trenton and Georgia were also in residence, and tomorrow the guests would arrive.

People, in this resort deliberately designed for solitude, would be a welcome advantage, Suzanne determined. It meant there would be plenty of opportunity to socialise, and less time spent alone with Sloane.

CHAPTER FIVE

THE PATH WAS CLEAR, but not well trodden, and Suzanne suspected it was deliberately kept that way by the resort management to provide the ambience of lush rainforest.

Sloane walked at her side, matching his stride to her own. How long would it take them to reach the main complex? Ten minutes? Longer? A lot depended on how the path was structured. The trip would be leisurely, she imagined, if the upward slant and winding curves were anything to go by.

'It probably would have been quicker to go back via the beach,' Suzanne offered, and he projected an indolent smile.

'At least this way we don't have to traverse a collection of boulders and rocks.'

She met his gaze with equanimity. 'They were relatively easy to navigate.'

He tipped his head and allowed his sunglasses to slip fractionally down the slope of his nose. One eyebrow lifted as he regarded her with a degree of quizzical humour. 'Yet you slipped and injured yourself.'

'It's the effect you have on people,' she declared with wicked mockery.

'People?'

'They either covet your company or choose to avoid it.'

'That's a particularly basic observation,' he said lazily. 'Would you care to elaborate?'

Her response was a succinct negative, and a husky chuckle emerged from his throat as she quickened her pace to step ahead of him.

The trees provided excellent shade, and did much to reduce the sun's heat. It was a lovely day, a beautiful island, and given different circumstances she would have considered herself in seventh heaven to be here alone with Sloane.

'Suppose you enlighten me as to precisely which verbal exchange, if not by whom, caused you so much grief?'

She drew in a deep breath and released it slowly. 'You don't give up, do you?'

'No.'

Whatever had made her think that he would? 'There's no point.'

'I beg to differ.'

She was mercilessly vengeful. 'I wasn't born into the social hierarchy.' She held up one hand, fingers extended, ready to provide a graphic example by ticking off each one as she cited the given reasons. 'No private schooling. At least, not at one of the few élite establishments. My mother still *works*, would you believe?' She was on a roll. 'How could someone like me dare to think she could compete with the *crème de la crème* of Sydney's society? For you to have a fling with me was quite acceptable, but marriage? *Never.*'

It was impossible to gauge anything from his expression. Dammit, didn't he care how each criticism had been like a finely honed barb that had speared through her heart? *Why* didn't he say anything?

'Your response was no doubt interesting.'

His drawled amusement set her teeth on edge, and she glared at him balefully when he brushed his knuckles across one cheekbone.

'I took the line of least resistance, smiled sweetly and assured her you kept me because I was incredibly good in bed.'

It was *he* who possessed incredible skill, *she* who became a willing wanton at his slightest touch.

'And the rest of it?'

'What makes you think there's more?'

'I can't imagine you taking notice of a few bitchy remarks.'

Verbal threats hadn't worried her. Written missives were something else entirely.

'I received an anonymous note in the mail.'

His eyes sharpened, and there was a still quality about him she found disquieting. 'What type of note?'

'Plain paper with an assemblage of cut-out letters from various news publications.'

'Pasted together and worded to say?'

'I had two days to get out of your life.' Even now she could recall it so vividly.

'Or?'

'I would be sorry.'

A muscle bunched at the edge of his jaw, and a string of pithy oaths escaped in husky condemnation. 'Why in hell didn't you tell me?'

'Because I didn't take it seriously.'

He barely restrained himself from shaking her. 'Something obviously occurred to persuade you otherwise?'

A few isolated incidents which had at first seemed coincidental. Except for one. And her mistake had been an attempt to deal with it herself.

'Suzanne.' Sloane's voice was too quiet. Ominous.

She suppressed a shiver, and held his gaze. 'I was driving home after work, and someone tried to run me off the road, then demonstrated very graphically that the next time I wouldn't be so fortunate.' She paused, and drew in a deep breath. 'It was followed by a personal confrontation demanding I get out of your life.'

'Why in *hell* didn't you tell me?'

She didn't flinch at the icy viciousness of his tone. 'You were away at the time.'

He was hard-pressed not to shake her within an inch of her life. 'That shouldn't have stopped you.'

Her eyes assumed an angry sparkle. 'And what could you have done?'

'Taken the next flight back.'

Knowing the importance of his London-based client and the seriousness of the case...

'Believe it,' Sloane assured her inflexibly.

'I dealt with it myself.'

'How, precisely?'

'Assuring her a full report would be lodged with the police and followed by legal action if I ever heard from her again.' Her eyes were dark crystalline sapphire, her features pale. 'Or if another suspicious accident should eventuate.'

And removing herself from his apartment, and to all intents and purposes from his life. Choosing not to confide in him, or seek external help. The silent rage deep within him intensified. Putting him through hell, not to mention herself.

Now, there was only one question.

'Who?' His tone hadn't altered, but she recognised the anger beneath the surface. And his immense effort to control it.

'It's my decision not to name her.'

His eyes held a ruthlessness that was frightening. Merciless, almost brutal with intent. 'It isn't your decision to make.'

He was a formidable force, but she refused to back down. 'Yes, it is.'

'You're aware I can override you? Initiate enquiries, and eventually obtain the answer I need?'

Her gaze didn't falter. 'To what end? What charges can you lay? I wasn't molested, or hurt.' Just very badly shaken by a vindictive woman who should have been seeking professional help for a sick obsession.

'Harassment constitutes a threat that, proven, is punishable by law.' His eyes were so dark they resembled obsidian shards.

'I'm as much aware of that as you are.' Her resolve was determined. 'Her father has a very high profile which would be irreparably damaged should this come out. It's out of my respect for him that I've chosen to keep quiet.'

He held onto control by a bare thread, and wondered if she knew just how close he was to full-blown anger. Twelve inches less in height and half his weight didn't diminish her stance in comparison to his own. Nor did she reflect any fear. Just steadfast intent that would be difficult to bend. But not impossible.

'You disappoint me.'

She was already ahead of him, for she'd had weeks to prepare for this moment. 'A psychological shift into skilled tactician mode, Sloane?' Her chin tilted fractionally. 'Don't waste your time. Or attempt to persuade me that *love conquers all*. We're heavily into reality, not fantasy. That combination is immiscible.'

'You want *reality*, Suzanne?'

His head lowered down to hers, his breath warm as it fanned her lips before his mouth settled over hers in a kiss that tore at the foundations of her being.

In an imitation of the sexual act itself, his tongue teased hers in a mating dance so evocatively persuasive that her bones seemed to liquefy, and she lifted her arms and held on as her body instinctively arched into his.

One arm curved across her back, while a hand tangled in her hair, holding her head fast as he deepened the kiss into something so incredibly erotic she lost track of time and place.

Her skin felt alive, each sensory nerve-ending so acutely attuned to this one man's touch that she groaned out loud as one hand cupped her bottom and he lifted her up against his body so that his mouth could pay homage to the slope of her neck, the soft hollows at the base of her throat, before tracing a path to the delicate curve of her breast.

She was incapable of offering any protest as he pulled up her top and undid the clip fastening of her bikini bra, nor when he pushed the thin Lycra aside and sought one rosy peak, taking it into his mouth and suckling it until she cried out at the wealth of sensation that swept through her body.

It wasn't enough, not nearly enough. And her hands clung to his deeply muscled shoulders, then slid down his chest in a tactile exploration of the dark whorls of hair stretching from one male nipple to the other.

She felt the flex of sinew beneath the pads of her fingers as she slid her hands over his ribcage to the back of his waist, slipped beneath the elasticated band of his shorts, then curved low over tensely muscled buttocks to hold him close.

His arousal was a potent entity, a powerfully male shaft pressing against the softness of her belly.

An anguished moan escaped her lips as his hand slid beneath her shorts and bikini briefs and teased the soft curling hair at the apex of her thighs, and she cried out as he sought and found the damp folds guarding entrance to her feminine core.

A touch was all it took. *His* touch. And she climbed a mental wall as he stroked the highly sensitised folds, sending her mindless with a desire so strong it was almost too much to bear.

Her whole body seemed to throb as acute sensation

took possession of every nerve-ending, and the blood pulsed through her veins to a quickened beat as awareness transcended onto a higher plane.

Sloane knew he could take her now, here, and she wouldn't stop him. It would be so easy, the act so primal, so intensely satisfying, it took all his strength not to take the final step that would make it happen.

He felt the damp heat of her climax, exulted in her soft, throaty cries, the warm savagery of her mouth on his as she lost herself to him with stunning completeness.

Slowly, gradually, Suzanne became aware of where she was and with whom. And what had almost transpired.

Warmth coloured her cheeks, and he watched as her eyes darkened, then became shadowed as long lashes swept down to form a protective veil.

She didn't struggle as he allowed her to slip down to her feet, and he saw a lump form and rise in her throat, only to fall as her mouth worked silently in an effort to form a few words.

'Don't,' Sloane cautioned gently, and pressed a forefinger to her lips. 'What we share is more powerful than mere sexual gratification.' His eyes darkened, and became almost black. '*That* is the reality I have no intention of abandoning.' His finger slid to the corner of her mouth, then traced the curve of her jaw.

He smiled, a soft, slightly humorous, warm curve of his mouth that melted every bone in her body. 'Until the day you can look at me and say the love isn't there any more. Then…' he paused, and depressed her lower lip with one forefinger '…I might listen to you.'

Suzanne felt as ambivalent as a feather floating in a fragile breeze. Surely he didn't—couldn't be implying what she thought he meant?

'Shall we head back?'

Her lips parted, then closed again. 'Sloane, I don't think—'

'You want to stay here?'

Oh, God, no. She didn't dare. To risk a repeat of the past—how long? Ten, twenty minutes? A slight shiver shook her slim shoulders as she remembered with vivid clarity just how deep her involvement had been.

Total wipe-out, she accorded silently. If she allowed him to kiss, *touch* her again, she would be reduced to begging for the wildness of total consummation. And that was a divine madness she could ill afford if she was to walk away from this weekend with her dignity intact.

Sloane watched the fleeting emotions chase across her expressive features, and interpreted each and every one of them.

He extended his hand, and she took it, all too aware of the way he curled her fingers within the enveloping warmth of his own.

They followed the path along its winding curve through the rainforest until it took a steady downward slant to the beach adjacent to the main complex. Their conversation was, as if by tacit consent, confined to inconsequential subjects unrelated to family or anything personal.

It was, Suzanne determined from a quick glance

at her watch, almost five. Allowing thirty minutes to shower and wash her hair, then dress for dinner, she had half an hour to spare.

'Want to try out the pool?'

Had he guessed she was hesitant to return to their villa? Determined the reason why?

Tension created knots inside her stomach, and a tiny bubble of faintly hysterical laughter rose in her throat. She was fast becoming an emotional mess. A wicked irony considering she was almost entirely to blame.

It was the *almost* part that bothered her most. Sloane's participation couldn't be ignored, and she could only wonder why. The convenience of casual sex for old times' sake? An attempt to show her what she was missing?

Somehow neither reason seemed to fit the man, and introspection didn't help at all.

Suzanne turned towards Sloane with a brilliant smile. 'Why not?' Suiting words to action, she moved towards the tiled surround area bordering the pool, shrugged off her shirt and shorts, and executed a neat dive.

The water was deliciously cool, and she stroked several lengths with leisurely ease before turning onto her back and allowing her body to float at will.

She could close her eyes and shut out the world. It was so quiet, it was almost possible to believe that everything was right, and here on this idyllic island they were inviolate from the pressures of business and social obligations. No one could get to them, unless they chose to allow it. Paradise, she mused.

A splash sounded loud in the stillness, and seconds later a dark head surfaced a short distance from her own.

'Sleeping in water isn't a good idea,' Sloane drawled, flicking cool, salty droplets onto her midriff.

'I wasn't asleep.'

'First one out gets exclusive use of the shower.' He lifted a hand and trailed idle fingers across her cheek. 'Unless you feel inclined to share?'

Heat suffused her body and pooled deep within, a sensual flaring over which she had no control.

Suzanne caught his dark, gleaming gaze, glimpsed the faint curl of humour tilt the edge of his mouth. Dammit, he was enjoying this.

She offered him a languid smile. 'Do I get a head start?'

His mouth widened and showed his even white teeth. 'I'm feeling generous.'

She jackknifed into racing position. 'First one out, huh?'

She was a strong swimmer, but Sloane had the superior advantage of height and male power. They reached the pool's tiled edge together, and in one synchronised movement levered themselves up onto its perimeter.

'A perfect finish,' Sloane accorded with indolent amusement as he rose to his feet, watching as she smoothed back the streaming length of her hair while matching her movements with his own.

Suzanne bent to collect her clothes. 'Now why doesn't that surprise me?'

'No shared shower, I take it?'

Her fingers stilled at the sudden graphic image, then

shook slightly as she thrust first one arm into a sleeve of her shirt, then the other. 'In your dreams, Sloane.'

'That's the problem—they're remarkably vivid.' His voice was silk-soft and dangerous. 'What about yours?'

Glorious Technicolor complete with sound and emotional effects.

Without a further word she turned and stepped quickly towards the path leading to their villa, uncaring whether he followed her or not, grateful that she'd had the foresight to pick up the duplicate key on their way out.

Inside she made straight for the upper level, collected fresh underwear and a silk robe, then entered the *en suite*.

She set the temperature dial to warm, stripped off her clothes, then stepped beneath the cascade of water.

Ten minutes later she emerged into the bedroom, a towel wound turban-fashion around her hair, to discover Sloane in the process of selecting casual trousers and shirt.

'Finished?'

He'd discarded his shirt, if in fact he'd opted to put it on when leaving the pool area, and the cotton-knit shorts moulded firm-muscled buttocks, gave credence to the power of his manhood, and accentuated long, heavily muscled thighs. To say nothing of the exposed breadth of chest and shoulder.

Suzanne dragged her eyes away from him. 'I need to use the hair-drier when you're done.' She crossed to the wardrobe and extracted an elegant trouser suit in deep aqua, added matching heeled sandals, and slowly expelled the breath she'd unconsciously held as she heard the *en suite* door close behind him.

Just when she thought she had a handle on which way he would move and when, he did the opposite. If she was of a suspicious mind, she could almost swear he was being deliberately unpredictable.

Suzanne discarded her robe, stepped into the trouser suit, then slid her feet into the sandals, and reached for her make-up bag, only to realise she'd left it in the bathroom earlier.

Damn. What would be Sloane's reaction if she invaded his privacy? After all, it wouldn't be anything new. They'd shared a lot more than a bathroom in the past. Except then the game had been love and they'd been unable to keep their hands off each other.

Whereas now... Now, it was an entirely different ball game. The rules had shifted, and both players had regrouped.

Almost ten minutes later Sloane emerged, showered and freshly shaven, a towel hitched low on his hips.

One eyebrow rose in silent query as he examined her bare complexion. 'Too shy to share the bathroom with me, Suzanne?'

She wanted to hit him. 'You allowed me sole use.'

His husky laughter brought a soft tinge of colour to her cheeks. 'Only because you'd have fought me tooth and nail if I hadn't.' He reached for briefs, loosened the towel, and stepped into them. Trousers followed, and his eyes met hers as he slid home the zip fastener. 'And there isn't enough time to enjoy the fight.' He reached for his shirt and shrugged into it. 'Or its aftermath. If we're to make dinner.'

Anger flared, deepening her colour to a rosy hue, and her eyes assumed the brilliance of dark sapphire. 'There wouldn't *be* an aftermath,' she vouched with unaccustomed vehemence.

His gaze didn't waver for endless seconds, then he conducted a slow, sweeping appraisal of her body.

Suzanne felt as if he touched her. Her skin tingled beneath his probing assessment, and her pulse leapt to a faster beat she was sure had to be visible at the base of her throat. Even her breath seemed to catch, and she had to make a conscious effort to prevent her chest from heaving in tell-tale evidence of his effect on her.

His eyes when they met hers again were dark, faintly mocking and held vague cynicism. 'No?'

Sloane wondered if she knew just how appealing she looked with her hair all damply tousled, her cheeks flushed with an intriguing mix of temper and desire.

It made him want to tumble her down onto the bed and show her, *prove* that what they had together was good. Too good to allow anything or anyone to come between them.

Except afterwards she wouldn't thank him for it, and only hate herself.

He wanted her. Dear heaven, *how* he wanted her. His body ached, painfully, with need. But he was after the long haul, not a short transitory ride.

Suzanne drew herself up to her full height and glared at him balefully. 'If you think that sharing this villa, this *bedroom*, means I'll agree to sex, then you can go to hell!'

Did she imagine he hadn't been there? Ever since the evening he'd entered his apartment and discovered she had gone.

'Go dry your hair, Suzanne. Then I'll take a look at your hand.'

His voice was deceptively quiet, and didn't fool her in the slightest. What she'd perceived as being a dangerous situation had just moved up a notch or two.

Five minutes with the hair-drier was sufficient, a further five took care of her make-up, then she emerged into the bedroom.

Sloane was waiting, standing at the full-length window, and he turned as she crossed the room.

'I have some antiseptic in my wet-pack.'

'It's fine.' She dismissed his offer, and her breath caught as he reached her side. 'Really. There's no need to play nurse.'

'Humour me.'

'This is ridiculous!' Exasperation was a mild word for describing how she felt at being shepherded back into the bathroom, and having her hand examined and dabbed with anti-bacterial solution.

'There. All done,' Sloane said with satisfaction.

'I could easily have done that myself!' She wanted to *hit* him.

'Don't,' he warned with dangerous softness, reading her mind.

'Or you'll do *what*?' she flung, incensed.

'Take all your fine anger,' he threatened in a voice

that was pure silk, 'and ensure you expend it in a way you won't forget.'

Her stomach executed a torturous somersault, and for a few endless seconds she forgot to breathe. 'By displaying masculine strength and sexual superiority?' She managed to keep her voice even. 'I don't find caveman tactics a turn-on.'

His eyes were dark, so impossibly dark she found them unfathomable. 'Make no mistake, Suzanne,' Sloane drawled with hateful cynicism. 'There would be no need for coercion of any kind.'

Tension filled the room, an explosive, dangerous entity just waiting for the trigger to let a certain hell break loose.

With considerable effort she banked down her anger, then she turned towards him and marshalled her voice to an incredibly polite level. 'Shall we leave?'

'Wise, Suzanne,' he taunted silkily.

How long would such wisdom last? she wondered with a sense of desperation. Sooner or later she was going to lose control of her temper. With every hour that passed she could feel the pressure of it building, and she hated him for deliberately stoking the fire.

They walked in silence to the main complex and joined Georgia and Trenton for a drink in the lounge before entering the restaurant.

Dinner was a casual meal eaten alfresco on the terrace, their choice a selection of varied seafood with delicate accompanying sauces. They enjoyed salads, fresh bread brought daily onto the island, and they settled on fresh fruit from a selection of succulent pineapple, cantaloupe, sweet melon, and strawberries, served with a delightful lemon and lime sorbet, for dessert.

They declined coffee, and lingered over tall glasses containing deliciously cool piña colada.

'We thought we might take a walk along the beach,' Trenton declared. 'Care to join us?'

And play gooseberry? 'I've challenged Sloane to a game of tennis,' Suzanne indicated, casting the source of that challenge a singularly sweet smile. 'Haven't I, darling?'

Sloane reached forward and brushed gentle fingers down the length of her bare arm. And smiled as he glimpsed the way her eyes dilated in damnable reaction. 'Indeed. I'll even grant a handicap in your favour.'

'How…' she hesitated fractionally '…kind.' She touched a hand to his, and summoned a doting look. 'Especially when we both know you could run me off the court.'

He didn't miss an opportunity, and his eyes were openly daring as he lifted her hand to his lips and kissed each finger in turn.

'We need to go change first.'

There was hardly any point in saying she'd changed her mind. 'We should wait half an hour.' Her eyes took on a wicked gleam. 'Exercise so soon after a meal isn't advisable.' Her mouth curved into a winsome smile. 'I don't want you to collapse with a heart attack.'

Trenton laughed, and Georgia's eyes twinkled as she rose to her feet. 'I don't think that's likely, darling. Come for a walk with us. That'll fill in some time.'

'Sloane?' Suzanne deferred to him, sparing him a level glance.

'An excellent suggestion, Georgia.' He stood and together they strolled along the path leading down to the beach.

Suzanne slipped off her sandals and held them in one hand, watching as Sloane followed her actions with his shoes, aware that Georgia and Trenton did the same.

It was a beautiful evening, the sky a deep indigo with a clear moon and a sprinkle of stars. The sort of night for lovers, Suzanne perceived as she stepped onto the sand and felt its firm crunch beneath her feet.

There wasn't much she could do about the hard, masculine arm that curved along the back of her waist as they formed a foursome and began following the gentle curve of the bay.

'Do you have everything ready for tomorrow, Mama?' Suzanne queried, conscious of the man who walked at her side. The arm that bound her to him would tighten if she attempted to put some distance between them. For a moment she almost considered it, simply for the sake of enforcing her position, only to discard it as she thought of the consequences.

'Yes.' Georgia cast her a warm glance in the semi-darkness. 'Although I probably won't sleep tonight as I go through everything again and again in my mind.'

'I have a remedy for that,' Trenton declared, and Georgia laughed.

'Perhaps we'll join you later for a game of tennis. How long do you intend to play?'

'I'll leave it up to Suzanne,' Sloane drawled, and she

turned towards him with a sweet smile that was lost in the fading light.

'Passing the buck, darling? What if I'm feeling particularly energetic?' As soon as the words left her mouth she wanted to curse herself for uttering them.

'I think I can match you.'

In more ways than one. Silence, she decided, was golden. Something she intended to observe unless anyone asked her a specific question.

The ocean resembled a dark mass that merged with the sky. There were no visible lights, no silvery path reflected from a low-set moon. Tonight it rose high, a clear milk-white orb in the galaxy.

Suzanne felt the increased pressure of Sloane's fingers at the edge of her waist, and a tiny spiral of sensation unfurled inside her stomach.

'I think we'll turn back,' Sloane declared, drawing to a halt. 'If we don't see you on the court, we'll meet for breakfast. Eight, or earlier?'

'Eight,' Trenton agreed. 'Enjoy.'

As soon as they had progressed out of earshot Suzanne broke free from Sloane's grasp. Lights were visible through the trees, and as they drew close the main complex came into view.

Within minutes they reached their villa, and indoors she quickly changed into shorts and a top, added socks and trainers, aware that Sloane was doing likewise.

Securing the court wasn't a problem, because there were no other guests to compete with. The hiring of racquets and balls was achieved in minutes, and Suzanne preceded Sloane into the enclosure.

CHAPTER SIX

'ONE SET, or two?'

'Two,' Suzanne declared as she crossed the court and took up her position at its furthest end.

'A practice rally first,' Sloane called. 'Best of three gets to serve. OK?'

'Sure.'

He had the height, the strength and the expertise to defeat her with minimum effort. It was the measure of the man that he chose not to do so in the following hour as she returned one shot after another, won some, lost most, and while it was an uneven match she managed to finish with two games to her credit in the first set and three in the second. A concession, she was sure, that was as deliberate as it was diplomatic.

'Your backhand has improved.'

Suzanne caught the towel he tossed her, and patted the faint film of sweat from her face and neck. He, damn him, didn't show any visible sign of exertion. Not a drop of sweat, and he was breathing as evenly as if he'd just taken a leisurely walk in the park.

'I expected your serve to singe the ball.'

Sloane's eyes gleamed with latent humour. 'Were you disappointed that it didn't?'

Expending physical energy had been a good idea. The heat was there, but banked down to a level she could deal with.

'You played as I expected you to,' she responded sweetly, and waited a beat. 'Like a gentleman.'

He rubbed the towel over the back of his neck, and sent her a musing smile. 'Ah, a mark in my favour.'

'Are we keeping score?'

'Believe it.'

Why did she get the instinctive feeling he had his own hidden agenda?

Her agenda was to survive the weekend with her emotions intact. *His* she could only guess at.

'Let's get a drink from the bar, shall we?' Sloane suggested smoothly.

A diversionary tactic which Suzanne let pass only because she was thirsty.

It was an unexpected surprise, and a welcome one, to see Georgia and Trenton seated comfortably at a table adjacent to the well-stocked bar. Surprise, because she'd thought not to see them again before breakfast, and the welcome part was a definite plus, for it meant she wasn't alone with Sloane.

'We thought we'd join you for a game of doubles,' Georgia said as Suzanne slid into a seat at her mother's side.

'Georgia's idea,' Trenton drawled with amused resignation. 'I had another form of exercise in mind.'

'Don't tease, darling. You'll embarrass the children.'

Children? Suzanne looked at Georgia in keen surprise. Those beautiful eyes the colour of her own bore a faintly wicked gleam that promised much to the man seated at her side. Loving sex without artifice, a joyous sharing and caring.

Suzanne felt a lump rise in her throat at the latent emotion evident, and she took a generous sip from the tall glass of iced water a waiter had placed in front of her only moments before.

She risked a glance at Sloane and glimpsed his wry amusement. 'The *children*, of course,' she ventured conversationally, 'are less likely to score a handsome win after expending their energy on court.'

Trenton sent her a devilish smile. 'Georgia and I need any advantage we can get.'

'So sharing a drink is seen as a five-minute break for refreshment?'

'Definitely.'

'Of course, we're playing two sets?'

'One,' Trenton decreed.

'In that case,' Sloane drawled, collecting his racquet as he rose to his feet, 'let's get started.'

Father and son chose not to play competitively, and Georgia and Suzanne were fairly evenly matched. It was a lot of fun. Suzanne couldn't remember ever seeing her mother appear so brilliantly alive, or so happy.

After an hour and a narrow win in Suzanne and Sloane's favour, they exited the floodlit court and crossed to the lounge bar.

Trenton led the way, his arm curved round Georgia's

shoulders, and there was little Suzanne could do about the casual arm Sloane placed at her waist.

'A cool drink?' Trenton suggested as they selected a table and sank down into individual chairs. 'Or would you prefer an Irish coffee?'

It was after ten when Trenton and Georgia got to their feet.

'We'll see you at breakfast. Eight o'clock,' Trenton said. He clasped Georgia's hand in his and brought it up to his lips with a warm intimacy. Suzanne felt her heart flip with something she refused to acknowledge as envy.

'Want to follow them, or stay here for a while?'

Suzanne spared Sloane a considering glance from beneath her long-fringed lashes. 'We could take a walk in the moonlight.'

'A delaying tactic, Suzanne?'

Her lashes swept upwards, and she regarded him with ill-concealed mockery. 'How did you guess?'

'Afraid?' His voice was so quiet it sent shivers down her spine.

That was an understatement. But it was fear of herself that made her reluctant to be alone with him. 'Yes.'

'Such simple honesty,' Sloane said with unmistakable indolence. He rose to his feet and extended his hand. It had been a long day. An even longer night lay ahead.

A swift retort rose to her lips, and remained unuttered. 'It's one of my more admirable traits.' She wanted to take hold of his hand, feel it enclose her own, and bask in the warmth of his intimate smile. Yet to do so would amount to a fine madness of a kind she dared not afford.

'One of many.'

She rose, ignored his outstretched hand, and skirted the table *en route* to the entrance. 'Flattery will get you nowhere.'

He drew level with her. 'Try sincerity.'

She spared him a sideways glance, and chose not to comment. She quickened her step, and felt mildly irritated at the ease with which he lengthened his to match it.

They reached their villa, and inside she crossed the lounge and quickly trod the stairs to the bedroom. She paused only long enough to collect her nightshirt before entering the *en suite*, and carefully closed the door behind her.

A foolish, childish action that nevertheless afforded her a measure of satisfaction. Until it was time to emerge some ten minutes later, when all of the former fire had died and wary apprehension reposed in its place.

Sloane was standing at the window, looking out into the darkness.

'Bathroom's all yours.'

He turned to face her, aware of the moment she'd entered the bedroom via the darkened glass reflection.

She looked about sixteen, her skin scrubbed clean, her hair tied back in a pony-tail. Did she have any idea how sexy she looked in that mid-thigh-length tee shirt? As a cover-up the soft cotton merely moulded her firm breasts and was more provocative than designer silk and lace.

'How's the hand?'

Oh, hell, she'd almost forgotten. 'Fine.'

'And your hip?'

Painful, and showing the promise of a nasty bruise. 'OK.' She moved towards the bed she'd nominated as her own, turned back the cover, and slid between the sheets. 'Goodnight.'

'Sweet dreams, Suzanne.'

She didn't care for the mocking humour in his voice, and as soon as the bathroom door closed behind him she propped herself up on one hand and plumped the pillow vigorously with the other, then she shifted onto her left side and almost groaned out loud as her bruised hip came into contact with the mattress.

She was tired, and, if she closed her eyes and willed herself to believe she was comfortable, surely she should sleep.

Suzanne heard the shower run, then stop minutes later. The bathroom door opened, a shaft of light illuminated the room, then there was darkness, the soft pad of Sloane's feet on the polished floorboards as he crossed to the bed, the faint slither of cotton percale, and the almost inaudible depression of mattress springs settling beneath a solid male frame.

Despite counting imaginary sheep and practising various relaxing techniques, Suzanne found sleep remained elusive.

Her hip ached. Throbbed, she corrected, deep into

specific analysis in the darkness of night. Pain-killers would dull the pain's keen edge and help her sleep.

If only she had some. Maybe there was a foil strip in her vanity bag, or, failing that, it was possible Sloane had some in his wet-pack.

Damn, damn, *damn*. If she lay wide awake for much longer, she'd be in a fine state by the end of Georgia and Trenton's wedding festivities.

You would think, she ruefully decided as she slid carefully from the bed, that an over-abundance of emotional and nervous tension together with long walks, rock-clambering, and three sets of tennis, would fell the fittest of the physically fit.

Instead, she felt as if she'd trebled a daily dose of caffeine.

Suzanne crept to the bathroom, closed the door, then switched on the light and rummaged through her vanity bag to no avail. Her fingers delved into Sloane's wet-pack, hesitated, then, driven more by need than courtesy, she separated compartments and almost cried out with relief when she discovered a slim pack of paracetamol.

She broke off two, part-filled a glass with water and swallowed them, then she replaced the glass and switched off the light. She'd allow a few seconds for her eyes to adjust, then she'd open the door and tiptoe back to bed.

It was a remarkably simple plan. Except in attempting to give Sloane's bed a wide berth she veered too far and brushed against a chair.

A soft curse fell from her lips at the same time Sloane activated the bed-lamp.

'What in sweet hell are you doing?'

Suzanne threw him a dark glance, and resorted to flippancy. 'Rearranging the furniture.'

He slid into a sitting position and leaned against the headboard. His dark hair was slightly tousled and he was bare to the waist.

Probably bare beneath the waist as well, she reflected a trifle ruefully, all too aware of his penchant for sleeping nude.

It was too much. *He* was too much.

'You should have turned on the light.'

Oh, sure. The last thing she'd wanted to do was to wake him. Coping with a darkly brooding male wasn't a favoured option.

Suzanne pushed in the chair and took the few steps necessary to reach her bed, then slid carefully between the sheets.

'Headache?'

She should have known he wouldn't leave it alone. The look she cast him held such fulsome anger it was a wonder he didn't *burn*. *'Yes.'* In this instance she had no compunction in resorting to fabrication.

'Want me to give you a neck and scalp massage?'

Oh, God. 'No.' Would he detect the faint desperation in her voice? She hoped not. 'Thank you.'

'Seduction isn't part of the deal,' he drawled with musing cynicism, and she closed her eyes, then opened them again.

He read her far too easily, and it rankled unbearably. 'Well, now, that's a relief,' she said with pseudo-sweetness.

'Unless you want it to be,' Sloane added with killing softness.

The thought of that hard male body curved over her own in a tasting, teasing supplication of each and every pleasure spot filled her with such intense longing it was all she could do to respond, let alone keep her voice even.

'If you come anywhere near me,' she warned in a tense whisper, 'I'll render you serious bodily harm.'

His husky chuckle further enraged her. 'It might almost be worth it.'

Without thought Suzanne picked up the spare pillow and threw it at him, watching in seemingly slow motion as he fielded it and unhurriedly tossed the bed-covers aside.

'Dammit—don't.' She turned and scrambled to the furthest side of the bed, only to give a sharp cry as her hip dragged painfully against the mattress.

It was no contest. She simply didn't have a chance as Sloane's hands caught hold of her shoulders and turned her back to face him.

For a long moment she gazed at him in open defiance, aware that the slightest move, the faintest word would invite crushing retribution.

His eyes were impossibly dark, their depths unfathomable as he reached for the edge of the bedcovers and wrenched them off with one powerful pull of his hand, then drew her down onto the mattress.

His head lowered and she felt one hand grasp hold of her thigh, then slide to her hip.

Her gasp of pain was very real, and he paused, his mouth only inches from her own. She saw his eyes narrow, glimpsed the tiny lines fanning out from each outer edge, and felt him tense for a few long seconds before he slid the hem of her nightshirt to her waist.

It was a long bruise, red, purpling, and growing more ugly with every hour.

He swore, words she'd never heard him use before, and she flinched as he traced the line of her hip-bone, then probed the surrounding flesh.

'You walked through the rainforest,' Sloane said with deadly softness, 'played three sets of tennis, nursing *this*?'

'It didn't hurt much then.'

His eyes appeared as dark obsidian shards, infinitely forbidding. 'It does now.' He levered himself off the bed and descended the stairs to the lower floor.

She heard the chink of glass, the bar-fridge door close, then he was back with a chilled half-bottle in his hand.

'What are you doing?'

'Applying the equivalent of an ice-pack.'

'A magnum of champagne?' Suzanne queried in disbelief, and shivered as the cold frosted glass touched her skin.

'It'll serve the purpose. Now, lie still.'

She didn't plan on moving. Besides, fighting him would prove a futile exercise.

'What did you find to take in the bathroom?'

'Paracetamol,' she said huskily as he adjusted the bottle. 'Two. In your wet-pack,' she added. An icy numbness settled in, minimising the pain, and she closed her eyes so she didn't have to look at him.

The proximity of his male body was a heady entity, despite the skimpy black silk briefs providing a modicum of decency. As a concession to her?

She could smell the clean scent of expensive soap and male deodorant on skin only inches away from her own. All her senses were acutely attuned, almost in recognition of a rare and special alchemy existent in two separate halves that were meant to make a perfect whole.

It didn't make sense. Nothing made sense.

The pain slowly ebbed, and her eyelids grew heavy. Gentle fingers soothed, kneaded, and dispensed with the tight knots in the muscles of her shoulders, back and thighs.

Heaven, she acknowledged as she relaxed and let him work his magic. She made only a token protest when he lifted her into his arms and transferred her to the other bed.

His bed. Her eyes sprang open, and she made to scramble to the edge as he climbed in beside her.

'I don't think this is a good idea,' she said helplessly as he curved an arm beneath her shoulders and drew her close.

'Just shut up and let it be.' He pillowed her head against his chest, then curled an arm round her waist.

He was deliciously warm, and she cautiously moved one arm so that it rested across his midriff.

It was like coming home. *Déjà vu*, she reflected.

With one exception. Lacking was the satiation of love-making.

The temptation to begin a tactile exploration was strong. Just the slight movement of her fingers and she could trace the outline of his ribcage, tease one brown nipple, then trail a path to his navel.

He possessed a strong-boned frame, with symmetrical muscle structure, textured skin that emanated its own musky male aroma. Clean and slick with sweat at the height of sexual possession, it became an aphrodisiac that drove her wild. Sensual heat, raw and primal. As primitive as the man himself.

Don't even think about it, an inner voice cautioned. Unless you want to dice with dynamite.

Soon he'd fall asleep, then she'd gradually ease free and slip into her own bed.

It was the last coherent thought she had, and she woke to find warm sunshine filtering through the curtains, the smell of fresh coffee teasing her nostrils. One quick glance was all it took to determine she was alone in the bed. Another to see Sloane's broad back curved over a newspaper spread out on the buffet bar.

At that precise moment he turned towards her, almost as if he was acutely attuned to her every move, and his warm smile melted her bones.

'Good morning.'

Suzanne felt awkward, sleep-rumpled, and she dragged a hand over her tousled hair. 'Hi.'

He had the advantage, dressed and freshly shaven, and she watched him step from the stool and cross to the edge of the bed. 'How is the bruise?'

She caught hold of the sheet in a compulsive movement, almost as if she expected him to insist on a personal inspection. She flexed her leg. 'It doesn't seem to hurt as much.'

'Want to try another makeshift ice-pack?'

In the clear light of day, she didn't want to be beholden to him in any way. *Too late.* You slept with him, remember? *Sleep* being the operative word…but how much more *beholden* could you get?

'I doubt it's necessary,' Suzanne said quickly. Thinking on her feet seemed a vast improvement to staying in bed, and she managed it in one dignified movement. *Dignity* was the key, she assured herself, and being dressed would be better than wandering around in an over-large tee shirt.

She collected underwear, tailored cream linen trousers and a light cotton top *en route* to the *en suite*, emerging ten minutes later feeling refreshed after a quick shower. And in control. Well, she corrected wryly, as much in control as she could hope for in the circumstances!

Sloane checked his watch. 'It's almost eight. If you're ready, we'll go down to the restaurant.'

Lipstick was all it would take, and perhaps a light touch of blusher. 'Give me a minute.'

Georgia and Trenton were already seated beneath the large airy veranda when Suzanne and Sloane arrived.

'We went for a walk along the beach. It was so quiet and peaceful. Heaven,' Georgia enthused warmly.

Suzanne caught the sparkle in her mother's eyes, glimpsed the soft curve of her mouth as she smiled, and deduced that while the island possessed a magic all its own, *heaven* to Georgia was the man at her side.

'No pre-wedding nerves?' she queried teasingly as she accepted the waitress's offer to fill her cup with coffee.

'A few,' her mother conceded. 'Last-minute doubts about what I've chosen to wear for the ceremony. Whether my heels are too high, and hoping I'll remember to tread carefully so as not to trip. And whether I should wear the hat the salesgirl insisted was just perfect.' Her mouth shook slightly, then widened into a helpless smile. 'I can't decide whether to wear a bright lipstick or go for something pale.'

Suzanne looked at Trenton and grinned. 'Ah, serious stuff, huh?'

He spread his hands wide and responded with an easy smile. 'My assurance that I don't give a damn what she wears doesn't appear to hold much weight.'

'The mysterious vagaries of the female mind,' Sloane remarked, and met Suzanne's mocking glare with gleaming humour.

'Men,' Suzanne denounced him, 'simply have no idea.' She shot her mother a stunning smile. 'After we finish here, I'll come and give you my considered opinion, shall I?'

'Oh, darling. Please. I'd be so grateful.'

'You can safely say goodbye to a few hours,' Sloane inferred aloud to his father, and Suzanne couldn't suppress the bubble of laughter that emerged from her throat.

'At least.' And was totally unprepared for the brush

of his fingers across one cheek, and the warm intimacy of his smile.

'Then I suggest we go eat, so you can get started.'

Why, when she lapsed into a comfort zone, did he do something to jolt her out of it? Her eyes clouded. It's an act, just an act. For Georgia and Trenton's benefit.

The breakfast smorgasbord was a delight, comprising several varieties of cereal, fresh fruit, yoghurt, as well as croissants and toast. Sausages, steak, eggs, hash-browns, mushrooms. A veritable feast.

It was almost nine when they emerged into the sunshine, and the two men opted to retire to the lounge on the pretext of discussing business, while Suzanne and Georgia made their way to the villa Georgia shared with Trenton.

The design was identical to that of their own villa, although the soft furnishings were different, Suzanne noticed as they entered the air-conditioned interior.

Georgia crossed the lounge. 'Come upstairs, darling.'

Suzanne followed and stood to one side as her mother opened the wardrobe, the drawers, and reverently draped each item of apparel over the bed.

'Let's do the fashion parade thing,' Suzanne suggested, shaking her head as Georgia wrinkled her nose. 'It's the only way I can get the complete picture.'

Fifteen minutes later Suzanne stood back and expressed her admiration. 'Perfect. Everything.'

'Even the hat?'

'Especially the hat,' she assured her mother. 'It's stunning.'

Georgia's eyes moistened with gratitude. 'Do you really think so?'

'Really.'

Suzanne stood still, her head tilted to one side as she regarded the slim, beautiful woman in front of her. 'Now, let's take off the hat, get rid of the shoes, and we'll try each lipstick and decide which one suits best.'

The deep rose, definitely. Pale was too pale, and the coral too bright.

'OK,' Suzanne declared as Georgia carefully divested herself of her wedding suit, and hung it back on padded hangers beneath its protective bag. 'All done.' She grinned, and caught hold of her mother's hands. 'You're going to knock 'em dead.'

A warm smile tugged the edges of Georgia's mouth. 'How nice of you to say so, darling.' She drew a deep breath. 'Now, shall we have a cold drink, and talk girl-talk?' A light laugh spilled out, and her eyes danced. 'Isn't that what the prospective bride and her maid of honour are supposed to do?'

Suzanne fetched a bottle of mineral water from the bar-fridge, poured the contents into two glasses and handed one to her mother.

'Here's to health and happiness. A wonderful day. A wonderful life,' she added gently.

Georgia touched the rim of Suzanne's glass in silent acknowledgement. 'You, too, sweetheart.'

They each took an appreciative sip. 'It'll be nice that we'll be living in the same city,' Georgia said a trifle wistfully. 'I can meet you for lunch. We'll attend a lot of the same functions, too, I imagine. And we'll be able to shop together.'

An arrow of pain pierced Suzanne's stomach. The lunch and the shopping part were fine, but attending the same social functions wouldn't be a good idea. In all probability Sloane would be there, and she would rather die than have to watch him with another woman at his side.

'Tell me where you're staying in Paris.' The honeymoon was a safe topic. 'The shops there are supposed to be marvellous. The Eiffel Tower,' she enthused. 'Make sure you take plenty of photos, and write up a diary. I want to hear everything.'

Georgia laughed. 'Not quite everything, darling.'

Suzanne's eyes danced with impish humour. 'Well, no, I guess not.'

Her mother possessed a rare integrity. And charm. Something that came from the heart. Trenton Wilson-Willoughby was a very fortunate man. But then, she guessed he knew that. It explained why he wanted his ring on Georgia's finger without delay.

'Do you remember when we lived in St Lucia in Brisbane?' Georgia reminisced. 'That adorable little terrace house?'

'And the cat who called both adjoining houses *home*?' Suzanne queried, laughing. 'We fed him mince for breakfast, the man next door gave him fresh fish for lunch, and dear old Mrs Simmons dished out tinned salmon for his tea. He was such a gorgeous bundle of grey fluff.'

The school years, carefree for the most part, with increasing study as she decided on the legal fraternity as her profession. University, law school. Dating. Friends.

Hers had been a happy childhood, despite the lack of a father-figure, and there were many memories to cherish. She and Georgia were so close, *friends* and equals rather than mother and daughter. They had shared so much.

And now it was going to change. Don't go down that path, Suzanne mentally chided herself. Today was meant to be happy, joyous.

CHAPTER SEVEN

THE LAUNCH DEPOSITED the wedding guests, together with the photographer and celebrant, each of whom had undergone a security check at Dunk Island before boarding the chartered launch to ensure no unwanted media were able to intrude.

Suzanne could only admire Trenton's determination that their weekend sojourn, and particularly the wedding itself, remain a strictly private affair.

There would be time for the guests to check into their respective villas, enjoy a leisurely lunch, and explore Bedarra's facilities before assembling next to the main complex for an outdoor marriage ceremony.

Trenton and Sloane joined the guests in the restaurant for lunch, while Georgia and Suzanne ate a light salad together in Georgia's villa.

It ensured there was plenty of time for them to style their hair, complete their make-up, then dress.

Georgia was ready ahead of time, looking lovely, if slightly nervous. Suzanne gave her mother's hand a reassuring squeeze, then quickly stepped into the elegant pale blue silk slip-dress she'd chosen to wear.

There was a matching jacket and shoes, and she opted to leave her hair loose. Make-up was kept to a minimum, except for skilful application of eyeshadow and mascara, and she selected a clear rose lipstick to add colour.

Then she spared her watch a quick glance. 'This is it.' She cast her mother an impish grin. 'Are you OK?' There was no need to ask if there were any last-minute doubts.

Georgia smiled a trifle shakily. 'In half an hour, I'll be fine.'

Suzanne crossed to tuck a hand beneath her mother's elbow. 'Then let's get this show on the road, shall we?'

The short walk to the main complex was achieved in minutes. Georgia didn't falter as she crossed the lawn to where Sloane stood waiting at the head of a stretch of red carpet dividing three small rows of seated guests and leading to an artistically decorated archway, where Trenton waited with the celebrant.

Suzanne felt her breath catch as Sloane turned towards her with a slow, warm smile, then he took Georgia's hand in his and walked her down the carpeted aisle.

Suzanne followed, and when they reached the archway she moved to Sloane's side as Trenton took hold of Georgia's hand.

Glorious sunshine, the merest hint of a soft breeze, and a small gathering of immediate family and close friends assembled on an idyllic island resort. What more could a bride ask for?

Nothing, if Georgia's radiant expression was anything to go by, Suzanne decided, unable to still a faint stirring of wistful envy.

Her mother looked beautiful, and much younger than her forty-seven years as she stood at Trenton's side while the celebrant intoned the words of the marriage ceremony.

Georgia's response was clear, Trenton's deep and meaningful, and his incredibly gentle kiss at the close of the ceremony tugged Suzanne's heartstrings.

She moved forward to congratulate and hug them both, and the faint shimmer of tears in Georgia's eyes was reflected in her own.

Sloane did the unexpected and kissed Suzanne briefly, but hard, and the pressure of his mouth on hers sent her lashes sweeping wide in silent disapproval.

His answering smile didn't come close in explanation, and she stood at his side, almost *anchored* there as they greeted guests, made social small talk, and accepted the occasional gushing compliment about the happiness of the bride and groom.

The encroaching dusk meant everyone moved indoors, and it was essentially *smile* time. In fact, Suzanne smiled so much and so often, her facial muscles began to ache from sheer effort.

'You're doing well,' Sloane drawled as she took a further sip from her flute of champagne.

'Why, thank you, darling. *Wonderfully* well is what I'm aiming for.'

'And a hair's breadth from overkill.'

She cast him a stunning glance. 'No more than anyone else. Even as we speak, deals are being implemented by two of the country's top business moguls.' Her eyes sparkled wickedly. 'Their respective second wives are at daggers drawn beneath the soph isticated façade as they size up *who* is wearing the more expensive designer outfit.'

'Second and third wife,' Sloane corrected, and she inclined her head in mocking acceptance.

'Sandrine Lanier and Bettina—?' She arched her eyebrows speculatively. 'Just *who* in Sydney's social élite tied the knot with Bettina?'

He lowered his head and brushed his lips against her temple. 'Cynicism doesn't suit you.'

'Ah, but given the right context it can be fun,' she declared solemnly.

'Sandrine works very hard at being the successful wife.'

It was true. The former actress was delightful, and devoted herself tirelessly to charitable causes. She was also an excellent hostess who enjoyed entertaining her husband's business associates. Michel Lanier was a very fortunate man.

Bettina, however, fell into an entirely different category. The glamorous blonde had frequented every social event Suzanne had attended with Sloane. And had taken great pleasure in flirting with him outrageously at every opportunity. As well as with every wealthy eligible man on the social circuit in a bid to cover her options.

'Just who did Bettina choose?' There could be no doubt on that issue!

'Frank Kahler. They married two weeks ago.'

She didn't need to ask. 'You attended the wedding.'

'Yes.' Sloane's acquiescence held a certain wryness for the occasion that had been far too over the top to be described as being in good taste.

What excuse had he given for her absence?

'You were visiting your mother in Brisbane for the weekend.'

Suzanne looked at him, and glimpsed the fine lines fanning out from the corners of his eyes, then her gaze travelled to the vertical crease slashing each cheek, the wide, sensual mouth, and the strong set of his jaw.

'Feasible, in the circumstances, wouldn't you say?'

Very feasible, she silently agreed. 'You could easily have admitted our relationship was over.'

'Now why would I do that?'

'Because it was. *Is.*'

'No.'

'What do you mean, *no*?'

He leaned forward and brushed his lips against her own, and then he raised his head fractionally. His eyes were dark, and appeared so incredibly deep she became momentarily lost.

Her heart thudded in her chest, and for a split second she forgot to breathe. Then reality kicked in, and she took in a deep, ragged breath, then shakily released it.

'Did you honestly think I'd let it rest on the basis of the explanation you presented to me?' Sloane queried, and saw her eyes dilate with something akin to apprehension, then be replaced with an attempt at humour.

'Impossible, of course, that I might have had a hissy

fit about the number of women who fawn over you, and acted on impulse?'

His lips parted to show even white teeth behind an amused smile. 'A hissy fit?' The edge of his mouth curved. 'Now that's an expression which conjures up an interesting image.'

'Doesn't it just?'

His eyes became even darker, and something moved deep within. Something she dared not define. 'Not your style, Suzanne.'

No, it wasn't. Nor did she act on impulse.

'Nor was your note,' Sloane continued in a dangerously mild voice.

'You *know* why I left,' she said fiercely.

'*Whatever* the motivation, the action was all wrong.'

'Sloane. Suzanne. We need you for photographs.' Trenton's voice intruded, and Suzanne drew a deep breath and collected her scattered thoughts as they moved across the room to the position the photographer indicated.

The man was a hired professional, and aware of the scoop his work would create. He wanted the best shots.

It took a while. The eye of the camera was very perceptive, and Suzanne should, she felt, have earned an award for her performance in playing the loving fiancée of the bride's stepson. Not to mention the groom's son.

Afterwards trays of exquisitely presented hors d'oeuvre were proffered and the champagne flowed like water. Background music from a selection of CDs filtered from strategically placed speakers as the guests mixed and mingled.

'Sloane, so *nice* to see you again.'

Suzanne turned at the sound of a breathy feminine voice, and summoned a stunning smile for the second— no, *third* wife of one of Trenton's friends.

'Bettina,' Sloane acknowledged her. 'You've met Suzanne?'

Bettina's laugh was the closest thing to a tinkling bell that Suzanne had ever heard. 'Of course, darling.'

Kittenish, Suzanne decided. Definitely cultivated kitten. The short, tight shell-pink skirt, the almost-too-tight matching camisole top covered by a designer jacket one size too small. Her hair and make-up were perfection, her lacquered nails a work of art, and the jewellery she wore just had to be worth a small fortune. Bored, and with an inclination to flirt.

'Such a cute idea to have an island wedding.' She touched careless fingers to Sloane's sleeve and deliberately fluttered her lashes. 'You will save a dance for me, won't you?' The *moue* was contrived. 'Frank isn't the partying type.'

Frank Kahler was a substantial catch, Suzanne mused, and felt a pang of sympathy for the much older entrepreneur whose fame and fortune were Bettina's main attraction.

'I doubt Suzanne would be willing to share,' Sloane responded with a musing smile.

'Oh, *darling*, of course you must dance with Bettina,' she said in mild reproach, and her eyes shimmered with simmering sensuality. 'After all, I'm the one who gets to take you home.'

He caught hold of her hand and lifted it to his

lips, then kissed each finger in turn. 'Indeed,' he intoned softly.

Oh, my, he was good. She could almost believe he meant it. Then she came to her senses, and she smiled, aware that *her* acting ability was on a par with his own.

'I think I'll have some more champagne.' Bettina cast Sloane an arch look from beneath artificially curled lashes. 'You'll fetch another for me, won't you?'

Interesting, Suzanne decided, that Bettina should use such a well-used ploy. Sloane's eyes gleamed in silent recognition, and Suzanne derived a certain pleasure from handing him her flute. 'I think I'll join Bettina. Thank you, *darling*.' The emphasis was very slight, but there nonetheless.

'He's a hunk, isn't he?' Bettina sighed as Sloane turned and began threading his way to the bar.

And then some. 'Yes,' Suzanne agreed, waiting for the moment Bettina would slip in the knife.

'Sloane came alone to my wedding. Were you sick, or something, darling?' A dimple appeared in one cheek, although there was no humour apparent in Bettina's expression. 'For a moment there, I thought you were no longer an item.'

Suzanne hated fabrication, but she refused to give Bettina any satisfaction by differing her story from the one Sloane had provided. 'I was in Brisbane visiting Georgia.'

'Quite a coup.' The almost-green eyes hardened and her expression became brittle. 'Mother and daughter snaring both father and son.'

'Yes, isn't it?' Suzanne's smile was in place, and she appeared perfectly at ease.

'You must have worked very hard.'

'Impossible, of course,' Suzanne said with the utmost charm, 'that Trenton and Georgia could have fallen genuinely in love?'

'Oh, really, Suzanne. No one falls *in love* with a wealthy man. Steering them into marriage involves an extremely delicate strategy.'

'Of the manipulative kind?' There were no rules in this game, and, as loath as she was to play it, she was damned if she'd allow Bettina a victory. 'Is that how you snared Frank?'

'I cater to his needs.'

Suzanne deserved an award for her performance as she touched a finger to the diamond-encrusted watch fastened on Bettina's wrist. 'Catering obviously pays well. Perhaps I should try it.'

'What,' a familiar deep voice drawled, 'should you try?'

Suzanne turned slightly and met Sloane's indolent gaze. She accepted a flute of champagne and watched as he handed another to Bettina.

'Bettina and I were discussing catering to our men's needs.' Her eyes sparkled with deliberate guile. 'My car has been playing up lately, darling. I rather fancy a Porsche Carrera. Black.' Her mouth widened into a beautiful pout as she lifted a finger to her lips, licked it suggestively, then placed it against the centre of his lower lip. 'Perhaps we could negotiate—later?'

Sensation spiralled from her central core as he nipped

her finger, then drew it into his mouth and swirled the tip with his tongue before releasing it.

His eyes were dark, gleaming depths reflecting desire and thinly disguised passion. 'I'm sure we can reach an agreeable compromise.'

Are you mad? a tiny voice taunted. Don't you know you're playing with *fire*?

'One imagines you intend tying the knot *soon*?'

'Trenton and Georgia's arrangements have taken precedence over our own,' Sloane informed Bettina smoothly, and incurred her tinkling laugh.

'Don't wait *too* long, darling. There's quite a few who would be happy to push Suzanne out of the way.'

Suzanne saw Sloane's eyes narrow slightly, sensed the predatory stillness, and felt all her muscles tense.

'Should that happen, they'd have me to deal with.' His voice was ominously soft, and intensely dangerous.

Bettina's light laugh held a slight note of incredulity. '*Figuratively* speaking. Not literally, for heaven's sake.'

Sloane's expression didn't change. 'I'm relieved to hear it.' His eyes hardened measurably. 'Any threat, impulsive or premeditated, is something I'd take very seriously.'

His meaning was unmistakable, and Bettina blinked rather rapidly.

'Well, of *course*.' She sipped her champagne, then offered a brilliant smile. 'If you'll excuse me, I really should get back to Frank.'

'Wasn't that just a bit too menacing?'

His eyes were still hard when they swept over Suzanne's features. 'No.'

She opened her mouth, only to have it pressed closed by his in a brief, hard kiss.

'Don't argue.'

Mixing and mingling was a social art form, and Sloane did it extremely well, slowly circulating between guests as he enquired about various family members, listened to an amusing anecdote or two, and shared a few reminiscences.

Dinner was served at seven. Tables in the restaurant had been assembled to ensure the bridal party of four were easily visible to the guests, and the food, comprising several courses, was superb.

There were two speeches: one which Sloane delivered welcoming Georgia into the family, and the other a response from Trenton.

The wedding cake was an exquisite work of art, with intricately iced orchids so incredibly lifelike that one almost wanted to touch a petal to see if it was authentic.

When it was cut, sliced and handed to each guest, Sloane bit into his before feeding some of it to Suzanne in a sensual display she opted to return, for the benefit of their audience. Or so she told herself, for there was a part of her that wished it were real.

The kiss was something else. Evocative and incredibly thorough; there was absolutely nothing she could do about it without causing a stir.

When he lifted his head she could only look at him with a measure of reflected hurt, and just for a second she thought she glimpsed regret beneath the gleaming purpose, then it was gone.

The music changed and Trenton led Georgia onto the floor to dance.

'We'll follow suit,' Sloane indicated, rising to his feet and catching her hand in his.

Now *this*…this was dangerous, she mused as she moved into his arms. It was like coming home. Heaven. Her body fitted his with intimate familiarity, and she felt it quiver in recognition of something beyond which she had little control.

Sexuality. Heightened sensuality. Potent alchemy. If love was like a river, then theirs ran deep. And fast.

She was acutely aware of her own response and, held close like this, she found it impossible to ignore the evidence of desire in his.

It was all she could do not to link her hands together at his nape, and her eyes held bemusement as his lips trailed to one temple.

Suzanne heard her mother's soft laugh, and Sloane's hold loosened as each couple came to a brief halt in order to switch partners.

'It's a beautiful wedding,' Suzanne commented as Trenton led her into another waltz. Other guests began to join them on the floor.

'Georgia is a beautiful woman. On the inside, where it counts,' he said gently. 'As you are.'

It was a lovely compliment. 'Thank you.'

'I can promise to take good care of her.'

'I know.' It was nothing less than the truth. 'Just as I know you'll both be very happy together.'

They circled the floor again, then Sloane effected the change. Five minutes later another guest cut in, and during the ensuing hour Suzanne danced with almost every man in the room.

Bettina manoeuvred things very skilfully so that she got to dance with Sloane. Suzanne saw each move the glamorous blonde made, and had to commend her tactics.

To anyone else in the room Bettina looked a vivacious guest, and their fleeting attention would have admired the practised smile, the faint flutter of perfectly manicured lacquered nails.

Suzanne, whose examination was much more precise, saw the subtle promise in Bettina's almost-green eyes, the apparent accidental brush of her generous and silicone-enhanced breasts, the inviting part of those perfectly painted lips, and had to still the desire to tear Bettina's eyes out.

Three minutes, four? They each seemed to acquire a tremendous magnitude before Sloane executed a change in partners and drew Suzanne close.

She held herself stiffly within the circle of his arms, and she moved her head slightly so that his lips brushed her ear and not her cheek as he intended.

'Bettina,' Sloane drawled with stunning accuracy.

'You're *so* perceptive.'

'It's an inherent trait,' he declared musingly. 'Do you know you quiver when you're angry?'

Quiver? 'Really?' She wanted to hit him.

'Which one of us did you want to tear limb from limb?'

'Bettina,' she declared with soft vehemence, and heard his husky chuckle.

'Claws, when there's absolutely no need?'

'Careful,' Suzanne warned. 'I haven't sheathed them yet.'

She leaned into him a little, and heard the strong beat of his heart, felt the strength of his body, and enjoyed the moment for as long as the slow music lasted. Then she joined Georgia and Trenton for a few minutes before slipping to the powder-room to freshen up.

When she returned most of the couples had drifted off the floor to sit in groups at various tables. Sloane was deep in conversation with Bettina's husband, Frank, and Suzanne made her way out onto the terrace where a breeze teased its way in from the ocean.

At this time of year the tropical far north was close to perfection. Lovely sunny days, cool clear nights, and little or no rain. Ideal for those who lived in southern states where winter tended to be cold and wet with winds that gusted round corners and buffeted buildings.

In two days Georgia would fly to Paris. The city for lovers, with its historic buildings and magnificent art collections. Haute couture, food, the total ambience. She'd read about it, viewed the travel documentaries on film, and felt vaguely envious.

No, that wasn't strictly true. There were always goals in life, some achievable, others merely dreams. The aim was to strive for the dream, but not lose sight of the reality.

There was also avarice and greed, which she deplored, along with artificial superficiality. And those who sought and fought for it. Love had been destroyed, lives wrecked, even lost, in pursuit of an abundance of wealth and all it could provide.

A slight shiver shook her slim frame. She'd tasted it, felt the fear and opted to remove herself from its orbit. Had she been right to handle it herself? The doubts, ever present, rose to the surface.

'Voluntary solitude, or an escape?'

Suzanne straightened at the sound of Sloane's drawled query, and she didn't move as he slid his arms round her waist and drew her back against him.

'A little of both,' she answered honestly.

'Want to share?'

Her eyes sprang open at that quietly voiced query. Share her innermost thoughts? That would give the *danger* a new dimension.

'I'll take a rain check.'

She felt his chin rest down on top of her head. 'You realise I'll call it in?'

Yes, he would. But not now. 'Perhaps we should go inside.'

'I came out to find you,' Sloane said. 'Trenton and Georgia intend to retire soon.'

'Leaving the guests to party on?' Was it that late?

'It's almost midnight.'

Where had the evening gone? 'Time flies when you're having fun,' she said lightly, and felt her stomach curl as Sloane moved one hand towards her breast while the other splayed across her hip.

They were, she knew, visible to the guests inside. 'Don't. Please,' she added quietly.

'Then come indoors, and bid our respective parents goodnight.'

Out of the way of temptation. But not for long. Sooner or later they'd return to their villa. What then? She couldn't afford the ecstasy of one long night of loving, or the resulting agony when she had to leave him.

Without a word she slipped free of his hold and led the way indoors.

'Oh, there you are, darling,' Georgia said warmly. 'Trenton and I are about to leave.' She leant forward and gave her daughter a fond hug. 'It's been a splendid party, hasn't it?'

'Really lovely,' Suzanne agreed as she caught hold of her mother's hands.

'Most of the guests are meeting around nine for a champagne breakfast. You'll join us, of course.'

'Of course, Mama.'

'Now we're going to get out of here,' Trenton declared as he bestowed upon his new wife a look of passionate warmth.

Georgia's eyes held a delightful sparkle, and her cheeks bore the faintest tinge of colour.

Trenton took care of their escape by simply declaring, 'Goodnight,' and led Georgia from the restaurant.

'Would you like me to get you some coffee?' Sloane queried.

'Please,' Suzanne replied, and within seconds of his return they were joined by Bettina, which, Suzanne decided, was stretching coincidence a bit far.

'Frank doesn't want to stay and party on. We thought

we might go for a walk along the beach. Maybe go for a swim. Want to join us?'

And watch Bettina strip down to nothing and display those voluptuous curves, cavort in the moonlight and attempt to capture more than one man's attention?

'Thanks, but no.' Sloane tempered the refusal with a quizzical smile, then cast Suzanne a dark, gleaming look. 'We have other plans.'

'A party?'

'For two,' he responded evenly. He took Suzanne's cup and saucer and deposited them down onto a nearby table, then he caught hold of her hand. 'If you'll excuse us?'

'We should,' Suzanne admonished mildly, 'say goodnight to the guests.'

'We shall. Very briefly.'

'And have them speculate why we're in such a hurry to leave?'

'Do you want to stay?'

Not really. But she wasn't sure she wanted to go back to the villa, either. Nor did she want to walk along the beach and encounter Bettina.

'No.'

Ten minutes later Sloane unlocked their door, then closed it behind them. Suzanne watched as he shrugged off his suit jacket and draped it over a nearby chair, tugged free his tie and loosened the top two buttons of his shirt.

Then he crossed to the bar-fridge, extracted a magnum of champagne, opened it, filled two flutes, then handed her one. He touched the rim of her flute with his own, then lifted it in silent salute before sipping the contents.

Suzanne was acutely aware of him, and the raw, primitive chemistry that was his alone. There was a brooding sensuality apparent that fired a deep answering need inside her.

She could almost *feel* the blood move more quickly through her veins, the fine hairs on her skin rise as sensitised nerve-ends came alive, and slow heat radiated throughout her whole body.

Imagining how it would be with him almost brought her to a state of climax. Three weeks seemed an eternity, each night apart so long and lonely she'd lain awake aching in solitary pain.

CHAPTER EIGHT

SLOANE GLIMPSED THE faint fleeting shadows, determined their cause, and fought the urge to sweep Suzanne into his arms. The sex would be a wonderful release…for both of them. Wild, wanton, and uninhibited. He could almost smell the bloom of sensual heat on her skin, taste her exotic scent. The thought of sinking into her, hearing the soft purr in her voice change to something deep and driven, the cries of ecstasy as he took her with him…

'It was a lovely wedding.' She had the feeling she'd already said those words, and fought to keep the wistfulness out of her voice, the awkward hesitancy. Dammit, it must be the champagne's eroding effect on her self-confidence. Warm and fuzzy wasn't a feeling she wanted to cultivate. 'Georgia looked radiant.'

'Yes, she did.'

'And Trenton—'

'Wouldn't allow anything or anyone to interfere with their plans,' Sloane interceded. He was silent for a few long seconds, and when he spoke his voice held an inflexible edge. 'Any more than I will.'

There was something in his eyes, the powerful set of his features that triggered alarm bells in her brain.

She regarded him carefully, apprehension uppermost as it merged with sickening knowledge. 'You've discovered who she is, haven't you?'

His expression hardened, muscles sculpting broad facial bones into a daunting mask. 'Yes. I had the answer I needed this morning.'

Suzanne didn't have to ask *how*. He had the power and the contacts to elicit any information he wanted. It was impossible to believe that he wouldn't take action. 'What are you going to do?'

'It's already done. Zoe's father is now aware of the facts. And extremely grateful we've chosen not to prosecute. He will personally ensure she seeks professional help.'

Her eyes searched his, and she almost died at the ruthlessness apparent. There was something else she couldn't define, and it frightened her.

'No one,' Sloane intoned with brutal mercilessness, 'threatens me. Directly, or indirectly.' He kept his anger under tight rein. The e-mail report had listed extensive repairs to her car. He could only imagine the verbal assault.

Suzanne saw his clenched fists, evidenced the cold fury in those dark eyes, and placed her partly empty flute onto a nearby pedestal.

She needed to get out of this room, away from him, even if it was only briefly. 'I'm going for a walk.'

'Not alone.'

She tilted her head to look at him, uncaring that the

conversation had taken a dangerous shift. 'Don't play the heavy, Sloane.' She walked across the room to the door, her anger so intense she knew she'd *hit* him if he tried to stop her.

Outside the darkness seemed like a shroud, and she followed the lit path down to the beach. When she reached the sand she stepped out of her heeled shoes and bent to collect them in one hand.

Sloane was a short distance behind her, and it was all she could do not to throw something at him. If he wanted to follow her, he could. But she was damned if she'd allow him to dictate her actions, or when she'd return to the villa. *If* she returned, she decided darkly. There were plenty of beach loungers that would make an adequate place to rest for what remained of the night.

The moonlight bathed the beach with an eerie glow, and she trod the crunchy sand to the water's edge, then followed its curve towards the outcrop of rocks.

The tide eddied and flowed at her feet, and on impulse she paused, shed her clothes and dropped them onto dry sand, then turned and walked into the sea.

The water felt silky and wonderfully cool against her skin, and when it reached her waist she eased into a lazy breast-stroke parallel to the shore. Then she turned onto her back and floated, idly counting the sprinkle of stars.

A faint splash alerted her bare seconds before Sloane's dark head appeared less than a metre away.

He didn't say a word, didn't need to, and she moved away from him and rose to her feet. If he was intent on invading her space, then she'd simply shift it somewhere else!

She had only taken two steps towards the shore when hard hands grasped hold of her shoulders and turned her back to face him. 'Let me—'

Anything else she might have said remained locked in her throat as his mouth closed over hers in a kiss that *possessed*...mind, body and soul.

She tried to struggle, and got nowhere. Dear Lord, he was strong. If she could only bite him...but his jaw had possession of her own, dictating its movements as he ravaged the inner tissues with his tongue, his teeth, in a deliberate assault on her senses.

One hand curved down to cup her bottom, while the other held fast her head. She pummelled his back with her fists, and attempted to kick his shin...with totally ineffectual results.

Just when she thought she couldn't bear any more, he loosened his hold, only to change it as he hefted her over one shoulder and walked out of the sea onto the sand.

'What in *hell* do you think you're doing?'

He bent down and she automatically clutched the back of his waist. And found no purchase.

'Collecting our clothes.'

'Put me down!'

He stood upright, adjusted his hold of her, then calmly strode towards the path. 'No.'

'For heaven's sake,' Suzanne hissed. 'Someone might see us.'

'I don't give a damn.'

'At least give me your shirt.' The request came out as a hollow groan.

'I happen to be holding it in front of a vulnerable part of my anatomy,' he responded drily.

'You'd better pray we make it undetected,' she threatened direly. 'Or I'll never forgive you.'

The path to their villa was reasonably short, but Suzanne was conscious of every step Sloane took until they were safely indoors.

'You fiend! How *dare* you?' She pummelled his back with her fists, and attempted to kick him. 'Put me *down*.'

He kept walking, ascended the steps to the bedroom, paused long enough to toss their clothes onto the bed, then he crossed into the *en suite* and turned on the shower.

'What in sweet hell do you think you're doing?'

'Precisely what it looks like.' He stepped into the shower stall and closed the glass sliding door. Then he pulled her down to stand in front of him.

Without thought she lifted a hand and slapped his jaw. Anger, sheer helpless rage, exuded from every pore, and when she lifted her hand a second time he caught it mid-air in a punishing grip.

'You want to fight, Suzanne?'

'*Yes*, damn you!'

'Then go ahead.' He released her hand and stood still, his arms folded across his chest.

His eyes gleamed darkly, silently daring her to thwart him, and she lashed out, both fists flailing as she connected with his chest, his shoulders, anywhere she could land a punch.

He took each and every one, and only grunted once.

Hot, angry tears filled her eyes, then spilled to run in twin rivulets down to her chin. Her knuckles hurt from where she'd struck strong muscle and sinew. And bone. He didn't move, and her arms slowed, then dropped to her sides.

'Are you done?'

The water lashed his shoulders and coursed down his back, and she turned blindly towards the glass door, only to halt as he prevented her escape.

Without a word he pulled her into his arms, effectively stilling any further struggle.

'Let me go.' To stay like this was madness.

Fingers splayed across the base of her spine began a subtle movement, sufficient to make her breath catch, and she tried to pull away from him without success.

The hand that held her nape slid to capture her head, tilting it so she had no defence against his descending mouth.

She expected a devastating invasion, and was unprepared for the soft slide of his tongue against her own. Teasing, tantalising, he made it a sensual assault as he explored and caressed, encouraging her response in a manner that soon left her weak-willed and malleable.

Uncaring of the consequences, she lifted her arms and twined them round his neck, melting into him as she kissed him back. Slowly, tentatively, then with an increasing urgency that left both of them labouring for breath.

'Please.' *Now.* She didn't think she could wait a second longer, and an exultant laugh broke free from her throat as he parted her thighs and lifted her high to straddle his waist.

With one supple action he buried himself inside her, and she gloried in the hard, deep thrust that stretched silken tissues to a level where she gasped at his degree of penetration.

For several seconds he remained still, then he began to move, slowly at first, each thrust deeper than the last as he increased the pace until their actions became a synchronised match leading to an explosive climax.

Suzanne had thought she'd experienced every facet of his lovemaking, but this had held a wild quality, almost unbridled, as if he was barely retaining a hold on his emotions.

She could only bury her head against his neck as he cradled her close, his lips warm and evocative as they traced a path across one exposed cheek.

How long they stood like that, she had no idea. Long seconds, *minutes* maybe. Eventually her breathing steadied, and with infinite care he set her down onto her feet.

Then he reached for the soap and slowly lathered every inch of her body before turning his attention to his own.

Suzanne felt as if she wasn't capable of moving, much less uttering a single word, and when he switched off the water she stepped out from the shower stall and caught up a towel, only to have him take it from her to blot their skin free of moisture.

Not once did his eyes leave hers, and she became

lost in the darkness, every cell flaring brilliantly *alive* in the knowledge of what would follow.

She wanted him. Dear heaven, so much. But what about afterwards? How could she board the launch on Monday and return to Sydney, her own apartment, and attempt to get on with her life as if this weekend had never happened?

It would be a living nightmare of unfulfilled needing, wanting...*empty*. She doubted if she could survive.

'Sloane—' She couldn't say the words, and she lifted a hand then let it fall helplessly down to her side.

He brushed gentle fingers against her cheek, then let them drift to trace the pulsing cord at her neck.

She was melting inside, subsiding into a state of sensual inertia where all she wanted was for him to continue until the slow warmth heated to white-hot fire.

He knew. She could see it in his eyes, feel it in his touch as his hand slid to her breast and caressed the soft contours before wreaking havoc with the sensitive peak.

His head lowered and his mouth closed over hers in a deep evocative kiss that tore what little defences she had left to shreds. His mouth left hers and followed a sensual path to her breast, savouring, suckling on the tender nub as she arched her neck in silent invitation.

One night, she groaned silently. Just one night.

Her hands reached for him, the movement compulsive as she began exploring tight muscle and sinew, touching, tasting, and wanting more. So much more.

The blood flowed through her veins like quicksilver, feeding every nerve-cell until her whole body ached with need. Sensual heat at its zenith.

Sloane carried her into the bedroom and sank down with her onto the bed. She looked magnificent, her eyes deep blue crystalline, her soft mouth slightly swollen and parted from his kiss. There was a faint sheen on her skin, and her hair hung in tousled disarray.

She leaned forward and initiated a deep kiss, enjoying the feeling of power as he allowed her free rein. Then in one smooth movement she arched her body and took him deep inside, gasping faintly as she felt inner tissues stretch to accommodate him.

Dear God, he felt good. *This* was so good, the feeling of completeness, the joining of two bodies in perfect accord. Sensation spiralled, and she began to move, creating a deep penetrating rhythm as old as time.

His hands reached for her waist, and he joined in the ride, taking her higher and higher until she cried out her release.

Slowly she raised her head and looked down at him, met the dark, slumberous depths and defined the degree of passion evident.

Extending a hand, she touched a gentle finger to his lower lip and traced its outline, then slid it down his chin to his throat, trailing a central line past his chest, his stomach, to where they were still joined, before travelling a similar path to her own mouth.

Slow, sweet warmth swirled deep within, heating her body, and she gave a soft laugh as his hands reached up to bring her head down to his.

This time there was no gentleness in his kiss. It became a foray that was claim-staking, possession at its most damnable as she met and matched the dramatic primitiveness that lay deep within him.

It transcended mere sexual gratification. It was much more than sensual satiation.

A faint groan emerged from her throat as he shifted position and rolled so that she lay on her back.

The control was his, and she wrapped her legs round his hips and pulled him down to her, glorying in his strength.

Afterwards she could only lie still, unable to move as he let his fingers drift idly over the softness of her skin.

She must have slept, for she came awake to the touch of his lips exploring the delicate contours of her body, tasting the spent bloom on her skin as he trailed lower to savour the intimate heart of her.

A banked flame flared into pulsating life, licking through her veins, igniting nerve-ends as she came achingly alive. Consummate skill took her high and tipped her over the edge, and she cried out as she fell.

Afterwards she pleasured him, exulting in the faint sheen of sweat that heated his skin, the quivering muscles of his stomach, the way his breath caught in his throat.

For much of what remained of the night, they indulged in lovemaking, creating a sensual ecstasy that was alternately wild and untamed and slow and evocative.

Suzanne didn't want the magic to end. With the dawn came sleep, and afterwards a long, lingering loving that was so incredibly gentle it made her want to weep.

'We should shower and go down to breakfast,' she

said reluctantly as she swept a glance to the digital radio clock.

Sloane's eyes held a mocking gleam that didn't fool her in the slightest. 'Should we?'

'I think so.'

He touched her mouth with his own, savoured its inner sweetness, then trailed soft kisses along the softly swollen contours of her lower lip. 'Why is that?'

Assertiveness was the key. Definitely. For to stay here any longer would be a madness she could ill afford. 'Because I'm hungry.' His eyes became dark and slumberous. 'For food. Sustenance,' she elaborated with an impish grin. 'And I'd almost kill for a cup of strong coffee.' She slid to her feet, stretched her arms high... and felt the pull of muscles. 'I'll hit the shower first.' She directed him a faintly wry glance. 'Alone. Otherwise we'll never get out of here.'

He reached out a hand and pulled her back down to him for a brief, hard kiss, then he let her go. 'Five minutes, then I join you.'

It was almost nine when they entered the restaurant, and Suzanne chose a table on the terrace, ordered coffee, then helped herself to a selection of fresh fruit and cereal from the smorgasbord.

'You're looking rather fragile this morning, darling. Had a hard night?'

She turned and met Bettina's deliberately guileless smile, and proffered one of her own. 'Surely that's rather a personal question?'

'Why pretend? I have my eye on a magnificent emerald and diamond ring.' Her eyes glittered acquisitively. 'Frank needs a little persuasion to buy it for me.'

'Which you have every intention of providing.'

'Why, of course. Women have traded sexual favours for gifts since—*forever*.' Bettina's lashes swept wide. 'Aren't you working hard to persuade Sloane to buy you a Porsche Carrera?'

'*Repaying* me will become a lifetime commitment.'

Suzanne turned at the sound of Sloane's drawling voice, caught his faintly wry, musing smile, glimpsed the dark gleam in his eyes, and opted to respond in kind.

'Not necessarily. My tastes are simple.'

'So are mine,' he said solemnly. *'You.'*

Her pulse tripped and raced to a faster beat. He saw the evidence of it in the hollow at the base of her throat, the dilation of those sapphire depths, the soft parting of her lips.

'The Porsche was meant to be a joke,' she said as she carried her plate back to their table.

'I know.'

'If you gave me one,' she declared fiercely, 'I'd hand it straight back.'

Sloane sank into his chair and ordered fresh coffee. 'I do believe you would.'

'Sloane—'

'You think I don't know Bettina enjoys making mischief?' His dry, mocking tone was matched by a hardness in his eyes.

She was all too aware of the tensile steel beneath the sophisticated veneer. Only a fool would believe he wasn't aware of every angle, and adept in determining the foibles of human nature.

'She has her eye on you.'

His soft laughter brought a fiery sparkle to her eyes. 'Bettina needs confirmation of her attraction to the opposite sex. Her choice of clothes, make-up, jewellery is a blatant attempt at attention-seeking.' His expression assumed a degree of cynicism. 'Any man will do.'

'I disagree,' Suzanne declared as she reached for her coffee. 'That should amend to any well-connected, wealthy man.' She lifted her cup, took an appreciative sip, then replaced it back on its saucer and cast him a wry look. 'And you're more sought after than most.'

'But spoken for,' Sloane asserted tolerantly.

'"A hunk" were her exact words,' she continued as if he hadn't spoken.

'Really?'

He was amused, damn him. 'Definitely *mistress* material.'

'Now why,' he drawled lazily, 'would I covet a mistress, when I have you?'

Suzanne took the time to spear a segment of fresh fruit, which she savoured, then slowly chewed and swallowed, before voicing a response. She chose her words with care, and tempered them with a faint smile. 'You don't *have* me.'

He placed his fork down carefully on his plate, then leant back in his chair, looking, she decided, indolently relaxed and not poised to deliver a verbal sally. 'I retain a particularly vivid memory of how we spent the night.'

His dark brown eyes held gleaming humour. 'And the early dawn hours.'

So did she. So much so that it was all she could do to contain the stain of colour spreading high on each cheek. 'I don't think that's entirely relevant.'

She saw one eyebrow lift to form a mocking arch. 'No? I beg to disagree.'

'It was just sex.' Albeit very good sex, she acknowledged silently. And knew she lied. *Sex* didn't even begin to describe what they'd shared.

'I think I should take you back to bed,' Sloane drawled with musing mockery. 'It's the one place where we're in perfect accord.'

She captured another portion of fruit with her fork. 'Our absence would be noticed.'

His regard was warm and infinitely sensual. 'I fail to see that as a problem.'

'You possess a one-track mind,' she admonished him, and reached for her coffee once more.

'Three weeks' abstinence tends to have that effect on a man.'

Not only a man. Even thinking about what they'd shared through much of the night was enough to flood her veins with telling warmth.

The damnable thing was that he knew. The knowledge was apparent in the way his eyes lingered on her mouth, then slid slowly to the heavily beating pulse at the edge of her neck, the slight thrust of each breast.

'I think,' she began, hating the faint raggedness in her voice, 'I've had enough to eat.'

'Georgia and Trenton have just arrived,' Sloane advised quietly, 'and indicated they'll join us.'

The meal became a leisurely affair with the connotation of a champagne brunch as the champagne flowed and staff provided a selection of finger food.

'Tennis this afternoon, definitely,' Georgia declared as she sipped a second cup of black coffee. 'And I think I'll just have fruit for lunch, or forgo it altogether.'

'Likewise.' Followed by a swim, and a nap on the beach, Suzanne decided. A lazily spent afternoon was just what she needed. After last night.

An arrow of pain pierced her body. What of tonight? Would Sloane...? Yes, a silent voice taunted. Of course he will. How would she survive another night of loving without breaking into a thousand pieces? Perhaps if she explained, maybe pleaded with him...

She spared him a quick glance, and then wished she hadn't. His gaze was focused on her features, reading each and every fleeting expression...with damning accuracy, unless she was mistaken.

Did anyone else guess she was a mass of nervous tension beneath the composed exterior? After last night the boundaries she'd imposed had been moved, and she was unsure of their position.

What would happen when she returned to Sydney? *No*, don't think about it, she told herself. *Thinking* wasn't a good idea, for there were just two scenarios. Neither of which she wanted to explore right now.

Her stomach executed a series of painful somersaults, and she forcibly controlled her breathing into a steady, regulated rise and fall. Her heart felt heavy in her chest, and she was sure her contribution to the conversation sounded terribly inane.

In a way it was a relief to circulate among the guests, to lose herself, even briefly, in a social exchange with women whose main topics of conversation seemed to be whose hairdresser was the best, which fashion designer would take out the annual award, and whose parties on the social circuit were *de rigueur* for the remainder of the winter season.

Sloane seemed similarly immersed with Trenton's, and doubtless his own, associates. Twice she glanced in his direction only to have him meet her gaze.

'No hint of a date yet, Suzanne?' one woman asked, while another ventured,

'Paul and I have a very tight schedule until Christmas. Get those invitations out early, darling.'

'You *must* visit Stefano; he'll do wonders with your hair,' an elegant brunette assured Suzanne, and a glossy dark-haired sylph advised,

'Marie-Louise is without equal for the nails.'

'Gianfranco,' the stylish redhead insisted. 'You must see him about your dress, darling. Tell him Claudia sent you.'

'Of course, there is only O'Neil for the flowers.'

'Frank spent almost a million on my reception,' Bettina offered, and didn't notice the electric silence that followed her announcement.

Suzanne sensed their momentary withdrawal, and their disapproval. Any mention of actual amounts of money among the upper social echelon was *de trop*. One could mention the yacht, the villa in France, the apartment in Venice, Rome or Milan. The Swiss chalet, the New York Fifth Avenue apartment, the London Knightsbridge town house or the mansion in Surrey. *Anything*, except how much it cost. Unless it was an outrageous bargain. Delusions of grandeur were not entertained among society's élite.

It was almost eleven when the guests departed to board the launch that would transfer them to Dunk Island to connect with their flight south.

Suzanne and Sloane joined Georgia and Trenton on the jetty to see them off.

CHAPTER NINE

'Now I CAN RELAX.' Georgia wound an arm round Trenton's waist and leaned in against him. 'It's been a wonderful weekend. Thank you, darling.'

The look he directed at her mother brought a lump to Suzanne's throat. So much love, so clearly visible. It made her heart ache. 'I don't think I could eat or drink a thing,' she declared lightly. 'I'm going to take a book down onto the beach, then go for a dip in the ocean.'

'We'll meet for tennis,' Trenton indicated. 'Four o'clock, OK?'

'You could,' Sloane drawled minutes later as they entered their villa, 'relax here.'

Suzanne twisted her head to look at him. 'Uh-uh. I don't think our ideas of *relaxation* match.' She ran quickly up the steps to the bedroom and extracted a black bikini.

'Afraid to be alone with me?'

He posed a tremendous threat to her equilibrium, but *fear* had no part in it. 'No.'

Sloane crossed to her side and placed his hands at

the base of her nape, initiating a soothing massage that felt so good…too damned good. 'Tired?'

She wanted to close her eyes and sink back against him, have him hold her, kiss her. Slow, oh, so slowly. If she gave in to such feelings, they'd never get out of the villa before nightfall.

'A little.'

'Let me indulge you,' he commanded quietly.

Need curled deep inside her, then twisted into a spiral that radiated through her body. Her smile was incredibly sad, and tinged with regret. 'I don't think that's such a good idea.'

His breath feathered her temple. 'No?'

His fingers skimmed beneath the hair at her nape, lifting it aside as he traced his lips down to the sensitive spot behind one ear, savoured it, then trailed the pulsing cord to the edge of her neck.

'Sloane.' The protest fell from her lips in scarcely more than an agonised whisper as his fingers loosened tight shoulder muscles.

'Shh,' he bade her gently. 'Just relax.'

Dared she? Maybe just for a few minutes. There was no harm in just a few minutes, surely?

Suzanne closed her eyes and let all her muscles relax as he began weaving a subtle magic that seemed to seep into her very bones.

She was hardly aware of him sliding the zip free at the back of her dress, or the faint slither as it slipped to the floor. Her bra clasp undid with ease, and his hands smoothed her slip down over her hips.

'I don't think—'

'Don't *think*,' Sloane said huskily. 'Just feel.'

His lips tasted her skin, embraced it, and roamed at will over her neck, her shoulders, then trailed down one arm to the sensitive hollow at her elbow, before tracing the delicate veins down to the inside of her wrist.

A despairing groan escaped her throat as he rendered a similar treatment to the other arm, and when he turned her into his arms she had no will of her own to prevent him laying her gently down on the bed.

What followed was a long, slow supplication of every pleasure point, each pulse. The curve of her hip, the inside of one thigh, the hollow behind each knee. The sensitive slope of her calf, the tender hollows at her ankle, the acutely vulnerable arch of her foot.

She felt as if she was slowly dying as pleasure radiated from every pore, each nerve-cell, as his hands, his lips roved at will. Her breasts, their sensitised peaks, the soft concave of her stomach. The rapidly discolouring bruise at her hip. Nothing escaped his attention.

Her blood leapt as he brushed the most intimate crevice of all, and her limbs slid against the sheet in agitation, then her whole body jerked as he began effecting a simulation of the sexual act itself.

His hands cupped her hips and held them as he wreaked a havoc that was so incredibly tender, so intensely evocative, her body seemed to sing as one vibration after another shook her central core and radiated in all-consuming waves.

He felt her shudder in release, and gifted her an openmouthed kiss before travelling a slow path to her waist, then the soft contour of one breast.

It was a torturous journey until his mouth reached hers, and the kiss was so gentle she felt the prick of tears and their warm spill as they trickled slowly across each cheekbone and disappeared into her hair.

Sloane felt the faint tremor as her body shook, and he lifted his head fractionally, glimpsed the drenched sapphire pools and removed the trail of moisture with his tongue.

Then he stretched out close and gathered her in against him. 'Better?'

Dear Lord, did he have any conception of how she felt? 'There's only one problem,' she murmured shakily.

His fingers brushed against her cheek. 'What's that?'

Her mouth trembled as she reached for him. 'You're wearing too many clothes.'

His smile was infinitely warm and sensual. 'You could have fun taking them off.'

'Is that an invitation?'

Lips traced the clean line of her jaw. 'Do you need one?'

This was special. Something so precious, the memory would last her for the rest of her life. Through all the lonely, empty nights, an inner voice sighed in sorrow.

His shoes came first, then she took time with the buckle of his trousers, the zip fastening, silently encouraging his help as she slid the garment free. Undoing each shirt button became a tantalising exercise as her fingers tangled with the springy hair curling in a sparse pattern across his tightly muscled chest.

All that remained was a pair of silk briefs, and she traced the waistband as it stretched across his hip-bone, the firm plane of his stomach, and allowed her fingers to brush fleetingly over his arousal.

Control. He had it. Part of her wanted to see what it would take to break it as she tucked her fingers into the waistband and eased the briefs free.

With incredible slowness she copied his example, teasing, tasting, glorying in the soft tremor of his stomach, each flexed muscle as she traversed every inch of his body.

The most vulnerable, the most erotic part of his anatomy she left until last, laving it with such delicate artistry, he groaned in the effort to maintain control.

Minutes later his breath rasped in one husky exhalation, and hard hands grasped her shoulders as he rolled her onto her back and drove into her in one deep thrust.

Suzanne gave an exultant laugh and met his mouth as it came down in possession of her own, and together they climbed to each crest as raw, primitive sensation took them high in a mutual climax so devastatingly flagrant there were no words to define it.

Afterwards he cradled her against him as his fingers trailed a soothing pattern up and down her back, tracing each indentation of her spine.

She slept, drifting into blissful somnolence, secure in the knowledge that she was safe. *His*. Undoubtedly his.

Suzanne came awake at the soft pressure of lips brushing against her own, and she opened her eyes slowly, allowing the lashes to drift wide as she focused on the man who was intent on disturbing a dreamy ambience she was loath to leave.

'It's almost four,' Sloane informed her huskily, and she offered him a slow, sweet smile.

'Time to shower, dress, and meet Trenton and Georgia for tennis.'

'I could ring through to their villa and cancel.'

'We shouldn't disappoint them,' she opined solemnly, and he uttered a faint laugh. 'Should we?'

'Witch.' He levered himself off the bed, and extended a hand. 'Come on, then, or we'll be late.'

They were, but only by ten minutes, and Georgia and Trenton were already on the court, quite happily enjoying a relaxing rally.

Together, they agreed on one set, and although both men were evenly matched the pace was laid-back rather than competitive, ending an hour later with a seven-five win in favour of Sloane and Suzanne.

'A drink in the bar?' Sloane suggested as they exited the court, and Trenton clapped a hand to his son's shoulder in silent agreement.

'I must be feeling my age,' Georgia declared with a sparkling laugh as they entered the main complex and sank into comfortable chairs.

Trenton signalled to the waiter and within minutes they were each sipping something long and cool.

'Dinner at six-thirty?' Trenton proposed. 'I'll have someone alert the dining room.'

That would give them time to shower and change. Their final night on the island, Suzanne reflected, unsure whether to feel relieved or regretful that the extended weekend sojourn was almost at an end.

What had begun as something she'd have given anything to avoid had become quite different in many respects from anything she'd envisaged.

The anger, the resentment was gone. Yet what was in its place? The sex was great. Better than great...magnificent. But was that *all* it was?

She wanted to ask, but she was afraid of the answer. *Knew* that if she was to survive emotionally she had to cull some form of self-preservation.

'It'll be the last night we spend with Georgia and Trenton for a while,' Sloane reflected with indolent ease. 'Shall we view a video, play cards, or just take a leisurely stroll along the beach for a while after dinner?'

Trenton looked from his wife to his stepdaughter for confirmation. 'Georgia? Suzanne?'

Georgia's smile was infectious. 'Cards. Suzanne and I are rather good, aren't we, darling?'

It was, Suzanne decided gratefully, the more mentally stimulating choice. 'Yes,' she conceded with droll humour. 'Let's pit our combined skills and see if we can beat them.'

Sloane arched an eyebrow and spared his father a wry look. 'Men against the women?'

Trenton indulged in a husky chuckle. 'You do play, Sloane? Otherwise we're in deep trouble.'

'Your villa or ours?'

'Yours,' Trenton drawled, and shot Georgia a wicked glance. 'Then we can leave when we want to.'

'Bring matchsticks,' Suzanne bade them solemnly. 'Georgia and I never play for money.'

They finished their drinks and wandered out into

the cool evening air. Darkness was falling, and already the garden lights illuminated the complex and grounds.

Trenton and Georgia paused at a fork in the path leading to their villa. 'We'll meet in the restaurant in half an hour.'

Once indoors, Suzanne made straight for the *en suite*, stripped off her clothes, and stepped beneath the warm pulsing water. Then gasped in surprise when Sloane followed close behind her.

His presence triggered a spiral of electric energy, and she reached for the soap only to have it removed from her hand.

What followed became an incredibly sensual assault that heightened every nerve-ending until her entire body seemed to pulse with sensory awareness.

When he finished he silently handed her the soap, and she returned his ministrations, then stood still as he rinsed the lather from his skin.

He reached for the water dial and closed it, then he cupped her face and kissed her hard and all too briefly before reaching out for a towel.

'I don't think we need dress up. Something casual will do.'

Nevertheless she did, selecting black silk evening trousers and a matching silk singlet top. She kept make-up to a minimum, and added a slim gold chain Georgia had gifted her on her twenty-first birthday. Medium-heeled strappy sandals completed the outfit.

Wearing immaculate ivory linen trousers and a deep blue cotton shirt, Sloane exuded a vibrant energy that was intensely male, and her senses leapt when he enfolded her hand in his as they made their way to the restaurant.

Dinner was a convivial meal, and they each chose locally caught seafood, garnished with a variety of fresh salad greens. They opted out of dessert and selected the cheeseboard instead, with fresh grapes and cantaloupe, followed by a sinfully rich liqueur coffee.

A leisurely walk among the lamp-lit grounds and gardens extended the time it took to reach the villa, and once inside they seated themselves comfortably at the table while Trenton extracted and shuffled a pack of cards.

It wasn't so much the game, or winning, Suzanne mused as she collected the cards she'd been dealt. She found the pitting of mental skills honed by chance to be an enjoyable challenge. Predicting how the suits and the numbers would run, and the odds. She didn't believe in tricks, or sleight of hand, and abhorred players who utilised any system.

As a pair, she and Georgia won the first game, then the second. When the third meant another loss for the men, there was keen speculation about the fourth game.

'I think we're about to go down,' Trenton declared, meeting Sloane's musing smile with one of his own.

'If we win, we'll split up and change partners,' Georgia offered generously.

'Now that could make things interesting,' Sloane drawled, and Suzanne spared him a wicked grin.

'Must we, Mama? This might be the only advantage we'll ever gain over them.'

Sloane lifted a hand and brushed his knuckles across

her cheek. 'Oh, I don't know,' he intoned tolerantly. 'I can think of other advantages.' His eyes were dark with lambent warmth, his meaning unmistakable, and there was absolutely nothing she could do about the soft tinge of colour that flared high across her cheekbones.

'You'll embarrass my mother,' she chided, and Trenton laughed.

'Doubtful, darling,' Georgia assured her.

Suzanne looked from one gleaming gaze to another, and conceded defeat. 'I think we should play on.' Afterwards, when they were alone, she'd pay Sloane back. And relish every second of it. She shot him a silently threatening glance from beneath her lashes, and glimpsed the teasing gleam in those dark depths.

It gave her a degree of satisfaction to win, and she chose to be paired with Trenton against Georgia and Sloane in a series of games that brought a finish so close, the margin was minuscule in Georgia and Sloane's favour.

Being seated opposite him provided the opportunity to watch every move, glimpse each facial expression, the faint narrowing of his eyes as he considered which card to play, which one to discard.

He was a superb tactician, a supreme strategist. And he learned really fast. Too fast. It made her wonder if he hadn't deliberately played to lose earlier.

'Anyone for coffee?'

'No, thank you, darling.' Georgia spared a glance at her watch, then rose to her feet. 'We'll see you at breakfast. Around eight?'

Sloane walked at Suzanne's side to the door. 'We'll be there.'

Georgia leaned forward and brushed her daughter's cheek with her own. 'Sleep well.'

As soon as the door had closed behind them, Suzanne crossed to the table and gathered up the pile of matchsticks, then collected the cards.

'Leave them.'

His smile was warm with implied intimacy, and she almost melted at its mesmerising quality. 'It'll only take a minute. Then I'll pack.'

His expression didn't change. 'There's plenty of time to do that in the morning.'

She looked at him helplessly. 'Sloane—' How could she say she was a mass of nerves, relieved in one way the weekend was almost over, yet deep inside fighting off a feeling of inconsolable grief? Wanting him, but reluctant to add another night of loving that would only add to the heartache? She shook her head in silent remonstrance, then drew on inner strength. 'It won't take long.'

He was close, much too close. Her breathing seemed to hang suspended as her pulse raced into overdrive.

'Look at me.'

Her stomach executed a painful flip. 'Sloane—'

'Look at me, Suzanne,' he commanded in a voice that was deceptively mild—too mild.

She turned from her task of clearing the table, and hugged her arms together in an involuntary defensive gesture.

'You're as skittish as a newborn foal.' And consumed

by a confusing mix of contrary emotions, he added silently, aware of almost every one of them. 'Want to talk about *why*?'

How did she begin, and *where*? Or should she even begin at all? *Words* seemed superfluous and contradictory, yet there were things that needed to be said.

She looked at his strongly etched features, and felt as if she was teetering on the edge of a bottomless pit.

'I'd like to go to bed. It's late, and I'm tired.'

He reached out a hand and took hold of her chin, then tilted it. 'You're avoiding the issue.'

Her eyes darkened, and she felt them begin to ache with suppressed emotion. 'Tomorrow we go back to Sydney and lead separate lives.'

'If you believe I'm going to let that happen, then you're sadly mistaken.'

He lowered his head and angled his mouth over hers in a gentle possession that soon hardened into something deep and incredibly erotic.

It was all she could do not to respond, and she fought against the dictates of her own traitorous body, almost hating herself for being so mindless, so incredibly vulnerable where he was concerned.

Want; need. The two were entwined, yet separate. With differing meanings, depending on the gender.

A man could want, and use seducing skills to achieve sexual satisfaction. Was that what Sloane was doing? Making the most of the weekend?

Yet it was two-sided. She hadn't exactly displayed too much reluctance.

When he lifted his head she could only stand in silence, her eyes wide and hiding her pain.

His arm slid down her back, and she tried to put some distance between them. Without success. 'Please, don't.'

'Don't *what*, Suzanne? Take you to bed? Is that what this is all about?' His eyes searched hers, and glimpsed the slight flaring evident in her own.

'Sex isn't the answer to everything.'

He noted the faint wariness in the set of her beautiful mouth, the bruised softness in those crystalline blue eyes, and wanted to wipe away all the indecision, the doubt, and replace it with the uninhibited emotion she'd gifted him in the beginning.

'I don't call what we share *sex*,' Sloane opined gently.

No, it was never just sex. Shared intimacy, lovemaking, a sensual exploration and satiation of the senses with *love* the ultimate goal.

'Last night—'

'Last night was a mistake.'

His eyes hardened to dark obsidian shards, and his expression became a bleak, angry mask.

CHAPTER TEN

'THE HELL IT WAS.'

'Sloane—'

'What excuse are you going to try for, Suzanne? Too much champagne, when you barely touched a second glass? It seemed like a good idea at the time?' His dark eyes bored into her with relentless and deadly anger. 'What?'

Oh, God. She closed her eyes, then opened them again. 'It wasn't like that.'

'Then explain how it was.'

Magical, euphoric. Devastating in more ways than one. She tried for an ineffectual shrug and almost got it right. 'I let the pretence become reality.' The burning need to experience heaven one last time.

'You expect me to believe that?' His voice was dangerously quiet.

'Dammit, Sloane. What do you want? A blow-by-blow analysis of my emotions?'

'The truth might help.'

'What truth?'

'There were two people in that bed. And you were with me every inch of the way.'

'So what does that prove, other than you're a skilled lover?'

'Are you saying you'd respond to any man the way you respond to me?'

No. Never. So deep was her certainty, it robbed the power from her voice.

'Suzanne?'

His eyes sharpened, homing in on the thinly disguised bleakness. 'You didn't answer the question.'

Her eyes blazed, and she lifted her chin to a defiant angle. 'What would you do if I said *yes*?'

His expression frightened her. 'Be tempted to beat you within an inch of your life.'

'You're not a violent man,' she said with certainty, only to have that conviction waver at the brilliant flare of intense emotion evident in his eyes, the deep set of his features projecting a mask that made her feel suddenly afraid. Which was ridiculous.

'Try me.' The silky softness of his voice sent a chill chasing the length of her spine.

Gone was the cool, implacable control of the courtroom barrister. Absent, too, was the veneer of sophistication. In its place was a man intent on fighting—if not physically then verbally—to the bitter end to effect a resolution. Here, now. No matter what the outcome.

Suzanne moved her shoulders in an infinitely weary gesture. 'Can't this wait until morning?' It had been a long night, and an even longer day.

He folded both arms across his chest. 'No.'

'Sloane—'

'No,' he reiterated with dangerous softness.

She was almost at the end of her tether, tired in spirit, physically, emotionally. All she wanted to do was undress, curl into bed and sleep.

Then, when she woke in the morning, the long weekend would be over. She'd board the launch, take the flight back to Sydney, and attempt to take up with her life again. Without Sloane.

'What do you *want* from me?' It was a tortured cry straight from the heart.

A muscle bunched at the edge of his jaw. 'You. Just you.'

Her throat ached with emotion, and she was willing to swear her heart stopped beating.

'As my wife, my partner, the twin half of my soul. For the rest of my life.'

She could only look at him in silence as she tried to assemble a few words that made sense.

He didn't give her the chance. 'I have a Notice of Intention to Marry in my possession.' He let his arms fall to his sides. 'All you have to do is attach your signature prior to the service tomorrow morning.' Her voice emerged from her throat with difficulty. 'Tomorrow?' The single query was little more than a soundless gasp. 'Are you mad?'

'Remarkably sane.'

Suzanne felt as if she needed to sit down. 'We can't possibly—'

'We can,' Sloane insisted. 'You're as aware of the legalities as I am.' He paused fractionally, then touched a gentle finger to the corner of her mouth, traced its outline, then let his hand fall. 'Georgia and Trenton will act as witnesses.'

'You expect me to agree to all this?' she questioned weakly.

He looked at her for long, timeless minutes, examining the fall of clean blonde hair, the fine-textured skin with minimum make-up coverage, the beautiful crystalline blue eyes. And played his last card.

'We can go back to Sydney tomorrow and begin organising the *social event of the year*. Plan the date, the venue, the marquee, the guest list, your designer gown, the media. If that's what you want, I'll go along with it. Happily.' He paused, his voice softening. 'As long as it means I get *you*.' He lifted a hand and brushed gentle fingers down her cheek, then cupped her jaw. 'Or we can marry quietly here, tomorrow.' His smile held incredible warmth. 'The choice is yours.'

Life with Sloane. Life without Sloane. There really wasn't any choice at all. Never had been.

'Tomorrow?' she reiterated in stunned disbelief.

'Tomorrow,' Sloane insisted.

Suzanne's brain whirled with numerous implications. 'You planned it like this,' she said unsteadily. 'Didn't you?'

He touched a forefinger to her lips. 'I planned to marry you. The time, the place were irrelevant.'

She searched his features and glimpsed the strength of purpose evident. 'Georgia and Trenton's wedding, this remote island resort—' She faltered, absently lifting a hand to push a lock of hair behind her ear. 'Their plans made it easy for you to—'

'Discover the truth,' he finished.

'But what if—'

There was a faint edge of tension beneath the surface of his control that he fought hard to subdue. Losing her temporarily had nearly cost him his sanity.

'You said you needed time and space,' Sloane declared quietly. 'Something I vowed to give you…within reason.'

Suzanne digested his words, and perceived the meaning behind them. 'You had that much faith in me?'

A slight tremor in her voice brought a faint smile, and he lifted a hand and tucked another loose tendril of hair behind her ear. 'Yes.'

She saw the passion visible in those dark, arresting features, and her bones began to melt. 'Thank you,' she said simply.

His mouth curved with sensual warmth, deepening the darkness of his eyes as he leaned forward and trailed his lips along her cheekbone, then traced her jaw and settled near the edge of her mouth.

Without hesitation she shifted slightly and parted her lips to meet his in a kiss that merged from warmth to flaring heat in the space of a heartbeat.

It seemed an age before he lifted his head. 'We have a wedding to organise.'

Suzanne's eyes gleamed as she sought to tease him a little. 'I don't have anything suitable to wear.'

'Yes, you do.'

In her mind's eye she skimmed the clothes she'd

brought with her. 'I do?' The pale blue silk slip dress she'd worn the day before would suffice...providing the resort staff could work a cleaning miracle in time.

'Trust me.'

She opened her mouth, then closed it again.

He smiled, and it sent lines fanning out from the corners of each eye. 'Do I take that to mean a *yes*?'

Suzanne tried for solemnity, and failed. 'It depends what I'm saying *yes* to.'

He leaned forward and brushed his lips to the curve of her neck. His mouth moved lower, trailed a path up her throat and hovered above her lips. He angled his mouth down to hers and took his fill, plundering, possessing, until she could be in no doubt of his feelings, *hers*.

'Marrying me.'

His mouth was intent on wreaking such delicious havoc with her senses, savouring the delicate flavour of her skin, while his hands sought and found the acutely sensitised pleasure spots that drove her wild.

'Tomorrow.'

Yes, she cried silently. There were words she wanted to say, assurances she felt the need to give.

'Sloane.'

His hands stilled at the way her voice caught in saying his name, and his mouth paused in its downward path. He lifted his head and took in the soft fullness of her lips, the dilated depths of her eyes.

'I love you.' Words, just three of them. Yet in saying them she gifted more than her body. Her heart, her soul. Everything.

His hands shook slightly as they slid up to cup her face, and his expression was devoid of any artifice.

Joy, *love*, slow-burning deep emotion. Passion. Just for her.

'Thank you,' he said gently.

The anger, the frustration, the sheer helplessness that had coloured the past few weeks disappeared. He knew he never wanted to experience them again.

No one would ever be permitted to diminish what they shared, or seek to damage it in any way. There would be no more doubts, no room for any insecurity. He would personally see to it. Every day of his life.

Suzanne watched the changing emotions and successfully read every one of them. The resolution, the caring. And love.

His thumb moved across the fullness of her lower lip with a reverence that made her want to cry. 'I'm yours,' he said softly. 'Always.' His lips curved into a slow smile that melted her bones. 'For ever.'

She had to blink rapidly to dispel the suspicious moistness behind her eyes. 'Then I guess we get married tomorrow.' Her mouth moved to form a shaky smile. 'What on earth will Georgia and Trenton think?'

Sloane kissed the tip of her nose. 'Be delighted, I imagine.'

She leaned into him, overwhelmed by the sheer feel and power of him. 'Let's—' She paused slightly as Sloane's hand slid beneath the hem of her top and worked an evocative path towards one hip.

'Make love?' His husky chuckle was low and infinitely sensual.

'Go for a walk along the beach afterwards?' In the moonlight, in the stillness of night, with the sound of water lapping softly against the sand. Enjoying the magic of an island that was removed from civilisation, where solitude and privacy were guaranteed.

'Sure,' Sloane agreed easily.

'Providing you have sufficient energy left, of course,' she said with demure amusement, and had her laugh cut short as his mouth closed over hers in a kiss that promised total ravishment.

'Planning on wearing me out, huh?' he teased as he carried her upstairs, then laid her down on the bed.

As he undressed his eyes were so dark, magnificent. And alive with a passion that made her catch her breath. Slowly, and with a sensuality that wasn't contrived, she lifted the hem of her top, pulled it over her head and dropped it onto the floor.

He eased himself down onto the bed beside her and she lowered her head and kissed his shoulder, trailing her mouth down to one hard male nipple, savoured it, then followed the dark hair arrowing down to his navel.

Beneath the fine black silk briefs his arousal was a potent force, and she caressed its outline with the tip of her tongue. It created a slight friction that made him catch his breath, and with a boldness she didn't pause to question she took the waistband between her teeth and gradually eased them down, inch by inch until the briefs were reduced to a narrow fold across the top of his thighs.

There was a tremendous beauty in the aroused male

form, the knowledge of what that harnessed power could achieve in the pleasure stakes. For each of them.

Suzanne felt as if she wanted to laugh and cry, both at the same time, with the intense joy of being with this man, for she couldn't remember feeling so *alive*, so complete. It was like coming home, the knowledge of everything being *right*. She wanted to tell him, show him.

And she did. With infinite care, and a passion unfettered by uncertainty or reservation.

She wasn't sure when Sloane took control. Only that together they experienced emotions at their zenith again and again during the ensuing night hours.

Suzanne stirred as fingers trailed a light path across the flat plane of her stomach, and nuzzled the warm flesh beneath her cheek.

She didn't want to move. Didn't think she *could* move.

'I guess the moonlit walk along the beach will have to wait.'

Suzanne registered Sloane's amused drawl, felt his warm breath tease her temple, and slowly opened her eyes to discover an early dawn fingering soft light into the room.

'Well,' she murmured, 'there's always the early morning swim.'

His soft laughter reverberated beneath her ear, and she lifted her head to look at him, glimpsed the teasing warmth evident in the generous curve of his mouth, the liquid darkness of his eyes, and wrinkled her nose.

'Don't you think I'm capable?'

The corners of his eyes creased, and the darkness intensified. 'I should come along in case you drown.'

'You, of course, are a bundle of energy this fine morning?' She trailed her fingers across his midriff, felt the muscles tighten and created a playful pattern with the dark hair there.

'Go any lower, and I won't answer to the consequences,' Sloane warned huskily.

'Just checking,' she told him with impish mischievousness, then gasped as he lifted her across his chest, rolled her onto her back, and fastened his mouth on hers with devastating accuracy.

She clung to him, meeting his ardour with her own, loving the fierceness before it altered and softened into something that was incredibly gentle.

'A swim,' she said with a shaky smile. 'Definitely a swim. Otherwise we'll never get out of here.'

They rose, donned minimum swimwear, and Suzanne caught up a cotton wrap as Sloane collected a towel.

Outside it was still, and there wasn't a sound. No birdlife, not so much as a breeze to riffle the foliage as they made their way onto the sand.

A new day, she mused, watching as the colours around her gradually intensified. Crisp white sand, the sea changing hue from blue to aqua, clearly defined from an azure sky. The air was warm and devoid of the sun's heat.

As she watched, the golden orb's outer rim crept above the horizon, bringing with it the clarity of light, and she heard the first twitter as birds awoke.

Sloane watched her expressive features, the way her mouth curved slightly open, the softness in those vivid blue eyes as she stood there.

'Want to walk along the shoreline?'

She turned slowly towards him, and her eyes teased his. 'Dip our toes in the water, skim a few shells out over the surface?'

'Commune with Nature, and maybe sacrifice a swim for a long warm shower?'

Suzanne gave a throaty laugh as she caught hold of his hand. 'Chicken,' she teased. 'A bracing cold swim, a hearty breakfast...' She trailed off with a grin. 'Just what we need to kick-start the day.' Her eyes sparkled with humour. 'Last one in—' She didn't get to finish as she was swept off her feet and carried into the water. 'Sloane. Don't you *dare.*'

Cool, not cold, and definitely bracing. The hearty breakfast came way after the long warm shower.

Then things seemed to move very swiftly into action.

The celebrant didn't turn a hair when asked to perform another ceremony. Georgia and Trenton were thrilled with the news. The restaurant management appeared completely unfazed at the request to prepare a small but sumptuous midday wedding feast.

Suzanne gasped out loud when Georgia removed a pale ivory creation of silk and lace from its protective covering, added shoes, and a fingertip veil.

Sloane's contingency plan.

She reached out a hand and touched the exquisite lace overlay. 'It's beautiful.' The correct size, the right length, perfect.

'Did you—?'

'Help?' Georgia queried. 'No, I swear.'

'You're not going to ask if I have doubts?'

'I don't need to,' her mother said gently. 'You wouldn't be about to do this if you had them.'

No, Suzanne agreed in contemplative silence as she crossed to the mirror and began tending to her make-up.

It was almost eleven-thirty when she made the final adjustment to her veil and stood back from the mirror.

'You take my breath away,' Georgia said with a tremulous smile.

'Don't you dare cry,' Suzanne admonished her with a shaky grin. 'Or I will too, then we'll have to redo our make-up, which will make us late, and Sloane will send Trenton on a rescue mission, only to follow closely on his heels with the celebrant in tow.' Her eyes danced with expressive mischief. 'Not exactly a scene I would choose. Besides, we can't have this hastily arranged service misconstrued as a kidnap attempt of the bride by the groom, can we? Think what a field day the gossip columns would have with that!'

Georgia's mouth quivered as she caught hold of her daughter's outstretched hand. 'Unthinkable,' she agreed solemnly.

Tables had been cleared at one end of the restaurant to make room for an elegant archway threaded with hibiscus and frangipani in brilliant shades of pink. Soft music filtered from a stereo system, and red carpet formed a temporary aisle.

Suzanne took a deep breath, accepted the reassuring squeeze from her mother's fingers, then began walking slowly towards the archway where Sloane and Trenton waited with the celebrant.

Father and son were similar in height and stature, their breadth of shoulder outlined by superb tailoring, and almost in unison both men turned to watch the two women in their lives walk towards them.

Suzanne felt as if time stood still. Her eyes met Sloane's, and clung. Everything else faded to the periphery of her vision as she drew close, and there was him, only him.

The expression in those liquid brown eyes held a warmth that threatened to melt her bones. There was a wealth of emotion apparent as he smiled, and her step almost faltered as she reached his side.

Sloane caught hold of her hand and lifted it to his lips, then he kissed each finger in turn, slowly, as her heart went into overdrive.

She was barely aware that Georgia moved to one side, and she endeavoured to focus on the celebrant's voice as he intoned the words, elicited their individual responses, then solemnly accorded them man and wife after the exchanging of rings.

'You may now kiss the bride.'

Sloane lifted the fine veil with infinite care, then his hands slid to cup her face, and his head descended as he took possession of her mouth in a kiss that claimed and pleasured with such thoroughness, her skin tinged a delicate pink at the blatant promise apparent.

Afterwards they sipped Cristal champagne from slim crystal flutes, posed for the essential few photographs, then took their seats at an elegantly decorated table where they were served the finest seafood in delicate sauces, fresh salads, an incredible pavlova decorated with fresh cream and fruit for dessert, followed by the pièce de résistance, an iced wedding cake. Which necessitated more champagne, a toast, followed by coffee.

As weddings went, it had to be one of the smallest, most intimate affairs on record, Suzanne mused as they stood and thanked Georgia and Trenton, the staff, the celebrant, then led the way from the restaurant.

Sadly, the romantic idyll was almost over, for in half an hour the launch would leave for Dunk Island, where the family jet was on standby to fly them to Sydney.

Inside the villa Sloane caught hold of her hands and drew her close.

'I don't think we have time for this,' Suzanne said a trifle breathlessly as his head descended to hers.

'Depends on your definition of *this*,' Sloane teased, touching his lips to the corner of her mouth as he trailed a tantalising path along the contours of her lower lip.

A groan escaped her throat, and she angled her mouth so that it fitted his, encouraging a possession he didn't hesitate to give.

It seemed an age before he lifted his head, and she could only look at him in total bemusement. 'I think,' she managed huskily, 'we should change and pack.'

His lips brushed across her forehead. 'Change, but not pack.' He lingered at her temple, then traced the edge of her jaw. 'We're staying here.'

'How can we stay? I'm due back at work tomorrow.' Her eyes widened. 'You must have court appearances.' Her voice husked down to a mere whisper. 'It's not possible.'

He lifted his head and surveyed her features with musing indulgence. 'Yes, it is.' He placed a forefinger beneath her chin and lifted it. 'All it took was a few phone calls.'

'But you can't—'

'I just have.'

'My job—'

'Secure,' Sloane assured her. 'For as long as you want it.'

She drew in a shaky breath, then released it. 'What did you tell them?'

His thumb traced the column of her throat, felt the convulsive movement as she swallowed, and soothed it with the gentle brush of his fingers. 'The truth.' He explored the hollow at the edge of her neck, and felt her quivering response. 'You have a week's leave with their blessing.'

It was feasible her work could be shared around. Sloane, however, was in a vastly different position. 'But what about you?'

'Forward planning,' he declared, and effected a slight shrug. 'I did a bit of shuffling, called in a few favours.'

'How long?' It couldn't possibly be more than a day or two.

'I'm not due in court until Friday.'

She wanted to kiss and hug him, both at the same time. 'I love you,' she said reverently. 'Later, I intend to show you just how much.'

'Promises?'

She offered him a brilliant smile. 'Oh, yes. Definitely. But now,' she declared, 'we change, then we'll go see Georgia and Trenton onto the launch.'

His mouth quirked with humour, playing her game. 'And after?'

'A girl's wedding day is special.' Her smile was infinitely wicked. 'Something of which memories are made and reminisced over down the years.' She lifted both hands and ticked off her fingers, one by one. 'There's the champagne, the bridal waltz, and the throwing of the bridal bouquet.' Irrepressible humour intensified the blue of her eyes. 'You planned the first half of the day. Are you willing to leave the second half to me?'

Sloane caught hold of her hands, and kissed the inside of each wrist before releasing them. 'I guess I can do that.'

CHAPTER ELEVEN

THEY REACHED THE jetty a few minutes before Georgia and Trenton, together with the celebrant, were due to board the launch. Goodbyes were affectionate, but brief.

'I want postcards from Paris,' Suzanne insisted gently as she kissed Georgia.

'Done.'

Suzanne stood within the circle of Sloane's arms as the launch moved out of sight, then she turned and curved an arm around his waist.

'Let's walk along the beach.'

He looked down at her expressive features, caught the faint shadows beneath her eyes and experienced a faint pang of regret that he was the cause. She needed to catch up on sleep. Dammit, they both did.

'No rock-climbing,' he warned, and she laughed, a light, infectious sound that curled round his heart.

'Intent on preserving the energy levels?'

The smile he slanted her held warm humour. 'Yours, as well as my own.'

They trod the soft sand to the first promontory, then turned and slowly retraced their steps. The pool looked inviting, and they stroked a few lengths in lazy rhythm before emerging to lie supine side by side on two loungers, allowing the soft warm breeze to dry the brief, thin pieces of silk they each wore.

Suzanne must have slept, for she dreamt of isolated incidents that had no common linkage, and woke to the drift of fingers tracing a soft pattern down her forearm.

The sun was low in the sky, and there were long shadows deepening the colour of the sand.

'It's late.'

'Does it matter?' Sloane queried, propping himself up on one arm.

She rose to her feet in one fluid movement. 'We have a dinner reservation in half an hour.' She stretched a hand towards him. 'Time to rise and shine and shower and dress.'

They made it with barely a minute to spare, and were seated out on the terrace overlooking the bay.

Suzanne requested champagne, conferred with Sloane over the menu choices, and they opted for a light meal, preferring entrée servings with salads and fresh fruit.

The scallops mornay were superb, the oysters kilpatrick divine, and the prawns delectable.

They delighted in feeding each other morsels of food in a feast that equally fed their palates and their senses.

Anticipation was a powerful aphrodisiac, and they deliberately lingered, delaying the return to their villa by tacit consent.

There was background music, and Suzanne smiled as Sloane stood and held out his hand.

'You mentioned something about dancing.'

Heaven didn't get any better than this, she decided dreamily as she slipped into his arms. His hold was hardly conventional, and his lips grazed her temple, creating an evocative pattern that heated her blood to fever pitch.

It would be all too easy to whisper, Let's get out of here.

He sensed the moment she almost wavered, and brushed a kiss down the slope of her nose. There were other nights, a whole lifetime of them. He closed his eyes, then opened them again. *Thank God*, he thought in silent reverence.

Did she realise how much she meant to him? How the prospect of a life without her was akin to slowly dying?

He had known from the first moment they met that she was special. Courting her should have been easy. Never once had he even had to *try* with a woman. They were there for the taking, the selection entirely his. Suzanne had been different. There was no façade, no games, no emotional baggage. Just honesty, and a beautiful soul.

In retrospect, he acknowledged he'd moved too fast. The *image* of Wilson-Willoughby had proved to be a deterrent, for instead of enticing it had earned unaccustomed caution.

The night he'd walked into an empty penthouse and discovered she'd gone had been the worst night of his life. In the space of mere minutes he'd experienced very real fear, devastating loss, and a slow-mounting rage, the like of which he'd never known before. The note had left no phone number, no address, and no way of contacting her until eight-thirty the next morning when she arrived at the office.

'It's time to throw the bridal bouquet.'

He relaxed his hold and let her slip out from his arms, watching as she scooped up a display of frangipani and hibiscus from a nearby table centrepiece.

'To whom do you intend to throw it?'

'Ah, now there's a thing,' she said solemnly. 'The waiter? The waitress at the bar?'

All he had to do was raise his hand, murmur his request, and within minutes there were five staff members forming a line.

'It's not really a bouquet.'

'I don't think they'll care.'

They didn't, not at all, and she gave an infectious laugh as the flowers sailed a few metres and then separated easily between two pairs of hands.

Suzanne turned towards Sloane, and her eyes shone with mischief. 'Now we get to leave.'

There was a moon, bathing everything with a dim light, and halfway along the path she reached up and kissed him, only to gasp when he pulled her close and turned the impulsive gesture into something infinitely sensual.

They had almost an entire week of lazily spent days and long nights of lovemaking ahead of them, Suzanne reflected dreamily as they reached their villa. Time out for romance, before the return to reality in a cosmopolitan southern city and a faster pace of life. Somehow their inevitable social obligations no longer seemed daunting.

Sloane unlocked the door, then switched on the light. Suzanne stepped inside, then came to an abrupt halt.

Inside, both downstairs and visible in the bedroom, grouped in vases, were masses of deep red roses, filling the villa with their delicate perfume.

She felt her eyes widen with sheer pleasure, then mist with the threat of tears. Slowly she turned to face him, her mouth shaky with emotion as she looked at him in silent query.

'While you were planning,' Sloane declared gently, 'I did a little planning of my own.'

'So many,' she said breathlessly, as she moved forward and touched a gentle finger to one velvet bud.

He crossed to stand behind her, curving her close into his body. His warm breath teased the hair at her temple as she sank back against him.

'A dozen to represent every year for the rest of our lives.'

Her heart seemed to turn over in her chest. She turned in his arms and reached up to link her hands together at his nape. His eyes were dark, so darkly gleaming she could almost see herself in their reflection.

'I love you. So much,' Suzanne whispered. 'I always have.'

His lips grazed hers, then lifted fractionally. 'I know,' he said gently. Her lips parted, and he pressed them closed. 'It was the only thing that kept me sane.'

His mouth closed over hers, seeking, finding everything she had to give and more, as he gave in return.

It wasn't enough, not nearly enough. Suzanne groaned as her fingers sought the hard flesh beneath his clothes, and she gasped as he swung an arm beneath her knees and lifted her high against his chest.

Her lips were slightly swollen, and her eyes deep and slumberous, as he strode towards the steps leading up to the bedroom.

'I am capable of walking,' she teased, and nearly died at the depth of passion evident in his gaze.

'Isn't the groom supposed to carry the bride over the threshold?'

'Something like that,' she said with mock seriousness. She lifted a hand and trailed her fingers down the edge of his cheek. 'What other traditions do you have in mind?'

He reached the upper level, crossed to the large bed, and lowered her down to stand within the circle of his arms. 'One or two.'

His fingers freed the loops attaching two tiny buttons at her nape, then he slid the zip fastening down the length of her back. The pale silk whispered to the floor to pool at her feet.

Soft opaque lining had negated the need to wear a bra, and she quivered beneath the intensity of his gaze, all too aware of her body's reaction. Only lace bikini briefs remained, and her eyes widened as he reached out a hand and extracted a single rose from a nearby vase.

With exquisite care he touched the velvet-petalled bud to her cheek, then trailed it gently to the edge of her mouth.

The delicate scent teased her nostrils, and she felt

all her fine body hairs rise in acute sensual expectation as he traced an evocative pattern to the valley between each breast.

Slowly, with infinite care, he gently outlined one breast, then the other, before trailing down to rest at her navel.

Suzanne's breath caught as desire arrowed through her body, igniting each erogenous zone in a conflagrant path and sending fire coursing through her veins.

With one deliberate movement he reached forward and pulled the covers from the bed, and she watched in mesmerised fascination as he lifted the rosebud to his lips.

Her eyes widened, dilating into huge pools of dark blue sapphire as he carefully peeled one petal free and let it flutter down on the bedsheets. Then another, and another, slowly, until only the rose stem and its stamen remained.

Suzanne thought her bones would melt, and a slow, sweet smile curved her generous mouth as she stepped out of her shoes.

She reached for the buttons on his shirt and undid them one by one, then discarded it. Her fingers moved to the buckle at his waist, dispensed with it, then she freed the zip fastening his trousers. Shoes and socks slid off easily.

Without a word she collected a rose, then, giving his chest a gentle push, she tumbled him down onto the bed.

His husky laughter brought forth a wickedly teasing gleam and her eyes danced at the thought of what she had in store for him.

Mirroring his actions, she slowly peeled one petal and let it drift down onto his torso. Then another, and another, with infinite care, until there was none.

With a witching smile she reached forward and plucked another rose from a nearby vase, and gently placed it against his mouth.

Sloane doubted he would ever be able to look at a rose again without experiencing a damning and very intimate reaction. Petals softer than a woman's touch, their brush against sensitive skin incredibly evocative, the eroticism so intense it took all his will-power to lie supine while she conducted the sensual stroking. Much more of this...

Suzanne saw the instant his eyes darkened, and she gave a soft, throaty laugh as he pulled her down on top of him.

The rose slipped from her fingers and fell to the floor as he surged into her, and she reached for his forearms as he caught hold of her hips, commanding a ride that had no equal in her experience.

Moisture filmed her skin, his, as he took her to a place where control had no meaning and the senses exploded in a starburst of heat so intense she thought she might *burn* with it.

Afterwards she collapsed against his chest in a state of emotional exhaustion. She could feel the drift of his fingers against her skin as he caressed the indentations of her spine.

Gradually her breathing steadied, and her heart slowed to an even beat.

She wanted to stay close to him like this for ever.

To feel, to know that their loving would always be so intense, so emotive. A true meshing of the emotions, physical, mental and spiritual.

Suzanne lifted her head and looked down into those dark, passion-filled eyes, and felt her body turn to jelly.

'I love you,' Sloane said with heartfelt simplicity. 'I know I couldn't survive a life without you in it. You're everything there is, and more. So much more.'

Tears filmed her eyes, and she lifted a hand to brush gentle fingers across his mouth. 'Same goes.'

He parted his teeth and nipped one finger, then drew it into his mouth and laved it with his tongue.

Awareness swirled into active life, spiralling through her body with damning ease, and she shifted slightly, exulting in the quickening power of his arousal as it swelled inside her.

In one smooth movement he rolled over and pinned her against the mattress.

The scent of crushed rose petals was strong, and she curved her legs around his hips, drawing him in close as she linked her hands together and pulled his head down to hers.

'Thank you.' She brushed his mouth with her own. 'For today. The roses. Everything. *You*, especially you.'

'My pleasure,' Sloane murmured against her lips, aware the pleasure was mutual. As it always would be.

* * * * *

THE BRIDAL BED
HELEN BIANCHIN

CHAPTER ONE

GABBI EASED THE car to a halt in the long line of traffic banked up behind the New South Head Road intersection adjacent to Sydney's suburban Elizabeth Bay. A slight frown creased her forehead as she checked her watch, and her fingers tapped an impatient tattoo against the steering wheel.

She had precisely one hour in which to shower, wash her hair, dry and style it, apply make-up, dress, and greet invited dinner guests. The loss of ten minutes caught up in heavy traffic didn't form part of her plan.

Her eyes slid to the manicured length of her nails, and she dwelt momentarily on the fact that time spent on their lacquered perfection had cost her her lunch. An apple at her desk mid-afternoon could hardly be termed an adequate substitute.

The car in front began to move, and she followed its path, picking up speed, only to depress the brake pedal as the lights changed.

Damn. At this rate it would take two, if not three attempts to clear the intersection.

She *should*, she admitted silently, have left her office earlier in order to miss the heavy early evening traffic. Yet stubborn single-mindedness had prevented her from doing so.

As James Stanton's daughter, she had no need to work. Property, an extensive share portfolio and a handsome annuity placed her high on the list of Sydney's independently wealthy young women.

As Benedict Nicols' *wife*, her position as assistant management consultant with Stanton-Nicols Enterprises was viewed as nepotism at its very worst.

Gabbi thrust the gear-shift forward with unaccustomed force, attaining momentary satisfaction from the sound of the Mercedes' refined engine as she eased the car forward and followed the traffic's crawling pace, only to halt scant minutes later.

The cellphone rang, and she automatically reached for it.

'Gabrielle.'

Only one person steadfastly refused to abbreviate her Christian name. 'Monique.'

'You're driving?'

'Stationary,' she informed her, pondering the purpose of her stepmother's call. Monique never rang to simply say 'hello.'

'Annaliese flew in this afternoon. Would it be an imposition if she came to dinner?'

Years spent attending an élite boarding-school had instilled requisite good manners. 'Not at all. We'd be delighted.'

'Thank you, darling.'

Monique's voice sounded like liquid satin as she ended the call.

Wonderful, Gabbi accorded silently as she punched

in the appropriate code and alerted Marie to set another place at the table.

'Sorry to land this on you,' she added apologetically before replacing the handset down onto the console. An extra guest posed no problem, and Gabbi wasn't sufficiently superstitious to consider thirteen at the table a premise for an unsuccessful evening.

The traffic began to move, and the faint tension behind her eyes threatened to develop into a headache.

James Stanton's remarriage ten years ago to a twenty-nine-year-old divorcee with one young daughter had gifted him with a contentment Gabbi could never begrudge him. Monique was his social equal, and an exemplary hostess. It was unfortunate that Monique's affection didn't extend to James's daughter. As a vulnerable fifteen-year-old Gabbi had sensed her stepmother's superficiality, and spent six months agonising over why, until a friend had spelled out the basic psychology of a dysfunctional relationship.

In retaliation, Gabbi had chosen to excel at everything she did—she'd striven to gain straight As in each subject, had won sporting championships, and graduated from university with an honours degree in business management. She'd studied languages and spent a year in Paris, followed by another in Tokyo, before returning to Sydney to work for a rival firm. Then she'd applied for and won, on the strength of her experience and credentials, a position with Stanton-Nicols.

There was a certain danger in allowing one's thoughts to dwell on the past, Gabbi mused a trifle wryly as she swung the Mercedes into the exclusive Vaucluse street, where heavy, wide-branched trees

added a certain ambience to the luxurious homes nestled out of sight behind high concrete walls.

A few hundred metres along she drew the car to
a halt, depressed a remote modem, and waited the
necessary seconds as the double set of ornate black
wrought-iron gates slid smoothly aside.

A wide curved driveway led to an elegant two-
storeyed Mediterranean-style home set well back from
the road in beautiful landscaped grounds. Encompassing four allotments originally acquired in the late
1970s by Conrad Nicols, the existing four houses had
been removed to make way for a multi-million-dollar
residence whose magnificent harbour views placed it
high in Sydney's real-estate stratosphere.

Ten years later extensive million-dollar refur-
bishment had added extensions providing additional
bedroom accommodation, garages for seven cars, re-
modelled kitchen, undercover terraces, and balconies.
The revamped gardens boasted fountains, courtyards,
ornamental ponds and English-inspired lawns bordered by clipped hedges.

It was incredibly sad, Gabbi reflected as she released one set of automatic garage doors and drove beneath them, that Conrad and Diandra Nicols had been
victims of a freak highway accident mere weeks after
the final landscaping touches had been completed.

Yet Conrad had achieved in death what he hadn't
achieved in the last ten years of his life: His son and
heir had returned from America and taken over Conrad's partnership in Stanton-Nicols.

Gabbi slid the Mercedes to a halt between the sleek
lines of Benedict's XJ220 Jaguar and the more staid
frame of a black Bentley. Missing was the top-of-the-

range four-wheel drive Benedict used to commute each day to the city.

The garage doors slid down with a refined click and Gabbi caught up her briefcase from the passenger seat, slipped out from behind the wheel, then crossed to a side door to punch in a series of digits, deactivating the security system guarding entry to the house.

Mansion, she corrected herself with a twisted smile as she lifted the in-house phone and rang through to the kitchen. 'Hi, Marie. Everything under control?'

Twenty years' service with the Nicols family enabled the housekeeper to respond with a warm chuckle. 'No problems.'

'Thanks,' Gabbi acknowledged gratefully before hurrying through the wide hallway to a curved staircase leading to the upper floor.

Marie would be putting the final touches to the four-course meal she'd prepared; her husband, Serg, would be checking the temperature of the wines Benedict had chosen to be served, and Sophie, the casual help, would be running a final check of the diningroom.

All *she* had to do was appear downstairs, perfectly groomed, when Serg answered the ring of the doorbell and ushered the first of their guests into the lounge in around forty minutes.

Or less, Gabbi accorded as she ascended the stairs at a rapid pace.

Benedict's mother had chosen lush-piled eau-de-nil carpet and pale textured walls to offset the classic lines of the mahogany furniture, employing a skilful blend of toning colour with matching drapes and bedcovers, ensuring each room was subtly different.

The master suite was situated in the eastern wing with glass doors opening onto two balconies and commanding impressive views of the harbour. Panoramic by day, those views became a magical vista at night, with a fairy-like tracery of distant electric and flashing neon light.

Gabbi kicked off her shoes, removed jewellery, then quickly shed her clothes *en route* to a marble-tiled *en suite* which almost rivalled the bedroom in size.

Elegantly decadent in pale gold-streaked ivory marble, there was a huge spa-bath and a double shower to complement the usual facilities.

Ten minutes later she entered the bedroom, a towel fastened sarong-style over her slim curves, with another wound into a turban on top of her head.

'Cutting it fine, Gabbi?' Benedict's faintly accented drawl held a mocking edge as he shrugged off his suit jacket and loosened his tie.

In his late thirties, tall, with a broad, hard-muscled frame, his sculpted facial features gave a hint of his maternal Andalusian ancestry. Dark, almost black eyes held a powerful intensity that never softened for his fellow man, and rarely for a woman.

'Whatever happened to "Hi, honey, I'm home"?' she retaliated as she crossed the room and selected fresh underwear from a recessed drawer, hurriedly donned briefs and bra, then stepped into a silk slip.

'Followed by a salutatory kiss?' he mocked with a tinge of musing cynicism as he shed his shirt and attended to the zip of his trousers.

She felt the tempo of her heartbeat increase, and she was conscious of an elevated tension that began in the pit of her stomach and flared along every nerve-end, firing her body with an acute awareness that was entirely physical.

Dynamic masculinity at its most potent, she acknowledged silently as she snatched up a silk robe, thrust her arms through its sleeves, and retraced her steps to the *en suite*.

Removing the towelled turban, she caught up the hair-drier and began blow-drying her hair.

Her attention rapidly became unfocused as Benedict entered the *en suite* and crossed to the shower. Mirrored walls reflected his naked image, and she determinedly ignored the olive-toned skin sheathing hard muscle and sinew, the springy dark hair that covered his chest and arrowed down past his waist to reach his manhood, the firmly shaped buttocks, and the powerful length of his back.

Her eyes followed the powerful strength of his shoulders as he reached forward to activate the flow of water, then the glass doors slid closed behind him.

Gabbi tugged the brush through her hair with unnecessary force, and felt her eyes prick at the sudden pain.

It was one year, two months and three weeks since their marriage, and she still couldn't handle the effect he had on her in bed or out of it.

Her scalp tingled in protest, and she relaxed the brushstrokes then switched off the drier. Her hair was still slightly damp, its natural ash-blonde colour appearing faintly darker, highlighting the creamy smoothness of her skin and accentuating the deep blue of her eyes.

With practised movements she caught the length of

her hair and deftly swept it into a chignon at her nape, secured it with pins, then began applying make-up.

Minutes later she heard the water stop, and with conscious effort she focused on blending her eye-shadow, studiously ignoring him as he crossed to the long marbled pedestal and began dealing with a day's growth of beard.

'Bad day?'

Her fingers momentarily stilled, then she replaced the eyeshadow palette and selected mascara. 'Why do you ask?'

'You have expressive eyes,' Benedict observed as he smoothed his fingers over his jaw.

Gabbi met his gaze in the mirror, and held it. 'Annaliese is to be a last-minute guest at dinner.'

He switched off the electric shaver and reached for the cut-glass bottle containing an exclusive brand of cologne. 'That bothers you?'

She tried for levity. 'I'm capable of slaying my own dragons.'

One eyebrow lifted with sardonic humour. 'Verbal swords over dessert?'

Annaliese was known not to miss an opportunity, and Gabbi couldn't imagine tonight would prove an exception. 'I'll do my best to parry any barbs with practised civility.'

His eyes swept over her slim curves then returned to study the faint, brooding quality evident on her finely etched features, and a slight smile tugged the edges of his mouth. 'The objective being to win another battle in an ongoing war?'

'Has anyone beaten *you* in battle, Benedict?' she queried lightly as she capped the mascara wand, re-

turned it to the drawer housing her cosmetics and concentrated on applying a soft pink colour to her lips.

He didn't answer. He had no need to assert that
he was a man equally feared and respected by his
contemporaries and rarely, if ever, fooled by anyone.

Just watch my back. The words remained unuttered as she turned towards the door, and minutes
later she selected a long black pencil-slim silk skirt
and teamed it with a simple scoop-necked sleeveless
black top. Stiletto-heeled evening shoes completed
the outfit, and she added a pear-shaped diamond pendant and matching ear-studs, then slipped on a slim,
diamond-encrusted bracelet before turning towards
the mirror to cast her reflection a cursory glance. A
few dabs of her favourite Le Must de Cartier perfume
added the final touch.

'Ready?'

Gabbi turned at the sound of his voice, and felt her
breath catch at the image he presented.

There was something about his stance, a sense of
animalistic strength, that fine tailoring did little to
tame. The dramatic mesh of elemental ruthlessness
and primitive power added a magnetism few women
of any age could successfully ignore.

For a few timeless seconds her eyes locked with
his in an attempt to determine what lay behind the
studied inscrutability he always managed to portray.

She envied him his superb control…and wondered
what it would take to break it.

'Yes.' Her voice was steady, and she summoned a
bright smile as she turned to precede him from the
room.

The main staircase curved down to the ground

floor in an elegant sweep of wide, partially carpeted marble stairs, with highly polished mahogany bannisters supported by ornately scrolled black wrought-iron balusters.

Set against floor-to-ceiling lead-panelled glass, the staircase created an elegant focus highlighted by a magnificent crystal chandelier.

Marble floors lent spaciousness and light to the large entry foyer, sustained by textured ivory-coloured walls whose uniformity was broken by a series of wide, heavily panelled doors, works of art, and a collection of elegant Mediterranean-style cabinets.

Gabbi had just placed a foot on the last stair when the doorbell pealed.

'Show-time,' she murmured as Serg emerged from the eastern hallway and moved quickly towards the impressively panelled double front doors.

Benedict's eyes hardened fractionally. 'Cynicism doesn't suit you.'

Innate pride lent her eyes a fiery sparkle, and her chin tilted slightly in a gesture of mild defiance. 'I can be guaranteed to behave,' she assured him quietly, and felt her pulse quicken as he caught hold of her hand.

'Indeed.' The acknowledgement held a dry softness which was lethal, and an icy chill feathered across the surface of her skin.

'Charles,' Benedict greeted smoothly seconds later as Serg announced the first of their guests. 'Andrea.' His smile was warm, and he appeared relaxed and totally at ease. 'Come through to the lounge and let me get you a drink.'

Most of the remaining guests arrived within minutes, and Gabbi played her role as hostess to the hilt, circulating, smiling, all the time waiting for the moment Monique and Annaliese would precede her father into the lounge.

Monique believed in making an entrance, and her arrival was always carefully timed to provide maximum impact. While she was never unpardonably late, her timing nevertheless bordered on the edge of social acceptability.

Serg's announcement coincided with Gabbi's expectation and, excusing herself from conversation, she moved forward to greet her father.

'James.' She brushed his cheek with her lips and accepted the firm clasp on her shoulder in return before turning towards her stepmother to accept the salutatory air-kiss. 'Monique.' Her smile was without fault as she acknowledged the stunning young woman at Monique's side. 'Annaliese. How nice to see you.'

Benedict joined her, the light touch of his hand at the back of her waist a disturbing sensation that provided subtle reassurance and a hidden warning. That it also succeeded in sharpening her senses and made her incredibly aware of him was entirely a secondary consideration.

His greeting echoed her own, his voice assuming a subtle inflection that held genuine warmth with her father, utter charm with her stepmother, and an easy tolerance with Annaliese.

Monique's sweet smile in response was faultless. Annaliese, however, was pure feline and adept in the art of flirtation. A skill she seemed to delight in practising on any male past the age of twenty, with scant respect for his marital status.

'Benedict.' With just one word Annaliese managed to convey a wealth of meaning that set Gabbi's teeth on edge.

The pressure of Benedict's fingers increased, and Gabbi gave him a stunning smile, totally ignoring the warning flare in the depths of those dark eyes.

Dinner was a success. It would have been difficult for even the most discerning gourmand's palate to find fault with the serving of fine food beautifully cooked, superbly presented, and complemented by excellent wine.

Benedict was an exemplary host, and his inherent ability to absorb facts and figures combined with an almost photographic memory ensured conversation was varied and interesting. Men sought and valued his opinion on a business level, and envied him his appeal with women. Women, on the other hand, sought his attention and coveted Gabbi's position as his wife.

A MATCH MADE IN HEAVEN, the tabloids had announced at the time. THE WEDDING OF THE DECADE, a number of women's magazines had headlined, depicting a variety of photographs to endorse the projected image.

Only the romantically inclined accepted the media coverage as portrayed, while the city's—indeed, the entire country's—upper social echelons recognised the facts beneath the fairy floss.

The marriage of Benedict Nicols and Gabrielle Stanton had occurred as a direct result of the manipulative strategy by James Stanton to cement the Stanton-Nicols financial empire and forge it into another generation.

The reason for Benedict's participation was clear...

he stood to gain total control of Stanton-Nicols. The bonus was a personable young woman eminently eligible to sire the necessary progeny.

Gabbi's compliance had been motivated in part by a desire to please her father and the realistic recognition that, given his enormous wealth, there would be very few men, if any, who would discount the financial and social advantage of being James Stanton's son-in-law.

'Shall we adjourn to the lounge for coffee?'

The smooth words caught Gabbi's attention, and she took Benedict's cue by summoning a gracious smile and rising to her feet. 'I'm sure Marie has it ready.'

'Treasure of a chef', 'wonderful meal', 'delightful evening'. Words echoed in polite praise, and she inclined her head in acknowledgement. 'Thank you. I'll pass on your compliments to Marie. She'll be pleased.' Which was true. Marie valued the high salary and separate live-in accommodation that formed part of the employment package, and her gratitude was reflected in her culinary efforts.

'You were rather quiet at dinner, darling.'

Gabbi heard Monique's softly toned voice, and turned towards her. 'Do you think so?'

'Annaliese is a little hurt, I think.' The reproach was accompanied by a wistful smile, and Gabbi allowed her eyes to widen slightly.

'Oh, dear,' she managed with credible regret. 'She gave such a convincing display of enjoying herself.'

Monique's eyes assumed a mistiness Gabbi knew to be contrived. *How did she do that?* Her stepmother had missed her vocation; as an actress she would have excelled.

'Annaliese has always regarded you as an elder sister.'

There was nothing *familial* about Annaliese's regard—for Gabbi. Benedict, however, fell into an entirely different category.

'I'm deeply flattered,' Gabbi acknowledged gently, and incurred Monique's sharp glance. They had lingered slightly behind the guests exiting the dining-room and were temporarily out of their earshot.

'She's very fond of you.'

Doubtful. Gabbi had always been regarded as a rival, and Annaliese was her mother's daughter. Perfectly groomed, beautifully dressed, perfumed...and on a mission. To tease and tantalise, and enjoy the challenge of the chase until she caught the right man.

Gabbi was saved from making a response as they entered the lounge, and she accepted coffee from Marie, choosing to take it black, strong and sweet.

With a calm that was contrived she lifted her cup and took a sip of the strong, aromatic brew. 'If you'll excuse me? I really must have a word with James.'

It was almost midnight when the last guest departed, a time deemed neither too early nor too late for a mid-week dinner party to end.

Gabbi slid off her heeled sandals as she crossed the foyer to the lounge. Her head felt impossibly heavy, a knot of tension twisting a painful path from her right temple down to the edge of her nape.

Sophie had cleared the remaining coffee cups and liqueur glasses, and in the morning Marie would en-

sure the lounge was restored to its usual immaculate state.

'A successful evening, wouldn't you agree?'

Benedict's lazy drawl stirred the embers of resentment she'd kept carefully banked over the past few
hours.

'How could it not be?' she countered as she turned
to face him.

'You want to orchestrate a post-mortem?' he queried with deceptive mildness, and she glimpsed the
tightly coiled strength beneath the indolent façade.

'Not particularly.'

He conducted a brief, encompassing appraisal of
her features. 'Then I suggest you go upstairs to bed.'

Her chin tilted fractionally, and she met his dark
gaze with equanimity. 'And prepare myself to accommodate you?'

There was a flicker of something dangerous in the
depths of his eyes, then it was gone, and his movements as he closed the distance between them held a
smooth, panther-like grace.

'Accommodate?' he stressed silkily.

He was too close, his height and broad frame an
intimidating entity that invaded her space. The clean,
male smell of him combined with his exclusive brand
of cologne weakened her defences and lodged an attack against the very core of her femininity.

He had no need to touch her, and it irked her unbearably that he knew it.

'Your sexual appetite is...' Gabbi paused, then
added delicately, 'Consistent.' Her eyes flared slightly,
the blue depths pure crystalline sapphire.

He lifted a hand and caught hold of her chin, lifting it so she had little option but to retain his gaze. 'It's a woman's prerogative to decline.'

She looked at him carefully, noting the fine lines fanning out from the corners of his eyes, the deep vertical crease slashing each cheek, and the firm, sensual lines of his mouth.

The tug of sexual awareness intensified at the thought of the havoc that mouth could wreak when it possessed her own, the pleasure as it explored the soft curves of her body.

'And a man's inclination to employ unfair persuasion,' Gabbi offered, damning the slight catch of her breath as the pad of his thumb traced an evocative pattern along the edge of her jaw, then slid down the pulsing cord to the hollow at the curve of her neck, cupping it while he loosened the pins holding her hair in place.

They fell to the carpet as his fingers combed the blonde length free, then his head lowered and she closed her eyes as his lips brushed her temple, then feathered a path to the edge of her mouth, teasing its outline as he tested the soft fullness and sensed the faint trembling as she tried for control.

She should stop him now, plead tiredness, the existence of a headache…say she didn't want to have to try to cope with the aftermath of his lovemaking. The futility of experiencing utter joy and knowing physical lust was an unsatisfactory substitute for love.

His body moved in close against her own, its hard length a potent force she fought hard to ignore. Without success, for she had little defence against the firm pressure of his lips as he angled her mouth and possessed it, gently at first, then with an increasing depth of passion which demanded her capitulation.

She didn't care when she felt his hands slide the length of her skirt up over her thighs, and she cared even less when he shaped her buttocks and lifted her up against him.

There was a sense of exultant pleasure as she curved her legs around his hips and tangled her arms together behind his neck, the movement of his body an exciting enticement as he ascended the stairs to their bedroom.

She was on fire, *aching* for the feel of his skin against her own, and her fingers feverishly freed his tie and attacked the buttons on his shirt, not satisfied until they found the silken whorls of hair covering his taut, muscled chest.

Her mouth slid down the firm column of his throat, savoured the hollow at its base, then sought a tantalising path along one collarbone.

At some stage she became dimly aware she was standing, her clothes, and *his*, no longer a barrier, and she gave a soft cry as he pulled her down onto the bed.

Now, hard and fast. No preliminaries. And afterwards he could take all the time he wanted.

His deep, husky laugh brought faint colour to her cheeks. A colour that deepened at the comprehension that she'd inadvertently said the words out loud.

He sank into her, watching her expressive features as she accepted him, the fleeting changes as she stretched and the slight gasp as he buried his shaft deep inside her.

He stayed still for endlessly long seconds, and she felt him swell, then he began to withdraw, slowly, before plunging even more deeply, repeating the action and the tempo of his rhythm until she went up in flames.

The long, slow after-play, his expertise, the wicked treachery of skilful fingers, the erotic mouth, combined to bring her to the brink and hold her there until she begged for release—and she was unsure at the peak of ecstasy whether she loved or *hated* him for what he could do to her.

Good sex. Very good sex. That's all it was, she reflected sadly as she slid through the veils of sleep.

CHAPTER TWO

'VOGEL ON LINE TWO.'

Gabbi's office was located high in an inner city architectural masterpiece and offered a panoramic view beyond the smoke-tinted glass exterior.

It was a beautiful summer morning, the sky a clear azure, with the sun's rays providing a dappled effect on the harbour. A Manly-bound ferry cleaved a smooth path several kilometres out from the city terminal and vied with small pleasure craft of varying sizes, all of which were eclipsed by a huge tanker heading slowly into port.

With a small degree of reluctance Gabbi turned back to her desk and picked up the receiver to deal with the call.

Five minutes later she replaced it, convinced no woman should have to cross verbal swords with an arrogant, *sexist* male whose sole purpose in life was to undermine a female contemporary.

Coffee, hot, sweet and strong, seemed like a good idea, and she rose to her feet, intent on fetching it herself rather than have her secretary do it for her. There were several files she needed to check, and she extracted the pertinent folders and laid them on her desk.

The private line beeped, and she reached for the receiver, expecting to hear James's or Benedict's voice. A lesser possibility was Marie and—even more remote—Monique.

'Gabbi.' The soft, feminine, breathy sound was unmistakable.

'Annaliese,' she acknowledged with a sinking feeling.

'Care to do lunch?'

Delaying the invitation would do no good at all, and she spared her appointment diary a quick glance. 'I can meet you at one.' She named an exclusive restaurant close by. 'Will you make the reservation, or shall I?'

'You do it, Gabbi,' Annaliese replied in a bored drawl. 'I have a meeting with my agent. I could be late.'

'I have to be back in my office at two-thirty,' Gabbi warned.

'In that case, give me ten minutes' grace, then go ahead and order.'

Gabbi replaced the receiver, had her secretary make the necessary reservation, fetched her coffee, then gave work her undivided attention until it was time to freshen up before leaving the building.

The powder-room mirror reflected an elegant image. Soft cream designer-label suit in a lightweight, uncrushable linen mix, and a silk camisole in matching tones. Her French pleat didn't need attention, and she added a touch of powder, a re-application of lipstick, then she was ready.

Ten minutes later Gabbi entered the restaurant foyer where she was greeted warmly by the maître d' and personally escorted to a table. She ordered mineral water and went through the motions of perusing the menu, opting for a Caesar salad with fresh fruit to follow.

Three-quarters of an hour after the appointed time Annaliese joined her in a waft of exclusive perfume. A slinky slither of red silk accentuated her model-slender curves. She was tall, with long slim legs, and her skilfully applied make-up enhanced her exotic features, emphasised by dark hair styled into a sleek bob.

No apology was offered, and Gabbi watched in silence as Annaliese ordered iced water, a garden salad and fresh fruit.

'When is your next assignment?'

A feline smile tilted the edges of her red mouth, and the dark eyes turned to liquid chocolate. 'So keen to see me gone?'

'A polite enquiry,' she responded with gentle mockery.

'Followed by an equally polite query regarding my career?'

Gabbi knew precisely how her stepsister's modelling career was progressing. Monique never failed to relay, in intricate detail, the events monitoring Annaliese's rise and rise on the world's catwalks.

'It was you who initiated lunch.' She picked up her glass and took a deliberate sip, then replaced it down on the table, her eyes remarkably level as she met those of her stepsister.

Annaliese's gaze narrowed with speculative contemplation. 'We've never been friends.'

In private, the younger girl had proven herself to

be a vindictive vixen. 'You worked hard to demolish any bond.'

One shoulder lifted with careless elegance. 'I wanted centre stage in our shared family, darling. *Numero uno.*' One long, red-lacquered nail tapped a careless tattoo against the stem of her glass.

Gabbi speared the last portion of cantaloupe on her plate. 'Suppose you cut to the chase and explain your purpose?'

Annaliese's eyes held a calculated gleam. 'Monique informed me James is becoming increasingly anxious for you to complete the deal.'

The fresh melon was succulent, but it had suddenly lost its taste. 'Which deal are we discussing?'

'The necessary Stanton-Nicols heir.'

Gabbi's gaze was carefully level as she rested the fork down onto her plate. 'You're way out of line, Annaliese.'

'Experiencing problems, darling?' The barb was intentional.

'Only with your intense interest in something that is none of your business.'

'It's *family* business,' Annaliese responded with deliberate emphasis.

Respect for the restaurant's fellow patrons prevented Gabbi from tipping a glass of iced water into her stepsister's lap.

'Really?' Confrontation was the favoured option. 'I have difficulty accepting my father would enrol you as messenger in such a personal matter.'

'You disbelieve me?'

'Yes.' The price of bravery might be high. Too high? *'Darling.'* The word held a patronising intonation that implied the antithesis of affection. 'The only difference between daughter and stepdaughter is a legal adoption decree. Something,' she continued after a deliberate silence, 'Monique could easily persuade James to initiate.'

Oh, my. Now why didn't that devious plan surprise her? 'James's will is watertight. Monique inherits the principal residence, art and jewellery, plus a generous annuity. Shares in Stanton-Nicols come directly to me.'

One delicate brow arched high. 'You think I don't know that?' She lifted a fork and picked at her salad. 'You've missed the point.'

No, she hadn't. 'Benedict.'

Annaliese's eyes assumed an avaricious gleam. 'Clever of you, darling.'

'You want to be his mistress.'

Her soft, tinkling laugh held no humour. 'His wife.'

'You aim high.'

'The top, sweetheart.'

Iced water or hot coffee? Either was at her disposal, and she was sorely tempted to initiate an embarrassing incident. 'There's just one problem. He's already taken.'

'But so easily freed,' her stepsister purred.

'You sound very sure.' How was it possible to sound so calm, when inside she was a molten mass of fury?

'A wealthy man wants an exemplary hostess in the lounge and a whore in his bedroom.' Annaliese examined her perfectly lacquered nails, then shot Gabbi a direct look. 'I can't imagine *passion* being your forte, or adventure your sexual preference.'

Gabbi didn't blink so much as an eyelash. 'I'm a quick study.'

'Really, darling? I wonder why I don't believe you?'

Gabbi summoned the waiter, requested the bill, and signed the credit slip. Then she rose to her feet and slid the strap of her bag over her shoulder.

'Shall we agree not to do this again?'

'Darling,' the young model almost purred. 'I'm between seasons, and where better to take in some rest and relaxation than one's home city?' Her eyes gleamed with satisfaction. 'As family, we're bound to see quite a lot of each other. The social scene is *so* interesting.'

'And you intend being included in every invitation,' Gabbi responded with soft mockery.

'Of course.'

There wasn't a single word she wanted to add. A contradiction—there were several…not one of which was in the least ladylike, and therefore unutterable in a public arena. It was easier to leave in dignified silence.

Three messages were waiting for her on her return. Two were business-oriented and she dealt with each, then logged the necessary notations into the computer before crossing to the private phone.

There was a strange curling sensation in the pit of her stomach as she waited for Benedict to answer.

'Nicols.'

His voice was deep and retained a slight American drawl that seemed more noticeable over the phone. The sound of it caused her pulse to accelerate to a faster beat.

'You rang while I was out.'

She had a mental image of him easing his lengthy frame in the high-backed leather chair. 'How was lunch?'

Her fingers gripped the receiver more tightly. 'Is there anything you don't know?'

'Annaliese requested your extension number.' He relayed the information with imperturbable calm.

Any excuse to have contact with Benedict; Gabbi silently derided her stepsister.

'You didn't answer my question.' His voice held a tinge of cynicism and prompted a terse response.

'Lunch was fine.' She drew a deep breath. 'Is that why you rang?'

'No. To let you know I won't be home for dinner. A Taiwanese associate wants to invest in property, and has requested I recommend a reputable agent. It would be impolite not to effect the introduction over dinner.'

'Very impolite,' she agreed solemnly. 'I won't wait up.'

'I'll take pleasure in waking you,' he mocked gently, ending the call.

A tiny shiver slithered the length of her spine as she recalled numerous occasions when the touch of his lips had woken her from the depths of sleep, and how she'd instinctively welcomed him, luxuriating in the agility of his hands as they traversed a tactile path over the slender curves of her body.

With concentrated effort she replaced the receiver down onto the handset, then focused her attention on work for what remained of the afternoon.

It was almost five-thirty when she left the building, and although traffic was heavy through the inner city it had begun to ease when she reached Rushcutter's Bay, resulting in a relatively clear run to Vaucluse.

The sun's rays were hot, the humidity level high. Too high, Gabbi reflected as she garaged the car and entered the house.

A long, cool drink, followed by a few lengths in the pool, would ease the strain of the day, she decided as she slipped off her jacket and made her way towards the kitchen.

Marie was putting the finishing touches to a cold platter, and her smile was warm as she watched Gabbi extract a glass and cross to the large refrigerator.

'Are you *sure* all you want is salad?'

Gabbi pushed the ice-maker lever, filled the glass with apple juice, then crossed to perch on one of four buffet stools lining the wide servery.

'Sure,' Gabbi confirmed as she leaned forward and filched a slice of fresh mango from the tastefully decorated bed of cos lettuce, avocado, nuts, and capsicum. 'Lovely,' she sighed blissfully.

Marie cast her an affectionate glance. 'There's fresh fruit and *gelato* to follow.'

Gabbi took a long swallow of iced juice, and felt the strain of the day begin to ebb. 'I think I'll change and have a swim.' The thought of a few laps in the pool followed by half an hour basking in the warm sunshine held definite appeal. 'Why don't you finish up here? There's no need for you to stay on just to rinse a few plates and stack them in the dishwasher.'

'Thanks.' The housekeeper's pleasure was evident, and Gabbi reciprocated with an impish grin.

It wasn't the first evening she'd spent alone, and

was unlikely to be the last. 'Go,' she instructed. 'I'll see you at breakfast in the morning.'

Marie removed her apron and folded it neatly. 'Serg and I'll be in the flat, if you need us.'

'I know,' Gabbi said gently, grateful for the older woman's solicitous care.

Minutes later she drained the contents of her glass, then went upstairs to change, discarding her clothes in favour of a black bikini. Out of habit she removed her make-up, applied sunscreen cream, then she caught up a multi-patterned silk sarong and a towel and made her way down to the terraced pool.

Its free-form design was totally enclosed by non-reflective smoke-tinted glass, ensuring total privacy, and there were several loungers and cushioned chairs positioned on the tiled perimeters.

Gabbi dropped the sarong and towel onto a nearby chair, then performed a racing dive into the sparkling water. Seconds later she emerged to the surface, cleared excess moisture from her face, then began the first of several leisurely laps before slipping deftly onto her back to idle aimlessly for a while, enjoying the solitude and the quietness.

It was a wonderful way to relax, she mused, both mentally and physically. The cares of the day seemed to diminish to their correct perspective. Even lunch with Annaliese.

No, she amended with a faint grimace. That was taking things a bit too far. Calculating her stepsister's next move didn't require much effort, given the social scene of the city's sophisticated élite.

Stanton-Nicols supported a number of worthy charities, and Benedict generously continued in

Diandra and Conrad Nicols' tradition—astutely aware
that as much business was done out of the office as
in it, Gabbi concluded wryly.

The thought of facing Annaliese at one function or
another over the next few weeks didn't evoke much
joy. Nor did the prospect of parrying Monique's subtle hints.

Damn. The relaxation cycle was well and truly
broken. With a deft movement, Gabbi rolled onto her
stomach and swam to the pool's edge, hauled her slim
frame onto the tiled ledge, then reached for the towel
and began blotting her body.

Faced with a choice of eating indoors or by the
pool, she chose the latter and carried the salad and a
glass of chilled water to a nearby table.

The view out over the harbour was spectacular,
and she idly watched the seascape as numerous small
craft cruised the waters in a bid to make the most of
the daylight-saving time.

On finishing her meal, scorning television, Gabbi
made herself some coffee, selected a few glossy magazines and returned to watch the sunset, the glorious
streak of orange that changed and melded into a deep
pink as the sun's orb sank slowly beneath the horizon providing a soft pale reflected glow before dusk
turned into darkness.

A touch on the electronic modem activated the
underwater light, turning the pool a brilliant aqua-
blue. Another touch lit several electric flares, and she
stretched out comfortably and flipped open a magazine, scanning the glossy pages for something that
might capture her interest.

An article based on the behind-the-scenes life of a prominent fashion guru provided a riveting insight, and endorsed her own view on the artificiality of a society where one was never sure whether an acquaintance was friend or foe beneath the token façade.

The publishers had seen fit to include an in-depth account by a high-class madam, who, the article revealed, had procured escorts for some of the country's rich and famous, notably politicians and visiting rock stars, for a fee that was astronomical.

Somehow the article focusing on cellulite that followed it seemed extremely prosaic, and Gabbi flipped to the travel section.

Paris. What a city for ambience and *joie de vivre.* The language, the scents, the fashion. French women possessed a certain *élan* that was unmatched anywhere else in the world. And the food! *Très magnifique,* she accorded wistfully, recalling fond memories of the time she'd spent there. For a while she'd imagined herself in love with a dashing young student whose sensual expertise had almost persuaded her into his bed. Gabbi's mouth curved into a soft smile, and her eyes danced with hidden laughter in remembrance.

'An interesting article?'

Gabbi looked up at the sound of that deep, drawling voice and saw Benedict's tall frame outlined against the screened aperture leading into the large entertainment room.

His jacket was hooked over one shoulder, and he'd already removed his tie and loosened a few buttons on his blue cotton shirt.

Her eyes still held a hint of mischief as they met his. 'I didn't realise it was that late,' she managed lightly, watching as he closed the distance between them.

'It's just after ten.' He paused at her side, and scanned the open magazine. 'Pleasant memories?'

Gabbi met his gaze, and sensed the studied watchfulness beneath the surface. 'Yes,' she said with innate honesty, and saw his eyes narrow fractionally. 'It was a long time ago, and I was very young.'

'But old enough to be enchanted by a young man's attentions,' Benedict deduced with a degree of cynical amusement. 'What was his name?'

'Jacques,' she revealed without hesitation. 'He was a romantic, and he kissed divinely. We explored the art galleries together and drank coffee at numerous sidewalk cafés. On weekends I visited the family vineyard. It was fun,' she informed him simply, reflecting on the voluble and often gregarious meals she'd shared, the vivacity and sheer camaraderie of a large extended family.

'Define "fun".'

The temptation to tease and prevaricate was very strong, but there seemed little point. 'He had a very strict *maman*,' she revealed solemnly. 'Who was intent on matching him with the daughter of a neighbouring vintner. An *Anglaise* miss, albeit a very rich one, might persuade him to live on the other side of the world.'

Amusement lurked in the depths of his eyes. 'He married the vintner's daughter?'

'Yes. His devoted *maman* despatches a letter twice a year with family news.'

'Did you love him?' The query was soft, his voice silk-smooth.

Not the way I love you. 'We were very good friends,' she said with the utmost care.

His intense gaze sent a tiny flame flaring through her veins, warming her skin and heating the central core of her femininity.

'Who parted without regret or remorse when it was time for you to leave?' Benedict prompted gently.

A winsome smile curved the edges of her mouth. 'We promised never to forget each other. For a while we exchanged poetic prose.'

'Predictably the letters became shorter and few and far between?'

'You're a terrible cynic.'

'A realist,' he corrected her with subtle remonstrance.

Gabbi closed the magazine and placed it down on a nearby table. With an elegant economy of movement she rose to her feet, caught up the sarong and secured it at her waist. 'Would you like some coffee?'

'Please.'

He turned to follow her, and the hairs on the back of her neck prickled in awareness. She subconsciously straightened her shoulders, and forced herself to walk at a leisurely pace.

In the kitchen she crossed to the servery, methodically filled the coffee-maker with water, spooned ground beans into the filter basket, then switched on the machine.

The large kitchen was a chef's delight, with every conceivable modern appliance. A central cooking island held several hobs, and there were twin ovens, two microwaves, and a capacious refrigerator and freezer.

With considerable ease Gabbi extracted two cups and saucers, then set out milk and sugar.

'How was dinner?'

'Genuine interest, or idle conversation, Gabbi?'

Was he aware of the effect he had on her? In bed, without doubt. But out of it? Probably not, she thought sadly. Men of Benedict's calibre were more concerned with creating a financial empire than examining a relationship.

It took considerable effort to meet his lightly mocking gaze. 'Genuine interest.'

'We ate Asian food in one of the city's finest restaurants,' Benedict informed her indolently. 'The business associate was suitably impressed, and the agent will probably earn a large commission.'

'Naturally you have offered them use of the private jet, which will earn you kudos with the Taiwanese associate, who in turn will recommend you to his contemporaries,' she concluded dryly, and his lips formed a twisted smile.

'It's called taking care of business.'

'And *business* is all-important.'

'Is that a statement or a complaint?'

Her eyes were remarkably steady as she held his gaze. 'It's a well-known fact that profits have soared beyond projected estimates in the past few years. Much of Stanton-Nicols' continuing success is directly attributed to your dedicated efforts.'

'You didn't answer the question.' The words held a dangerous softness that sent a tiny shiver down her spine, and her eyes clashed with his for a few im-

measurable seconds before she summoned a credible smile.

'Why would I complain?' she queried evenly, supremely conscious of the quickening pulse at the base
of her throat.

'Why, indeed?' he lightly mocked. 'You have a
vested interest in the family firm.'

'In more ways than one.'

His eyes narrowed fractionally. 'Elaborate.'

Gabbi didn't hedge. 'The delay in providing James
with a grandchild seems to be the subject of family
conjecture.'

For a brief millisecond she caught a glimpse of
something that resembled anger, then it was lost beneath an impenetrable mask. 'A fact which Annaliese
felt compelled to bring to your attention?'

One finger came to rest against the corner of her
mouth, while his thumb traced the heavy, pulsing cord
at the side of her throat.

'Yes.'

His hand trailed lower to the firm swell of her
breast, teased a path along the edge of her bikini top,
then brushed against the aroused peak before drop-
ping back to his side.

'We agreed birth control should be your prerogative,' Benedict declared with unruffled ease, and she
swallowed painfully, hating the way her body reacted
to his touch.

'Your stepsister is too self-focused not to take any
opportunity to initiate a verbal game of thrust and
parry. Who won?'

'We each retired with superficial wounds,' Gabbi
declared solemnly.

'Dare I ask when the game is to continue?'

'Who can tell?'

'And the weapon?'

She managed a smile. 'Why—Annaliese herself. With *you* as the prize. Her formal adoption by James would make her a *Stanton*. Our divorce is a mere formality in order to change Stanton to *Nicols*.'

He lifted a hand and brushed light fingers across her cheek. 'Am I to understand you are not impressed with that scenario?'

No. For a moment she thought she'd screamed the negative out loud, and she stood in mesmerised silence for several seconds, totally unaware that her expressive features were more explicit than any words.

'Do you believe,' Benedict began quietly, 'I deliberately chose you as my wife with the future of Stanton-Nicols foremost in mind?'

Straight for the jugular. Gabbi had expected no less. Her chin tilted slightly. 'Suitable marriages are manipulated among the wealthy for numerous reasons,' she said fearlessly. '*Love* isn't a necessary prerequisite.'

His expression didn't change, but she sensed a degree of anger and felt chilled by it.

'And what we share in bed? How would you define that?'

A lump rose in her throat, and she swallowed it. 'Skilled expertise.'

Something dark momentarily hardened the depths of his gaze, then it was gone. 'You'd relegate me to the position of *stud*?'

Oh, God. She closed her eyes, then opened them

again. 'No. *No*,' she reiterated, stricken by his deliberate interpretation.

'I should be thankful for that small mercy.'

He was angry. Icily so. And it hurt, terribly.

Yet what had she expected? A heartfelt declaration that *she* was too important in his life for him to consider anyone taking her place?

Gabbi felt as if she couldn't breathe. Her eyes were trapped by his, her body transfixed as though in a state of suspended animation.

'The coffee has finished filtering.'

His voice held that familiar cynicism, and with an effort she focused her attention on pouring coffee into both cups, then added sugar.

Benedict picked up one. 'I'll take this through to the study.'

Her eyes settled on his broad back as he walked from the kitchen, her expression pensive.

Damn Annaliese, Gabbi cursed silently as she discarded her coffee down the sink. With automatic movements she rinsed the cup and stacked it in the dishwasher, then she switched off the coffee-maker and doused the lights before making her way upstairs.

Reaching the bedroom, she walked through to the *en suite*, stripped off her bikini, turned on the water and stepped into the shower.

It didn't take long to shampoo her hair, and fifteen minutes with the blow-drier restored it to its usual silky state.

In bed, she reached for a book and read a chapter before switching off the lamp.

She had no idea what time Benedict slid in beside

her, nor did she sense him leave the bed in the early-morning hours, for when she woke she was alone and the only signs of his occupation were a dented pillow and the imprint of his body against the sheet.

CHAPTER THREE

GABBI GLANCED AT the bedside clock and gave an inaudible groan. Seven-thirty. Time to rise and shine, hit the shower, breakfast, and join the queue of traffic heading into the city.

Thank heavens today was Friday and the weekend lay ahead.

Benedict had accepted an invitation to attend a tennis evening which Chris Evington, head partner in the accountancy firm Stanton-Nicols employed, had arranged at his home. Tomorrow evening they had tickets to the Australian première performance at the Sydney Entertainment Centre.

The possibility of Annaliese discovering their plans for tonight was remote, Gabbi decided as she slid in behind the wheel of her car. And it was doubtful even Monique would be able to arrange an extra seat for the première performance at such short notice.

It was a beautiful day, the sky clear of cloud, and at this early-morning hour free from pollution haze.

Gabbi was greeted by Security as she entered the car park, acknowledged at Reception *en route* to her office, and welcomed by her secretary who brought coffee in one hand and a notebook in the other.

As the morning progressed Gabbi fought against giving last night's scene too much thought, and failed.

During the afternoon she overlooked a miscalculation and lost valuable time in cross-checking. Consequently, it was a relief to slip behind the wheel of her car and head home.

Benedict's vehicle was already parked in the garage when she arrived, and she felt her stomach clench with unbidden nerves as she entered the house.

Gabbi checked with Marie, then went upstairs to change.

Benedict was in the process of discarding his tie when she reached the bedroom.

'You're home early.' As a greeting it lacked originality, but it was better than silence.

She met his dark gaze with equanimity, her eyes lingering on the hard planes of his face, and settling briefly on his mouth. Which was a mistake.

'Dinner will be ready at six.'

'So Marie informed me.' He began unbuttoning his shirt, and her eyes trailed the movement, paused, then returned to scan his features.

Nothing there to determine his mood. Damn. She hated friction. With Monique and Annaliese it was unavoidable—but Benedict was something else.

'I should apologise.' There, it wasn't hard at all. Did he know she'd summoned the courage, wrestled with the need to do so, for most of the day?

A faint smile tugged at the edges of his mouth, and the expression in his eyes was wholly cynical. 'Good manners, Gabbi?'

He shrugged off the business shirt, reached for a

dark-coloured open-necked polo shirt and tugged it over his head.

Honesty was the only way to go. 'Genuine remorse.'

He removed his trousers and donned a casual cotton pair.

He looked up, and she caught the dark intensity of his gaze. 'Apology accepted.'

Her nervous tension dissolved, and the breath she'd unconsciously been holding slipped silently free. 'Thank you.'

Retreat seemed a viable option and she crossed to the capacious walk-in wardrobe, selected tennis gear, then extracted casual linen trousers and a blouse.

The buzz of the electric shaver sounded from the *en suite* bathroom, and he emerged as she finished changing.

Gabbi felt the familiar flood of warmth, and fought against it. 'What time do you want to leave?' It was amazing that her voice sounded so calm.

'Seven-fifteen.'

They descended the stairs together, and ate the delectable chicken salad Marie had prepared, washed it down with mineral water, then picked from a selection of fresh fruit. A light meal which would be supplemented by supper after the last game of tennis.

Conversation was confined to business and the proposed agenda at the next board meeting.

Chris and Leanne Evington resided at Woollahra in a large, rambling old home which had been lovingly restored. Neat lawns, beautiful gardens, precisely clipped hedges and shrubbed topiary lent an air of a past era. The immaculate grassed tennis court merely added to the impression.

A few cars lined the circular forecourt, and Gabbi slid from the Bentley as Benedict retrieved their sports bags from the boot.

Social tennis took on rules of its own, according to the host's inclination and the number of participating guests.

The best of seven games would ensure a relatively quick turn-around on the court, Chris and Leanne determined. Partners were selected by personal choice, and it was accepted that two rounds of mixed doubles would precede two rounds of women's doubles and conclude with two rounds of men's doubles.

Gabbi and Benedict were nominated first on the court, opposing a couple whom Gabbi hadn't previously met. All four were good players, although Benedict had the height, strength and skill to put the ball where he chose, and they emerged victorious at the end of the game with a five-two lead.

Chris and Leanne's son Todd had nominated himself umpire for the evening. A prominent athlete and law student, he had any number of pretty girls beating a path to his door. That there wasn't one in evidence this evening came as something of a surprise.

Until Annaliese arrived on the scene, looking sensational in designer tennis wear.

'Sorry I'm late.' Annaliese offered a winning smile.

'Mixed has just finished,' Leanne informed her. 'The girls are on next.'

Annaliese turned towards Gabbi. 'Will you be my partner? It'll be just like the old days.'

What old days? Gabbi queried silently. Surely Annaliese wasn't referring to an occasional mismatch during school holidays?

Leanne allocated the pair to the second round, and Gabbi accepted a cool drink from a proffered tray.

The guests reassembled as Todd directed play from the umpire's seat. The men gravitated into two groups, and in no time at all Annaliese had managed to gain Gabbi's attention.

'I had a wonderful afternoon phoning friends and catching up on all their news.'

'One of whom just happened to mention the Evington tennis party?' Gabbi queried dryly.

'Why, *yes.*'

'Who better to know the guest list than Todd?'

'He's a sweet boy.'

'And easily flattered.'

Annaliese's smile was pure feline. 'Aren't most men?'

'Shall we join the others?'

It was thirty minutes before they took their position on the court, and evenly matched opponents ensured a tight score. Deuce was called three times in the final game before Annaliese took an advantage to winning point by serving an ace.

An elaborate seafood supper was provided at the close of the final game, followed by coffee and a selection of delicious petits fours.

Gabbi expected Annaliese to commandeer Benedict's attention. What she didn't anticipate was an elbow jolting her arm.

It happened so quickly that she was powerless to

do anything but watch in dismayed silence as coffee spilled onto the tiled floor.

'I'm fine,' Gabbi assured Benedict as he reached her side. She bore his swift appraisal with a determined smile.

Only a splash of hot liquid was splattered on her tennis shoes, and a cloth took care of the spillage.

'You could have been burnt,' Annaliese declared with apparent concern.

'Fortunately, I wasn't.'

'Are you sure you're OK, Gabbi?' Leanne queried. 'Can I get you some more coffee?' Her eyes took on a tinge of humour. 'Something stronger?'

She was tempted, but not for the reason her hostess imagined. A ready smile curved her mouth and she shook her head. 'Thanks all the same.'

It was almost midnight when she slid into the passenger seat of the Bentley. Benedict slipped in behind the wheel and activated the ignition.

'What happened in there?'

The car wheels crunched on the pebbled driveway, and Gabbi waited until they gained the road before responding.

'Could you be specific?'

He shot her a quick glance that lost much of its intensity in the darkness. 'You're not given to clumsiness.'

'Ah, *support*.'

'Annaliese?'

Tiredness settled like a mantle around her slim shoulders. Indecision forced a truthful answer. 'I don't know.'

'She was standing beside you.'

'I'd rather not discuss it.'

Gabbi was first indoors while Benedict garaged the car, and she went upstairs, stripped off her clothes and stepped into the shower-stall.

A few minutes later Benedict joined her, and she spared him a brief glance before continuing her actions with the soap. They each finished at the same time, emerged together and reached for individual towels.

Ignoring Benedict, especially a naked Benedict, was impossible, and there was nothing she could do to slow the quickened beat of her heart or prevent the warmth that crept through her body as she conducted her familiar nightly ritual.

A hand closed over her arm as she turned towards the door, and she didn't utter a word as he pulled her round to face him.

Eyes that were dark and impossibly slumberous held her own and she bore his scrutiny in silence, hating her inner fragility as she damned her inability to hide it.

More than anything she wanted the comfort of his arms, the satisfaction of his mouth on her own. Slowly she lifted a hand and traced the vertical indentation slashing his cheek, then pressed her fingers to the edge of his lips.

Her eyes flared as he took her fingers into his mouth, and heat unfurled deep inside her as he gently bit the tip of each finger in turn.

Unbidden, she reached for him, drawing him close, exulting in the feel of his body, his warm, musky scent, and she opened her mouth in generous acceptance of his in a deep, evocative kiss that hardened in irrefutable possession, wiping out any vestige of conscious thought.

Gabbi gave a husky purr of pleasure as he drew her into the bedroom and pulled her down onto the bed, lost in the sensual magic only he could evoke.

If business commitments didn't intrude, Benedict elected to spend Saturdays on the golf course, while Gabbi preferred to set the day aside to catch up on a variety of things a working week allowed little time for.

Occasionally she took in a matinée movie, or had lunch with friends.

Today she chose to add a few purchases to her wardrobe and keep an appointment with a beautician and her hairdresser.

Consequently it was almost six when she turned into their residential street and followed Benedict's four-wheel drive down the driveway.

He was waiting for her as she brought the car to a halt.

'Great day?' Gabbi asked teasingly as she emerged from behind the wheel.

'Indeed. And you?'

'I flashed plastic in a few too many boutiques,' she said ruefully, indicating several brightly assorted carrier bags on the rear seat.

He looked relaxed, his height and breadth accentuated by the casual open-necked shirt that fitted snugly over his well-honed muscles.

His potent masculinity ignited a familiar response deep within her as he reached past her and gathered the purchases together.

Maybe one day he wouldn't have quite this heightened effect on her equilibrium, she thought wryly as she followed him indoors. Then a silent laugh rose and died in her throat. Perhaps in another lifetime!

It was after seven when they left for the Entertainment Centre to witness the New Jersey-born son of a menswear storekeeper, who was known to mesmerise an audience with any one of the two hundred and fifty magic illusions in his repertoire.

Gabbi adored the show. Pure escapism that numbed the logical mind with wizardry and chilled the spine.

The fact that Annaliese was nowhere in sight added to her pleasure—a feeling that was compounded the next day when Gabbi and Benedict joined friends on a luxury cruiser.

Monday promised to be busier than most, Gabbi realised within minutes of arriving at the office and liaising with her secretary.

The morning hours sped by swiftly as she fed data into the computer. Concentration was required in order to maintain a high level of accuracy, and she didn't break at all when coffee was placed on her desk.

It was after midday when Gabbi sank back against the cushioned chair and flexed her shoulders as she surveyed the computer screen. The figures were keyed in, all she had to do was run a check on them after lunch.

A working lunch, she decided, fired with determination to meet a personal deadline. James had requested the information by one o'clock tomorrow. She intended that he would have it this afternoon.

Gabbi rose from her desk, extracted the chicken

salad sandwich her secretary had placed in the concealed bar fridge an hour earlier, selected a bottle of apple juice and returned to her seat.

The bread was fresh, the chicken soft on a bed of crisp salad topped with a tangy mayonnaise dressing. Washed down with juice, it replenished her energy store.

The phone rang and she hurriedly plucked free a few tissues from the box on her desk, then reached for the receiver.

'Francesca Angeletti on line one.'

Surprise was quickly followed by pleasure. 'Put her through.' Two seconds ticked by. 'Francesca. Where are you?'

'Home. I flew in from Rome yesterday morning.'

'When are we going to get together?' There was no question that they wouldn't. They had shared the same boarding-school, the same classes, and each had a stepmother. It was a common bond that had drawn them together and fostered a friendship which had extended beyond school years.

Francesca's laugh sounded faintly husky. 'Tonight, if you and Benedict are attending Leon's exhibition.'

'Leon's soirées are high on our social calendar,' she acknowledged with an answering chuckle.

'James will be there with Monique?'

'And Annaliese,' Gabbi added dryly, and one eyebrow lifted at Francesca's forthright response. 'Nice girls don't swear,' she teased in admonition.

'This one does,' came the swift reply. 'How long has your dear stepsister been disturbing your home turf?'

'A week.'

'She is fond of playing the diva,' Francesca commented. 'I had the misfortune to share a few of the same catwalks with her in Italy.'

'Fun.'

'Not the kind that makes you laugh. Gabbi, I have to dash. We'll catch up tonight, OK?'

'I'll really look forward to it,' Gabbi assured her, and replaced the receiver.

For the space of a few minutes she allowed her mind to skim the years, highlighting the most vivid of shared memories: school holidays abroad together, guest of honour at each other's engagement party, bridesmaid at each other's wedding.

The automatic back-up flashed on the computer screen, and succeeded in returning her attention to the task at hand. With determination she drew her chair forward, reached for the sheaf of papers, and systematically began checking figure columns.

An hour later she printed out, collated, then had her secretary deliver copies to James and Benedict. She was well pleased with the result. The reduction of a percentage point gained by successful negotiations with the leasing firm for Stanton-Nicols' company car fleet could be used to boost the existing employee incentive package. At no extra cost to Stanton-Nicols, and no loss of tax advantage.

It was after five when she rode the lift down to the car park and almost six when she entered the house.

'Benedict just called,' Marie informed Gabbi when she appeared in the kitchen. 'He'll be another twenty minutes.'

Time for her to shower and wash and dry her hair. 'Smells delicious,' she complimented as she watched

Marie deftly stir the contents of one saucepan, then tend to another.

'Asparagus in a hollandaise sauce, beef Wellington with vegetables and lemon tart for dessert.'

Gabbi grabbed a glass and crossed to the refrigerator for some iced water.

'A few invitations arrived in the mail. They're in the study.'

'Thanks,' she said, smiling.

A few minutes later she ran lightly up the stairs, and in the bedroom she quickly discarded her clothes then made for the shower.

Afterwards she donned fresh underwear, pulled on fitted jeans and a loose top, then twisted her damp hair into a knot on top of her head. A quick application of moisturiser, a light touch of colour to her lips and she was ready.

Benedict entered the bedroom as she emerged from the *en suite*, and she met his mocking smile with a deliberate slant of one eyebrow.

'A delayed meeting?'

'Two phone calls and a traffic snarl,' he elaborated as he shrugged off his jacket and loosened his tie.

She moved towards the door. 'Dinner will be ready in ten minutes.'

The gleam in those dark eyes was wholly sensual. 'I had hoped to share your shower.'

Something tugged at her deep inside, flared, then spread throughout her body. 'Too late,' she declared lightly as she drew level with him.

His smile widened, accentuating the vertical lines slashing each cheek. 'Shame.'

Her breath rose unsteadily in her throat as she

attempted to still the rapid beat of her pulse. Did he take pleasure in deliberately teasing her?

'A cool shower might help.'

'So might this.' He reached for her, angling his mouth down over hers in a kiss that held the promise of passion and the control to keep it at bay.

Gabbi felt her composure waver, then splinter and fragment as he drew deeply, taking yet giving, until she surrendered herself to the evocative pleasure only he could provide.

A tiny moan sounded low in her throat as he slowly raised his head, and she swayed slightly, her eyes wide, luminous pools as she surveyed his features. Her breathing was rapid, her skin warm, and her mouth trembled as she drew back from his grasp.

'You don't play fair,' she accused him shakily, and stood still as he brushed the backs of his fingers across her cheek.

His lips curved, the corners lifting in a semblance of lazy humour. 'Go check with Marie,' he bade her gently. 'I'll be down soon.'

Dinner was superb, the asparagus tender, the beef succulent and the lemon tart an excellent finale.

'Coffee?' Marie asked as she packed dishes onto a trolley.

Gabbi spared her watch a quick glance. It would take thirty minutes to dress, apply make-up and style her hair. 'Not for me.'

'Thanks, Marie. Black,' Benedict requested as Gabbi rose from the table.

CHAPTER FOUR

GABBI CHOSE RED silk evening trousers, matching camisole and beaded jacket. It was a striking outfit, complete with matching evening sandals and clutch-purse. The colour enhanced her delicate honey-coloured skin, and provided an attractive contrast for her blonde hair.

With extreme care she put the finishing touches to her make-up, donned the trousers and camisole, then brushed her hair. Loose, she decided, after sweeping it high and discarding the customary French pleat.

Her mirrored image revealed a confident young woman whose clothes and jewellery bore the exclusivity of wealth. There was a coolness to her composure, a serenity she was far from feeling.

Which proved just how deceptive one's appearance could be, she decided wryly as she slid her feet into the elegant sandals.

'Is the colour choice deliberate?'

'Why do you ask?' Gabbi countered as she met Benedict's indolent gaze.

'I get the impression you're bent on making a statement,' he drawled, and she directed a deceptively sweet smile at him.

'How perceptive of you.'

He looked the epitome of male sophistication, the dark evening suit a stark contrast to the white cotton shirt and black bow tie.

It was almost a sin, she reflected, for any one man to exude such a degree of sexual chemistry. The strong angles and planes of his facial features bore the stamp of his character. The unwavering eyes were hard and inflexible in the boardroom, yet they filled with brooding passion in the bedroom. And the promise of his mouth was to die for, she concluded, all too aware of the havoc it could cause.

He possessed the aura of a predator, arresting and potentially dangerous. Compelling, she added silently.

A tiny thrill of excitement quivered deep inside her at the thought of the pleasure it would give her to pull his tie free and help discard his clothes. And have him remove her own.

'Why the faint smile?'

The desire to shock deepened the smile and lent her eyes a tantalising sparkle. 'Anticipation,' she enlightened him wickedly.

'Of Leon's exhibition?'

She doubted he was fooled in the slightest, for he seemed to find her achingly transparent. 'Naturally.'

'We could always arrive late,' Benedict suggested in dry, mocking tones, and the edges of her mouth formed a delicious curve.

'Leon would be disappointed.' Not to mention Annaliese, she added silently, mentally weighing up which might be the worst offence.

'I could always placate him by making an exorbitant purchase.'

She gave it consideration, then shook her head with apparent reluctance.

'Teasing incurs a penalty,' Benedict declared with soft emphasis.

'I am suitably chastened.'

'That compounds with every hour,' he completed silkily, and saw the momentary flicker of uncertainty cloud those beautiful eyes. It made him want to reach out and touch his hand to her cheek, see the uncertainty fade as he bent his head to claim her mouth. He succumbed to the first but passed on the latter.

Gabbi collected her clutch-purse and preceded him from the room, and, seated inside the Jaguar, she remained silent, aware that the latent power of the sports car equalled that of the man seated behind the wheel.

To attempt to play a game with him, even an innocuous one, was foolish, she perceived as the car purred along the suburban streets. For even when she won she really lost. It didn't seem quite fair that he held such an enormous advantage. Yet the likelihood of tipping the scales in her favour seemed incredibly remote.

'How did James react to your proposal?' Business was always a safe subject.

Benedict turned his head slightly and directed a brief glance at her before focusing his attention on the road. 'Small talk, Gabbi?'

'I can ask James,' she responded steadily.

'I fly to Melbourne in a couple of weeks.'

I, not *we*, she thought dully. 'How long will you be away?'

'Three, maybe four days.'

She should have been used to his frequent trips interstate and overseas. Yet she felt each absence more keenly than the last, intensely aware of her own vulnerability, *and*, dammit, incredibly insecure emotionally.

Gabbi wanted to say she'd miss him, but that would
be tantamount to an admission she wasn't prepared to
make. Instead, she focused her attention on the scene
beyond the windscreen, noting the soft haze that had
settled over the city, the azure, pink-fringed sky as the
sun sank beyond the horizon. Summer daylight-time
delayed the onset of dusk, but soon numerous street-
lamps would provide a fairy tracery of light, and the
city would be lit with flashing neon.

The views were magnificent: numerous coves and
inlets, the grandeur of the Opera House against the
backdrop of Harbour Bridge. It was a vista she took
for granted every day as she drove to work, and now
she examined it carefully, aware that the plaudits acclaiming it one of the most attractive harbours in the
world were well deserved.

Traffic at this hour was relatively minimal, and
they reached Double Bay without delay. There was
private parking adjacent to the gallery, and Benedict
brought the Jaguar to a smooth halt in an empty bay.

Gabbi released the door-latch and slid out of the
passenger seat, resisting the urge to smooth suddenly
nervous fingers over the length of her hair. It was
merely another evening in which she was required to
smile and converse and pretend that everything was
as it appeared to be.

She'd had a lot of practice, she assured herself silently as she walked at Benedict's side to the entrance.

The gallery held an interesting mix of patrons,

Gabbi could see as she preceded Benedict into the elegant foyer.

Their presence elicited an ebullient greeting from the gallery owner, whose flamboyant dress style and extravagant jewellery were as much an act as was his effusive manner. A decade devoted to creating an image and fostering clientele had paid off, for his *'invitation only'* soirées were considered *de rigueur* by the city's social élite.

'Darlings, how are we, *ça va?*'

Gabbi accepted the salutatory kiss on each cheek and smiled at the shrewd pair of eyes regarding her with affection.

'Leon,' she responded quietly, aware that the Italian-born Leo had acknowledged his French roots after discovering his ancestors had fled France during the French Revolution. 'Well, *merci.*'

'That is good.' He caught hold of Benedict's hand and pumped it enthusiastically. 'There are some *wonderful* pieces. At least one I'm sure will be of immense interest. I shall show it to you personally. But first some champagne, *oui?*' He beckoned a hovering waiter and plucked two flutes from the tray, then commanded a uniformed waitress to bring forth a selection of hors d'oeuvres. 'Beluga, smoked salmon, anchovy.'

Gabbi selected a thin wafer artfully decorated with smoked salmon topped with a cream cheese and caper dressing. 'Delicious,' she complimented. 'Franz has excelled himself.'

'Thank you, darling,' Leon said gently. 'Now, do mingle. You already know almost everyone. I'll be back with you later.'

She moved forward, conscious of the interest their presence aroused. It was definitely smile-time, and she greeted one fellow guest after another with innate charm, pausing to indulge in idle chatter before moving on.

How long would it be before James made an entrance with Monique on one arm and Annaliese on the other? Ten, fifteen minutes?

Twenty, Gabbi acknowledged when she caught sight of her father, caught his smile and returned it as he threaded his way through the throng of guests.

'Hello, darling.' He squeezed her hand, then turned to greet his son-in-law. 'Benedict.'

'Monique.' Gabbi went through with the air-kiss routine. 'Annaliese.'

Her stepsister's perfume was subtle. Her dress, however, was not. Black, it fitted Annaliese's slender curves like a glove, the hemline revealing an almost obscene length of long, smooth thigh and highlighting the absence of a bra.

There wasn't a red-blooded man in the room whose eyes didn't momentarily gleam with appreciation. Nor was there a woman in doubt of her man who didn't fail to still the slither of alarm at the sight of this feline female on the prowl.

Gabbi could have assured each and every one of them that their fears were unfounded. Benedict was the target, *she* the victim.

'Have you seen anything you like?'

To anyone overhearing the enquiry, it sounded remarkably genuine. Gabbi, infinitely more sensitive, recognised the innuendo in Annaliese's voice and searched for it in Benedict's reply.

'Yes. One or two pieces have caught my interest.'

'Are you going to buy?' asked Monique, intrigued, yet able to portray dispassionate detachment.

Gabbi doubted if James was aware of his step-daughter's machinations, or her collusion with his wife.

'Possibly,' Benedict enlightened her smoothly.

'You must point them out to me,' Annaliese purred in a voice filled with seductive promise.

Gabbi wanted to hit her. For a wild second she envisaged the scene and drew satisfaction from a mental victory.

'Numbers five and thirty-seven,' Benedict was informing Annaliese.

'Gabbi, why don't you take Monique and Annaliese on a tour of the exhibits?' James suggested. 'I have something I'd like to discuss with Benedict.'

Oh, my. Did her father realise he'd just thrown her to the lions?

'The girls can go,' Monique said sweetly. 'I'll have a word with Bertrice Osterman.'

How opportune for one of the society doyennes to be within close proximity. Gabbi offered Annaliese a faint smile. 'Shall we begin?'

It took two minutes and something like twenty paces to reach Benedict's first choice. 'It leans towards the avant garde,' Gabbi declared. 'But it will brighten up one of the office walls.'

'Cut the spiel, Gabbi,' Annaliese said in bored tones. 'These art exhibitions are the pits.'

'But socially stimulating, wouldn't you agree?'

'Monique came along to be seen, and—'

'So did you,' Gabbi interceded quietly.

'By Benedict.'

She felt the breath catch in her throat, and willed her expression not to change.

'Surely you didn't doubt it, darling?'

'I expected nothing less,' she managed civilly.

'Then we understand each other.'

Gabbi extended a hand towards a row of paintings. 'Shall we pretend to look at the other exhibits?' She even managed a credible smile. 'It will provide you with a topic of conversation.'

Annaliese was, Gabbi conceded, a consummate actress. No one in the room would guess there was no love lost between the two stepsisters. And Gabbi hated participating in the façade.

For fifteen minutes they wandered, paused and examined, before rejoining James and Benedict. Monique was nowhere in sight.

'Wonderful choice, Benedict,' Annaliese said in a deliberately throaty tone. 'There's a sculpture that would look incredible in the corner of your office. You must come and see it.' She turned towards Gabbi. 'It is quite spectacular, isn't it, darling?'

'Spectacular,' Gabbi conceded, taking a fresh flute of champagne from the tray proffered by a waiter. She lifted the glass to her lips and took a pensive sip, then dared to raise her eyes to meet those of her husband. They were dark and faintly brooding, with just a tinge of latent humour. He was amused, damn him!

'Then I shall have to take a look.'

'Talk to James, darling, while I drag Benedict away.'

It was a beautiful manoeuvre, Gabbi applauded silently as Annaliese drew Benedict across the room.

'She's grown into a very attractive girl,' James said quietly, and Gabbi inclined her head.

'Very attractive,' she agreed solemnly.

'Incredibly successful, too.'

'Yes.' She took a careful sip of champagne and steeled herself not to glance towards where Anna-liese held Benedict's attention.

'I looked at those figures you submitted. They're excellent.'

'Thank you,' she accepted, pleased at his praise.

'You possess your mother's integrity, her sense of style,' he said gently. 'I'm very proud of you, Gabbi. And of what you've achieved.'

She brushed a quick kiss over his cheek. 'I love you too.'

'James.'

Gabbi turned at the sound of an unfamiliar voice, smiled, and stood quietly as her father completed an introduction. A business associate who seemed intent on discussing the effects of an upcoming state elec-tion. With a murmured excuse, she left the two men to converse and began threading her way towards the opposite side of the room.

There were quite a few people present whom she knew, and she paused to exchange greetings.

A painting had caught her eye shortly after they'd arrived, and she wanted to take another look at it.

'Gabbi.'

'Francesca!' Her smile was genuinely warm as she embraced the tall, svelte auburn-haired model. 'It seems ages since I last saw you.'

'Too long,' Francesca agreed. 'The catwalks were

exhausting, and—' she paused fractionally '—the family daunting.'

'Do we get to talk about this over lunch?'

Francesca's smile was infectious. 'Tomorrow?'

'Love to,' Gabbi agreed, and named a fashionable restaurant a short distance from the office. 'Twelve-thirty?'

'Done.' Francesca took hold of her arm. 'Do you particularly *want* to watch Annaliese's attempt to snare Benedict?'

'No.'

'Then let's do the unexpected and examine the art exhibits for any hidden talent!' An eyebrow arched in a sardonic gesture as she cast a glance at a nearby sculpture. 'There has to be *some*, surely?'

'It's a case of beauty being in the eye of the beholder,' Gabbi vouchsafed solemnly as they moved from one painting to another.

'The prices are scandalous,' Francesca opined in a quiet aside. 'Does anyone actually make a purchase?'

'You'd be surprised.'

'Utterly.'

'Some of the city's rich and famous are known to buy on a whim, then years later make a killing when the artist becomes well-known.'

'And if the artist doesn't?'

Gabbi smiled. 'They place it in the foyer of their office and pretend its obscure origin makes it a curiosity piece. The added advantage being the item then becomes a legitimate tax deduction.'

'Oh, my,' Francesca breathed. 'When did you become so cynical?'

'I grew up.' It shouldn't hurt so much. But it did.

'And Benedict?'

She hesitated a moment too long. 'We understand each other.'

'That's a loaded statement, darling. I rather imagined he was your knight in shining armour.'

'That myth belongs in a story book.'

'Not always,' Francesca disagreed gently. 'I experienced a brief taste of it.'

Too brief. Francesca's marriage to a world-famous Italian racing-car driver had lasted six months. A freak accident three years ago on a tight turn had claimed his life and that of another driver, the horrific scene captured for ever on news-film.

Gabbi had flown to Monaco to attend the funeral, and hadn't been able to express adequate words then, any more than she could now.

'It's OK,' Francesca said quietly, almost as if she knew. 'I'm learning to deal with it.'

Gabbi had witnessed the magic, *seen* for herself the rare depth of their shared love, and wondered if it was possible to cope with such a loss.

'Mario was—'

'One of a kind,' Francesca interrupted gently. 'For a while he was mine. At least I have that.' She pointed out a glaring canvas whose colours shrieked with vivid, bold strokes. 'Was that a kindergarten tot let loose with brush and palette, do you suppose? Or is there some mysterious but meaningful symmetry that momentarily escapes the scope of my imagination?'

'It's an abstract,' an amused male voice revealed. 'And you're looking at the kindergarten tot who took an afternoon to slash the canvas with paint in the hope someone might pay for the privilege of putting bread on my table.'

'Expensive bread,' Francesca remarked without missing a beat. 'The artist favours hand-stitched shoes, a Hermes tie and wears a Rolex.'

'They could be fake,' he declared.

'No,' Francesca asserted with the certainty of one who *knew* designer apparel.

Gabbi watched the interplay between her friend and the tall, broad-framed man whose dark eyes held a piercing brilliance.

'Next you'll tell me where I live and what car I drive.'

'Not what people would expect of an artist,' Francesca considered with scarcely a thought. 'Northern suburbs, overlooking water, trees in the garden, a detached studio and a BMW in the garage.'

Gabbi sensed Benedict's presence an instant before she felt the touch of firm fingers at the edge of her waist, and she summoned a dazzling smile as she turned slightly towards him.

The eyes that lanced hers were dark and impossible to fathom so she didn't even try.

'Benedict,' Francesca greeted him warmly. 'It's been a while.'

'Indeed,' he agreed urbanely. 'You've met Dominic?'

'We haven't been formally introduced.' Francesca's smile was deliberately warm as she turned her head towards the man at her side.

'Dominic Andrea. Entrepreneur and part-time artist,' Benedict informed her. 'Francesca Angeletti.'

'How opportune. The designer luggage won't require a change of initials.'

Gabbi registered Dominic's words and heard Francesca's almost inaudible gasp one second ahead of Benedict's husky chuckle.

'You must come to dinner,' Dominic insisted. 'Bring Francesca.'

'Gabbi?' Benedict deferred, and she caught her breath that the decision should be hers.

'Thank you, we'd love to.'

'No,' the glamorous widow declined.

'I have yet to nominate a night,' Dominic said in mild remonstrance. 'And with Benedict and Gabbi present you'll be quite safe.' His smile was dangerously soft and filled with latent charm. 'Aren't you in the least curious to see if you're right?'

Gabbi watched Francesca's eyes narrow and heard her voice chill to ice. 'Where you live doesn't interest me.'

'Tomorrow,' he insisted gently. 'Six-thirty.' He turned and threaded his way to the opposite side of the gallery.

'What a preposterous man,' Francesca hissed disdainfully the moment he was out of earshot.

'A very rich and successful one,' Benedict added mildly. 'Who dabbles in art and donates his work to worthwhile charities.'

'He's a friend of yours?'

'We occasionally do business together. He spends a lot of time overseas. New York, Athens, Rome,' Benedict enlightened her.

'Champagne, caviare and camaraderie aren't my style,' Francesca dismissed.

'You share something in common,' Benedict informed her with a degree of cynical amusement.

'Then why the dinner invitation?'

'He admires your charming wit,' Benedict responded wryly, and his mouth curved to form an amused smile.

'An attempt to charm wasn't my intention,' Francesca declared with an expressive lift of one eyebrow.

'Perhaps he is sufficiently intrigued to want to discover why not?' Benedict ventured in a dry undertone.

'I presume women rarely refuse him.'

A low chuckle escaped Benedict's throat. 'Rarely.'

Gabbi witnessed the faint sparkle evident in her friend's eyes, and was unable to repress a winsome smile. 'So you'll accept?'

'It's a long time since I've been offered such an interesting evening,' Francesca conceded. 'I'll let you know at lunch tomorrow.'

Benedict drew their attention to an intricate steel sculpture that was garnering a great deal of notice, and after a few minutes Francesca indicated her intention to leave.

'Do you want to stay for Leon's party?' Benedict queried minutes later, and Gabbi cast him a studied glance.

'I imagine you've already presented him with a sizeable cheque, sufficient to appease any regret he might express at our absence?' The words were lightly voiced and brought a faint smile to his lips.

'Exhibits five and thirty-seven, plus the sculpture Annaliese admired.'

A knife twisted inside her stomach.

'A gift for James,' he added with gentle mockery.

She held his gaze with difficulty, unsure what interpretation to place on his words, or if there was *any* hidden innuendo in them. 'I'm sure he'll be most appreciative,' she said after a measurable silence.

'You didn't answer my question,' Benedict reminded her gently.

'James, Monique and Annaliese have yet to leave.' It was amazing that her voice sounded so calm, equally surprising that she was able to project an outward serenity. But then she'd had plenty of practice at conveying both.

Humour tugged at the edges of his mouth. 'I was unaware that their presence, or absence, dictated our own,' he countered with deceptive mildness.

It didn't, but she hadn't quite forgiven him for being so easily led away by Annaliese or for being caught so long in conversation.

She effected a slight shrug he could interpret any way he chose. 'If you want to leave—'

'You're not going?' Monique intervened, her voice tinged with mild reproach, and Gabbi wondered if lip-reading was one of her stepmother's acquired skills. 'Leon will be most upset if you miss his party.'

'A headache,' Benedict invented smoothly.

Monique spared Gabbi a penetrating look. 'Oh darling, really?' Her eyes sharpened suspiciously.

Annaliese's mouth formed a pretty pout. 'What a shame to end the evening so early.' She turned sultry eyes towards Benedict. 'Perhaps Gabbi won't mind if you drop her home and come back for the party?'

Benedict's smile didn't quite reach his eyes. 'I'm the one who is suffering,' he informed her, subjecting Gabbi to a deliberate appraisal that left no one in any doubt that his suffering was of a sexual nature.

Monique's expression didn't change and James's features remained deliberately bland, although Gabbi thought she glimpsed a fleeting humorous twinkle in his eyes. Annaliese, however, shot her a brief, malevolent glare before masking it with a faint smile.

'Have fun,' Annaliese murmured, pressing her scarlet-tipped fingers to Benedict's arm in a light caress.

Gabbi prayed that the soft flood of warmth to her cheeks wasn't accompanied by a telling tide of pink as Benedict smoothly uttered the few necessary words in farewell, and her fingers clenched against his in silent retaliation as he caught hold of her hand and began threading his way across the room to where Leon was holding court with a captive audience.

'Oh, darlings, you're leaving?'

'You don't mind?'

'I'm so pleased you were able to attend.' Leon's smile was beatific, courtesy of Benedict's cheque in his wallet.

Gabbi waited until Benedict had steered the Jaguar clear of the car park before launching into a verbal attack.

'That was unforgivable!'

'What, precisely, did you find unforgivable?' Benedict drawled in amusement as he joined the traffic travelling eastward along the New South Head road.

She wanted to rage at him, physically *hit* him. Instead she chose to remain silent for the time it took him to reach Vaucluse, garage the car and enter the house.

'Coffee?' Benedict enquired as he turned from re-setting the alarm system.

'No,' she refused tightly, raising stormy eyes to meet his as he closed the distance between them.

He made no attempt to touch her, and she stood firmly resolute, hating him for a variety of reasons that were too numerous to mention.

'So much anger,' he observed indolently.

'What did you expect?'

'A little gratitude, perhaps, for initiating a premature escape?'

Words warred with each other in her mind as she fought for control. More than anything she wanted to lash out and hit him, and only the silent warning apparent in those dark features stopped her.

'You take exception to the fact I want to make love with you?' he queried silkily. Lifting a hand, he slid it beneath the curtain of her hair.

'I didn't expect a clichéd announcement of your intention,' she threw at him angrily, gasping as he cupped her nape and angled his head down to hers. *'Don't.'*

The plea went unheeded as his mouth closed over hers, and she strained against the strength of his arm as it curved down her back and held her to him.

Slowly, insidiously, warmth coursed through her veins until her whole body was one aching mass, craving his touch, and she opened her mouth to accept the possession of his own.

Passion replaced anger, and a tiny part of her brain registered the transition and wondered at the traitorous dictates of her own heart.

It wasn't fair that he should have quite this effect

on her, or that she should have so little control. Sex motivated by lust wasn't undesired, but *love* was the ultimate prize.

She wanted to protest when he swept an arm beneath her knees and lifted her against his chest. She knew she should as he climbed the stairs to the upper floor. And when he entered their bedroom and let her slip down to her feet she stood, quiescent, as he gently removed her beaded jacket and tossed it over a nearby chair.

The soft light from twin lamps reflected against the mirror and she caught a momentary glimpse of two figures—one tall and dark, the other slender in red, then she became lost in the heat of Benedict's impassioned gaze, her fingers as dexterous as his in their quest to remove each layer of clothing.

Yet there was care apparent, almost a teasing quality as they each dealt with buttons and zip-fastenings, the slide of his hands on her exposed flesh increasing the steady spiral of excitement.

He wasn't unmoved by her ministrations either, and she exulted in the feel of tightening sinews as she caressed his muscled chest, the taut waist and the thrust of his powerful thighs.

His heartbeat quickened in tempo with her own as he pulled her down onto the bed and she rose up above him, every nerve, every *cell* alive with anticipation. She sought to give as much pleasure as she knew she'd receive, taking the path to climactic nirvana with deliberate slowness, enjoying and enhancing each step of the emotional journey until there was no sense of the individual, only the merging of two souls so in tune with each other that they became one.

And afterwards they lay, arms and legs entwined, exchanging the soft caress of fingers against warm flesh, the light, lingering brush of lips, in an after-play that held great tenderness and care, until sleep claimed them both.

CHAPTER FIVE

THE SUN'S RAYS were hot after the controlled coolness of the building's air-conditioning, and Gabbi felt the heat come up from the pavement combined with the jostle of midday city staff anxious to make the most of their lunch hour, elderly matrons *en route* from one shopping mall to another and mothers with young children in tow.

Sydney was a vibrant city alive with people from different cultures, and Gabbi witnessed a vivid kaleidoscope of couture and grunge as she walked the block and a half to meet Francesca.

The restaurant was filled with patrons, but she'd rung ahead for a reservation, and the maître d' offered an effusive greeting and ushered her to a table.

There was barely time to order iced water before Francesca slid into the opposite seat in a soft cloud of Hermes Calèche perfume.

'The traffic was every bit as bad as I expected,' Francesca commented as she ordered the same drink as Gabbi. 'And securing a parking space was worse.'

Gabbi smiled in commiseration. 'City commuting is the pits.' She picked up the menu. 'Shall we order?'

'Good idea. I'm starving,' Francesca admitted with

relish, selecting the *soupe du jour* followed by a Greek salad and fresh fruit.

Gabbi also selected her friend's choice, but opted for linguini instead of soup as a starter.

'How long will you be Sydney-based?' Her smile was warm, her interest genuine.

Ice-cubes chinked as Francesca picked up her glass. 'Not long. A few weeks, then I'll head back to Europe.'

True friendship was rare, and with it came the benefit of dispensing with the niceties of idle conversation. 'So, tell me about Rome.'

Francesca's expression became pensive. 'Mario's mother was diagnosed with inoperable cancer.'

Gabbi's heart constricted with pain, and she reached out and covered her friend's hand with her own. 'Francesca, I'm so sorry.'

'We had a few short weeks together before she was hospitalised, and after that it was only a matter of days.' Francesca's eyes darkened with repressed emotion. 'She bequeathed me everything.'

'Mario was her only child,' Gabbi reminded her gently.

'Nevertheless, it was—' she paused fractionally '—unexpected.'

The waiter's appearance with their starters provided an interruption.

'What's new with the family?' Francesca asked as soon as he was out of earshot.

'Not a thing.'

'Benedict is to die for, Monique superficially gracious, Annaliese a bitch and James remains oblivious?'

The assessment was so accurate, Gabbi didn't

know whether to laugh or cry. 'Selectively oblivious,' she qualified.

'A clever man, your father.'

'And yours, Francesca?'

'Consumed with business in order to keep my dear stepmama in the incredible style she insists is important.' She managed a tight smile. 'While Mother continues to flit from one man to the next with time out in between for the requisite nip and tuck.'

They finished the starters and began on the salads.

'Dominic Andrea,' Francesca ventured speculatively. 'Greek?'

'Second generation. His mother is Australian.'

'Irritating man.'

Dominic was many things, but irritating wasn't one of them. 'Do you think so?'

'And arrogant.'

Perhaps. Although Gabbi would have substituted self-assured. 'You want to opt out of dinner tonight?'

Francesca forked the last mouthful of salad, took her time with it, then replaced the utensil onto her plate. 'No,' she said thoughtfully, her gaze startlingly direct. 'Why deny myself an interesting evening?'

Gabbi's mouth curved with humour. 'A clash between two Titans?'

Francesca's eyes assumed a speculative gleam. 'It will be an intriguing challenge to beat the man at his own game.'

Indeed, Gabbi accorded silently. Although she wasn't sure that Francesca would win.

The waiter brought a fruit platter and they ordered coffee.

'Shall I give you Dominic's address?' Gabbi queried as she picked up the bill, quelling Francesca's protest. 'Or will we collect you?'

'I'll meet you there.' She extracted a pen and paper from her handbag and took down the address. 'Six-thirty?'

'Yes,' Gabbi confirmed as they emerged out onto the pavement. She accepted Francesca's light kiss on each cheek, and touched her hand as they parted. 'It's been great to catch up. Take care.'

'Always,' Francesca promised. 'See you tonight.'

There were several messages on Gabbi's desk when she returned, and she dealt with each, dictated several letters and worked on streamlining overheads in a subsidiary company. Systematic checking was required to discover alternative suppliers who, she was convinced, could provide an equal service for a more competitive price. She made a list of relevant numbers to call.

The intercom buzzed, and Gabbi depressed the button. 'Yes, Halle?'

'There's a parcel in Reception for you. Shall I bring it down?'

She eased her shoulders and pushed a stray tendril of hair behind one ear. 'Please.'

A minute later her secretary appeared carrying a flat rectangular parcel wrapped in brown paper. 'There's an envelope. Want me to open it?'

It couldn't be…could it? Gabbi rose to her feet and crossed round to the front of her desk. 'No, I'll take care of it. Thanks, Halle.'

She placed the attached envelope on her desk, then undid the wrapping, pleasure lighting up her features as she revealed the painting she'd admired at Leon's gallery.

It was perfect for the southern wall of her office.

The card held a simple message: 'For you.' It was signed 'Benedict.'

Gabbi reached for the private phone and punched in Benedict's coded number.

He answered on the second ring. 'Nicols.'

'You noticed my interest in the painting,' she said with evident warmth. 'I love it. Thanks.'

'Why don't you take a walk to my office and thank me in person?' The lazy drawl held mild amusement, and a soft laugh emerged from her throat.

'A momentary diversion?'

'Very momentary,' Benedict agreed with light humour. 'An associate is waiting in my private lounge.'

'In that case, you shouldn't delay seeing him,' she chastised him sweetly, and heard his husky chuckle in response.

'Tonight, Gabbi.'

She heard the faint click as he replaced the receiver.

The rest of the afternoon went quickly, and at five she shut down the computer, signed the completed letters then collected her briefcase and took the lift down to the car park.

Benedict's four-wheel drive was in the garage when she arrived home, and as they were to dine out she bypassed the kitchen and made for the stairs.

It would be nice to strip off and relax in the Jacuzzi, she thought longingly as she entered the master suite, but there wasn't time. Twenty-five minutes in which to shower, dress, apply make-up and style her hair didn't allow for a leisurely approach.

The sound of an electric razor in action could be heard from the bathroom and she quickly shed her clothes, pulled on a silk robe and pushed open the door.

Benedict was standing in front of the wide mirror dispensing with a day's growth of beard, a towel hitched at his waist. It was evident from his damp hair that he hadn't long emerged from the shower.

'Hi.' It irked her that her voice sounded vaguely breathless. Maybe in another twenty years she would be able to view his partly naked form and not feel so completely *consumed* by the sight of him.

If, that far down the track, she was still part of his life. The thought that she might not be brought a stab of unbearable pain.

He looked up from his task and met her eyes in the mirror. 'Hi, yourself.'

His appraisal was warm and lingered a little too long on the soft curve of her mouth. With determined effort she reached into the shower-stall, turned on the water, slipped off her robe and stepped beneath the warm jet-spray. When she emerged it was to find she had sole occupancy of the bathroom.

Ten minutes later her hair was swept into a sleek pleat, her make-up complete. In the bedroom she crossed to the walk-in closet and selected silk evening trousers in delicate ivory, added a beaded camisole and slid her arms into a matching silk jacket. Gold jewellery and elegant evening sandals completed the outfit, and she took time to dab her favourite perfume to a few exposed pulse-points before catching up an evening purse.

'Ready?'

With a few minutes to spare. She directed a cool glance at him. 'Yes. Shall we leave?'

Dominic's home was a brilliant example of architectural design in suburban Beauty Point overlooking the middle harbour.

Dominic greeted them at the door and drew them into the lounge.

High ceilings and floor-to-ceiling glass lent the room spaciousness and light, with folding white-painted wooden shutters and deep-cushioned furniture providing a hint of the Caribbean.

There was no sign of Francesca, and Gabbi wondered if she was deliberately planning her arrival to be a fashionable, but excusable, five minutes late.

Ten, Gabbi noted, as the bell-chimes pealed when she was partway through a delicious fruit cocktail. Dominic allowed his housekeeper to answer the door.

It would seem that if Francesca had a strategy Dominic had elected to choose one of his own.

Stunning was an apt description of Francesca's appearance, Gabbi silently applauded as she greeted her friend. Francesca's expression was carefully bland, but there was a wicked twinkle apparent in those dark eyes for one infinitesimal second before she turned towards her host.

'Please accept my apologies.'

'Accepted,' drawled Dominic. 'You'll join us in a drink?'

'Chilled water,' Francesca requested with a singularly sweet smile. 'With ice.'

'Bottled? Sparkling or still?'

'Still, if you have it.'

Gabbi hid a faint smile and took another sip of her cocktail.

Francesca had dressed to kill in black, designed perhaps to emphasise her widowed state? She looked every inch the successful international model. The length of her auburn hair was swept into a careless knot, with a few wispy tendrils allowed to escape to frame her face. The make-up was perfection, although Gabbi doubted it had taken Fran more than ten minutes to apply. The perfume was her preferred Hermes Calèche, and there was little doubt that the gown was an Italian designer original bought or bargained for at an outrageously discounted price.

Gabbi wondered how long it would take Dominic to dig beneath Francesca's protective shell and reveal her true nature. Or if Francesca would permit him to try.

Dinner was a convivial meal, the courses varied and many, and while exquisitely presented on the finest bone china they were the antithesis of designer food. There was, however, an artistically displayed platter of salads adorned with avocado, mango and sprinkled with pine nuts. A subtle concession to what Dominic suspected was a model's necessity to diet? Gabbi wondered.

Francesca, Gabbi knew, ate wisely and well, with little need to watch her intake of food. Tonight, however, she forked dainty portions from each course, declined dessert and opted for herbal tea instead of the ruinously strong black coffee she preferred.

'Northern suburbs, overlooking water and trees in the garden,' Francesca mocked lightly as she met

Dominic's level gaze over the rim of her delicate tea-cup.

'Three out of five,' he conceded in a voice that was tinged with humour. 'Are you sufficiently curious to discover if you're right about the remaining two?'

Her eyes were cool. 'The detached studio and a BMW in the garage?'

'Yes.'

One eyebrow lifted. 'A subtle invitation to admire your etchings?'

'I paint in the studio and confine lovemaking to the bedroom.'

Gabbi had to admire Francesca's panache, for there was no artifice in the long, considering look she cast him.

'How—prosaic.'

Give it up, Francesca, Gabbi beseeched silently. You're playing with dynamite. Besides, the 'BMW' is a Lexus and although the studio is detached it's above the treble garage and linked to the house via a glass-enclosed walkway.

'More tea?' Dominic enquired with urbanity.

'Thank you, no.'

Benedict rose to his feet in one smooth movement, his eyes enigmatic as they met those of his wife. 'If you'll excuse us, Dominic?' His smile was warm, and tinged with humour. 'Dinner was superb. Do give our compliments to Louise.'

'It's been a lovely evening,' Gabbi said gently, collecting her purse. She spared Francesca a brief, enquiring glance and could determine little from her friend's expression. Their imminent departure provided an excellent excuse for Francesca to leave, and

Gabbi's interest intensified when her friend failed to express that intention.

Perhaps, Gabbi speculated, Francesca was determined not to cut and run at the flimsiest excuse to avoid being alone with Dominic.

'Francesca is quite able to handle herself,' Benedict assured her as he eased the car through the electronically controlled gates and turned onto the street.

'So is Dominic,' Gabbi reminded him as she spared him a frowning glance.

'That worries you?'

'Yes,' she answered starkly. 'I wouldn't like to see Francesca hurt.'

'I failed to see any hint of coercion on Dominic's part,' Benedict returned tolerantly. 'And she chose not to take the opportunity to leave when we did.' He brought the car to a halt at a traffic-controlled intersection.

'Next you'll predict we'll dance at their wedding,' Gabbi declared with a degree of acerbity, and heard his subdued splutter of laughter.

'It wouldn't surprise me.'

'Mario—'

'Is dead,' Benedict stated gently. 'And Francesca is a beautiful young woman who deserves to be happy.'

The lights changed and the car picked up speed. Gabbi turned her attention to the tracery of electric lights on the opposite side of the harbour. It was a picture-postcard scene, and one she'd admired on many occasions in the past. Tonight, however, it failed to hold any attraction.

'You don't think she could fall in love again?'

Gabbi was silent for several long seconds. 'Not the way she loved Mario,' she decided at last.

'Affection, stability and security can be a satisfactory substitute.'

She felt something clench deep inside her, and she caught her breath at the sudden pain. Was that what he thought about *their* marriage? The fire and the passion...were they solely *hers*?

The car traversed the Harbour Bridge, then turned left towards the eastern suburbs. Soon they would be home. And, like the nights that had preceded this one, she would go to sleep in his arms. After the loving.

To deny him was to deny herself. Yet tonight she wanted to, for the sake of sheer perversity.

Gabbi made for the stairs as soon as they entered the house. 'I'll go change.' And slip into the Jacuzzi, she decided as she gained the upper floor. The pulsating jets would ease the tension in her body and help relax her mind.

It didn't, at least not to any satisfactory degree. The doubts that were ever-present in her subconscious rose to the surface with damning ease.

One by one she examined them. Benedict wanted her in his bed, but did he *need* her? *Only* her? Probably not, she admitted sadly, all too aware that there were a hundred women who would rush to take her place. With or without marriage.

One couldn't deny the security factor...for each of them. In her, Benedict had a wife who one day would inherit a share of a billion-dollar corporation, thereby doubling *his* share. Yet, conversely, she also stood to gain.

And stability would be cemented with the addition of children. Why, then, did she continue to take precautions to avoid conception?

Gabbi closed her eyes as images swirled in her mind. The shared joy of early pregnancy, her body swollen with Benedict's child, and afterwards the newborn suckling at her breast.

But it was more than that. Much more. The newborn would develop and grow into a child who became aware of its surroundings, its parents. Financial security would not be an issue. But emotional security?

Divorce had a traumatic effect, and having to accept a stepparent in the place of a loved one was infinitely worse.

Fiercely protective, she wanted desperately for her child to grow up in a happy home with two emotionally committed parents. A marriage based on a business merger lacked the one ingredient essential for a mutually successful long-term relationship: love.

A one-sided love wasn't nearly enough.

Damn. Introspection didn't help at all.

'Sleeping in a Jacuzzi isn't a good idea.'

Gabbi didn't open her eyes. 'I wasn't sleeping.'

'I'm relieved to hear it. Do you intend staying there long?'

'A while.'

He didn't comment, and she sensed rather than heard him leave. Perhaps he'd go downstairs and peruse the latest financial bulletin faxed through from London, New York and Tokyo.

Somehow she doubted he'd simply undress and slide between the sheets, for he was a man who could maintain maximum energy on six hours' sleep in any given twenty-four.

The warm, pulsating water had a soporific effect, and she allowed her thoughts to drift. To her childhood, early treasured memories of her mother, and James. After James followed Monique, and—Gabbi's eyes flew open as a foot brushed her own. Her startled gaze met a pair of dark brown, almost black eyes heavy with slumberous, vaguely mocking humour.

'What are you doing here?' Why did she sound so—shocked? It was hardly the first time they'd shared the Jacuzzi.

'Is my presence such an unwelcome intrusion?'

'Yes.' Except that wasn't strictly true. 'No,' she amended, unable to tear her eyes away from the strong features within touching distance of her own. Broad cheekbones, a well-defined jaw and the sensual curve of his mouth.

The mouth tilted slightly, and she caught sight of strong white teeth. 'You sound unsure.'

Her gaze didn't waver. 'Perhaps because I am.'

Sinews moved beneath the smooth skin sheathing the powerful breadth of his chest as he extended a hand to trail a gentle pattern across her cheek.

The faint aroma of his cologne had a tantalising effect on her equilibrium, and her pupils dilated as one finger traced the outline of her lower lip.

Please, she begged silently. Don't do this to me. Slowly, with infinite patience, he began to erode her defences, breaking them down one by one with the brush of his fingers against the pulse at the base of her throat where it beat in an increasingly visible tattoo.

Those same fingers trailed the contours of each

breast, cupped and weighed them in his palm, then teased each tender nub.

Her lips parted and her eyelids drooped low.

No one person should have this much emotional control over another, she thought. There should be some in-built mechanism in one's psyche to prevent such an invasion.

Possession, she substituted as her bones began to liquefy.

Strong hands settled at her waist, and with no effort at all he turned her round to sit in front of him. She felt caged by the strength of his shoulders, the muscled arms that curved beneath her own.

There was warmth, a heat that had nothing to do with the temperature of the water, and when his lips grazed the delicate hollow at the edge of her neck Gabbi sighed in unspoken acceptance.

He had the touch, she mused dreamily, and the knowledge to arouse a woman to the brink of madness. And the control to hold her on the edge until she almost wept for release.

It was a sensual journey that traversed many paths, along which Gabbi had no desire to travel with anyone but him. She knew she'd give up her fortune, her *life*, *everything*…if only he felt the same.

His hands slid to her shoulders, shifting her so that she faced him, and his mouth took possession of her own.

Her arms lifted to encircle his neck, her fingers burying themselves in the thickness of his hair as she held him close.

There was passion as he tasted and took his fill, and she met his raw energy with matching ardour, then let her mouth soften beneath the teasing influence of his, savouring the lingering sweetness, all too aware of the leashed power as he traced the full curve with the tip of his tongue.

She wanted to tease him, test the level of his control. And see if she could break it.

Gabbi let her arms drift down, trailing her fingers over the muscled cord of his neck, taking time to explore the hard ridges, the strong sinews stretching down to each shoulder.

Dark, springy hair covered his chest, and she played with the short curls, twisting them round her fingers, pulling gently, only to release them as she moved to capture a few more.

She lowered her head and touched her lips to his shoulder, then gently trailed a path inch by inch to his ear, using the tip of her tongue with wicked delight on the hollow beneath the lobe before nuzzling and nipping at the sensitive flesh.

With extreme care she caressed the length of his jaw, traced a path across his cheek, then moved to brush each eyelid closed before trailing the slope of his nose.

The sensual mouth was a temptation she couldn't resist, and she touched her lips to its edge, nibbling and tasting as she explored the lower fullness before traversing the upper curve, withdrawing as she felt it firm in preparation to take control.

Gabbi shook her head in silent remonstrance, then slid to her feet and stepped out of the Jacuzzi, grabbed a towel and wrapped it round her slender form, reaching for another as she turned and extended a beckoning hand.

Benedict held her gaze for a few heart-stopping seconds, and she saw his eyes darken with smouldering passion as he reared to his feet.

He loomed large, his frame a testament to male magnificence, muscled sinew moving with easy fluidity, darkened whorls of hair glistening on his water-drenched skin.

His movements were deliberate as he stepped onto the marble-tiled floor, his pace slow as he shortened the distance between them, and his eyes never left hers for a second.

He held out his hand for the towel, and she shook her head, bunching it in her hand as she reached forward to blot the moisture from his skin.

Gabbi began with one shoulder, then the other, and moved to his chest, taking time and care as she slowly traversed his ribcage, his waist, the lean hips, then the muscled length of his powerful thighs. With deliberate casualness she stepped behind him and tended to the width of his back, watching the play of muscles as they flexed and tensed at her touch.

'Nice butt,' she teased gently as she trailed the towel down the back of each thigh.

'You're playing a dangerous game,' Benedict warned with ominous softness as she moved round to stand in front of him.

'Really?' Her lips tilted slightly as she feigned a lack of guile. 'I haven't finished yet.'

'And I haven't even begun.'

Each word possessed the smoothness of silk, and a slight tremor slithered across the surface of her skin.

Was she mad? In setting out to smash his control, was she inviting something she couldn't handle?

Yet she couldn't, *wouldn't* throw in the towel. Literally, she established with a choked laugh as she brushed the thick cotton pile over the matt of dark, curling hair at the apex of his thighs.

A man's arousal was a potent erotic testimony to his sex, his power and his strength. And instrument of a woman's pleasure. With knowledge and expertise, it could drive a woman wild.

Gabbi looked at it with fascination. Unbidden, she trailed the length, gently traced the tip, and brushed a light finger down the shaft.

She wanted to taste him, to use her tongue and her mouth as if she were savouring an exotic confection.

'Do you know what you're inviting?'

Did he read minds? And was it her imagination, or did his voice sound husky and vaguely strained?

She lifted her head and met the burning intensity of his darkened gaze. 'Yes.'

A thrill of anticipatory excitement arrowed through her body at the thought of what demands he might make when caught in the throes of passion. With it came a sense of fear of his strength if it was ever unleashed without restraint.

She swallowed, the only visible sign of her nervousness, and his eyes registered the movement then flicked back to trap her own.

'Then what are you waiting for?' he queried softly. The silent challenge was evident in the depth of his eyes and apparent in the sensual slant of his mouth.

She'd begun this; now she needed to finish it.

Without a word she held out her hand, and felt the enclosing warmth as he clasped it in his own.

In silence Gabbi led him into the bedroom. When

she reached the bed she leant forward and dragged the covers free. She turned towards him and placed both hands against his chest, then gently pushed until he lay sprawled against the pale percale sheets.

This was for his pleasure, and she slid down onto her knees beside him.

Slowly she set about exploring every inch of his hair-roughened skin, tangling the tip of her tongue in the whorls and soft curls, the smooth texture that was neither soft nor hard, but wholly male and musky to the taste.

She felt a thrill of satisfaction as muscles tensed and contracted, as she heard the faint catch of his breath, the slight hiss as it was expelled, the soft groan as her hands sought the turgid length of his arousal. With the utmost delicacy she explored the sensitive head, traced the shaft and flicked it gently. Then she lowered her mouth and began a similar exploration with a feather-light touch, allowing sheer instinct to guide her.

Not content, she trailed a path to his hip, traversed the taut stomach, and traced a series of soft kisses to his inner thigh.

With deliberately slow movements she raised her head and looked at him, then she loosened the pins from her hair and shook its length free.

A tiny smile curved her lips as she bent her head and trailed her hair in a teasing path down his chest, past his waist, forming a curtain for the delights her lips offered to the most vulnerable, sensitive part of his anatomy.

Control. He had it. Yet she could only wonder for

how long as she lifted her head and lightly traced his moistened shaft with the tips of her fingers.

Her eyes never left his as she brought her fingers up to her mouth, and his eyes flared as she sucked each tip, one by one. Then she rose to her knees and straddled his hips with a graceful movement.

He didn't touch her, but his eyes were dark, so dark they were almost black, and his skin bore the faint flush of restrained passion.

She wanted to kiss him, but didn't dare. This was her game, but there was no doubt who was in charge of the score.

The element of surprise was her only weapon, and she used it shamelessly as she shifted slightly and teased his length with the moist, sensitive heart of her femininity. Then she arched against him, savouring the anticipation of complete possession for a few heart-stopping seconds before she accepted him in a long, slow descent.

Totally enclosed, she felt him swell even further, and gasped at the sensation. Then she began to move, enjoying the feeling of partial loss followed by complete enclosure in a slow, circling dance that tore at the level of her own control.

Her fingers tightened their grip on his shoulders as she fought against the insidious demands of desire, and she cried out when his hands caught hold of her hips and held them, steadying her as he thrust deep inside her, then repeated the action again and again until she became lost to the rhythm, mindless, in a vortex of emotion.

When she was spent he slid a hand behind her nape and brought her head down to rest against him.

Gabbi lay still, her breathing gradually slowing in tune with his. There was a sense of power, of satisfaction that had little to do with sexual climax in her post-orgasmic state. His skin was warm and damp and tasted vaguely of salt. She savoured it, and felt the spasm of hard-muscled flesh within her own.

Did a man experience this sensation of glory after taking a woman? That the sexual symphony he'd orchestrated and conducted had climaxed with such a wondrous crescendo?

And when it was over, did he want an encore?

Gabbi lifted her head and stared down at the slumberous warmth in Benedict's dark eyes, glimpsed the latent humour in their depths and caught the soft slant of his mouth.

'Thank you,' he murmured gently as he angled her mouth down to meet his in a possession that was a simulation of what they'd just shared.

His hand slid down her spine, and she gasped as he rolled with her until she felt the mattress beneath her back.

It was a long while before she lay curled in the circle of his arms. As an encore, it had surpassed all that had gone before. And, she reflected a trifle sadly, it was she who had lost control, she who had cried out in the throes of passion.

On the edge of sleep, she told herself she didn't care. If pleasure was the prize, it was possible to win even when you lost.

CHAPTER SIX

WHY WAS IT that some days were destined to be more eventful than others? Gabbi wondered silently as she entered the house and made her way through to the kitchen.

She'd been very calm at the board meeting when Maxwell Fremont had verbally challenged her to explain in minute detail why it would be beneficial to re-finance a subsidiary arm to maximise the company's tax advantage. The initial margin was narrow, given the re-financing costs involved, but the long-term prospect was considerably more favourable than the existing financial structure. Her research had been thorough, the figure projections carefully checked, and there had been a degree of satisfaction when the proposal had gained acceptance.

The afternoon had concluded with a misplaced file and a computer glitch, and on the way home a careless motorist hadn't braked in time and her car had suffered a few scratches and a broken tail-light. Which was a nuisance, for insurance red tape meant that the Mercedes would be out of action while the damage was assessed, and again when it went into the workshop for repair.

A few laps of the swimming pool, followed by an alfresco meal on the terrace, held more appeal than dressing up and attending a formal fund-raising ball. However, the ball was a prominent annual event for which Benedict had tickets and a vague disinclination to attend was not sufficient reason to initiate a protest. Although the thought of crossing verbal swords with Annaliese over pâté, roast beef and chocolate mousse wasn't Gabbi's idea of a fun evening.

And any minute now Benedict would drive into the garage, see a smashed tail-light and demand an explanation.

She crossed to the refrigerator, filled a glass with fresh orange juice and took a long, appreciative swallow.

'Care to tell me what happened?'

Right on cue. She looked at him and rolled her eyes. 'Heavy traffic, a driver more intent on his mobile phone conversation than the road, the lights changed, I stopped, he didn't.' That about encapsulated it. 'We exchanged names and insurance details,' she concluded.

He crossed to where she stood and his fingers probed the back of her neck. 'Headache? Any symptoms of whiplash?'

'No.' His concern was gratifying, but his standing this close didn't do much to stabilise her equilibrium. 'Traffic was crawling at the time.'

'Want to cancel out on tonight?'

She looked at him carefully. 'What if I said yes?'

'I'd make a phone call and we'd stay at home.'

'Just like that?' One eyebrow rose. 'I didn't realise I held such power. Aren't you worried I might misuse it?'

His hand slid forward and captured her chin, tilting it slightly so that he could examine her expression. 'Not your style, Gabbi.'

At this precise moment she felt disinclined to pursue an in-depth evaluation. 'What time do you want to leave?'

He released her and crossed to the refrigerator. 'Seven.'

She had an hour, part of which she intended to spend indulging in a leisurely shower.

In the bedroom she stripped down to her underwear then crossed to the bathroom and activated the water.

Bliss, she acknowledged several minutes later as she rinsed off shampoo and allowed the water to stream down her back. Scented soap freshened her skin with a delicate fragrance, and she lifted her hands to slick back her hair.

The glass door slid open and Benedict stepped into the stall. His naked body ignited a familiar fire deep inside her, and she attempted to dampen it down. 'I've almost finished.' How could her voice sound so calm, so matter-of-fact, when inside she was slowly going up in flames? she wondered.

Would he...? No, there wasn't time. Unless they were to arrive late...

Gabbi subconsciously held her breath as he moved behind her, then released it as his hands settled on her shoulders. Firm fingers began a soothing massage that felt good. So good that she murmured her appreciation.

She let her head fall forward as he worked the tense muscles and she relaxed, unwilling to move.

'Fremont gave you a hard time at the board meeting this morning.'

'Anticipating his queries kept me on my toes.'

'You came well prepared.'

'Being *family* isn't regarded by some as an advantage,' she responded dryly.

'Should it be?'

'You obviously didn't think so.'

Benedict's fingers didn't still. 'My father was a very powerful man. I chose not to compete on his turf.'

'Yet you're where he wanted you to be.'

'There was never any question I wouldn't eventually take his place.'

No, just a matter of when, Gabbi added silently, and wondered whether destiny had played a part. For if Conrad hadn't died Benedict would still be living in America. And the marriage between Benedict Nicols and Gabbi Stanton would not have taken place. It was a sobering thought.

She lifted her head and moved away from him. 'I must get ready.' He made no attempt to stop her as she stepped out of the stall.

It took fifteen minutes to dry and style her hair, a further fifteen to complete her make-up. The gown she'd chosen to wear was dramatic black in a figure-hugging design with shoestring shoulder-straps. Long black gloves added glamour, as did jewellery, black hosiery and stiletto-heeled evening shoes. A few dabs of her favourite perfume completed the image.

Benedict's frame, height and looks were guaranteed to weaken a woman's knees no matter what he wore...or didn't wear. In a tailored black evening suit and white cotton shirt he was positively awesome.

Gabbi cast him a studied glance, and felt the familiar trip of her pulse as it leapt to a quickened beat. The heat flared inside her stomach and slowly spread, licking each nerve-ending into vibrant life.

Less than an hour ago she'd stood naked with him in the shower, yet she felt more acutely vulnerable *now*, fully clothed, than she had then.

To dispel the feeling she spread her arms, completed a full turn and summoned a mischievous smile. 'What do you think?'

His eyes were dark, and his mouth tugged wide over gleaming teeth as he deliberated.

Perhaps she should have worn her hair down, instead of caught into a carelessly contrived knot? Was black too dramatic, too stark?

'Stunning,' Benedict complimented, and saw relief beneath her carefully guarded expression.

'Flattery is an excellent way to begin the evening,' Gabbi said lightly as she turned away to collect her evening bag.

Thirty minutes later a parking valet swept the Bentley down into the vast concrete cavern beneath the hotel as she walked at Benedict's side through the main entrance.

Smile-time, show-time. She knew she shouldn't be such a cynic at twenty-five. Yet *years* spent taking an active part in the social scene had taught her she was expected to play a part. And she'd learned to do it well—the radiant smile, the light-hearted greeting, the spontaneous small talk.

The Grand Ballroom looked resplendent with its decorative theme, the DJ had unobtrusive mood-music playing, and impeccably uniformed waiters and waitresses hovered dutifully, taking and delivering drink orders.

A sell-out, one of the committee members delighted in informing Benedict as she directed him to their appointed table.

Gabbi entertained the slight hope that Annaliese might bring a partner, and she brightened visibly for all of two seconds before recognising the man on her stepsister's arm as none other than Dominic Andrea. More of a mismatch was difficult to imagine, and hot on the heels of that thought was...*what about Francesca*?

'A migraine,' Dominic said for her ears only as he seated Annaliese on his right and then slid into the seat beside Gabbi. 'Annaliese's date will be late.'

A smile curved her mouth. 'You read minds?'

'I anticipated your reaction.'

'Am I that transparent?'

His smile was slow and his eyes sparkled with devilish humour.

'Subtlety isn't my strong point.'

No, but determination was. She thought of Francesca and smiled. If Dominic was intent on pursuit, Francesca didn't have much of a chance.

'She intrigues me.'

Gabbi's smile widened. 'I had noticed.'

'Wish me luck?'

'All you need.'

James arrived with Monique and they took the

seats opposite, exchanged greetings, and placed orders with the drinks waiter.

Monique looked radiant in a royal blue gown and a matching evening jacket. Sapphire and diamond jewellery graced her neck and her wrist, and a large sapphire and diamond dress ring on her right hand almost eclipsed the magnificent diamond above her wedding band.

Annaliese had chosen deep emerald silk that hugged her curves like a second skin, with a side-split that bordered on the indecent.

The two remaining couples at their table slid into their seats as the DJ changed CDs and played an introductory number that was followed by the charity chairman's welcoming speech.

A prawn cocktail starter was served. Soft music filtered unobtrusively while the guests ate, providing a pleasant background.

The main course followed, comprising grilled chicken breast served with mango sauce and vegetables.

Delicious, Gabbi complimented silently as she forked delicate portions. A sandwich eaten at her desk around midday seemed inadequate sustenance by comparison.

A few sips of excellent Chardonnay proved relaxing, and she listened with interest as the host extolled the virtues of the charity, cited the money raised at this evening's event and thanked various sponsors for their generous donations.

A tall male figure slid into the empty seat beside Annaliese and, when the speech was concluded, Annaliese performed the necessary introductions.

Not that one was needed. Aaron Jacob was equally well-known as an eminently successful male model as he was as a star in a long-running television series.

A heartthrob and a hunk, Gabbi acknowledged in feminine appreciation of a near-perfect male specimen. Pity he had an inflated ego and a reputation for changing his dates as often as his socks!

As a couple, Annaliese and Aaron were guaranteed to have their photo prominently displayed on the society page in tomorrow's newspaper. Perhaps that was the purpose of their date? *Be nice,* Gabbi silently chided in self-admonishment as she sipped her wine.

Soon the DJ would increase the volume of the music and invite guests to take to the dance floor. It would be a signal for everyone to mix and mingle, dance and provide an opportunity for the society doyennes to flaunt their latest designer gowns.

'More wine?'

Gabbi turned slightly and met Benedict's warm gaze. 'No, thanks. I'd prefer water.'

One eyebrow lifted in silent enquiry, and she offered him a brilliant smile. 'I thought you might like me to drive home.'

'Considerate of you.' His quiet drawl held a degree of musing cynicism, aware as she was that he rarely took more than one glass of wine with an evening meal and that therefore the offer was unnecessary.

'Yes, isn't it?'

'Benedict.'

Monique's intrusion commanded his attention. 'I've managed to get a few tickets to *Phantom of the Opera*, Wednesday evening. You and Gabrielle will join us, won't you?'

Was it coincidence that Monique had tickets for the same night that Gabbi and Benedict had invited Francesca and Dominic to make up a foursome?

'Thank you, Monique. I already have tickets.'

'Perhaps we could arrange to meet afterwards for supper?'

Familial togetherness was a fine thing, Gabbi acknowledged. But Monique's stage-managing was becoming a little overt.

'Unfortunately we've made other arrangements.'

'Annaliese and Gabrielle are so close, and see so little of each other.' Monique injected just the right amount of regret into her voice then moved in for the figurative kill. 'It seems such a shame not to take advantage of every opportunity to get together while Annaliese is home.'

Oh, my, her stepmother was good. Gabbi almost held her breath, waiting for Benedict's response.

'Another time, Monique.'

'You must come to dinner. Just family. Monday, Tuesday? Either evening is free.'

Persistence, thy name is Monique!

'Gabbi?'

That's right, she thought wryly; pass the buck. Avoiding the dinner was impossible, therefore decisiveness was the only way to go. 'Monday. We'll look forward to it.' Were polite lies considered *real* lies? If so, she'd be damned in hell. Yet she felt justified in telling them for her father's sake.

'Shall we dance?'

Now there was a question. Dancing with Benedict inevitably became a dangerous pleasure. 'Thank you, darling.' She rose to her feet and allowed him to lead her onto the dance floor.

The Celine Dion number was perfect, the lyrics revealing a certain poignancy that echoed most women's hopes and dreams.

Gabbi's body fitted the contours of his with easy familiarity, and she had the crazy desire to discard her conventional hold and wind her arms round his neck.

Did he sense how she felt? He was the very air that she breathed. Everything she wanted, all she would ever need. In a way it was frightening. What if she ever lost him?

'Cold?'

She lifted her head and looked at him for a few seconds without comprehension.

'You shivered,' Benedict enlightened her gently.

Get a grip, Gabbi, she chided herself. She summoned a smile and dismissed it lightly. 'Old ghosts.'

'Want to go back to the table?'

'You think I need to conserve my strength?' she queried solemnly as he led her to the edge of the dance floor.

'Tomorrow's Saturday.'

She shot him a sparkling smile. 'An hour of morning decadence before enjoying a late breakfast on the terrace?'

'*Early*-morning decadence, breakfast on the terrace, followed by a drive to the airport.'

'We're *escaping*?' Gabbi looked at him with due reverence. 'Alone? *Where?* No, don't tell me. Someone might overhear.'

'Witch,' he murmured close to her ear.

Dessert was served as they resumed their seats, followed by coffee and after-dinner mints.

Annaliese drifted onto the dance floor with Aaron, then paused and posed for a vigilant photographer.

'May I?'

Gabbi glanced at Dominic and rose to her feet. Benedict broke his conversation with James and cast her a quick smile.

'Benedict is selective with men who want to partner his wife.'

Gabbi cast Dominic a startled glance as he led her towards the dance floor and pulled her gently into his arms.

'Don't you believe me?'

How did she respond to that? Her light, amused laugh seemed relatively noncommittal.

They circled the floor, twice, then Dominic stepped to one side as Aaron and Annaliese suggested an exchange in partners.

Gabbi smiled as she moved into Aaron's clasp, then winced as he pulled her close. Too close.

'Watch my show?' The query was smooth, and she felt reluctant to enter the game he expected every female to play.

'No, I don't.' She tried to sound vaguely regretful, but it didn't quite come off.

'You don't watch television?'

The temptation to take him down was difficult to resist. 'Of course. Mainly news and documentaries.'

'You're a brain.'

Gabbi wasn't sure it was a compliment. 'We all have one.'

'In my business you have to look after the body. It's

the visual thing, you know? Nutrition, gym, beauty therapist, manicurist, hair stylist. Waxing's the worst.'

'Painful,' she agreed.

'Oh, yeah,' he conceded with a realistic shudder. 'I'm jetting out to LA next week. Been offered a part in a film. Could be the big break.'

She attempted enthusiasm. 'Good luck.'

'Thanks.'

'Mind if I cut in?'

Gabbi heard the quiet, drawling tone and detected the faint edge to her husband's voice.

'Sure.' Aaron relinquished her without argument.

'You interrupted an interesting conversation,' she said mildly as Benedict drew her close.

'Define interesting.'

'Waxing body hair. His.'

'Up front and personal, hmm?'

She stifled a bubble of laughter. 'Oh, yeah,' she agreed in wicked imitation.

As they circled the floor she wondered how he would react if she said she hungered to feel his skin next to her own, his mouth in possession of hers in the slow dance towards sexual fulfilment.

'Darling Gabrielle. Isn't it about time I danced with my brother-in-law?'

No. And he isn't. At least, not technically. However, the words stayed locked in her throat as she graciously acknowledged Annaliese and moved into Dominic's arms.

'I was outfoxed,' Dominic murmured, and Gabbi offered a philosophical smile. 'Want me to complete a round of the floor, intervene and switch partners?'

'No, but thanks anyway.'

A few minutes later there was a break in the music and they returned to the table.

Gabbi collected her evening bag and with a murmured excuse she moved towards the foyer with the intention of freshening her make-up in an adjacent powder room.

There was a queue, and it was some time before she was able to find free space at the mirror to effect repairs.

A number of people had escaped the ballroom to smoke in the adjoining foyer, and Gabbi exchanged a greeting with one guest, then another, before turning to re-enter the ballroom.

'Ah, there you are, darling.' Annaliese projected a high-voltage smile. 'I was sent on a rescue mission.'

'By whom?'

Annaliese's eyes widened in artful surprise. 'Why, Benedict. Who else?'

'An absence of ten minutes hardly constitutes the need for a search party,' Gabbi said evenly.

Annaliese examined the perfection of her manicured nails.

'Benedict likes to guard his possessions.'

Attack was the best form of defence, yet Gabbi opted for a tactical sidestep. 'Yes.'

'Doesn't it bother you?'

'What, precisely?'

'Being regarded as an expensive ornament in a wealthy man's collection.'

This could get nasty without any effort at all. 'A trophy wife?' Gabbi arched one eyebrow and proffered a winsome smile. 'Did it ever occur to you to examine the reverse situation? In Benedict I have an

attentive husband who indulges my slightest whim.'
She ticked off the advantages one by one. 'He's attractive, socially eminent and he's good in bed.' She
allowed the smile to widen. 'I consider I made the
perfect choice.'

A flash of fury was clearly evident before Annaliese managed to conquer it. 'You seem a little peaky,
darling. Pre-menstrual tension?'

'Sibling aggravation,' Gabbi corrected her, resisting the temptation to add more fuel to her stepsister's
fire. 'Shall we return to the ballroom?'

'I intend to use the powder room.'

'In that case…' She paused, and effected a faint lift
of her shoulder. 'See you back at the table.'

The minor victory was sweet, but she entertained
no doubt that the war was far from over. However, a
weekend away would provide a welcome break from
the battlefield. The thought was enough to lighten her
expression and bring a smile to her lips.

Benedict was deep in conversation with Dominic,
Aaron and Monique were conducting animated small
talk and James seemed content being an observer.
Gabbi took the vacant seat beside her father.

'Would you like some more coffee?'

She shook her head. 'You could ask me to dance.'

A smile slanted his mouth. 'Dear, sweet Gabbi.
I'm honoured.' He rose to his feet and held out his
hand. 'Shall we?'

'Enjoying yourself?'

Gabbi considered his question as they circled the
dance floor, and opted to counter it. 'Are you?'

'Monique assures me such occasions are a social
advantage.'

'I suspect she considers you need a welcome break from wheeling and dealing,' she teased lightly, and incurred his soft laughter.

'More likely a woman's ploy to justify spending a small fortune on a new gown and half the day being pampered by a beautician and hairdresser.'

'Which men are content to allow, in the knowledge that said social occasions provide equal opportunity for proposing or cementing a business deal.'

He spared her a thoughtful glance. 'Do I detect a note of cynicism?'

'Perhaps.'

'Benedict adores you.'

She could accept respect and affection, but wasn't *adore* a little over the top? Fortunately with James there was no need to perpetuate the myth. 'He's very good to me.'

'I would never have sanctioned the marriage if I hadn't been convinced that he would take care of you.'

The music wound down for a break between numbers, and Gabbi preceded her father to their table.

Annaliese had taken an empty seat next to Benedict, Monique was conversing with Dominic and Aaron was nowhere in sight. Musical chairs, Gabbi decided with a touch of black humour as she slid into a vacant one.

Guests were slowly beginning to dissipate. In half an hour the bar would close and the DJ would shut down for the night. Any time soon they could begin drifting towards the foyer, take the lift to the main entrance and have the doorman summon their car.

Benedict lifted his head at that moment and cast her a searching glance, raised one eyebrow a frac-

tion, then smoothly extricated himself from Annaliese's clutches. Literally, as the scarlet-tipped fingers
of one hand trailed a persuasive path down the fabric
sheathing his forearm, followed by a coy smile and
an upward sweep of mascaraed eyelashes in a deliberate attempt at flirtation.

Gabbi tried to assure herself that it didn't matter.
But it did.

She smiled graciously all the way to the main entrance, completed the air-kiss routine with Monique
and Annaliese, brushed lips over her father's cheek,
bade Dominic and Aaron goodnight, then slipped into
the passenger seat of the Bentley.

Benedict eased the car towards the busy main
street, paused until he gained clear passage into the
flow of traffic then quickly increased speed.

Gabbi leaned her head back and focused her attention on the view of the city. Bright flashing neon
signs and illuminated shop windows soon gave way
to inner-city suburban streets and shuttered windows,
some dark, others showing a glimmer of muted elec-
tricity. And, as they began to ascend the New South
Head road, they gained a view of the harbour, its
waters darkened by night and tipped with ribbons of
reflected light.

'You're very quiet.'

She turned her head and examined Benedict's
shadowed profile. 'I was enjoying the peaceful silence after several hours of music and noisy chatter.'
It was true, but she doubted he was fooled by her explanation. 'If there's something you want to discuss…'
She trailed off, and gave a slight shrug.

'Annaliese.'

No doubt about it, he aimed straight for the main target. But two could play at that game.

The Bentley turned into their street, slowed as they reached the electronically controlled gates guarding their property, swept along the curved driveway and came to a halt inside the garage.

Gabbi released the seat belt, unfastened the door-clasp and slid out of the car, aware that Benedict was mirroring her actions. He attended to the house alarm and followed her indoors, keyed in the re-set code then drew her into the lounge.

'Would you like a drink?'

She looked at him carefully, and chose a light-hearted response. 'Champagne.'

He crossed to the bar, removed a bottle from the fridge, opened it, filled two flutes then retraced his steps.

Gabbi took one flute and raised it in a silent salute, then sipped the contents. 'What particular aspect of my stepsister's character do you want to discuss?'

She could read nothing in his expression, and she had no idea whether he intended to damn her with faint praise or offer a compliment on her remarkable restraint.

'Annaliese's determination to cause trouble.'

Gabbi allowed her eyes to widen measurably, and she placed a hand over her heart. 'Oh, my goodness. I hadn't noticed.'

'Don't be facetious.'

'It's *obvious*?'

'Stop it, Gabbi,' Benedict warned.

'Why? I'm on a roll.'

'Quit while you're ahead.'

'OK. Pick a scenario. Annaliese wants you, you want her. Annaliese wants you, you don't want her.'

'The latter.'

She hadn't realised she'd been holding her breath, and she released it slowly. 'Well, now, that's a relief. I can kiss goodbye visions of throwing out monogrammed towels, ruining your hand-stitched shoes and cutting up every one of your suits.' She gave him a hard smile that didn't quite match the vulnerability apparent in her eyes. 'I had intentions of being quite vicious if you decided on divorce.'

Humour gleamed in those dark eyes, and a deep chuckle emerged from his throat.

'It's not funny.'

'No.'

'Then don't laugh. I was serious.'

Benedict took a long swallow of champagne and placed his flute down on a nearby pedestal. 'Why in hell would I consider divorcing a sassy young woman who delights in challenging me on every level in favour of someone like Annaliese?' He removed her champagne flute and lowered it to join his own. Then he pulled her into his arms.

Gabbi didn't have a chance to answer before his mouth closed over hers, and she drank in the taste of him mingled with the sweet tang of vintage French champagne, generously giving everything he asked, more than he demanded, until mutual need spiralled to the edge of their control.

'I could take you here, now,' Benedict groaned huskily as his lips grazed a path down her throat, and she arched her head to allow him easy access to the sensitive hollow at its base, the swell of her breasts as he trailed lower.

A soft laugh choked in her throat as he freed one tender globe and took a liberty with its peak. Then she cried out as he lifted her over one shoulder and began striding from the room.

'Caveman tactics,' she accused as he ascended the stairs.

He gained the upper floor, then headed for the main suite. When he reached it, he released her to stand within the circle of his arms.

'Want to undress me?'

Her eyes sparkled with wicked humour. 'Might be quicker if you did it yourself.'

'That bad, huh?'

'Yes,' she said with honest simplicity, her own fingers as busy as his as clothes layered the carpet.

Their loving was all heat and hunger the first time round, followed by a long, sweet after-play that led to the slow slaking of mutual need.

Afterwards she lay with her head pillowed against his chest, the sound of his heartbeat beneath her cheek.

'I don't think I could bear to lose you,' Gabbi said, on the edge of sleep, and wasn't sure whether she heard or dreamed his response.

'What makes you think you will?'

CHAPTER SEVEN

QUEENSLAND'S GOLD COAST lay little more than an hour's flight north of Sydney, and the Stanton-Nicols' Lear jet ensured private airport access, luxurious cabin space and personalised service.

Cleared for take-off, the streamlined jet cruised the runway and achieved a rapid ascent before levelling out.

'No laptop?' Gabbi quizzed as she loosened her seat belt. 'No papers in your briefcase?'

Benedict sank back in his chair and regarded her with indolent amusement. 'Each within easy access.'

'Are you going to work during the flight?'

'Would you prefer me to?'

'No.' Her eyes assumed a mischievous gleam. 'It's not often I get one hour of your undivided attention.' She saw one eyebrow slant, and quickly qualified this. 'Alone. Out of the bedroom,' she added, then spread her hands in helpless acceptance at having stepped into a verbal quagmire. 'I'll give up while I'm ahead.'

'Wise.'

'Coffee, Mr Nicols? Juice, Mrs Nicols?'

'Thanks, Melanie.'

The cabin stewardess's intrusion was timely. Her

smile was professional as she unloaded the tray, then poured coffee and juice. 'I'll be in the cockpit. Buzz me if you need anything.'

Gabbi leaned forward, picked up the glass of fresh orange juice and took an appreciative sip. 'Tell me about the deal you and James are involved in with Gibson Electronics.'

He proceeded to do so, answering her queries as she debated various points.

'It's tight, but fair,' she conceded after a lengthy discussion. 'Think we'll pull it off?'

'Gibson needs Stanton-Nicols' proven reputation with the Asian market.'

'And in return we gain a slice of Gibson Electronics.'

Business. The common factor that forged the link between them. Without it, she doubted she'd be Benedict Nicols' wife. A chilling thought, and one she chose not to dwell on.

The 'fasten seat belt' sign flashed on as the jet began its descent towards Coolangatta airport.

A car was waiting for them, and it took only a few minutes to transfer the minimal luggage into the boot. Benedict signalled to the pilot and had a brief word with the driver while Gabbi took the passenger seat, then he strode round and slid in behind the wheel.

The Gold Coast was Australia's major tourist mecca. Long, sweeping beaches, surf, golden sands, towering high-rise buildings, modern shopping complexes and a subtropical climate all combined to make it a highly sought-after holiday destination. Theme parks, a casino, hotels, cruise boats, canal developments and luxurious prestige housing estates promoted a lifestyle that belonged in part to the rich and famous.

Gabbi loved the casual atmosphere, the spacious residential sprawl. A city with few disadvantages, she mused as Benedict joined the north-bound traffic.

High-rise apartment buildings lined the foreshore, their names varying from the prosaic to the exotic. Warm temperatures, sunshine, azure-blue sky, palm fronds swaying beneath a gentle breeze.

A smile curved her generous mouth, and her eyes filled with latent laughter. Paradise. And Benedict. They were hers for two days.

Conrad and Diandra Nicols had purchased a beach-front block of land and built a three-level vacation home in the days before prestigious real estate lining Mermaid Beach's Hedges Avenue had gained multi-million-dollar price-tags.

Benedict had chosen to retain it as an investment, persuaded from time to time to lease it short-term to visiting dignitaries who desired the privacy of a personal residence instead of a hotel suite or apartment block. Gabbi loved its location, its direct access onto the beach and the open-plan design.

A sigh of pure pleasure left her lips as Benedict drew the car to a halt before the electronically controlled gates, depressed the modem that released them and keyed in a code to operate the garage doors.

The three-car garage was backed by a games-room that led out to a terraced swimming pool. The first level comprised an office, lounge, kitchen and dining-room, with a master suite, three guest bedrooms and two bathrooms on the upper floor.

Each level was connected by a wide curved stair-

case leading onto a semi-circular, balustraded landing, providing a circular central space highlighted
by a magnificent chandelier suspended from the top-
level ceiling and reaching down to almost touching
distance from the ground-level entertainment room.
Lit up at night, it was a spectacular sight.

'You sound like a student let out of school,' Benedict commented as they ascended the stairs to the
uppermost floor.

'I love it here,' she said simply as she swung round
to face him.

'What do you suggest we do with the day?'

'Oh, my, what a responsibility.' Her eyes danced
with impish humour, and she pretended to deliberate. 'I could drag you off to visit a theme park. We
could hire a boat and cruise the broadwater. Do a bit
of sun-worshipping by the pool. Or take in a movie at
the cinema.' Her mouth curved into a winsome smile.
'On the other hand, I could be an understanding wife
and tell you to go set up a game of golf...something
you'd enjoy.'

Benedict reached out a hand and brushed light fingers across her cheek. 'And in return?'

'I get to choose where we have dinner.'

'Done.' He bent down and gave her a brief, hard
kiss. 'We'll go on to a show or the movies.'

'You ring the golf course while I unpack.' She had
a plan, and she put it into action. 'Do you want to take
the four-wheel drive or the sedan?'

'The four-wheel drive.'

Half an hour later she backed the sedan out of the
garage and headed for the nearest major shopping
complex. It was fun to browse the boutiques, sip a

cappuccino, before getting down to the serious business of shopping.

She had a list, and she entered the food hall, selected a trolley and began.

It was almost midday when she re-entered the house with no less than five carrier bags, the contents of which were systematically stored in the refrigerator and pantry.

The menu was basic. The accompanying sauces would be anything but. Wine, French breadsticks. A delicious tiramisu for dessert. Liqueur coffee. And she had hired a video.

At five she set the table with fine linen and lace, silver cutlery and china. Then she checked the kitchen and went upstairs to shower. After selecting fresh underwear, she donned elegant blue silk evening trousers and a matching top, then groomed her hair into a smooth knot on top of her head. She then tended to her make-up, which was understated, with just a hint of blusher, soft eyeshadow and a touch of clear rose-pink lip-gloss.

It was after six when the security system beeped, alerting her to the fact that the gates were being released, followed by the garage doors. She heard a refined clunk as the vehicle door closed, then Benedict came into view.

Gabbi stilled the nervous fluttering inside her stomach as she moved out onto the landing to greet him.

He looked magnificent. Dark hair teased by a faint breeze. Broad shoulders and superb musculature emphasised by a navy open-necked polo shirt. Strong facial features, tanned a deeper shade by several hours spent in the sun.

'Hi. How was the game?'

He looked intensely male, emanating a slight air of aggressive goodwill that spoke of achievement and satisfaction at having pitted his skill against a rival and won.

He reached the landing and moved towards her, pausing to bestow a brief, evocative kiss. 'I'll hit the shower.'

'Don't bother dressing.'

One eyebrow lifted and his lips twisted to form a humorous smile. 'My dear Gabbi. You want me to be arrested?'

'We're eating in.' Now that she'd taken the decision upon herself, she was unsure of his reaction. 'I've made dinner.'

He looked at her carefully, noting the slight uncertainty, the faint nervousness apparent, and her effort to camouflage it. 'Give me ten minutes.'

He rejoined her in nine. Freshly shaven, showered, and dressed in casual trousers and a short-sleeved shirt.

'Would you like a drink?'

Gabbi shook her head. 'You have one. I'll wait until we eat.'

He followed her into the kitchen, caught sight of numerous saucepans washed and stacked to drain. 'Looks professional. Smells delicious. Hidden talents, Gabbi?'

She wrinkled her nose at him, then swatted his hand as he reached forward to sample the sauce. 'No advance tasting, no peeking. Open the wine. It needs to breathe.'

She served the starter. Delicate stuffed mushrooms that melted in the mouth. French bread heated to crunchy perfection.

The main course was an exquisite *filet mignon* so tender that the flesh parted at the slightest pressure of the knife. With it they had asparagus with hollandaise sauce, baby potatoes in their jackets split and anointed with garlic butter and glazed baby carrots.

When they'd finished, Benedict touched his glass to hers in a silent salute. 'I haven't tasted better in any restaurant.'

'To the French, food is a passion. The meals I shared with Jacques's family were gastronomical feasts, visual works of art.' Her eyes sparkled with remembered pleasure. 'I made a deal with his mother,' she said solemnly.

'You kept your hands off her son, and she taught you to cook?'

Gabbi began to laugh. 'Close.'

'One look at you and any mother would fear for her son's emotional sanity,' Benedict drawled.

She met his gaze and held it. What about *his* emotional sanity? Was it so controlled that no woman could disturb it?

'I'll get dessert.' She rose to her feet and stacked his plate and cutlery with her own, then took them through to the kitchen.

Two wide individual crystal bowls held the creamy ambrosia of liqueur-soaked sponge, cream and shaved chocolate that was tiramisu.

It was good; she'd even have said delicious.

Benedict sat back in his chair and discarded his napkin. 'Superb, Gabbi.'

She lifted one shoulder in a negligible shrug. 'We dine out so often, I thought it would make a change to stay home.'

'I'll help with the dishes.'

'All done,' she assured lightly. 'I'll make coffee. There's a video in the VCR.'

When the coffee had filtered, she poured it, added liqueur and topped it with cream, then took both stemmed glasses through to the lounge.

Benedict had chosen one of three double-seater leather settees, and he indicated the empty space beside him.

The movie was a comedy, loosely adapted from the original *La cage aux folies*. It was amusing, well acted and entertaining.

Gabbi sipped her coffee slowly, then, when she had finished, Benedict took the glass and placed it together with his on a side table.

She relaxed and leaned her head back against the cushioned rest. Being here like this was magical. No guests, no intrusions.

An arm curved round her shoulders and drew her close. She felt his breath stir her hair. And she made no protest as he used a modem to switch off the lights.

The only illumination came from the television screen, and the electric candles reflected from the chandelier. Which he dimmed.

Awareness flared as his fingers brushed against her breast and stayed. His lips lingered at her temple.

She let her hand rest on his thigh, and didn't explore.

Occasionally his fingers would move in an absent pattern that quickened her pulse and triggered the heat deep inside her.

It was a delightful, leisurely prelude to a rhapsody that would gather momentum and crest in a passionate climax.

Gabbi wasn't disappointed. Just when she thought there were no more paths she could travel, Benedict took her along another, gently coaxing, pacing his pleasure to match her own before tipping her over the edge.

Close to sleep, she whispered, *Je t'aime, mon amour,* to the measured heartbeat beneath her lips. And wondered if he heard, if he knew.

They rose early and took a leisurely walk along the beach, then stripped down to swimwear and ventured into the ocean.

The water was cool and calm, the waves tame, and afterwards they sprinted back to the house and rinsed the sea from their skin and hair, donned casual clothes and ate a hearty breakfast out on the terrace.

'How do you feel about a drive to the mountains?'

Gabbi took a sip of coffee, then rested the cup between both hands. Visions of a picnic lunch and panoramic views were enticing. 'What of the call you're expecting?'

Benedict subjected her to a measured appraisal, then moved his shoulders in an indolent gesture. 'Divert the house phone to my mobile, sling the briefcase and laptop onto the rear seat.'

It wasn't often he took an entire weekend off. All too frequently his time was spent in the study in front of the computer, surfing various global financial sites on the Internet. Leisure was relegated to social occasions, and even then business was inevitably an ongoing topic of discussion.

Hesitation wasn't an option. 'Let's do it.' She replaced her cup on the table and rose to her feet. 'I'll make sandwiches.'

He put a restraining hand on her arm. 'We'll pick up something along the way.'

The phone rang, and Gabbi froze as Benedict crossed into the house to take the call. The day's pleasure disappeared as she heard the curt tone of his voice, saw him make notes on paper then fold the sheet into his shirt pocket.

Nice plans, she thought with wistful regret as she cleared their breakfast dishes onto a tray and carried them through to the kitchen. Pity they had to be abandoned.

She was determined not to show her disappointment. 'Shall I take more coffee through to the study?'

He shot her a sharp look. 'I need an hour, maybe less. Then we'll leave.'

'Can I help?'

He gave a brief nod of assent, and she followed him to the study.

The fax machine held paper, and Benedict collected it *en route* to the desk. Within seconds the laptop was up and running.

They worked together side by side and, when the document was done and checked, it was consigned to the printer then faxed through to the States.

'OK. Let's get out of here.'

Five minutes later Benedict reversed the four-wheel

drive from the garage and, once clear of suburbia, he headed west, taking the mountain road to Mount Tamborine.

'Thanks.'

'Whatever for?'

The terrain was lush green after seasonal subtropical rain. Grassed paddocks, bush-clad hills, homes on acreage, working farms.

They were gaining height as the bitumen road curved round the foothills and began its snaking ascent towards the peak.

'The weekend,' Gabbi elaborated. 'Today.' For the simple pleasures that cost only his time and therefore were infinitely more precious to her than anything money could buy.

'It's not over yet.'

No. The sun suddenly appeared much brighter, the sky a magical azure.

As the road wound higher there was a spectacular view of the hinterland, and in the distance lay the ocean, a sapphire jewel.

They reached the uppermost peak and travelled the road that traversed its crest, past houses of various ages and designs, an old-English-style hotel, and a quaint café.

The village was a mixture of shops with broad verandahs clumped together, and they stopped to purchase a large bottle of chilled mineral water, some delicious ham and salad rolls and fruit. Then they walked back to the four-wheel drive and drove to a grassed reserve with magnificent views over the valley.

It was isolated, picturesque, and Gabbi felt as if

they were perched on top of the world, removed from everything and everyone. It was a heady feeling, more intoxicating than wine, breathtaking.

Benedict unfolded a rug and spread it over the grass beneath the shade of a nearby tree. They ate until they were replete then sprawled comfortably, at ease with the vista and the silence.

A true picnic, it reminded Gabbi of the many she'd shared with Jacques in the days when laughter had risen readily to her lips and the only cares she had had were studying and excelling in her exams.

'Penny for them.'

Gabbi turned at the sound of Benedict's drawling voice, and gave him a slow smile. 'We should do this more often.'

'That's it?'

He sounded mildly amused, but she could play the faintly teasing game as well as he. 'You want my innermost thoughts?'

'It would be a start.'

'I love you' was so easy to say, so difficult to retract. Whispered in the deep night hours was one thing—voiced in the early afternoon on a mountaintop was something else.

'I was thinking this is a little piece of heaven,' she said lightly. 'Far away from the city, business pressures, people.'

'The place, or the fact we're sharing it?'

She offered him a wide smile that reached her eyes and lit them as vividly as the blue of the ocean in the distance. 'Why, *both*, of course. It wouldn't be nearly as much fun on my own.'

He curled a hand beneath her nape and brought his

mouth down over hers in an evocative kiss that teased, tantalised and stopped just short of total possession.

'Witch,' he murmured a few moments later against her temple. 'Do you want to stay here, or explore the mountain further?'

She pressed a kiss to the hollow at the base of his throat and savoured the faint taste that was his alone—male heat mingled with cleanliness and exclusive cologne.

'We're close to a public road, it's a public park, and we wouldn't want to shock anyone passing by,' she teased, using the edge of her teeth to nip his skin. 'Besides, there's a plane waiting to take us back to the rat race.'

'Tomorrow morning. Dawn.'

They had the night. 'We shouldn't waste a moment,' Gabbi said with mock reverence, and gave his chest a gentle push. 'When we reach the coast we'll get some prawns and Moreton Bay bugs which you can cook on the barbecue while I get a salad together. We'll open a bottle of wine, eat, and watch the sun go down.'

He let her go, watched as she rose lithely to her feet, then took her outstretched hand and levered himself upright in one fluid movement.

It was after five when they entered the house, and by tacit agreement they took a long walk over the damp, packed sand of an outgoing tide, then reluctantly turned and retraced their steps.

Her hand was held lightly clasped in his, and a faint breeze tugged her blouse and teased loose tendrils free from the careless knot of her hair. Her skin glowed from its exposure to the fresh sea air, and her eyes held a mystic depth that owed much to the pleasure of the day, and the anticipation of the night.

After preparing the meal there was time to change into swimwear and swim several lengths of the pool before emerging to dry the excess water from their skin.

The aroma of barbecued seafood heightened their appetite, and, seated out on the terrace, Gabbi reached for a prawn with her fingers, declared it ambrosia, then reached for another as she dug her fork into a delectable portion of salad.

'You've got prawn juice on your chin,' Benedict said lazily, and she directed a dazzling smile at him.

'Terribly inelegant.' She tore flesh from the shell of a perfectly cooked bug and ate it in slow, delicate bites. Monique would have been appalled. There wasn't a lemon-scented fingerbowl in sight. And paper napkins weren't an accepted substitute for fine Irish linen.

The sun began to sink, and the light dimmed, streaking the sky to the west with reflected pink that slowly changed to orange, a brilliant flare of colour that slowly faded, then disappeared, leaving behind a dusky glow.

Timed lights sprang up around the pool, lit the terrace, and cast a reflection that was almost ethereal until darkness fell and obliterated everything beyond their immediate line of vision.

Gabbi heard the phone, and watched as Benedict rose from his chair to answer it. She gathered the seafood debris together, stacked plates onto the tray, took it indoors to the electronic food trolley, then pressed the button that lifted it up to the kitchen. Then she closed the doors onto the terrace and activated the security system.

Dishes and cutlery were dispensed into the dishwasher, the kitchen soon restored to order. Her hair had long since dried, but needed to be rinsed of chlorine from the pool, and she made her way upstairs to the shower.

Afterwards she donned briefs, pulled on long white trousers in a soft cheesecloth, then added a matching sleeveless button-through blouse. Several minutes with the hair-drier removed the excess moisture from her hair, and she left it loose, added a touch of lip-gloss, then ran lightly down to the kitchen.

Coffee. Hot, strong and black, with a dash of liqueur.

The coffee had just finished filtering into the glass carafe when Benedict joined her, and she cast him a searching look.

'Problems?'

'Nothing I can't handle.'

She didn't doubt it. She poured the brew into a cup and handed it to him. 'Need me?'

His eyes flared. 'Yes.' His implication was unmistakable, and her heart skipped a beat, quickened, then slowly settled. 'But right now I have to make a series of phone calls.' He lowered his head and took her mouth in a soft kiss that made her ache for more. Then he turned and made his way across the landing to the study.

Gabbi took her coffee into the lounge, settled in a comfortable settee and switched on the television set. Cable TV ensured instant entertainment to satisfy every whim, and she flicked through the channels until she found a sitcom that promised lightness and mirth.

One programme ran into another, and she fought against an increasing drowsiness, succumbing without conscious effort.

There was a vague feeling of being held in strong arms, the sensation of being divested of her outer clothes, then the softness of a pillow beneath her cheek, and a warm body moulded against her back.

CHAPTER EIGHT

THE LEAR JET turned off the runway and cruised slowly into a private parking bay at Sydney's domestic airport.

Serg was waiting with the Bentley, and after transferring overnight bags into the boot he slipped behind the wheel and headed the car towards the eastern suburbs.

Gabbi sank back against the leather cushioning and viewed the scene beyond the windscreen. Traffic was already building up, clogging the main arterial roads as commuters drove to their places of work.

In an hour she'd join them. She looked at her casual cotton shirt, trousers and trainers. Soon she'd exchange them for a suit, tights and high heels.

Even now she could sense Benedict withdrawing, his mind already preoccupied with business and the day ahead.

Marie served breakfast within minutes of their arrival home, and shortly after eight Gabbi slid behind the wheel of her car and trailed Benedict's Bentley down the drive.

The day was uneventful, although busy, and lunch was something she sent out for and ate at her desk.

Waiting for a faxed confirmation and acting on it provided an unwanted delay, and consequently it was almost six when she garaged the car.

While Monique took liberties with time as a guest, as a hostess she insisted on punctuality. Six-thirty for seven meant exactly that. Which left Gabbi twenty minutes in which to shower, dress, apply make-up and tend to her hair.

She began unbuttoning her suit jacket as she raced up the stairs, hopping from one foot to the other as she paused to remove her heeled pumps. By the time she reached the bedroom she'd released the zip-fastener of her skirt and her fingers were busy with the buttons on her blouse.

Benedict looked up from applying the electric razor to a day's growth of beard and raised an enquiring eyebrow as she entered the *en suite* bathroom.

'Don't ask,' Gabbi flung at him as she slid open the shower door and turned on the water.

Black silk evening trousers, a matching singlet top and a black beaded jacket. High-heeled black pumps. Gold jewellery. Hair swept on top of her head, light make-up with emphasis on the eyes.

Gabbi didn't even think, she just went with it, relying on speed and dexterity for a finished result which, she accepted with a cursory glance in the cheval-glass, would pass muster.

She reached for her evening bag, pushed its long gold chain over one shoulder and turned to see Benedict regarding her with a degree of lazy amusement.

'No one would guess you achieved that result in so short a time,' he commented as they descended the staircase and made their way to the garage.

'I'll take three deep breaths in the car and think pleasant thoughts.'

She did. Not that it helped much. With every passing kilometre the nerves inside her stomach intensified, which was foolish, for Annaliese was unlikely to misbehave in Monique and James's presence.

'Darlings.' Annaliese greeted them individually with a kiss to both cheeks. 'Two of my favourite people.' Her smile was stunning as she moved between Gabbi and Benedict and linked an arm through each of theirs. 'Come through to the lounge.'

One eyebrow slanted as she ruefully glanced from Gabbi's black evening suit to her own figure-moulding black cocktail gown. 'Great minds, darling?' The light tinkling laugh held humour that failed to reach her eyes. 'We always did have an extraordinarily similar taste in clothes.'

Except I paid for my own, while you racked up Alaia and Calvin Klein on James's credit card, Gabbi added silently. *Stop it,* she chided herself.

Her father's home was beautiful, tastefully if expensively decorated, and a superb show-case for a man of James's wealth and social position. Why, then, did she feel uncomfortable every time she stepped inside the door? Was it because Monique had carefully redecorated, systematically replacing drapes, subtly altering colour schemes, until almost every memory of Gabbi's mother had been removed?

Yet why shouldn't Monique impose her own taste? James had obviously been willing to indulge her. And the past, no matter how idyllic a memory, had little place in today's reality.

'Gabbi. Benedict.' Monique moved towards them

with both hands outstretched. 'I was afraid you were going to be late.'

James gave his daughter a hug and laid a hand on Benedict's arm. 'Come and sit down. I'll get you both a drink.'

Innocuous social small talk. They were each adept at the art—the smiles, the laughter. To an outsider they resembled a happy, united family, Gabbi reflected as she took a seat next to Benedict at the dining table.

Monique's cook had prepared exquisitely presented courses that tantalised the taste buds. Tonight she excelled with *vichyssoise verte* as a starter.

'We arranged an impromptu tennis evening last night,' Monique revealed as they finished the soup. 'I put a call through, hoping you might be able to join us, but Marie informed me that you were away for the weekend.'

Monique possessed the ability to phrase a statement so that it resembled a question, and Gabbi fingered the stem of her water-glass, then chose to lift it to her lips.

'We flew to the coast,' Benedict drawled in response.

'Really?' Annaliese directed a brilliant smile at Gabbi. 'I'm surprised you were able to drag Benedict away from Sydney.' She switched her attention to Benedict and the smile became coquettish. 'I thought it was a requisite of the corporate wife to be able to entertain herself.'

Gabbi replaced her glass carefully. 'Surely not to the exclusion of spending quality time with her husband?'

The cook served a superb *poulet français*, with accompanying vegetables.

'Of course not, darling.' Annaliese proffered a condescending smile. 'It was very thoughtful of Benedict to indulge you.'

Gabbi picked up her cutlery and speared her portion of chicken, then she sliced a bite-size piece with delicate precision. 'Yes, wasn't it?' She forked the morsel into her mouth, savoured it, then offered a compliment that the chef deserved. 'This is delicious, Monique.'

'Thank you, Gabrielle.'

Gabbi completed a mental count to three. Any second now Monique would instigate a subtle third degree.

'I trust you had an enjoyable time?'

'It was very relaxing.'

'Did you take in a show at the Casino?'

'No,' Benedict intervened. 'Gabbi cooked dinner and we stayed home.' He turned towards Gabbi with a warm intimate smile which melted her bones.

Great, Gabbi sighed silently. You've taken control of Monique's game, and provided Annaliese with the ammunition to fire another round.

'You never cooked at home, darling.' The tinkling laugh was without humour.

'There was no need. We always had a chef to prepare meals.' Besides, Monique hadn't wanted her in the kitchen, even on the chef's night off.

'It could have been arranged, Gabbi.'

She looked at James and smiled. 'It was never that important.'

'You should give us the opportunity to sample your culinary efforts, Gabrielle.'

After all these years, Monique? 'I wouldn't think of hurting Marie's feelings by suggesting I usurp her position in the kitchen.'

'Marie *does* have a night off, darling,' Annaliese remonstrated in faintly bored tones.

'Yes,' she responded evenly. 'On the evenings Benedict and I eat out.'

Her stepsister examined the perfection of her lacquered nails, then spared Gabbi a teasing smile. 'You're hedging at extending an invitation.'

Venom, packaged in velvet and presented with pseudo-sincerity. Gabbi handled it with the ease of long practice. 'Not at all. Which evening would suit?'

It was a polite battle, but a battle nonetheless.

'Monique? James?' Annaliese was gracious in her deferral.

'Can I check my diary, darling, and get back to you?'

Gabbi was equally gracious. 'Of course.'

'I'm intrigued to learn what you will serve,' Annaliese purred.

'Marie can always be guaranteed to present an excellent meal,' Gabbi supplied, determined not to be backed into a corner.

Monique's eyes narrowed, as did her daughter's, and each man picked up on the tension, electing to defuse it by initiating a discussion totally unrelated to social niceties.

Bombe au chocolat was served for dessert. Afterwards they retired to the lounge for coffee.

'I thought we might play cards,' Monique suggested. 'Poker?'

'As long as it's not strip poker,' Annaliese teased with a provocative smile. 'I'll lose every stitch I'm wearing.'

And love every minute of it, Gabbi thought hatefully.

'We close the table at eleven-thirty. Winning hand takes the pool.' James deferred to Benedict. 'Agreed?'

'Agreed.'

The game wasn't about skill or luck, winning or losing. The stakes were minuscule, the ensuing two hours merely entertainment.

Annaliese seemed to delight in leaning forward at every opportunity in a deliberate attempt to display the delicate curve of her breasts and the fact that she wore nothing to support them.

Add a tantalising smile and sparkling witchery every time she looked at Benedict and Gabbi was feeling positively feral by the time the evening drew to a close.

'No comment?' Benedict ventured as he drove through the gates and turned onto the road.

Gabbi drew a deep breath then released it slowly. 'Where would you like me to begin?'

He spared her a quizzical glance, then concentrated on merging with the traffic. 'Anywhere will do, as long as you release some of that fine rage.'

'You noticed.'

'I was probably the only one who did.'

'It's such a relief to know that.' Dammit, she wanted to *hit* something.

'Don't,' Benedict cautioned with dangerous soft-ness, and she turned on him at once.

'Don't—*what*?'

'Slam a fist against the dashboard. You'll only hurt yourself.'

'Perhaps I should hit you instead.'

'Want me to pull over, or can it wait until we get home?'

'Don't try to humour me, Benedict.' She focused her attention on the scene beyond the windscreen: the bright headlights of oncoming traffic, fluorescent street-lamps and the elongated shadows they cast in the darkness.

Gabbi hurried indoors as soon as Benedict released the alarm system, not even pausing as he reset it. She made for the foyer and had almost reached the stair-case when a hand clamped on her arm.

Any words she might have uttered were stilled as he swung her round and caught her close. There was nothing she could do to halt the descent of his mouth, or deny its possession of her own.

Hard, hungry, almost punishing. It defused her anger, as he meant it to do. And when her body soft-ened and leant in against his he altered the nature of the kiss, deepening it until she clung to him.

A husky groan emerged from her throat as he swung an arm beneath her knees and lifted her into his arms. There wasn't a word she could think of ut-tering as he carried her up the stairs to their room. Or an action she wanted to take to stop him removing her clothes and his, before he drew her down onto the bed.

A long, slow exploration of the pleasure spots, the touch of his lips against the curve of her calf, the sensitive crease behind her knee, then the evocative path along her inner thigh... Gabbi felt her body begin to melt like wax beneath the onslaught of flame, until she was totally malleable, *his*, to do with as he chose.

Shared intimacy. Mutual sexual gratification. Was that all it was to Benedict?

Love. While her heart craved the words, her head ruled that she should be content without them.

Premium seating tickets for *Phantom of the Opera* were sold out weeks in advance. Benedict had undoubtedly wielded some influence to gain four tickets at such short notice, Gabbi mused as she took her seat beside him.

'Wonderful position,' Francesca murmured as the orchestra began an introductory number prior to the opening of the first act.

'Yes, isn't it?'

'You look stunning in that colour.'

The compliment was genuine, and Gabbi accepted it with a smile. 'Thanks.' Peacock-blue silk shot with green, it highlighted the texture of her skin and emphasised her blonde hair. 'So do you,' she returned warmly.

Deep ruby-red velvet did wonders for Francesca's colouring, and moulded her slim curves to perfection.

The music swelled, the curtain rose, and Act One began.

Gabbi adored the visual dimension of live performance—the presence of the actors, the costumes, the faint smell of greasepaint and make-up, the sounds. It was a totally different experience to film.

The interval between each act allowed sufficient

time for patrons to emerge into the foyer for a drink, or a cigarette for those who smoked.

Gabbi expected to see James, Monique and Annaliese in the crowd. What she didn't expect was for Annaliese to readily abandon Monique and James and spend the interval conversing with Francesca, Dominic and Benedict. Apart from a perfunctory greeting, Gabbi was barely acknowledged.

The buzzer sounded its warning for patrons to resume their seats. As soon as the lights dimmed Benedict reached for her hand and held it firmly within his own. At the close of the next act he didn't release it when they stood and moved towards the foyer.

'The powder-room?' Francesca queried, and Gabbi inclined her head in agreement a split second before she caught sight of Annaliese weaving a determined path towards them.

'Fabulous evening,' her stepsister enthused with a dazzling smile.

'Yes, isn't it?' Gabbi agreed as she slipped her hand free. 'If you'll excuse Fran and me for a few minutes?'

'Of course.' Annaliese's delight was almost evident. 'I'll keep Benedict and Dominic amused in your absence.'

And relish every second, Gabbi observed uncharitably.

'Doesn't give up, does she?' Francesca said quietly as she followed Gabbi through the crowd. 'Have you told her to get lost?'

'Yes.' They entered the powder-room and joined the queue.

'The polite version?' Francesca asked. 'Or the no-holds-barred cat-fight rendition?'

'Would you accept icily civil?' Gabbi countered with a smile.

'A little bit of fire wouldn't go amiss. Italians are very good at it.' A wicked gleam lit her eyes. 'We yell, we throw things.'

'I've never seen you in action,' Gabbi said with genuine amusement.

'That's because I've never been mad at you.'

'Heaven forbid.' They moved forward a few paces. 'Dare I ask how things are going between you and Dominic?'

'I shall probably throw something at him soon.'

A bubble of laughter rose in Gabbi's throat. 'Should I warn him, do you think?'

'Let it be a surprise.'

Dominic was a man of Benedict's calibre. Dynamic, compelling, *electrifying*. And mercilessly indomitable in his pursuit of the seemingly unattainable. Gabbi was unsure how much longer Dominic would allow Francesca to maintain an upper hand. The outcome, she decided with a secret smile, would be interesting.

The buzzer for the commencement of the following act sounded as they freshened their make-up, and they resumed their seats as the lights began to dim.

It was a faultless performance, the singers in excellent voice. As the curtain fell on the final act there was a burst of applause from the audience that succeeded in a further curtain call.

Emerging from the crush of the dispersing crowd took some time.

'Shall we go on somewhere for a light supper?' Dominic asked as they reached the car park.

'Love to,' Gabbi accepted. 'Where do you have in mind?'

'Benedict?'

'Your choice, Dom,' he drawled.

'There's an excellent place at Double Bay.' He named it. 'We'll meet you there.'

'Relax,' Benedict bade Gabbi as the Bentley by-passed the Botanical Gardens. 'I doubt Annaliese will embark on a club crawl in an effort to determine our whereabouts.'

'How astute,' Gabbi congratulated with a degree of mockery. 'Her enthusiasm hasn't escaped you.'

'And you, Gabbi,' he continued, 'are fully aware I provide Annaliese with no encouragement what-soever.'

'*Darling* Benedict, are you aware that you don't need to?'

'You sound like a jealous wife.'

'Well, of course.'

He slanted her a dark glance and chided softly, 'Don't be facetious.'

Her lips curved to form a wicked smile. 'One has to develop a sense of humour.'

'I could, and probably should, spank you.'

'Do that, and I'll seek my own revenge.'

He gave a husky laugh. 'It might almost be worth it.'

'I think,' Gabbi said judiciously, 'you should give the road your full attention.'

The restaurant was situated above a block of shops on the main Double Bay thoroughfare. The ambience was authentically Greek, and it soon became apparent that Dominic was not only a favoured patron but also a personal friend of the owner.

Gabbi declined strong coffee in favour of tea, and nibbled from a platter filled with a variety of sweet and savory pastries.

Dominic was a skilled raconteur, possessed of a dry sense of humour which frequently brought laughter to Gabbi's lips and, unless she was mistaken, penetrated a chink in Francesca's façade.

It was after midnight when they bade each other goodnight and slid into separate cars, almost one when Gabbi slid between the sheets and Benedict snapped off the bedside lamp.

CHAPTER NINE

STANTON-NICOLS SUPPORTED a few select charities, and tonight's event was in the form of a prestigious annual dinner held in the banquet room of a prominent city hotel.

Noted as an important occasion among the social élite, it achieved attendance in the region of a thousand patrons.

Haute couture was clearly evident as society doyennes strove to outdo each other, and Gabbi suppressed the wry observation that their jewellery, collectively, would probably fund a starving nation with food.

Men fared much better than women in the fashion stakes. They simply chose a black evening suit, white shirt and black bow-tie, albeit the suit might be Armani or Zegna, the shoes hand-stitched and the shirt expensive pure cotton.

Gabbi had chosen a full-length slimline strapless gown of multicoloured silk organza featuring the muted colours of spring. Cut low at the back, it was complemented by an attached panel and completed by a long, trailing neck-scarf in matching silk organza.

Tonight she'd elected to leave her hair loose, and

the carefree windswept style enhanced her attractive features.

Six-thirty for seven allowed time for those who chose to arrive early to mix and mingle over drinks in the large foyer. The banquet-room doors were opened at seven, and dinner was served thirty minutes later.

'A glass of champagne?'

'Orange juice,' Gabbi decided as a waiter hovered with a tray of partly filled flutes. She removed the appropriate flute and caught the glimmer of amusement apparent in Benedict's dark eyes.

'The need for a clear head?'

Her mouth curved to form a winsome smile. 'You read me well.' James, Monique and Annaliese would be seated at the same table, together with five fellow guests.

'Every time, *querida*,' he mocked softly, and saw the faint dilation of her pupils at his use of the Spanish endearment. Did he know the occasional use of his late mother's native language had the power to stir her emotions?

Her momentary disconcertion was quickly masked as Benedict greeted a colleague, and with skilled ease she engaged in small talk with the colleague's wife for the few minutes until Benedict indicated the necessity to locate their designated table.

Stanton-Nicols was one of several sponsors contributing to the event, and already seated at their table was the charity chairman and his wife and a visiting titled dignitary together with his wife and son.

The five minutes remaining before dinner was served were crucial for those who chose to make an entrance. James, Monique and Annaliese slid into their seats with barely one minute to spare, with the obligatory air-kiss, the smiles and the faint touch of a hand. Perfect, Gabbi noted silently. Monique had done it again, ensuring they were the last to arrive, and their passage, weaving through countless tables, observed by almost everyone in the room.

As the waiters distributed the first of three courses, the compère welcomed the guests, outlined the evening's programme, and thanked everyone for their patronage.

Light background music filtered unobtrusively from numerous speakers as Gabbi lifted her fork and started on an appetising prawn and avocado cocktail.

Someone—Monique, as a dedicated committee member? Gabbi pondered—had seen fit to seat Annaliese on Benedict's left and the visiting titled dignitary's son on Gabbi's right.

The seemingly careless placing of Annaliese's hand on Benedict's thigh during the starter could have been coincidental, although Gabbi doubted it.

'Pleasant evening,' the dignitary's son observed. 'Good turn-out.'

Hardly scintillating conversation, but it provided a necessary distraction, and Gabbi offered a polite rejoinder.

'An interesting mix,' he continued. 'A professional singer and a fashion parade.'

'Plus the obligatory speeches.'

His smile was disarming. 'You've been here before.'

Gabbi's mouth slanted to form a generous curve. 'Numerous times.'

'May I say you look enchanting?'

Her eyes held mild amusement as she took in his kindly features. 'Thank you.'

Their plates were removed, and she offered Benedict a wide smile as he filled her water glass. His eyes were dark, enigmatic, and she pressed a hand on his right thigh. 'Thank you, darling.'

'My pleasure.'

A *double entendre* if ever there was one, and she deliberately held his gaze, silently challenging him.

An announcement by the compère that they were to be entertained with two songs by the guest singer was a timely diversion, and Gabbi listened with polite attention.

The main course was served: chicken Kiev, baby potatoes and an assortment of vegetables.

'Wonderful food,' the dignitary's son declared as he demolished his serving with enthusiasm, and Gabbi tried not to notice Annaliese's scarlet-tipped fingers settling on Benedict's forearm.

The singer performed another medley, which was followed by dessert, then the charity chairman took the podium.

At that point Annaliese slid to her feet and discreetly disappeared to one side of the stage.

Coffee was served as the compère announced the fashion parade, and with professional panache three male and three female models appeared on the catwalk, displaying creations from prominent Sydney designers in a variety of styles ranging from resort, city and career, to designer day, cocktail and formal evening wear.

'Stunning, isn't she?'

Gabbi turned towards the titled dignitary's son and

saw his attention was focused on Annaliese's progress down the catwalk. 'Yes.' It was nothing less than the truth. Her stepsister exuded self-confidence and had the height, the body, the face...all the qualities essential for success in the modelling arena.

Most men took one look and were entranced by the visual package; most women recognised the artificiality beneath the flawless figure and exquisite features.

Annaliese participated in each section, her smile practised and serene. Although as the parade progressed it became increasingly obvious that she singled out one table for special attention...one man as the recipient of an incredibly sexy smile.

Gabbi's tension mounted with each successive procession down the catwalk, and it irked her unbearably that she was powerless to do anything about it. Except smile.

Benedict, damn him, took an interest in each model and every item displayed. Resort wear included swimwear. The bikini, the high-cut maillot. Annaliese looked superb in a minuscule bikini...and was well aware of her effect.

Gabbi felt the urge to kill and controlled it. The slightest hint of her displeasure at Annaliese's provocative behaviour would be seen as a victory, and she refused to give her stepsister that satisfaction.

Evening wear provided Annaliese with another opportunity to stun when she appeared in a backless, strapless creation that moulded her curves like a second skin.

The finale brought all the participating models on stage for one last turn on the catwalk.

'Is there anything that catches your eye?' Benedict enquired.

'The tall blond male model,' Gabbi responded with a deliberate smile, and glimpsed the amusement that lightened his features.

'Naturally you refer to the clothes he's wearing.'

She allowed her eyes to widen, and they held a glint of wicked humour. 'Naturally. Although the whole package is very attractive. He was magnificently *impressive* in swimwear.'

'Payback time?'

'Why, Benedict. Whatever do you mean?'

His expression held a degree of lazy tolerance. 'It'll keep.'

'You think so?'

A gleam lit his dark eyes. 'We could always leave and continue this conversation in private.'

'And commit a social *faux pas*?'

With indolent ease he reached for her left hand and raised it to his lips. 'I'm fortunate. I get to take you home.'

He kissed each finger in turn, then enfolded her hand in his on the table. Sensation flared and travelled like flame through her veins, but there was no visible change in his expression except for the crooked smile twitching the edges of his mouth as his thumb traced an idle pattern back and forth across the throbbing pulse at her wrist.

His eyes speared hers, faintly mocking beneath slightly hooded lids, and the breath caught in her throat.

'Some consolation,' she managed in an attempt at humour.

'The prize.'

She wanted quite desperately for it to be the truth, but she was all too aware it was part of the game. 'Ah,' she said with soft cynicism. 'You say the sweetest things.'

'*Gracias.*'

The waiters served another round of coffee as guests moved from one table to another, pausing to chat with friends as they made a slow progression towards the foyer.

'I've enjoyed your company.'

Gabbi heard the words and turned towards the dignitary's son. 'Thank you.' She included his parents. 'It's been a pleasant evening.'

'Most pleasant,' James agreed as he moved to his daughter's side and brushed a light kiss over her cheek. 'You look wonderful.'

'Thanks,' she murmured, and endeavoured to keep a smile in place as Annaliese rejoined them.

'A few of us are going on to a nightclub.' Her eyes focused on Benedict as she touched a hand to his shoulder. 'Why don't you join us?'

Gabbi wasn't aware that she held her breath as she waited for his reply.

'Another time perhaps.'

'We must do lunch, Gabrielle,' Monique insisted as she bade them goodnight. 'I'll ring.'

Gabbi felt a sense of remorse at wanting to refuse. It wasn't very often that her stepmother suggested a *tête-à-tête*. 'Please do.'

It was half an hour before they reached the car park and a further thirty minutes before Benedict brought the Bentley to a halt inside the garage.

'A record attendance,' he commented as they entered the house. 'The committee will be pleased.'

'Yes.'

'You sound less than enthused.'

'I'm disappointed.'

'Explain,' Benedict commanded as he reset the security alarm.

'I was just *dying* to go on to the nightclub.'

He turned and closed the distance between them, and her eyes took on a defiant gleam as he pushed a hand beneath her hair and captured her nape.

'Were you, indeed?'

He was much too close. His cologne teased her nostrils and melded with the musky male fragrance that was his alone.

'Yes. It would have been such *fun* watching Annaliese trying to seduce you.' She lifted a hand and trailed her fingers down the lapel of his suit.

'Your claws are showing.'

'And I thought I was being so subtle.'

'Do you want to debate Annaliese's behaviour?'

Her eyes glittered with inner anger, their depths darkening to deep sapphire. 'I don't think "debate" quite covers it.'

One eyebrow slanted in quizzical humour. 'It's a little late for a punishing set of tennis. Besides, I'd probably win.' His warm breath teased the tendrils of hair drifting close to one ear. 'And that,' he persisted quietly, 'wouldn't be the object of the exercise, would it?'

She wanted to generate a reaction that would allow her to vent her own indignation. 'At least I'd get some satisfaction from thrashing the ball with a racquet.'

His eyes were dark, fathomless. 'I can think of a far more productive way to expend all that pent-up energy.'

A thumb traced the edge of her jaw, then trailed lightly down the pulsing cord of her neck.

Gabbi could feel the insidious warmth spread through her veins, her skin begin to tingle as fine body hair rose in anticipation of his touch. 'You're not playing fair.'

He lowered his head and brushed his lips against her temple. 'I'm not *playing* at anything.'

Gabbi closed her eyes and absorbed the intoxicating feel of him as he angled his mouth over her own. His fingers tangled in her hair as he steadily deepened the kiss, intensifying the slow, burning heat of her arousal until it threatened to rage out of control.

Her body strained against his, pulsing, needing so much more, and she was hardly conscious of the small, encouraging sounds low in her throat as she urged him on.

Slowly, gently, he eased back and broke the contact, then swept an arm beneath her knees and crossed the foyer to the stairs.

'The bedroom is so civilised,' Gabbi breathed softly as she traced the lobe of his ear with her tongue and gently bit its centre.

When they reached their suite the door closed behind them with a satisfying clunk. 'You want *uncivilised*, Gabbi?' he demanded as he let her slide down to her feet.

The words conjured up a mental image so evocatively erotic that she had to fight to control the jolt of feeling that surged through her body.

'This is a very expensive gown,' she announced in a dismal attempt at flippancy. 'One I'd like to wear again.'

Something leapt in his eyes and remained there. A dark, primitive glitter that momentarily arrested the thudding beat of her heart before it kicked in at a wildly accelerated pace.

The breath caught in her throat as he reached for the zip-fastening and freed it so that the gown slid down to the carpet. With mesmerised fascination she stepped aside and watched as he carelessly tossed it over a nearby chair.

His eyes never left hers as he traced the swell of her breasts, teased each sensitive peak, then slowly slipped his fingers beneath the band of her briefs and slid them to her feet.

Her evening sandals came next, and she watched as he removed his jacket and tossed it across the valet-frame.

The bow-tie followed, and his shirt. Shoes and socks were abandoned, and his trousers landed on top of his jacket.

Then he captured her face in his hands and lowered his mouth to hers, initiating a kiss that took possession and demanded complete capitulation.

This was no seduction. It was claim-staking. Ruthless hunger and treacherous devastation.

She didn't fight it. Didn't want to. She rode the crest of his passion, and exulted in the ravishment of unleashed emotions.

It became a ravaging of body and mind—hers—as she gave herself up to him, her surrender complete as he tasted and suckled, tormenting her to the point of madness.

She had no control over her shuddering body, or the way it convulsed in the storm of her own passion. And she was completely unaware of the emotional sobs tearing free from her throat as she begged him not to stop.

A beautiful way to die, Gabbi decided with dizzying certainty as he dragged her down onto the bed. Then she was conscious only of unspeakable pleasure as he drove himself into her, again and again, deeper and deeper as she arched up to him in a dark, rhythmic beat that flung them both over the edge.

Afterwards she lay in a tangle of sheets, her limbs entwined with his, disinclined to move.

She didn't have the energy to lift a hand, and her eyes remained closed, for to open them required too much effort.

'Did I hurt you?'

She ached. Dear God, *how* she ached. But it was with acute pleasure, not pain. 'No.' A soft smile curved her lips. 'Although I don't think I'm ready for an encore just yet.'

He leaned forward and pressed a lingering kiss to the sensitive hollow at the base of her throat, then trailed a path to the edge of her mouth. 'Relax, *querida*. It's not an act I could follow too soon.'

'Some act.'

She felt him move, and the sheet settled down onto soft, highly sensitised skin. She sighed and let her head settle into the curve of his shoulder. Heaven didn't get any better than this.

* * *

Gabbi woke to the touch of lips brushing against her cheek, and she stretched, arching the slim bow of her body like a contented feline beneath the stroke of its master.

A smile teased her mouth and she let her eyes drift open.

'Is it late?'

'Late enough, *querida*.'

He was dressed, shaven and, unless she was mistaken, ready to leave.

Regret tinged her expression. 'I was going to drive with you to the airport.'

'Instead you can relax in the Jacuzzi, enjoy a leisurely breakfast and scan the newspaper before going in to the office.'

'You should have woken me,' she protested, and saw the gleam of humour evident in the dark eyes above her own.

'I just have.' He indicated a tray on the bedside pedestal. 'And brought orange juice and coffee.'

She eased herself into a sitting position and hugged her knees. A mischievous twinkle lightened her eyes. 'In that case, you're forgiven.'

'You can reach me on my mobile phone.'

He had assumed the mantle of business executive along with the three-piece suit. His mind, she knew, was already on the first of several meetings scheduled over the next few days in Melbourne.

She reached for the orange juice and took a long swallow, grateful for the refreshing, cool taste of freshly squeezed juice.

She'd wanted to wake early, share a slow loving,

join him in the Jacuzzi and linger over breakfast. Now she had to settle for a swift kiss and watch him walk out the door.

The kiss was more than she'd hoped for, but less than she needed, and her eyes were wistful as he disappeared from the room.

Four days, three nights. Hardly any time at all. He'd been gone for much longer in the past. Why now did she place such emphasis on his absence?

She finished the orange juice, slid from the bed and made for the bathroom. Half an hour later she ran lightly down the stairs and made her way to the kitchen.

'Morning, Marie.'

The housekeeper's smile held genuine warmth. 'Good morning. Do you want to eat inside, or on the terrace?'

'The terrace,' Gabbi answered promptly.

'Cereal and fruit, toast, coffee? Or would you prefer a cooked breakfast?'

'Cereal, thanks. I'll get it.' She plucked a bowl from the cupboard, retrieved the appropriate cereal container, added a banana, extracted milk from the refrigerator then moved through the wide sliding glass doors that led out onto the terrace.

The sun was warm on her skin, despite the early-morning hour. It would be all too easy to banish work from the day, stay home and spend several lazy hours reading a book beneath the shade of an umbrella…

CHAPTER TEN

'SERG ASKED ME to remind you to take the Bentley this morning.'

Gabbi looked up from scanning the daily newspaper and placed her cup down onto its saucer. She offered Marie a teasing smile. 'Not the XJ220?'

'We won't give him a heart attack,' Marie responded dryly, and Gabbi laughed.

'No, let's not.' The powerful sports car might be Benedict's possession, but it was Serg's pride and joy. Together with the Bentley and Mercedes, he ensured it was immaculately maintained. If the engine of any one of them didn't purr to his satisfaction, he organised a mechanical check-up. For the next few days the Mercedes would be in the panel shop having a new tail-light fitted and the scratches painted over.

The telephone rang, and Marie crossed to answer it. 'Nicols residence.' A few seconds later she covered the mouthpiece and held out the receiver. 'It's for you. Mrs Stanton.'

Gabbi rolled her eyes and rose to her feet to take the call. 'Monique. How are you?'

'Fine, Gabrielle. I thought we might do lunch today. Is that suitable?'

Exchanging social chit-chat with her stepmother over iced water and a lettuce leaf didn't rank high on her list of favoured pastimes. There had to be a reason for the invitation, and doubtless she'd find out what it was soon enough.

'Of course,' she responded politely. 'What time, and where shall I meet you?'

Monique named an exclusive establishment not too far from Stanton-Nicols Towers. 'Twelve-thirty, darling?'

'I'll look forward to it.' Oh, my, how you lie, an inner voice taunted. No, that wasn't strictly fair. Life was full of interesting experiences. Her relationship with Monique just happened to be one of them.

The traffic was heavy, drivers seemed more impatient than usual, and an accident at an intersection banked up a line of cars for several kilometres.

Consequently Gabbi was late, there was a message to say her secretary had reported in sick and the courier bag failed to contain promised documentation. Not an auspicious start to the day, she decided as she made the first of several phone calls.

By mid-morning she'd elicited a promise that the missing documentation would arrive in the afternoon courier delivery. It meant the loss of several hours, and if she was to assemble the figures, check and collate them for the board meeting tomorrow she'd need to work late, take work home or come in early in the morning.

Lunch with Monique loomed close, and with a resigned sigh she closed down the computer and retreated to the powder-room to repair her make-up.

Ten minutes later she emerged from the building

and set out at a brisk pace, reaching the restaurant with less than a minute to spare.

Gabbi followed the maître d' to Monique's table and slid into the seat he held out.

'Gabrielle.'

'Monique.'

Superficial warmth, artificial affection. Ten years down the track, Gabbi was resigned to it never being any different.

As always, Monique was perfectly groomed, with co-ordinated accessories. Chanel bag, Magli shoes, and a few pieces of expensive jewellery. Tasteful, but not ostentatious.

'Annaliese will join us. I hope you don't mind?'

Wonderful. 'Of course not,' she responded politely, and ordered mineral water from the hovering drinks waiter.

'Annaliese felt you might appreciate some family support while Benedict is away.'

Gabbi doubted it very much. The only person Annaliese considered was herself. 'How thoughtful.'

'The banquet dinner was very enjoyable.'

As a conversational gambit, it was entirely neutral. 'A well-presented menu,' she agreed. 'And the fashion parade was excellent.'

'Shall we order a starter? Annaliese might be late.'

Annaliese rarely arrived on time, so why should today be any different? Gabbi settled on avocado with diced mango served on lettuce, then took a sip of mineral water.

'I've managed to persuade James to take a holiday,' Monique began as they waited for their starters.

'What a good idea. When?'

'Next month. A cruise. The *QEII*. We'll pick it up in New York.'

The cruise would be relaxing for James, and sufficiently social to please Monique. 'How long do you plan on being away?'

'Almost three weeks, including flights and stopovers.'

'It'll be a nice break for you both.' And well deserved for her father, whose devotion to Stanton-Nicols' continued success extended way beyond the nine-to-five, five-day-a-week routine.

Their starters arrived, and they were awaiting the main course when Annaliese sauntered up to the table in a cloud of perfume.

'The showing went way over time,' she offered as she sank into the chair opposite her mother. Two waiters hovered solicitously while she made a selection, then each received a haughty dismissal. As soon as they were out of earshot she turned towards Gabbi.

'How are you managing without Benedict?'

The temptation to elaborate was irresistible. 'With great difficulty.'

Annaliese's eyes narrowed fractionally. 'If you were so—' She paused, then went on to add with deliberate emphasis, 'So desperate, you could have accompanied him.'

Gabbi determined to even the score. 'It's not always easy to co-ordinate time away together.'

Annaliese picked up her water-glass and took a delicate sip. 'Really, darling? Why?' She replaced the glass down on the table. 'Everyone knows you hold a token job and take a sizeable salary from a company which regards your services as superfluous.'

Two down. This wasn't looking good. And she was hampered from entering into a verbal cat-fight by Monique's presence.

'My qualifications earned me the token job and standard salary from in excess of twenty applicants,' she declared coolly, knowing she didn't need to justify anything. However, the barb had struck a vulnerable target. 'At the time, James made it very clear his final choice was based entirely on proven results and performance.'

'You expect me to believe he didn't wield any influence?'

It was time to end this, and end it cleanly. 'The directorial board would never sanction wasting company funds on a manufactured position.' Her gaze was level, with only a hint of carefully banked anger apparent.

She wanted to get up and leave, but a degree of courtesy and innate good manners ensured she stayed for the main course and coffee. The food was superb, but her appetite had disappeared, and there was a heaviness at her temple that signalled the onset of a headache.

As soon as she finished her coffee she extracted a credit card from her bag.

'Put that away, Gabrielle,' Monique instructed. 'You're my guest.'

'Thank you. Would you excuse me? I have a two o'clock appointment.'

Annaliese lifted one eyebrow in silent derision, then opined, 'Such dedication.'

'Consideration,' Gabbi corrected her quietly as she rose to her feet. 'To a client-company representative's known punctuality.'

As an exit note it served her reasonably well.

A pity Monique had been present, Gabbi mused as she walked back to the office. On a one-to-one with Annaliese she would have fared much better.

On her return, she found a single red rose in an elegant crystal vase on her desk, along with a white embossed envelope.

Gabbi tore it open and removed the card: 'Missing you. Benedict.'

Not as much as I miss you, she vowed silently as she bent to smell the sweet fragrance from the tight bud.

Tomorrow he would be home. She'd consult with Marie and arrange a special dinner à deux. Candles, fine wine, soft music. And afterwards...

The buzz of the intercom brought her back to the present, and she leaned across the desk and depressed the button.

'Michelle Bouchet is waiting in Reception.'

'Thanks, Halle. Have Katherine bring her down.'

Gabbi replaced the receiver and lifted a hand to ease the faint throbbing at her temple. A soft curse left her lips as she caught sight of the time.

It would take at least an hour before she finished reviewing the files on her desk, and a further thirty minutes to log them into the computer.

There were two options. She could take the files and the computer disk home and complete the work there, or she could stay on.

Let's face it, what did she have to rush home for? Besides, Annaliese's deliberate barbs had found their mark.

The decision made, she placed a call through to

Marie and let her know she'd be late. Then she sent out for coffee, took two headache tablets and set to work.

It was almost seven when Gabbi exited the program and shut down the computer. Freshly printed pages were collated ready for presentation, and there was satisfaction in knowing the board would be pleased with her analysis.

She collected her bag and vacated the office, bade the attending floor-security officer a polite good-night, then when the lift arrived she stepped into the cubicle and programmed it for the underground car park.

A swim in the pool, she decided as the lift descended in electronic silence. Followed by a long hot shower. Then she'd settle for a plate of chicken salad, watch television and retire to bed with a book.

The lift came to a halt, and she stepped out as soon as the doors slid open. The car park was well lit, and there were still a number of cars remaining in reserved bays. Executives tying up the day's business, appointments running over time. Dedication to their employer, a determination to earn the mighty dollar? Most likely the latter, Gabbi mused as she walked towards the Bentley.

Deactivating the alarm system, she released the locking mechanism and depressed the door-handle.

'Quietly, miss.' The voice was male, the command ominously soft.

She felt something hard press against her ribs in the same instant that a hand closed over her arm.

'Don't scream, don't struggle and you won't get hurt.'

'Take my bag.' Her voice was cool, calm, although her heart was hammering inside her ribs. 'Take the car.'

The rear door was wrenched open. 'Get in.'

He was going to *kidnap* her? Images flashed through her brain, none of which were reassuring. Dammit, she wasn't going *meekly.* 'No.'

'Listen, sweetheart,' the voice whispered coldly against her ear. 'We don't want anything except a few photos.'

'We'. So there was more than one. It narrowed her chances considerably.

'Now, you can co-operate and make it easy on yourself, or you can fight and get hurt.'

Hands pushed her unceremoniously onto the rear seat, and she gasped out loud as he came down on top of her.

'Get off me!'

Hands found her blouse and ripped it open. Gabbi fought like a wildcat, only to cry out in pain as first one wrist was caught, then the other, and they were held together in a merciless grip. She felt a savage tug as her bra was dragged down, and she twisted her head in a desperate bid to escape his mouth.

Her strength didn't match his, and an outraged growl sounded low in her throat as he ground his teeth against her lips.

Lights flashed as she twisted against him, and when he freed her hands she reached for his head, raking her nails against his scalp and down the side of his neck.

'You bitch!'

He lowered his mouth to her breast and bit hard.

It hurt like hell. Sheer rage and divine assistance

allowed her to succeed in manoeuvring her knee between his legs. The tight, upward jerk brought forth an anguished howl and a stream of incomprehensible epithets.

Then Gabbi heard the opposite door open, and two hands dragged her assailant out of the car.

'Come on, man. Let's get the hell out of here. I've got what I need.'

'Bloody little wildcat. I'm going to get her!'

'You were told to rough her up a little. Nothing else. *Remember*?' The door shut with a refined clunk, and Gabbi pulled the door closest to her closed and hit the central locking mechanism.

Then she wriggled over the centre console and slid into the driver's seat. The keys. Where were the keys? Oh, God, they were probably still in the lock.

The two men were walking quickly, one not quite as steadily as the other, and she watched them get into a van, heard the engine roar into life, then speed towards the exit ramp.

Only when the van was out of sight did she lower the car window and retrieve the keys.

Her blouse still gaped open, and she secured it as best she could. She was shaking so badly it took two attempts to insert the ignition key, then she fired the engine and eased the Bentley onto ground level.

Gabbi focused on the traffic, glad for once that there was so much of it. Cars, buses, trucks. Noise. People. They made her feel safe.

Home. She had never felt more grateful to reach the security of Benedict's palatial Vaucluse mansion.

Marie and Serg would be in their flat, and she had no intention of alarming them. Once indoors, she went straight upstairs to the bedroom and removed her clothes. Skirt, torn blouse, underwear. She bundled them together ready for disposal into the rubbish bin. She never wanted to see them again.

Then Gabbi went into the *en suite* bathroom and ran the shower. How long she stayed beneath the stream of water she wasn't sure. She only knew she scrubbed every inch of skin twice over, shampooed her hair not once, but three times. Then she stood still and let the water cascade over her gleaming skin.

Who? *Why?* The questions repeated themselves over and over in her brain as she replayed the scene again and again. Photos. *Blackmail?* The idea seemed ludicrous. Who would want to threaten her? What would they have to gain?

Then other words intruded...and she stood still, examining each one slowly with a sense of growing disbelief.

'You were told to rough her up a little. Nothing else. *Remember?*'

Who would want to frighten but not hurt her? *Dared* not harm her, to give such explicit instructions?

Gabbi shook her head as if to clear it. Photos. Damning shots taken with a specific purpose in mind.

Annaliese. Even her stepsister wouldn't go to such lengths... Would she?

Slowly Gabbi reached out and turned off the water. Then she froze. Someone was in the bedroom.

'Gabbi?'

Benedict.

She swayed, and put out a hand to steady herself. He couldn't be home. He wasn't due back until tomorrow. In a gesture born of desperation she reached for a towel and secured it above her breasts as he entered the *en suite* bathroom.

Her eyes skidded over his tall frame, registered his smile, and glimpsed the faint narrowing of his dark gaze as it swept over her features.

'You're back early.' Dear God. She had to get a grip on herself.

She was too pale, her eyes too dark, dilated and wide, and it was almost impossible to still the faint trembling of her mouth. Without benefit of make-up and a few essential seconds in which to adopt a nonchalant air, she didn't stand a chance.

His silence was ominous, filling the room until she felt like screaming for him to break it.

When he did, she almost wished he hadn't, for his voice was so quiet it turned the blood in her veins to ice.

'What happened?' No preamble, just a chilling demand that brooked no evasion.

Was she so transparent that he had only to take one look? she wondered. She fingered the towel, and fixed her attention on the knot of his impeccable silk tie. 'How was the flight?'

'It doesn't matter a damn in hell about the flight,' he dismissed with lethal softness. *'Tell me.'*

She heard the tension in his voice and was aware there was no easy way to say the words. 'I stayed back at the office to work on some figures.'

His eyes never left hers. 'Why did you do that, when you could easily have brought the disk home?'

Good question. Why *had* she? She swallowed, and saw his eyes follow the movement at her throat.

'Someone slipped through car park security.'

'Are you hurt?' The words held a deadly softness, and a tremor shook her body as his eyes raked every visible inch of her slender frame.

She lifted a hand, then let it fall. 'A few bruises.' He'd see evidence of them soon enough.

'Slowly, Gabbi,' Benedict bit out softly. He reached out a hand and soothed her cheek with his palm. 'From the beginning. And don't omit a single detail.'

His anger was palpable, and she felt afraid. Not for herself. But fearful of what might happen should that anger slip free.

'I unlocked the car door,' she revealed steadily. 'Then someone grabbed me from behind and pushed me onto the rear seat.'

'Don't stop there.' His voice sounded like the swish of a whip, and she flinched as if its tip had flayed her skin.

'He climbed in after me.'

A muscle tensed at the edge of his jaw. 'Did he touch you?'

She shivered at the memory of those brutal fingers manacling her wrists while he ripped open her blouse.

'Not the way you mean.'

Benedict's eyes hardened. 'You called the police?'

She shook her head. 'Nothing was stolen. The car wasn't damaged. I wasn't assaulted.'

His hands settled on her shoulders and slid gently down her arms. 'Assault is a multi-faceted term.' His fingers were incredibly gentle and thorough. Her breath caught when he touched her wrists, and she flinched as he carefully examined first one then the other before raising them to his lips.

His hands reached for the towel, and she froze, all

too aware of several deep pink smudges darkening the paleness of her breasts.

Naked fury darkened his features, and his hands clenched until the knuckles showed white.

Gabbi registered dimly that she had wanted to test his control and break it. But never like this.

'I scratched him rather badly,' she offered in explanation. 'And he retaliated.'

There was something primitive in his expression, a stark ruthlessness that frightened her. She needed to diminish it to something approaching civilised restraint. 'His purpose wasn't to harm me. He had an accomplice with a camera.'

Dark, nearly black eyes assumed an almost predatory alertness.

The shrill sound of the telephone made her jump, and she stared in mesmerised fascination at the bathroom extension.

'Pick it up when I lift the bedroom connection.'

Each word was a harsh directive she didn't think to ignore, and she watched, wide-eyed, as Benedict quickly crossed to the bedside pedestal. Her movements synchronised with his, she reached out and lifted the receiver.

'Gabbi Nicols.'

'Gabrielle.' Her name was a distinctive purr on the line, and Gabbi's fingers tightened measurably.

'Annaliese,' she greeted cautiously.

'I have in my possession photos which show you in a state of remarkable *déshabillé, mon enfant.*' It was almost possible to *see* Annaliese's cruel smile. 'Copies of them will be despatched to Benedict by courier an hour after his return tomorrow. Together with a file

on Tony detailing his career as a professional escort.'
She paused, then added with delicate emphasis, 'And
listing other services he's only too willing to provide
for a price.' Gabbi felt sick at the thought of being a
victim of so much hatred.

'Lost for words, darling?'

'Speechless.'

A tinkle of brittle laughter sounded down the line.
'If you had taken me seriously, it wouldn't have been
necessary to go this far.'

Gabbi tightened her grip on the receiver. 'Don't be
surprised if Tony hits you up for danger money. He
received a knee in the groin and a few deep scratches.'

'The photographs are worth it. Show a little wisdom and start packing,' Annaliese suggested with
saccharine sweetness.

'Benedict—'

'Will be shocked at the evidence.'

'Yes.'

There was a momentary silence.

'You can present me with the photos and the file
personally, Annaliese,' Benedict directed in a voice so
silk-smooth it sent shivers scudding down the length
of Gabbi's spine. 'If you're wise, you'll be waiting at
your front door with them in your hand ten minutes
from now. After which you'll explain to Monique and
James that you've received an urgent call from your
agent demanding your presence elsewhere. So urgent,'
he continued with deadly softness, 'that you need to
board a plane tomorrow. I'll arrange the airline ticket.

'If you should be sufficiently foolish to set foot
in Sydney again I'll lay charges against you for assault and extortion. And don't,' he advised icily, 'put

a warning call through to the infamous Tony. There isn't a place he can go that I won't eventually find him. Do we understand each other?'

Benedict replaced the receiver with such care, Gabbi felt afraid. With numbed fingers she replaced the bathroom receiver onto the wall handset.

Her eyes were impossibly large as he crossed the room, and she was powerless to utter so much as a word when he lowered his head down to hers and took reverent possession of her mouth.

'I'll be back.'

Then he was gone, with a swiftness that made her shiver. Within minutes she heard an engine start up, and the refined purr as the car headed towards the gates. Then silence.

Gabbi discarded the towel and selected a pair of ivory satin pyjamas. She crossed to the large bed and turned back the covering. Then she sank down onto the stool in front of the mirrored dressing table and picked up her hairbrush.

It was twenty-five minutes later when Benedict re-entered the bedroom, and her arm slowed to a faltering halt as he moved to her side.

Her mouth trembled when he removed the brush from her hand.

'Where are they?' Was that her voice? It sounded so hushed it was almost indistinct.

'I destroyed them,' Benedict said gently.

She had to ask. 'Did you look at them?'

His hands curved over her shoulders. 'Yes.'

Her eyes filled, and she barely kept the tears at bay. 'I imagine they were—'

'Damning.'

A muscle contracted in one cheek. 'Would you have believed—?'

'No.' He touched a finger to her cheek, then trailed its tip to the corner of her mouth. 'They were intended to be held against you as blackmail.' He traced the fullness of her lower lip. 'What was the price, Gabbi?'

'Me,' she enlightened him with stark honesty. 'Out of your life.'

His hand slid to her throat and caressed the soft hollows at its base.

'You imagined I would let you go?'

'Annaliese was counting on it.'

His fingers slid to the top button of her pyjama shirt and dealt with it, before slipping down to the next one. The second button slid free, as did the third and last. Gently, he pulled the satin shirt free from her arms.

Gabbi watched his eyes darken as they rested on the pink smudges marking each pale globe.

'It's to be hoped the infamous Tony was well paid. Expert medical care can be expensive.'

Her mouth opened, then closed again as he brushed it with his own.

She shivered at the extent of his power. At how quickly he could exert it, and how far it could reach.

'You came home early,' Gabbi whispered. 'Why?'

His lips curved. 'Because I didn't want to spend another night away from you.'

Unbidden, the tears welled up and spilled, trickling down each cheek in twin rivulets. Gentle fingers tilted her chin, and she felt the touch of his mouth as it trailed one cheek, then the other, before he kissed each eyelid in turn.

'Don't,' Benedict bade her quietly.

She wanted to say she loved him. The words hovered near the edge of her lips, but remained unspoken.

'Tomorrow morning we're flying out to Hawaii.'

A protest rose to her lips. 'The office—'

'Can get by without us,' Benedict assured her as he scooped her into his arms.

'The Gibson deal—'

'James will handle it.'

'Benedict—'

'Shut up,' he ordered softly as he sank down onto the bed with her cradled on his lap.

Her pulse leapt then accelerated to a faster beat as his mouth brushed her temple then slid to the sensitive hollow beneath her ear.

She felt secure. And protected. For now, it was enough.

Gabbi's fingers worked the knot on his tie, then slid to the buttons on his shirt. 'I need to feel your skin next to mine.'

Benedict placed her carefully against the nest of pillows, then straightened to his feet. He didn't hurry, and she watched every movement as he divested himself of one garment after the other.

Then he came down onto the bed and pulled her to lie beside him. He propped himself up on an elbow and examined the soft mouth, the blue eyes looking at him with unblinking solemnity.

'Do you want to talk?'

Gabbi considered the question, then slowly shook her head. Tomorrow, maybe. Tonight she wanted the reassurance of his arms around her, his body intimately joined to hers.

Lifting a hand, she trailed his cheek with tentative fingers, and her eyes widened fractionally as he caught and carried them to his lips.

With infinite care he kissed them, one by one, before traversing to the bones at her wrist. Then he released her hand and bent his head to her breast, caressing each bruise with his mouth.

'Benedict.'

He lifted his head and met her gaze in silent query.

'I *need* you,' she said quietly, and saw desire flare in the dark eyes close to her own.

Her hands lifted to encircle his neck, and her mouth trembled beneath the soft touch of his before the pressure increased.

His tongue was an invasive entity as it explored the soft tissues, and she felt him tense as he found the abrasions where Tony had briefly ground his mouth against her own, heard the low growl of his anger, and sought to soothe it.

The slow reverence of his lovemaking made her want to cry, and afterwards she slept in his arms, her head pillowed against his chest.

CHAPTER ELEVEN

WAIKIKI BEACH WAS a glorious sight. Deep blue ocean, white sand, with multi-level high-rise hotels and apartment buildings lining the foreshore.

There were beaches to equal and surpass it in Australia, and many believed Queensland's Gold Coast to be comparable to Honolulu.

The climate was similar, the designer boutiques many and varied, but it was the cosmopolitan population and the friendly Hawaiian people which fascinated Gabbi.

It wasn't her first visit nor, she hoped, would it be her last.

Benedict had chosen the Royal Hawaiian hotel, known as the 'pink palace' due to its pink-washed exterior. Originally home to Hawaiian royalty, it held an aura of tradition and timelessness, and was unique in comparison to the many modern hotels bordering the foreshore. Crystal chandeliers featured in the foyer, and there was an abundance of luxurious Oriental rose-pink carpets.

Gracious was a word that sprang to mind, Gabbi decided as she sank into a chair and ordered a virgin piña colada from the hovering drinks waiter.

Five days of blissful relaxation had done wonders to repair her peace of mind, she mused as she gazed idly out to sea. Careful sunbathing had coloured her skin to a warm honey-gold.

By tacit agreement, they'd avoided the tourist attractions, choosing instead to commission a limousine with driver for a day to drive round the main island.

Shopping wasn't a priority, although she had explored some of the boutiques and made a few purchases.

'Feel like sharing?'

Gabbi pushed her sunglasses up on top of her head as she turned towards Benedict.

'My piña colada?' she countered with a teasing smile.

'You've been deep in thought for the past five minutes,' he drawled.

Gabbi allowed her gaze to wander towards a young woman whose slender, model-proportioned curves were unadorned except for a black thong-bikini brief. Tall, gorgeous and tanned, she seemed intent on spending equal time anointing her firm body with oil and worshipping the sun.

'I was just surveying the scene,' she said easily. 'And wondering where you're taking me to dinner.'

'Hungry?'

For you. Only you. Was it such a sin to want to be with one man so badly? To laugh, pleasure, *love him* so much that he became the very air that she breathed?

'Yes.' She wrinkled her nose at him. 'I think it must be all the fresh sea air and sunshine.'

A smile lifted the edges of his mouth. 'You get to choose.'

'Somewhere exotic, I think.'

'Define "exotic".'

'Soft lights, dreamy music, exquisitely presented food and—' she paused, her eyes filling with wicked warmth '—black-suited waiters who look as if they're just waiting to be discovered by some international film-studio executive.'

His eyelids drooped fractionally, and his expression was deceptively indolent. 'You have a particular restaurant in mind?'

A soft bubble of laughter emerged from her throat. 'Yes. It will be interesting to discover if one particular waiter still works there. He displayed such flair, such panache.' Her eyes gleamed with irrepressible humour. 'Definitely *sigh* material.'

'And did he sigh over you?'

'No more than that attractive, scantily clad brunette is sighing at the sight of you.' She hadn't missed the veiled interest or the subtle preening as the slim-curved beauty displayed her perfect body.

Benedict's gaze skimmed to the girl in question, assessed and dismissed her, and returned to Gabbi.

'Pleasant to look at.'

'Is that all you have to say?'

His eyes were dark, slumberous. 'She's not *you*.'

A flippant response rose to her lips, and died before it could be voiced. 'Words are easy,' she managed after a long silence.

'There's an axiom about actions speaking louder than words,' he offered, and she held his gaze, suddenly brave.

'Maybe I need both.'

He leaned forward in his chair and surveyed her expressive features. 'A verbal attestation of love?'

Gabbi tried for nonchalance and failed. 'Only if you mean it.' She tore her eyes away from his and looked beyond the pink and white striped canopies fronting the terrace to the distant horizon.

It seemed as if she'd waited ages for this precise moment. But now that it had come she wasn't sure she was ready. The breath seemed locked in her throat, suspending her breathing, and she was oblivious to the people around them, the dull chatter of voices, the soft background music.

'Look at me.'

It was a softly voiced command she chose not to ignore.

His features appeared sculpted, the gleam of artificial and fading natural light accentuating the strong planes and angles, toning his skin a deeper shade and highlighting the darkness of his hair.

For one brief second she was reminded of boardroom meetings where a glance from those deep dark eyes could lance a colleague's façade and reduce him to a quivering, inarticulate fool.

'*Love*, Gabbi?' A slow, warm smile lightened his features, and she caught a glimpse of the passion, the desire. And the need. 'I don't want to spend a day, a night without you by my side. You're sunshine and laughter.' He took hold of her hand and brought her palm to his lips and bestowed an evocative, open-mouthed kiss on its centre. 'Warmth and love. Everything.'

Heat coursed through her veins, sensitising nerve

cells until her whole body was an aching entity demanding his touch.

The words that had lain imprisoned in her heart for so long seemed hesitant to emerge. She swallowed, and saw that his eyes followed the movement.

A faint smile tugged at the corners of his mouth. 'Is it so difficult to reciprocate?' he queried gently.

Gabbi looked at him carefully. She hadn't expected to find vulnerability in any form. Yet it was there, in his eyes. A waiting, watchful quality that allowed her a glimpse of his inner soul.

There was a sense of wonder in the knowledge that she was probably the only one who would ever be permitted to witness it.

'The first day you entered the boardroom,' she began quietly, 'it was the embodiment of every cliché.' An impish smile curved her mouth. '*Electric*. I don't remember a word I said. Yet your words stayed engraved in my mind. Every gesture, every smile.' She reached up and touched the palm of her hand to his jaw. 'When James invited you to dinner, I think I knew, even then, the idea formulating in his mind. It should have mattered. But it didn't,' she said simply.

Benedict watched the play of emotions in her expressive eyes. They held few secrets from him. Soon they would hold none.

'I fell in love with *you*. Not Conrad Nicols' son and heir. If I hadn't felt like that, I would never have agreed to marriage.'

'Yet you chose to establish a façade,' he pursued, and her eyes remained steady.

'Monique congratulated me after the wedding.' The words were almost painful as she forced them past the lump in her throat. 'On winning an eminently successful husband. I hadn't realised marrying you was a competition, or that Annaliese had been a contender.'

The leap of anger was clearly evident in the depths of his eyes. 'You believed her?'

'It all seemed to fit.' Too well, Gabbi reflected. 'Monique is James's wife. I would never say or do anything to destroy his happiness.'

'I don't share your generosity.'

'I can afford to be generous,' she said gently. And it was true.

The light was fading to dusk. Already the candles were being lit outside on the terrace tables, and electric lamps provided a welcome glow.

A faint smile tilted the edges of Gabbi's mouth. 'Are you going to feed me?'

His features softened. 'We could always order Room Service.'

The smile deepened. 'The food is superb at the Sheraton Waikiki's restaurant.' Set on a high floor, the restaurant offered panoramic views from every window. She cast him a teasing glance. 'We could dance a little, linger over coffee.'

'If that's what you want.'

She laughed, a light, bubbly sound that echoed her happiness and deepened the teasing gleam in her eyes. 'It'll suffice, for a few hours.'

'And afterwards?'

'We have the night.'

A low chuckle escaped from his throat. 'Sounds interesting.'

Gabbi fought the temptation to lean forward and kiss him. 'You can count on it.'

She made no protest as he stood and pulled her to her feet. Then together they walked down to the main entrance and crossed the path to the Sheraton Waikiki hotel.

It was early, and there was a choice of several empty tables. Gabbi chose one by the window, and Benedict ordered champagne—Cristal.

The food was presented with imaginative flair, and each course was a superb attestation to the chef's culinary skill.

'Magical,' Gabbi declared as she glanced at the fairy tracery of lit high-rise buildings lining the darkening foreshore as it curved towards Diamond Head.

'Yes.'

Except Benedict wasn't looking at the view. A delicate blush coloured her cheeks at the degree of warmth evident as his gaze lingered on her features.

'Shall we dance?'

When they reached the dance floor he gathered her close, and she melted against him, unselfconsciously lifting her arms to link her hands together at his nape.

The music was slow and dreamy, the lights low, and she rested against him as they drifted together. Her body stirred, warming with the promise of passion.

It was quite remarkable, she mused, how she could almost feel the blood coursing through her veins, the heavy, faster beat of her heart. And the kindling fire deep within her that slowly invaded every nerve, every cell, until she was aware of nothing else but a deep, physical need for more than his touch.

Yet there was a certain pleasure in delaying the moment when they would leave and wander back to their suite. It heightened the senses, deepened the desire, and slowly drove her wild.

His breath whispered against her ear. 'Let's get out of here.'

She lifted her face and brushed his lips with her own. 'Soon.'

As soon as they reached their table a waiter appeared.

'Would you care for coffee? A liqueur?'

Benedict deferred the decision to Gabbi, and his eyes assumed a musing gleam when she agreed with the waiter that a liqueur coffee would be an excellent choice with which to end the meal.

It was late when they entered their suite, and Gabbi slid off her heeled sandals, then reached to loosen the pins confining her hair.

His hands closed over her shoulders and pulled her close, then he lowered his head and took possession of her mouth.

Heat suffused her body, bringing it achingly alive. A tiny groan emerged from her throat as his lips slid down the sensitive cord of her neck, teased the hollows, then trailed the edge of her gown.

Layer by layer they slowly dispensed with their clothes, and Gabbi stifled a moan as Benedict began a slow tasting of each breast before tracing a path down to savour the most intimate crevice of all.

She felt the initial wave of sensation and gloried in it, and caught the next, exulting in each successive contraction as she rode higher and higher before soaring over the precipice to sensual nirvana.

It was so intensely erotic that her whole body shook with emotional involvement, and afterwards she lay still, enjoying the gentle drift of his fingers over her skin.

With one sinuous movement she rose up and placed her lips against his, initiating a long, evocative kiss. Now it was his turn, and she took her time, treasuring each indrawn breath, every tensed muscle, the faint sound deep in his throat as she teased and tantalised.

So much power, harnessed, yet almost totally beneath her control. It was a heady sensation to take him to the brink, and see how long she could hold him there before he tumbled her down beside him.

His possession was swift, and she gasped at the level of his penetration, arching again and again as she rose to meet each deep thrust.

Afterwards he rolled onto his back, carrying her with him, and he cradled her close, his lips brushing across her temple as he trailed his fingers lazily up and down her spine.

'I love you.' She felt fulfilled and at peace. Gone were the agonising afterthoughts, the wishful longing for something more.

Benedict slid a hand beneath her chin and sought her mouth with his own in a slow, sweet kiss.

Afterwards she settled her head down onto his chest.

'Comfortable?'

'Mmm,' she murmured sleepily. 'Want me to move?'

Gentle fingers stroked through her hair. 'No.'

Gabbi smiled and pressed her lips into the hollow

at the base of his throat. This was as close to heaven as it was possible to get.

'How do you feel about babies?'

'In general?'

'Ours.'

The fingers stilled. 'Are you trying to tell me something?'

Her lips teased a path along his collarbone. 'It should be a mutual decision, don't you think?'

'Gabbi.' Her name emerged as a soft growl, and she smiled.

'Is that a yes, or a no?'

'Of course—*yes*. The thought of you enceinte is enough to—'

A husky laugh escaped from her throat. 'Mmm,' she murmured appreciatively as she felt his length harden and extend deep within her. 'Such a positive reaction.'

Benedict's possession of her mouth was an evocative experience, and she sighed as she trailed a butterfly caress along the edge of his jaw.

'I'd like to continue my role with Stanton-Nicols. Flexibility, an office at home when I'm pregnant and afterwards...' She deliberated, her expressive eyes becoming pensive. 'Once the children are in school I'd like to return to the city. Part-time,' she added, knowing she'd want to be home to greet them, to be involved in their extra-curricular activities.

She indulged herself in a fleeting image of a small, dark-haired boy, a petite, pale-haired girl. Ball practice, swimming lessons, ballet, music, gymnastics. Homework. Walks in the park, picnics at the beach.

Laughter. *Family.* And Benedict. Dear God, always Benedict at her side.

'I love you,' Gabbi reiterated quietly.

Benedict kissed her deeply, then slowly rolled until she lay beneath him. 'You're my life,' he assured her simply, and kissed her again.

She gave a satisfied sigh as he began to move, and she linked her hands together behind his neck.

Magic, she concluded a long time later as she lay curved close against his side. Sheer magic. The merging of two bodies, two souls, in a mutual exploration of pleasure. And love. *Always* love.

* * * * *

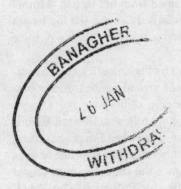